A DREAM FOR THE FUTURE

Stark grinned at her. 'If you had all the money in the world, what would you do with it, girl?'

Mina focused on him with difficulty. She could find nothing in the conversation relevant to her problem. 'I'd stay at the Savoy Hotel, in London,' she muttered, absently. 'And I'd travel. First class. Train and boat. To all the places I've read about. That's everywhere, Mr Stark. Round and round the world I'd go, staying at every first-class hotel on the way. Round and round.'

'There's an expensive dream,' he suggested, smiling.

She sat up, violently, suddenly angry that he should be laughing at her, when she had always been going to laugh at him. 'I'll make it come true,' she said. 'Somehow, I'll make it come true.'

Hotel de Luxe

CAROLINE GRAY

SPHERE BOOKS LIMITED

First published in Great Britain by
Michael Joseph Ltd 1985
Copyright © 1985 by F. Beerman B.V.
Published by Sphere Books Ltd 1986
27 Wright's Lane, London W8 5SW
Reprinted 1986

TRADE
MARK

Set in Baskerville

Printed and bound in Great Britain by
Cox & Wyman Ltd, Reading

To Chris Holifield,
for also dreaming about far away places.

Mina Doberley had a dream. Spurred on by misfortune, she defied God and Man to make that dream come true, regardless of the consequences.

Chapter 1

'There's this girl, Captain Stark,' the steward said, hovering in the doorway of the master's cabin a trifle nervously; when Captain Stark had been drinking, which meant most nights, he could be violent on arousal. 'Says she must talk to you.'

Charlie Stark opened one eye, regarded the boy, then opened the other eye and sat up. 'Girl?' He scoured the inside of his mouth with his tongue, listening; drunk as he might have been an hour before, he remained a seaman, and his ears were already taking in the swish of the sea and the creaking of the ship, the low growl of the engine, just as his senses were assimilating the movement of the vessel through the waves, and thus the probable wind force. All reassuringly normal. Then why had he been awakened? 'Girl?' he asked again. 'What girl?'

'My name is Wilhelmina Doberley, sir,' said a voice from the gloom. 'It really is most urgent that I speak with you.'

One of the steerage passengers. But he remembered her now, and not only on account of the name. She was not your usual steerage passenger by any means; both her clothes – at least when she had first come on board – and her voice identified her as someone who had once even aspired to be a lady, perhaps. As her parents had once counted themselves almost gentry. A priest, fleeing his parish!

But she was unusually pretty, for a steerage passenger. He waved his hand, and the steward stepped aside; the light from the lamp fell across Mina Doberley's face. Stark swung his legs away from his bunk – he slept in his clothes – and beckoned the girl to come closer. 'Someone tried to rape you?'

Mina Doberley gazed at him, and he flushed; she had a remarkably disconcerting stare. 'My parents are ill, sir,' she said. 'Very ill. Several of the people in the afterhold have been taken ill.'

1

Stark scratched his head, and wrinkled his nose. She stank. Well, who wouldn't, after two weeks in that overcrowded cesspool? 'What d'you expect me to do, lass? I take them from England to the Promised Land. I give them water. Everything else is their business. It says so on the ticket.'

'But they're sick,' Mina Doberley shouted. 'From your filthy water, like as not.'

The captain blinked at her, while Tommy, the steward gasped; Captain Stark had never been shouted at before, not on board his own ship.

'Please,' she begged. 'You must help them! You must!'

'Maybe I'll come and take a look at them,' he said. 'At sun-up.' But her ladyship needed to be taken down a peg or two. 'If you'll stay and have a drink with me now.' He grinned, as lecherously as he could, and reached into the drawer beneath his bunk for the half empty rum bottle. 'We'll send the boy away. Now.'

Her expression never changed, unless there was a slight, distasteful flaring of the nostrils. 'I will take a drink with you, Captain Stark,' she said, 'after you have attended to my parents, and the other sick people. And if you do so now.'

Stark regarded her for several seconds, more surprised by the calm manner in which she had accepted his proposal – although she had to know what he had in mind – than by her earlier lack of respect. Definitely she had aspirations. Or thought she had. Normally he wouldn't touch with a ten foot pole any of the human dregs he carried across the Atlantic. Most of them were diseased or were better at picking a man's pocket than attending to his needs. But he could not suppose this girl had ever come close enough to a man to pick his pocket in her entire life; it was even extremely probable that she was a virgin, as she was the daughter of a country parson. And she *was* pretty. Tall, but with a lot of body; he estimated long, strong legs, and a flat girlish belly – because she was, as he remembered from the manifest, only sixteen years old; but no matter how young she was, and despite the rumpled bodice of her gown, he reckoned there was a lot up there. She had splendid hair, too, long and yellow-brown, waving past her shoulders. He couldn't say she had a beautiful face, but the features were regular, with the nose a trifle long and the chin a trifle large, giving it both courage and character, which made for beauty of a sort. And green eyes. Cold green eyes, he observed. But a drink or two might warm them.

Because she could laugh. He remembered that about her more than anything else. Crossing the Atlantic steerage class in a tub like the *William McKinley* had to be the closest thing to hell on earth he could imagine, yet from the crowded afterdeck had come ripples of amusement wherever this girl had been standing; her delight in merely being alive had kept the other emigrants happy.

Until tonight. The absence of any suggestion of laughter was the principal indication that her parents might indeed be seriously ill. If only she didn't stink so. But that too could be cured. He thought that dumping this lovely creature in a hot tub would be the most pleasurable of experiences. And if she was in the mood to bargain, the sooner he got to that the better; his night's sleep was ruined anyway. That he would hardly be acting with the dignity required of a shipmaster, and that, where a sixteen-year-old girl like this one was concerned, there might conceivably be repercussions, was not relevant, at this moment – he was stale drunk, and liquor always made him randy. 'Then I'll come now,' he said, and pulled on his reefer jacket.

The girl stepped outside, waiting for him on the bridge wing, the breeze plucking at her hair; she wore a sort of shawl round her shoulders, because midnight in the North Atlantic, even in May, could be very cold. Stark inhaled the fresh air, looked forward at the bows rising and falling in the long swell. The *William McKinley* really carried far too grand a name for such a small and decrepit ship, but she had been launched, and christened, when the current President had still been Governor of Ohio. She was barely 2,000 tons displacement, just over a hundred feet long. She had a single steam engine, smoke from which was now belching from her after-funnel as it drove her across the ocean; the second funnel, regarded as obligatory by ship designers in the nineties, was a dummy, used as a storehouse. She had been designed for the coasting trade, and had been bought from that by her New York owners for the more lucrative business of carting unwanted human beings from Europe to the Promised Land; if, in this year of 1901, every company with ships on the Atlantic was in the emigrant business, from the great Cunarders and Hamburg-Americans down, there was always an overflow, unfortunates unable to pay the fares demanded by the larger and somewhat more comfortable – and certainly safer – vessels, but still determined to make the crossing. Thus the two holds, fore and aft of the central superstructure, which used to be packed with sacks of sugar or bales of cotton, were now packed with the poor and the criminal, the desperate and the optimistic, dreaming of a new start away from the dosshouses of England and Ireland, Russia and Poland – the *William McKinley* carried no cabin class passengers. It really was, Stark thought, no profession for a seaman who had also dreamed, once, of better things. But it was all the profession going for a seaman who had allowed his dreams to dissipate into a rum bottle.

Mina Doberley had moved aft, to stand by the ladder leading down. When she saw him behind her she hurried on; after fourteen days at sea she suffered from no uncertainty in her movements. The hatch cover was open, as Charlie Stark allowed his passengers as much fresh air as they could stand, save when it was actually blowing a gale, and even with the breeze flailing his hair he could smell the stench of unwashed bodies, of human vomit, and worse; he allowed his passengers on deck morning and afternoon, and sent his crew to their quarters so that the women could relieve themselves at least only in the company of their families, but there were always those who could not last the night. Now he frowned as he reached the deck itself; tonight there was something different about the smell.

'Rig a light here,' he grunted at the mate, who had hurriedly left the comfort of the chartroom as he realised his skipper was up and about.

'Aye-aye.' An electric cable was connected to the ship's generator, and a bulb was lowered into the hold. The girl sat on the hatch coaming with one leg already on the ladder, the wind doing attractive things with her skirts. But Charlie Stark no longer had eyes even for her, as he looked down, and met the gazes of those looking up. Only a few people scrambled to their feet in alarm at this intrusion into their precious sleep; most just lay, watching the light, pulling blankets and coats over themselves, men and women, children and babies, all huddled together.

'Please come down,' Mina Doberley said. 'They are very

sick. They . . .' She bit her lip and turned her head. Perhaps, in the few brief moments she had been away from the hold, she had realised how rank was the stench.

'Drop that light,' Stark commanded, and the naked bulb was lowered into the gloom. People protested, feebly, waved their arms and fists, tried to shade their eyes. Stark leaned over the coaming to peer down, eyes widening in horror as he saw the raw faeces on the deck, listened to the uncontrolled gasping and heaving beneath him. 'Jesus Christ!' he muttered, and straightened. 'That's cholera, Mr Lucas,' he said to the mate. 'Cholera!'

'Cholera!' whispered the mate. And then came to life. 'Close up the hatch,' he bawled, beckoning the watch. 'Haste now. Close up that hatch. Don't let anyone up. And then batten it down.'

'You cannot do that!' Mina Doberley screamed, scrambling back on deck and running at him. 'You said you would help them.'

'Nobody can help cholera, miss,' the mate protested, catching her wrists as she seemed about to strike him.

'Captain,' she begged. 'Captain,' she screamed.

'No one,' Stark muttered in agreement. 'Their guts are rotting. There's nothing to be done. You . . .' He checked himself before he pointed out that she should never have left the hold herself, in case she too was contaminated.

'There *is*,' she shouted, 'a lot that can be done. They don't *have* cholera. I'm sure of it. It's just an attack of dysentery. But either way, Captain, fresh air, clean water . . . they only started . . . they only came ill this afternoon. We thought it was sea sickness, until . . .' She bit her lip again. There were certain things that well brought up young ladies just did not talk about. 'But even if it *is* cholera . . . get them up on deck, to start with. Separate the sick from the well. I've read about cholera, Captain. Please. Get them up on deck.'

'Are you crazy?' he snapped. 'Once cholera gets in the air we'll all die.'

'That is utter *superstition*,' she shrieked, her voice cracking. 'No one has died yet. No one will die, if we can just clean them up, clean down there up, give them some clean water . . .'

Stark hesitated, pulling his ear.

'That's suicide, Captain,' the mate said. 'Once they comes up there'll be no stopping it.'

'I've read about it,' Mina moaned. 'Please believe me, Captain.'

Stark looked down again. Even though drink had ruined his career, he remained a God-fearing man. If he found it as impossible to keep his hands off a trim pair of hips as he did to keep them off a full bottle, he still suffered from the rule of his conscience. Not everyone in that hold had cholera, yet. So perhaps the girl was right and *they* could still be saved. Certainly he could not condemn nearly a hundred people to the most terrible of deaths without making some effort to save them.

'I'll nurse them,' Mina said. 'I'll nurse them all, Captain. Just get them up.' Tears rolled down her cheeks.

Stark thought he had never seen anything so beautiful. And so appealing. But she had still to be reminded who was in control here. He grinned at her. 'And you'll take a drink with me, after?' he suggested.

She stared at him, obviously unable to believe he could still be thinking of that. Then she nodded. 'I'll do anything you wish, after, Captain. Just get them up.'

Stark looked over the crew, who had retreated from the hatch as the argument had proceeded. 'So get them up,' he snapped.

'Us?' Heads began to shake. 'We'll all die.'

'I'll have you for mutiny,' Stark bellowed. 'You hear me? Get them up.' He threw one leg over the hatch coaming. 'I'll get them up myself, by God.'

Mina Doberley knelt on the afterdeck, wiped vomit and saliva from her mother's lips; most of it was black bile, anyway. She was no longer aware of the stench, only of exhaustion, and despair. She had said she would nurse them all; she had had time only for her own parents.

She was aware of crisis and torment all around her. The dreaded word 'cholera' had been whispered from ear to ear. Those of the passengers not actually seized by the paralysing stomach cramps had sought only to escape, but had been prevented from leaving the afterdeck by armed sailors manning the ladders and hatchways leading forward; now they huddled at the foot of those ladders, as far away as possible from the stern, moaning and begging and swearing. Other sailors manned the hoses, which they kept constantly playing over the deck, to the increased discomfort of the people lying or kneeling there; the hold itself had been flooded, to the destruction of even the few pitiful possessions down there, and, more important, the food which had been intended to last them the voyage. At least, now the sun was up, the water was no longer icy cold.

While from forward there came a tremendous hubbub; news of what was happening aft had reached the other hold, the rest of the passengers, and caused a panic, even if apparently no one forward had yet been taken ill.

But on the afterdeck calamity was no longer a rumour. There *was* cholera, and survival was only for the very fittest. One woman and two children were already dead, stretched on their backs, staring sightlessly at the sky. More than twenty others had been seized by the uncontrollable necessity to vomit and excrete, nothing but liquid now, while they begged for the water that merely made them the more ill.

'A judgement,' William Doberley muttered. 'A judgement.'

His face was ashen, and his mouth too dripped black bile, as his handsome features, his lively green eyes, seemed to have shrunk, while the rest of him . . . Mina could hardly bear to touch him. Yet she had to, swabbing his face, trying to hold her breath and as a result gasping for even more breath, praying for a gale, for a hurricane, if need be, to come and blow all the odours and the killing miasmas away. Killing miasmas! What nonsense. Just as to consider it some kind of judgement was equally nonsense. 'That is not so, Papa,' she said, tears dripping from her cheeks on to his. 'Not so. Cholera is a disease, not a judgement.'

Because she *had* read about it. She had read about so many things. She sometimes thought that all her life she had done nothing but read; the only thing Papa had managed to salvage from the wreckage of his life had been his library. Now even that was gone, but it had in its time provided a certain education for his daughter – the only education she had ever had.

She could understand his despair, even if she hated to hear him put it into words. It all should have been so different. John Doberley had made a fortune from his wine and spirit business;

his sons had been sent to Eton College, his daughters married to the younger aristocracy; all had the best of careers and marriages mapped out for them almost from birth. As the youngest, William had always been destined for the church. This he had accepted, however regretfully. But his father's choice of a plain, somewhat ill-tempered girl as a wife for him, simply because she was the daughter of a bishop, he had rejected in favour of marrying the pretty, but socially meaningless, daughter of a clerk in the wine office. His father had not forgiven him; John Doberley never forgave anything, or anyone, who opposed him.

By then William had already taken orders, and it had thus been too late to change his vocation. He had become a country curate and, in time, even a country vicar. But thus far and no farther. His bishop had been the same man whose daughter he had spurned, his wife was still regarded as an outcast by the Doberleys, and even the birth of a daughter named after her paternal grandmother had brought no word of recognition from the London mansion. All of which were crosses Papa might have been prepared to bear, had he truly had the vocation to which he had been directed. Certainly he was a sincere Christian. But he also possessed a keen and argumentative brain, which Mina felt, and hoped, she had inherited. He could discern all the inconsistencies and downright hypocrisies in the Bible as interpreted by generation after generation of Anglican ministers, and had wished to sweep them all aside. The bishop had been horrified. And Papa had seethed, for a few more years, until he had suddenly made his decision. He would preach the word of God in his own way, and if that way was not the Anglican way, then he would have to leave the Anglican communion.

Mina had supposed that such a decision, enormous in any parson, but unbelievable for a Doberley, would have brought *some* reaction from the London mansion. But the Doberleys had preserved a stony silence, as if accepting that such a step was no more than they had always expected, and feared, from such an apostate of family loyalty as well as of religion. How she hated them all! People she had never met, had never even seen, save in faded photographs. And how she dreamed of the day when Papa, become perhaps a great evangelical preacher in the

United States, should look down on them, and their puerile beliefs and consciences, their concern with form rather than substance. As he would. With her at his side. And Mama, of course. But Mama, while willing to follow her husband anywhere, and lend him all the immense reservoir of docile strength that she possessed, and which, from time to time, he so desperately needed, was essentially a passive prop. Papa would need *her* more; Mina never doubted it. If her reading had introduced her to a wide range of thoughts and ambitions, she knew that there was only one which truly mattered – to support and sustain Papa in his determination to prove himself right, and others wrong. This was noble. There was also an ignoble side to her ambitions, her determination. It was to have Papa make a great deal of money, an enormous amount of money, and return to England to show John Doberley that he *could* also be a worldly success. And the bishop, too. Mina was not sure that it was possible to be at once an evangelist and a successful man, financially. But if anyone could do it, Papa could, she was sure. And if he *did*, it would reveal to the world that God was on *his* side, after all.

So talk of being punished, of being judged, had to be absurd. 'You'll soon be well, Papa,' she said. 'You'll soon be well.'

'Harriet,' he muttered. 'Harriet . . .'

'She too, Papa,' Mina said, turning back to her mother, and catching her breath in sheer horror, as she gazed at the sagging mouth, the cold, pale cheeks. 'Oh, God,' she whispered. 'Oh, God!' She clutched her father's arm. 'Papa,' she shouted. 'Papa . . .' and gasped again. Her father was also dead.

'You reckon we'd better heave her over with the others, Captain?' asked Lucas, the mate.

Charlie Stark bent to look at the unconscious girl. For the past twenty-four hours he had been too busy even to think of her. And in all that time she had lain on the deck, indeed as if dead, soaked time and again by the hose which he had kept his men playing over the disease-darkened timbers. But she was still breathing, if heavily. She had been shocked into a condition of exhausted catalepsy, not death. 'She's alive,' he said. 'Thank God for that.'

'She'll sure as hell have it,' Lucas pointed out.

Stark shook his head. 'Then she'd have died. Anyway, mister, there's no sign of vomit.'

'Needn't be.' Lucas grinned. 'It could all be in her drawers.'

'Goddamned vulgar bastard,' Stark said, and knelt beside Mina Doberley. He lifted her head, sniffed her breath. 'Clean as a lady's.'

'You're likely committing suicide, Captain,' Lucas said. 'All for a pair of tits. And I'll lay you four to one that they'll be more trouble than they're worth, if you ever gets your hands on them.'

'Be off with you,' Stark growled. He thrust one arm under Mina's shoulders, the other under her knees, rose to his feet, swaying slightly. But he was cold sober this morning, and he was a powerful man.

'Captain!' Another man who had seen better days, like William Doberley, Stark estimated. But, as *he* had survived, he might even see better days again. 'I must protest about this food we are being served. It is inedible, sir. Quite inedible. Even were there enough of it.'

'Yeah?' Stark demanded. 'Well, mister, it's all you're going to get. Passengers provide their own food, it says so on your ticket.'

'But your men have ruined all our food, with their hoses.'

'To save your lives,' Stark pointed out. 'It was some of you people brought cholera on board my ship. Seems to me you should be thanking God you're still alive. And we're all going to suffer – that's my crew's rations you're gobbling up.'

'Does the girl live, Captain?' This was the wife, trying to keep the peace. 'My husband and I should be happy to care for the poor child, alone and helpless in this dreadful world . . .' Her voice tailed away as Stark gazed past her, at the two young men who waited behind their parents.

'A ready made daughter-in-law, eh,' the captain commented. 'Well, ma'am that may be. That may well be. Right now I'm putting Miss Doberley into the sick bay, and when she's strong again, she'll make her own decisions, eh? When she's strong again.'

He turned away before any of them could remember that the *William McKinley* did not have a sick bay, climbed the ladder to where Tommy, the steward, waited. 'You'll prepare a hot tub, boy,' he said. 'Lots of salt. Add salt. And then a broth. Hot and spicy, and thick. Put meat in it. You hear me?'

'Yes, sir, Captain Stark.' Tommy peered into Mina's face. 'Is she alive, then?'

'Of course she's alive,' Stark said, and carried her into his cabin.

Tommy hovered in the doorway. 'But . . . what are you going to do with her, Captain?' he asked. 'You don't mean to *bathe* her? She's a full grown woman.'

'Of course I have to bathe her,' Stark shouted. 'She could be contaminated. And who's going to do it, if not me?' He glared at the boy to stop him pointing out that there were at least thirty women on board the ship. 'Be off with you. I know my duty. Fetch the water, and the broth. Bring them here. Be off with you.'

His cabin contained two berths, on opposite sides of the room; masters in this line who were married were allowed to take their wives to sea. As if he would ever dream of taking Abigail to sea, Stark thought. And thanked God he had never done so. If she had been here now . . .

He laid Mina Doberley on the bunk opposite his own, stood above her, gazing down on that determined face, that flowing hair, that fluttering bodice. What he was about to do terrified him. But he had a right. More than that, he had a duty. If he returned her to the passengers, like the family which had accosted him, she'd be lost forever. He didn't know she wanted that. She was a cut above all those others. He'd seen that right away. She'd want to make the choice for herself. No doubt about that.

With trembling hands he began to unfasten her gown.

Water! Water everywhere, so hot it was stinging her flesh, soaking her hair, threatening to rise up her nostrils and choke her. She was drowning.

Mina jerked her head violently, and shook it from side to side, opened her eyes and gazed at the man who was kneeling beside her, a cake of soap in his hand. Her first thought was to wonder how long it must be since he had shaved. And how anxious he was; he looked positively terrified.

Of her? She sat up, and looked down at herself. 'Oh, my

11

God!' She drew up her legs, splashing more water from the tin tub, hugged her arms round her knees. 'You . . . you did this?'

'I was trying to help, Mina,' Charlie Stark said. 'I had to get you clean, to make sure . . . hell, girl, you could've had it. Cholera.'

She stared at him, not sure what he was saying, aware only that she had been stripped naked by a man who she knew had to be a lecher and a drunk, and then placed in a tub of hot salt water, and *soaped* . . . because she realised that there was soap everywhere. Everywhere! She slithered, even against herself.

Then what had happened *before* she had been sat in the tub?

'I will have you *hanged*,' she said, her voice low and angry.

'For saving your life?' Stark straightened, sat on his bunk. 'There's gratitude.'

Life, she thought. He keeps going on about life. Life! Papa! 'Papa,' she shouted, and leapt from the tub, standing up, scattering water, while his eyes gleamed at her, fascinated by every contour of the near perfect body he was staring at. She looked left and right, pulled the blanket from the other bunk, wrapped it round her waist and breasts, tucked the ends under her armpits. 'Where is Papa? Where is Mama?'

Stark sighed. 'They're dead.'

'Dead?' For a moment her jaw sagged, then her mouth clamped shut again. 'Dead?' Her voice rose an octave.

'They died of the cholera,' Stark explained. 'Thirty-one people died. I reckon that'll be all. Nobody's died these past twenty-four hours. So maybe it's done.'

'Where are they?' Mina went to the door, realised she was wearing only a blanket. 'Where are my clothes?'

'I threw them over,' he explained.

Once again her jaw sagged. 'You threw my clothes overboard?'

'Well . . . they was impregnated with the cholera. You could smell it.'

'You . . .' She squared her shoulders. There were more important things than clothes. 'Where are Mama and Papa?'

Stark uttered another sigh. 'Overboard.'

This time her jaw did not sag. She just stared at him, and he could see the explosion gathering behind her eyes.

'They died of cholera, Mina,' he said. 'Thirty-six hours ago.

12

They died of *cholera*. I couldn't just leave them lying about. All the dead have gone overboard.'

'You buried my father and mother, without telling me?' she screamed, and ran at him. The blanket slipped to the floor but she ignored it in her sudden spasm of blind anger. He caught at her hands, missed, grasped her body, hands slipping on the soapy flesh, evaded her fists and scratching nails, turned and rose at the same instant, throwing her on to the bunk.

'Keep out,' he bawled, as there came a knock on the door. But the door was already opening, to admit Tommy, carrying a tray on which there was a large bowl of soup. This he nearly dropped as he stared at the naked girl. 'Put it down,' Stark shouted. 'Put it down and get out.'

'Yes, sir, Captain,' Tommy said, laying the tray on the desk and slamming the door behind him as he bolted.

Mina said nothing, now merely panted, as she sat up. She had never been naked before another human being since the age of eleven. And now, in the space of seconds, before two men . . .

Stark was smiling at her, placatingly. 'You're making one hell of a mess of my bedding,' he pointed out. 'Why don't you rinse off? There's a towel. And I'll bet you're hungry.'

She gazed at him, trying to think, trying to remember, to understand. But he was right. She had never been so hungry in her life before, and thought was impossible while she could smell that delicious broth. Slowly she pushed herself from the bed, watching him as she went to the tub and knelt in it. Modesty hardly seemed relevant now, but she could still feel his fingers on her ribs and breasts where he had held her away from him, and she could still feel his eyes, watching her. If he were to attempt to touch her again . . . Because now she could remember as well. Everything she had said, every stupid promise she had made, in the foolish supposition that this man, this inept, drunken lout, could possibly help. And thus every crisis which had to be faced.

But not until she had eaten. She rinsed, and indeed felt better than she had done for days; being continually dirty was a new experience for her. Then she dried herself, wrapped herself in the towel as best she could, and sat at the desk. This meant she faced away from him, could not anticipate what he might do next, but it also allowed her to think. While the soup slipped down her throat like the most delicious of nectars.

Papa was dead! So was Mama, but she knew it was Papa she would weep for, when the tears finally came. When true realisation of what had happened came to her. Papa was dead, struck down, as he had said, by a vengeful God. For what, she thought angrily? What enormous crime had he committed, other than attempting to interpret the word of that same God in his own way? That had to have been a mistake, or not related to God at all.

Yet he *was* dead. In the prime of his life and health and strength and vigour, with every dream still ahead of him, with the determination to make all of those dreams come true, the hand of God had stretched out and snuffed him out. God, she thought bitterly. But for God none of them would have been on this God-forsaken tub anyway. Tears tumbled down her cheeks and splashed into the empty soup bowl.

And fingers suddenly settled on her shoulders, lightly, but causing every muscle to tense. 'You'll feel better now you've eaten,' Stark told her. 'More able to think. More able to cope with things. Because you've a lot to think about, girl. Oh, aye, a lot to think about.'

Oh, God, she thought. Oh, God! But not, oh God. Never, oh, God again. If God could so misunderstand Papa as to take away that precious life, there was no hope he would ever be able to understand *her*. And her life He had left, with utter careless contempt. He did not even count her of sufficient importance to destroy.

Well, she thought, she would show Him His mistake. Somehow, if it took her the rest of her life . . . because she realised with a start of surprise, however grief-stricken she was, that it had not actually occurred to her to want to die as well. She wanted to live. Even without Papa and Mama, she wanted to live. She was determined to live. And prosper. Just to show Him what a mistake He had made.

The fingers tightened. 'They was buried proper,' Stark said, soothingly. 'I read a prayer, and everything. I've a Bible, you know.'

And to live meant that firstly she had to survive this large, illiterate, shambling man, who seemed afraid of her and yet who so desperately wanted to get his hands on her body. She

14

had no idea what would happen if he succeeded; it was not a subject ever discussed in the Doberley household, and in the novels she had read what actually took place between a man and a woman when they 'retired' together was also encapsulated into three, or possibly five, little dots between scenes. But it would certainly have to do with lying down beside him, naked, and no doubt he would also be naked, which was an impossible thought, and with touching, and perhaps even kissing, which with a man like Charlie Stark was an even more impossible thought. When all she wanted to do was lie down, by herself, and weep, and sleep, and then try to think.

So, should she get up, throw off his hands, and run to the door, screaming? Where would that get her? Probably a box on the ears. The very best she could hope for, outside of this cabin, was a return to the hold, with the other survivors of the cholera. She thought that if that were to happen she would surely go mad. But it was that, or submitting. And surrendering herself, her virginity, her body, her every hope of the future, to this lout – would that not equally drive her mad?

'I know you're tired and upset,' Charlie Stark said. 'I know you want to sleep and have a good cry, Mina. There's a spare bunk in here. You can stay in here, for the time being, and sleep. Nobody's going to trouble you here, Mina.'

A respite? Because he was in no hurry? Why should he be in a hurry? She was utterly in his power.

But still, the promise of a respite. She pushed back the chair and stood up, and the fingers slipped from her shoulders. She faced him, realised that unlike last night, or the night before, or the night before that – she had no proper idea how long ago she had first come to this cabin seeking help, time seemed to have lost its meaning – today the captain was sober.

And the more dangerous for that? Quite the reverse, it appeared. He looked so eager to please, like a large, shaggy dog. She almost expected him to start wagging his tail.

But yet a dog who wanted. She could see that in his eyes. A want which would again become uncontrollable next time he took a drink. Yet surely there was never a dog which could not be tamed, guided . . . providing it knew its master. Or its mistress. And that meant providing she did not lose her head. She felt almost sick with a mixture of excitement and slowly returning confidence. She was surely the stronger, mentally.

15

Mentally, she had to be as far above this man as the moon above the earth. She had but to establish her superiority, and maintain it, no matter what happened, or threatened to happen. Above all, she must never show the slightest fear of him. Thus she must begin as if she was certain that nothing was ever *going* to happen.

She smiled at him. 'You don't really want me to stay here with you, Captain,' she said. 'I snore.'

He peered at her, uncertainly.

'On the other hand,' Mina went on, 'I *am* very tired, and that *is* a soft looking bunk. I tell you what. I'll hold my breath, all night.'

Now he scratched his head, totally unsure how to take what she was saying. She had not supposed it could be quite so easy. She stepped past him, dropped the towel, turned back the sheet on the bunk – and the ship lurched. She lost her balance and fell into his arms.

Immediately he held her close, his stale beer- and rum-laden breath playing on her face, his rope-calloused hands sliding over her shoulders, trying to come round in front and between their bodies, a space presently occupied by her own hands, and then abandoning that to slide down and hold her buttocks. 'Girl,' he muttered. 'Girl, but you are *beautiful*. The most beautiful thing I have ever seen. Oh, girl . . .'

She fought down the panic which was clawing at her mind, the desire to scream and to hit at him and scratch him. 'And suppose I have cholera, sir,' she gasped.

His hands slid away, and she fell backwards, on to the bunk, hastily drawing up her legs and inserting them beneath the sheet.

'Naw,' he said. 'You'd be dead. It goes through real quick, cholera does. You'd be dead.'

She had to keep him confused, unsure of himself, and make sure she avoided all future physical contact. 'I very probably am dead,' she told him. 'You're tired too, Captain. You can hardly keep your eyes open. You're imagining things. I don't think I'm here at all. I think I'm a figment of your imagination. If you close your eyes tight, I might go away altogether.'

He stared at her, obviously unable to grasp such a concept, and to her amazement actually did close his eyes, just for a moment, opening them again as the ship lurched the other way.

'Goddamn it,' he shouted. 'What are the fools at?'

As if someone had heard him the door burst open, and Tommy stood there, panting, desperately trying to prevent his gaze from drifting to the girl. 'Begging your pardon, Captain Stark,' he gabbled. 'But Mr Lucas asks if you'll join him on the bridge, sir. There's some real nasty weather come up.'

Stark hesitated, and then pulled his oilskins from the hook behind the door. 'You sleep,' he told Mina. 'You sleep, and be here when I gets back.'

The door banged shut, and she lay down and closed her eyes, aware that every muscle in her body, every nerve, too, had been taut, and was just slowly starting to relax, with an almost painful slowness.

She had been lucky. She should thank God for the sudden storm. But she was never going to thank God for anything ever again. She would cope with Charlie Stark, her own way, and for as long as it took. And then she would survive even New York, and she would prosper there, and make the name of Doberley famous throughout the world. New York was where millions were to be made. Papa had always said so, and Papa had surely been right about that, as he had been about everything else.

Millions, Mina thought, and fell asleep.

Mina became aware that the seas had got bigger, that the ship was not only lurching, but pitching, too, and rolling, to the accompaniment of creaks and groans; every so often the engine raced until it sounded about to tear itself loose from its bearing, then the propeller bit into the waves and it settled down into its low growl again.

The electric light remained on, but it did not keep her awake, any more than did the noise and the ferocity of the storm. It was more than exhaustion, she knew. She was in a state of shock, because she felt chilled even in the warmth of the cabin. And even more, for all her fine plans and determination, she was in a mood where she wanted to curl up and pretend the world wasn't there. When next she emerged from this bunk, as Stark had said, there were a whole number of things to be faced. Papa and Mama, dead! And then, Stark himself!

Stark! She awoke when he came in, muscles tensing as she knew he was bending over her, although she kept her eyes tight shut. Then she felt a blanket being placed over her, and was grateful, and then a kiss on the forehead. Then he was gone again. At some later time he returned, threw himself on to his own bunk, fully dressed as usual, and collapsed into a deep sleep. She did not know if she had been telling the truth when she had claimed to snore, but he certainly did.

Daylight, and the cabin was empty again. Outside the storm still raged; she could only imagine what conditions must be like in the holds. Tommy came in with food, a bowl of canned meat and vegetables, sloshing to and fro as the ship rolled, a hunk of ship-made bread, and a mug of lemon juice. 'Breakfast,' he announced.

She sat up, the blanket held to her throat. 'Will the weather get worse?' she asked.

He grinned at her. 'Most likely. But you don't have to worry. The skipper can drive a ship through anything. He's not as bad as he seems, the old man.'

His gaze shrouded her; he knew she was naked beneath the blanket. Now he waited for her to say something, to invite him, perhaps. Or more likely, she supposed, he was waiting for her to get out of bed to approach the food. He also wanted to be her 'friend'. He also no doubt thought that she was the most exciting thing that had happened to him in a long while – or could be. And he was a nice looking boy, and not only because of his youth. In every way he looked so much healthier and cleaner than the captain.

But her instincts told her that just because of that health and youth he would be more confident of her response than the captain, and thus less afraid. The captain's timidity towards her, his anxiety to have her enjoy whatever he finally intended to do to her, was her only real defence.

So she merely returned his gaze, and after a few seconds he flushed and looked away. 'You eat. You'll feel better.' He left the cabin.

She was in fact ravenous, and having already spent a fortnight at sea, in the most terrible conditions, she had no fears of sea sickness. She ate every scrap, then got back into the bunk, and stared at the deckhead. If only Papa and Mama had been able to afford a cabin like this. Even like *this*. No one could call this luxurious. But it was the Savoy compared with the hold. The Savoy! In the novels she had read, the more recent ones, anyway, the heroes and heroines had always stayed at the Savoy. It was the greatest hotel in the world, brand new, built even after she had been born, with every latest modern gadget, even its own printing press. Whenever she had managed at home to get hold of a newspaper, she had thumbed through it looking only for references to the Savoy, to great functions being held there, to the famous people who stayed there . . . she had never even seen the outside of the building, because she had never actually been to London. But she had long determined that she would stay there, one day.

Her eyes filled with tears. It had been going to be with Papa and Mama. Her entire life had been built around the dream of doing everything with Papa and Mama. She could imagine no other way of existence. Of course she had always known that one day she would have to get married. The thought had not troubled her, because she had assumed that her husband, an utterly formless and faceless representative male, would automatically make the trio into a quartet, without really changing her way of life at all. She knew that what she read in her novels, however romantic and exciting, was all invented, the product of someone's imagination. Reality was the *absence* of incidence and excitement, like life in the Devon vicarage, the cows pastured beyond the stile, the slowly changing seasons, Papa's fiery sermons on a Sunday morning, walking the downs and the moors, flirting with Harry Godden, who delivered the milk – knowing always, of course, that it was only a flirtation. In the course of time – not too distant time, she had been realising since her sixteenth birthday the previous December – Papa and Mama would bring someone home for her to meet, someone they had already met and had decided was right for her, and she would be married. But she had never supposed that life would then change that much, just as she had never even considered the possibility that she might not like the man they chose for her.

The intrusion, over the past few years, of other thoughts, of other awarenesses, of desires she had never known before, such as the warm day last summer when the heat and the stillness and the glorious feeling of being alive had so affected her that she had taken off all her clothes and gone swimming in the brook beyond the wood, had introduced into her life the first discordant element she had ever known – save, of course, for the distant, perpetual, rumbling discord between Papa and his family, between Papa and Bishop Aubrey, like an ever-present thundercloud, dominating their lives but not actually their waking moments. Swimming in the brook, feeling the delightful freedom of the water creating an awareness of her body such as she had never known before, had frightened her, threatening an introduction to a world beyond that conveyed by her books.

A world she had now actually entered? But without the comforting umbrella of Mama and Papa to turn to? She had been wild with excitement over the thought of emigrating to America. The Promised Land! Never had the future seemed so full of rose-coloured prospects. Even the possible husbands, fearsome creatures after that day in the brook, had suddenly seemed more acceptable. Now all those dreams were gone. All dwindled into rotting human flesh.

And now she lacked even the umbrella of God and religion. For the first time she understood what she might have done by her angry rejection of Him and all His works, and knew a tremendous urge to pray and beg forgiveness. And then remembered angrily that He had rejected her, because He had rejected Papa. So there *was* only herself to turn to, and she had no idea *where* to turn, save to the man who so strangely and so hugely loomed above her. When she had awakened in the tub – was it yesterday? – she had known the same feeling as in the brook, because of the soap. But wherever the soap had been, Stark's fingers had also been. Stark's *fingers!*

She shivered, and nestled deeper into the bed. She did not suppose she would ever get warm again. She slept, and awoke, to find Charlie Stark gazing at her. Immediately she knew that the second crisis was upon her. The movement of the ship had eased, the howl of the wind had dwindled, thus the storm was over. And he had been drinking. Indeed he held his rum bottle in his hand.

'Don't be afraid,' he said. 'I'm not going to hurt you, sweet little girl. Don't be afraid.'

She wanted to twist her fingers into the blanket, to hold it in place. But she was too late. He had already pulled it down from her chest, and now took the sheet as well, leaving her exposed.

'Christ,' he said, 'you are *beautiful*. Girl . . .' He frown-ed, watching her shiver. Because she could not stop her-self. Her body was seized with enormous shudders which

20

seemed to begin at her toes and rush to her mind, causing her teeth to chatter. She hated herself; she had not expected to be afraid. Indeed, she did not feel afraid. But she could not stop shivering, and the shivering was preventing her from thinking, when she desperately needed to think, to exert her personality, to dominate him and thus erect a wall between them . . .

Stark's hand stretched out, touched her cheek. 'Christ,' he said again. 'You're burning up.'

Her turn to frown. But suddenly she knew she was ill. Ill! God had sent for her after all, to join Mama and Papa. He had known He could not defeat her, so He had sent for her. 'I'm dying,' she whispered. 'Oh, God, I'm dying.'

Charlie Stark grinned at her. 'You're not dying, Mina, girl. You've caught a chill, lying on the deck, with that hose playing on you. You'll not die, girl. Not a healthy girl like you. And you've Charlie Stark to keep you alive.'

He fed her rum, which, to her surprise, she found quite palatable, and even enjoyable – she had never before tasted strong liquor. And he sat by her, and gazed at her. He would put his hand into her armpits, and once even between her legs. Taking her temperature, he said. And she believed him. He kept his fingers still, and was obviously desperate that she *should* get well. Charlie Stark, she thought. A man who, should she ever conceivably have encountered him on a street in England, she would have run away from, a mile if need be, to the nearest police station, panting and screaming. But in whose bed she now lay, frightened only when *he* was called away.

Even knowing that, as the fever died, and the wild, incoherent, obscene images dwindled in her mind, there was yet another crisis to be overcome. But a crisis she almost welcomed. She thought she could even like Charlie Stark, provided she could always keep him at arm's length.

And it was happening. 'We'll be in New York tomorrow,' he confided, holding the bowl of broth to her mouth. 'And not a cuddle . . .' He checked himself, eyes glooming at her.

'Still, you'll be glad to see the back of this voyage, Captain,' she said.

'Glad? Christ! They'll be crawling all over me. They'll be

wanting to know where that cholera came from. If it's still aboard. Christ! They'll take this ship apart.'

'There's been no further outbreak,' she reminded him. 'It can only have been that one water butt, contaminated.'

He frowned at her. 'You reckon?'

'Cholera doesn't just happen, Mr Stark,' she said. 'According to what I've read, it's a bacteria. It comes from, well, dirt. Dung.' She drew a long breath. 'Human . . . dung, Mr Stark. Someone must have contaminated a water butt.'

'Jesus,' he said, 'it's a theory. Christ, it might work . . .' Suddenly he held her hand, tightly, peered into her eyes. 'You know . . . I want to *fuck* you!' He flushed, perhaps realising that was not a word one usually spoke to the daughter of an English country parson.

Mina had never actually heard it before in her life, but instinctively she knew what it meant. Crisis Number Three. 'I know, Mr Stark,' she said. 'But you'd have been bored. I don't know anything about *that*.'

He grinned his delight, at least partly that he should be having so intimate a conversation with her. 'I'd have taught you, girl,' he said. 'By Christ, I'll teach you now.' His hands surged under the blanket.

She caught his fingers, never taking her gaze from his face. 'I couldn't, right this minute, Mr Stark. I'm not strong enough.'

He stared at her, knowing she was lying, afraid to say so.

'Maybe,' she said. 'Maybe, after we've landed . . .'

'After we've landed,' he said in disgust. 'They'll be crawling all over you, too, girl. Parson's orphan ! They'll have you on the next boat back to Britain.'

Back to . . . she couldn't allow that. She couldn't go back, not until Papa had somehow been avenged, been atoned for. To return, the penniless orphan of a failed and apostate parson . . .

Stark could see the distress in her eyes. 'You've no family?' he asked, hopefully.

'None who'd want me.' She bit her lip. Of course she shouldn't have said that. But she didn't want to go back to England, not until she had enough money to snub even Grandpa Doberley. On the other hand, she couldn't let Stark feel she had no friends or relatives at all.

But he appeared only sympathetic. 'You'll want to get some money,' he said. 'Money, that's the secret in this

22

world.' He grinned at her. 'If you had all the money in the world, what would you do with it, girl?'

Mina focused on him with difficulty. She could find nothing in the conversation relevant to her problem. 'I'd stay at the Savoy Hotel, in London,' she muttered, absently. 'And I'd travel. First class. Train and boat. To all the places I've read about. That's everywhere, Mr. Stark. Round and round the world I'd go, staying at every first-class hotel on the way. Round and round.'

'There's an expensive dream,' he suggested, smiling.

She sat up, violently, careless of the blanket which dropped away from her chest, suddenly angry that he should be laughing at her, when she had always been going to laugh at him. 'I'll make it come true,' she said. 'Somehow, I'll make it come true.'

'And grow grey trying to catch all those trains, trying to keep up with all your lost luggage and all those schedules,' he told her. 'Travel, even first-class, ain't all it's cracked up to be, girl. You'd do better to settle for something a little lower on the scale. A house and kids, maybe. And a man to love you.'

'Why?' she demanded. 'Maybe you're right, Mr. Stark. Maybe even first-class travel doesn't measure up. But it can, and it should. When I do it, there won't be any luggage going astray, any schedules missed, any wrong rooms. There'll be nothing but right. Everything will be right. And I'll have the right man, too.' She paused for breath, and a little uncertainly; she could not afford to offend him.

But he continued to be amused. 'Married to your prince,' he sneered. 'Or your multi-millionaire. You'll need at least one of each.'

Her eyes filled with tears. 'Yes,' she shouted. 'Married to my prince.' But it didn't have to be, surely, she thought. There weren't all that many princes and multi-millionaires in the world, but there were lots of people travelling first class. *They* didn't have any problems.

Or did they? Memory went back to Southampton, where they had embarked, waiting all night in the rain until they could board their glorified tramp steamer. There had been a huge liner alongside the next dock, a Cunarder or something like that. She had watched the boat train arrive from Victoria Station in London, the wealthy emerging, in their silks and

23

satins, their furs and their spats, with their lap dogs and their immense piles of luggage . . . and even they had been disgruntled and tired, complaining that their hotel rooms had been inadequate, that not all their suitcases had arrived, that the train had been late, one elderly woman that her dog had been left behind, complaining, all the time. And therefore not enjoying themselves. It was incredible, but true. She wondered what they would have made of the hold of the *William McKinley*?

But it was equally incredible that no one, no firm, no shipping company, no hotelier, had ever realised the fortune that was there to be made, both in slightly higher charges and in returning, because it was satisfied, custom, simply by taking care of all those troublesome details, making absolutely sure, guaranteeing, in fact, that there would be no delays and no missing suitcases, no pets gone astray and no wrong rooms.

So deep in thought had she been that she had released Stark's hands, and now they emerged above the blanket, to hold her breasts, with a gentleness which surprised her. 'Christ,' he said, as usual. 'Those tits. You have got to have the sweetest tits in all the world, girl.'

Her nipples were suddenly harder than she had ever known, even on the coldest winter evening. No one had ever touched her breasts before, save herself. No one had ever *seen* her breasts. Save herself. And therefore no one had been able to tell her how beautiful they were. She gazed at him, unsure whether to try to move his hands or not, mistrusting the sudden feeling which was seeping through her body.

'Listen, girl,' he said. 'I'd like to help you.' He forced a grin. 'I would, really. Seems like you and me, well, we've been thrown together by Fate, eh? I sure would like to help you, and . . . care for you, and . . .'

And fuck me, she thought, pleased with her own temerity in even thinking the word. Crisis Number Four. And by far the most serious, because suddenly she had no words with which to repel him. He was a lecher and he would surely be a monster to have make love to her. Yet he had gentle hands, and he was so sincere. And he had *tried* to help Mama and Papa, however ineffectually. But to let him . . .

He himself broke the spell. 'So I knows now's not the time,' he went on, still holding her flesh, still sending feeling racing

24

away from her nipples, leaving her incapable of thought. 'I know you're still upset about your Ma and Pa. About everything. But like I said, tomorrow we'll be in New York, and once we gets there . . . I'll have to let you go. Unless . . .'

'Unless what?' She was surprised at the sound of her own voice. She hadn't meant to ask.

'Well . . . if you was to say you're my niece, or something like that . . .'

'You'd take me home with you,' she suggested.

'Ah . . .no, I can't do that. There's well . . . there's Abigail, see. She wouldn't understand.'

'She'd understand too much, you mean.' This was better. The feeling was wearing off.

'You're a smart girl, Mina,' he said. 'Sure, she'd understand too much. Like you do. But I've been thinking. I've a place you can go. I have a brother . . .'

'No,' she said. One Stark was bad. Two would be impossible. 'No, Mr Stark. I think . . .'

'He works in an hotel. Works! He runs the goddamned thing. The Superb, on 7th Avenue. He's what they call the maître d'hôtel, right? He's in charge of everything. I'll take you to him, and he'll give you a job. I know he will. He'll give you a job until I can kind of sort things out. Make arrangements to look after you properly. Make arrangements for you to come to sea with me, next time I go. That'll be great, eh? You and me, at sea together. But meanwhile you'll be getting some money together.'

Mina stared at him, her eyes enormous.

'Because we're sort of meant for each other,' Stark said, faltering at her expression.

But she wasn't seeing him at all. He could get her a job, in an hotel. The Superb! That sounded even grander than the Savoy. She would be being paid to work there. To explore. To see. Money of her very own, for the first time in her life, to have the time of her life, inside the hotel. Okay, so Stark thought he was setting her up as his mistress. But once she was ashore, and in no danger of being sent back to England . . . once she was with other human beings . . . once she was earning her own money . . .

'It's that, or the cops when we land,' he reminded her. 'And then the voyage back, on a ship like this, only I won't be around to take care of you. Back to . . . well, whatever your dad was running away from, in the first place, right? He wouldn't want you to be doing that, lass.'

'No,' Mina breathed. 'He wouldn't want me to be doing that, Mr Stark.'

The Superb, she thought. That *had* to be better than the Savoy.

Chapter 2

The Superb Hotel was the tallest building Mina had ever seen. But then, all the buildings on Manhattan Island were the tallest she had ever seen; the Superb just happened to be taller than most of the others. Not all. But only the Superb mattered, at the moment.

Her neck ached from looking upwards. And sideways, and over her shoulder. There had been so much to look at that she no longer felt embarrassed, but when she had first been dressed in the ill-fitting and ill-assorted garments she now wore she had wanted to curl up and die. That had been when they had still been lying out in the East River, waiting for clearance by the health authorities. They had lain at anchor for two weeks, while the officials had fussed and fumed, examined and tested. No one had been allowed ashore, and no one except those in authority had been allowed on board, either, much to Charlie Stark's relief; Mina had gathered that his wife Abigail had been making a fuss on the distant dock.

It was during this period that Stark had had a collection taken from the other surviving emigrants, and found some clothes for her to wear – too large drawers and even large stockings, a gingham dress which hung on her like a sack – but at least she had her own boots, which Tommy the steward had done his best to polish. And a braid for her hair. She thought she looked about twelve. But maybe this was what Charlie had in mind.

Because it had been during that fortnight that he had also gone about creating the legend of his 'niece', establishing to everyone's satisfaction, he supposed, that he had given her his cabin and himself slept in the chartroom, that any gossip which might have been going about was at once malicious and slanderous.

He was a deep-thinking man, in his own very limited fashion, who was planning a long term future for them both. He was a lecherous, would-be adulterous scoundrel, with filthy personal habits and an even filthier mind, she was sure. Yet she went along with him, because, just over there, was New York, and the Superb. She *had* to keep looking at that, believing in it, because to look back was only to see Mama and Papa lying on the deck . . . and black despair.

She even thought of him as Uncle Charlie, now. Her life had, it seemed, ended, and then begun again, in the presence of Charlie. It was difficult to reconcile Devon and Mama and Papa with the waif she had now become, or with Charlie. Charlie was an ever-present threat, and yet a reassurance, too. He counted her already his, and was always touching her, and stroking her when they were alone together, as if she were a pet cat, just as he sought continual intimacies, would dress and undress in front of her, not that she ever looked properly, and encouraged her to bathe in his presence – but he counted her so much his that he never actually attempted to rape her. Charlie, in his own way, she was coming to understand, was a romantic. He liked to look even more than he wanted to touch. He might even have fallen in love with her. So when he finally came to her, he wanted her to want it as well, and he was sure he knew the way to her innocent but ambitious little heart. New York, and money, and perhaps even a soft bed and perfume.

She could understand his reasoning. Because even peering at the skyline of Manhattan from the river she had felt a growing sense of excitement. The Promised Land, Papa had always called it. It had been going to be *his* Promised Land. But God had failed him. So now it would be hers. Papa would approve of that. And if she had to run a few risks to get to it, then he would approve of that too. Had Papa not been prepared to run risks, he would never have embarked on the *William McKinley* at all.

Oh, if only he had not embarked on the *William McKinley* at all.

But she was here, and Charlie Stark was her passport to that glittering future. So him she must endure, and his lie she must perpetuate. The man and woman with the two vacant-eyed teenage sons, the Penders, kept seeking her out, telling how they had relatives here, who would be happy to care for her, frowning when she explained that she had to go with her Uncle

28

Charlie – they did not believe her. But there was nothing they could do, as long as she stuck by her story. There was nothing anyone could do. Not even the authorities, who looked at her hard and long, and insisted she go ashore on Ellis Island with the other passengers. Charlie had been quite happy about this, because when *he* went ashore, there would be Abigail. 'But I'll come for you afterwards,' he had said. 'I'll tell her there's business to be done.'

He was in a state of tremendous excitement. Mina did not suppose it had ever before occurred to him to betray his wife on such a scale, however much he might have indulged himself in foreign ports. But here was something – perhaps he even thought of her as a jewel, she thought with some pride – which he had picked up from a disease-ridden deck, and in which he had seen all his dreams of total possession of a beautiful female body turning to fruition. A lecher and a would-be adulterer, but also a dreamer and basically, she knew, a kindly man. She could do very much worse. But she was planning to betray him, because he did not fit into *her* dreams.

She wondered what Papa would think of that – and felt sure that he would approve. She need shed no tears for Charlie Stark. He was here reaching for something that was beyond his scope. Her mood of almost arrogant exhilaration was growing as she stared at the hotel. It was all behind her now, the dreadful medical examination, the searching questions, the contemptuous disbelief of the authorities . . . but they had not been inclined to press their disbelief. She had told them she was Captain Stark's niece, and was only waiting for him to come and fetch her, and take her home to his wife . . . and he *had* come to fetch her. If she so willingly wanted to go with him, there was no one wished to look further; the port authorities had more than enough to do coping with the other passengers, and with the prospect of trying to arrive at a decision about the future of the *William McKinley* – they were only too happy to have at least one unwanted responsibility off their hands.

Stark had had a cab waiting on the mainland, having, as he had promised, disposed of his wife's immediate company. 'Mind you,' he told Mina, 'I'm going to have to rush, as soon as I've settled you.' He squeezed her hand. 'But I'll be back, little Mina. Oh, I'll be back.'

A bridge she would cross when she came to it. Because now

the horse was stopping, and the cabbie was getting down to release the step. They were outside the Superb Hotel.

To Mina's disappointment, Charlie took her down the alleyway beside the hotel, and through the tradesman's entrance, instead of through the ornate revolving doors and the lobby. But she reflected that she would have lots of time to explore, and was immediately fascinated by what she found. They had to pass the inspection of an elderly man, all thin face and hook nose and wisecracks, who sat behind a pigeon-holed desk and was apparently responsible for keeping out undesirables. But he knew Charlie Stark, and used a speaking tube to send someone to find the great Joe, the maître d'. Then he let them through, having commented adversely on every visible article of Mina's clothing. She felt very much like sticking out her tongue at him, but decided against it, as she would be working here.

It was by now mid afternoon, and most of the guests would be out, Charlie told her, yet the huge building was filled with an enormous stealthy rustle. They climbed a flight of stairs, and her nostrils were assailed by the most delicious smells from a huge room opening on their right, and filled with white-coated, white-hatted men, great ranges, and long tables. 'The kitchen,' Charlie explained. 'They'll be starting tonight's dinners. But you won't want to be put in there.'

She didn't agree with him at all; rations had been very short indeed during the last few days at sea, and if, while they had been moored in the middle of the harbour, things had improved and they had even been given some fresh fruit and vegetables, she thought she would give a year of her life for one of the delicious lamb roasts her mother had prepared for Sunday lunch in the Devon vicarage.

But now they were in another hallway, and there were several white-uniformed girls hurrying by, casting her no more than a disinterested glance. They carried armfuls of snowy white linen, and disappeared into a vault in the wall, from behind which there came the clanking of machinery. 'Chambermaids,' Charlie told her. 'Taking the staff elevator up to make the beds. Now, there's a likely job for you.'

Taking the elevator? She didn't know what an elevator was.

And making beds? But she'd get to wear a white uniform, and be so clean and neat, and perhaps even meet some of the guests, she thought. And she would be being *paid*.

'Here we are,' Charlie said, turning down another corridor, at the end of which there was a closed door. 'Now, you just wait here, while I prepare the ground, like.'

She raised her eyebrows, but he was already stepping inside, hastily closing the door behind him. Mina hesitated, took a quick turn up and down, and discovered another short flight of stairs leading up, halfway along the corridor, and to the left. These she climbed, pausing just short of the top as she realised that they debouched into the lobby itself, a place of potted palms, of uniformed little boys, of comfortable armchairs, and the most elegantly clad people she had ever seen, while over to the far right there was a long counter with several frock-coated young men behind it, chatting gravely with various people in front of it, summoning the bellboys by imperiously flicking a little bell ... while on the *other* side, she discovered an orchestra, playing quiet and well-known tunes, mainly Offenbach.

In what seemed to be the *very* far distance, she saw the revolving doors, allowing brief glimpses of the avenue as they turned.

The lobby! It looked the most wonderful place in the world, a place to stroll through, dressed in the height of fashion, but to stroll through, anyway – she was disappointed to observe that none of the white-clad young women were visible, suggesting that this was a part of the hotel they did not service. And then, nearly jumped out of her skin as she received a hearty tug on her skirt. 'Mina!' Charlie hissed. 'Whatever are you doing?'

'Just looking, Mr Stark.' Hastily she ran back down the steps, beside him, to stop in front of a very grand looking individual, also wearing a frock-coat, and morning trousers, in matching black and grey stripes, and a pearl grey waistcoat, from which a gold watch chain peeped most noticeably; there were spats over his black shoes, and his hair was greased to a brilliant sheen. Yet his resemblance to Charlie Stark was unmistakeable, extending even to the way he looked at her, she observed with a sinking heart.

Although at the moment there was nothing but criticism in his gaze. '*This* is the girl, Charlie?' he asked.

'Well, you'll understand that she don't have any proper clothes,' Stark explained anxiously. 'She really is a looker, Joe. And refined. She's straight from an English vicarage. Say something, Mina.'

Mina gave a brief curtsy. 'I am most pleased to meet you, Mr Stark,' she said.

Joe Stark gazed at her for several seconds. 'Hm,' he said at last. 'Hm. You'd best come into my office, Miss Doberley.'

She ran behind him, heart pounding. So he looked even more of a lecher than his brother. But she had coped with his brother. The important thing was the job.

Joe Stark lowered himself into his chair behind his big mahogany desk, carefully flipping the tails of his coat over his thighs. Mina stood before him, Charlie at her side. 'Yes,' Joe said. 'She has possibilities.'

'You see, Mina,' Charlie said, obviously with enormous relief. 'I told you Joe would look after you. But you ain't forgetting that I brought her here, Joe.'

'Of course, Charlie, I quite understand,' Joe said, without embarrassment. 'She's clean?'

'Bathes twice a week.'

'That is not what I meant,' Joe observed, drily. 'But it is worth knowing. Hands, girl, hands.'

It took a second or two for Mina to understand *what* he meant, then, somewhat reluctantly, she held out her hands.

'Hm,' Joe Stark said. 'Hm. Nails.'

Even more reluctantly Mina turned her hands over; she knew her nails were dirty.

'She's been stuck on board ship for the past five weeks,' Charlie explained.

'I can see that,' Joe observed. 'Still, there's nothing wrong with her that a good brushing won't cure. All right, Charlie. I'll take her in.'

'You'll remember . . .'

'Of course I'll remember,' Joe said. 'She's *your* niece.'

Mina felt her cheeks flaring into heat; she might have been a side of beef up for sale.

'Well, then . . .' Charlie was also flushing. 'There's a to-do about the ship,' he explained. 'I have to be there. Board of Inquiry stuff. They're even talking about putting her into dry dock for a full refit. She ain't never had that. Then there's

Abigail . . . but I'll be back. Next week, I'll be back.'

'Thank you, Captain Stark,' she said.

'Yeah. Well . . .' He hesitated, then held her shoulders and kissed her on the forehead. 'You be a good girl, Mina. I'll be back.' But this time he was speaking more to his brother. He looked at Mina a last time, then left the room.

Mina watched Joe Stark. She did not doubt that Charlie was in her past, now; this man was her present. She could only hope that he was not also her future.

'Yes,' Joe Stark said, thoughtfully, allowing his eyes to strip her naked. 'My brother is an impressionable man. Always a problem. But the eldest, you know . . . I try to please him, Miss Doberley. Wilhelmina, is it? Well, Wilhelmina, you will do well at the Superb. Providing you behave yourself, and remember who you are and who are your superiors. But we like girls of breeding here. Yes, indeed. You've never been with a man?' He gave a deprecating cough. 'I mean, before my brother?'

Mina stared at him. It took her a few seconds to understand what he meant, and then she could not believe that a comparative stranger should ask her such a question. 'I've never *been* with your brother, Mr Stark,' she said.

For a moment his expression was confounded. 'Well,' he said. 'I shall have to discuss that with you, Wilhelmina. Yes, indeed. Meanwhile . . .' He felt in his fob pocket and found an enormous gold watch. 'Yes, duty calls.' He picked up the voice tube beside his desk and whistled into it. 'Peter,' he said. 'Ask Mrs Young to step down to my office? Right away, please.'

'We will start you as Mrs Young's assistant,' Joe Stark said. 'My brother told me that your father was a parson, in England.'

'Yes, sir,' Mina replied.

'Then you will have helped your mother about the house, no doubt. Think of Mrs Young as your new mother. She is the housekeeper, and has . . . ah, charge of all the girls in the hotel. You understand me?'

'Oh, yes, Mr Stark,' Mina said. What a splendid thought, to have suddenly accumulated a new mother. Perhaps she had made a mistake about him, perhaps . . . the door behind her opened, and she turned hastily – and realised that she had not make a mistake, about anything.

Mrs Young was tall and broad. Her face seemed all jutting nose and protruding chin, and she wore a little moustache on her upper lip. Her expression was aggressive. 'You sent for me, Mr Stark?' Her voice was matchingly harsh.

Mina felt her heart begin to sink into her stomach.

'We are employing this young lady,' Joe Stark said. 'A niece of mine who is unfortunately destitute.'

Mrs Young surveyed Mina. 'A *niece*?'

'Ahem,' Stark said. 'Actually, a niece of my brother's. You know, the sea captain. A niece by marriage.'

Mrs Young's lip curled. 'She looks as if she was rescued from a garbage dump.'

'She has had a difficult time,' Stark agreed. 'But she is a young lady of breeding and accomplishment. A parson's daughter, Mrs Young. Say something, Wilhelmina.'

Mina drew a long breath. 'I am very pleased to make your acquaintance, Mrs Young,' she said, using her best Sunday-morning-after-service voice.

Mrs Young seemed more offended than impressed. 'She's English,' she remarked.

'And all the better for that,' Stark pointed out. 'My grandfather was English. And so was yours, Mrs Young.'

'He was a scoundrel,' Mrs Young observed. 'What am I supposed to do with her?'

Stark's eyes became strangely hooded. 'That is something we shall have to discuss, Mrs Young. In the fullness of time. Remembering always that she is my *brother's* niece. For the moment, I should let her help you with the laundry. She will know about these things from helping her mother. And for heaven's sake find her something decent to wear.'

'Yes,' Mrs Young agreed, looking more doubtful than ever. 'Well, come along, girl.'

Mina drew another long breath. 'Captain Stark said that I would be paid.'

They stared at her. Then Joe Stark gave a brief laugh. 'Of course you'll be paid, Wilhelmina. In time. Now run along with Mrs Young.'

Mina hesitated a last time, but she dared not press the point any further. Mrs Young had already opened the door. She gave Stark a hasty smile and hurried behind her new . . . mother? That was an impossible thought.

But at least it was exciting. Mrs Young took her to the same vault in the wall into which she had earlier seen the chambermaids disappearing, and a moment later they were climbing steeply through the building. So an elevator was actually a lift. She had read about lifts. But had never actually ridden in one. She had to gasp to allow her stomach to catch up with the rest of her, found herself staring at Mrs Young, who was gazing at her with a most speculative expression on her face.

'This is the ninth floor,' Mrs Young informed her as they stepped out into a narrow corridor. 'The staff quarters are on this floor. The senior staff, that is. There are also some of the cheaper guest bedrooms along there. Now . . .' she opened a door and went inside, beckoned Mina to follow her, into a very comfortably furnished bed-sitting room. 'This is *my* apartment. When did you last have a bath?'

Mina found she was standing on one leg. This was elegance. Oh, if they were to give her a room like this . . .

'I am speaking to you, girl.'

'Oh . . . last night, Mrs Young.'

'You will call me ma'am,' Mrs Young commanded. 'Last night. That will not do at all. My girls must smell sweet at all times. That means you will take a shower first thing every morning, and again every afternoon before commencing your second round.'

'My . . . a shower?' Mina asked, having no idea what the woman was talking about.

Mrs Young waved her hand. 'You could use one now. Take a shower now. I will see if I can find you some clothes to wear.'

Mina had never seen a shower bath before. It took her several experimental twisting of taps to obtain water at all, and then the gush was scalding hot, which sent her leaping on to the bathmat. She located the cold tap after some further experimenting, and discovered that she had soaked her hair. Well, she reflected, it desperately needed washing anyway, and Mrs Young had some very sweet-smelling shampoo. She soaked herself, enjoying the feeling of standing up while the water pounded on her skin, scooped her hair and squeezed it dry before soaking it again, oblivious of the passage of time,

35

and was brought back to reality by a sudden barked 'Out!' from the bathroom doorway.

She switched off the water, peered round the screen at Mrs Young, discovered that her clothes, even the towels on the rack, were out of reach – somehow she was even more embarrassed to appear in the nude before Mrs Young than before Charlie Stark and Tommy the steward.

'You little wretch,' Mrs Young remarked. 'You've soaked the floor. And you've been using my shampoo.'

'Well . . . it was there,' Mina said. 'And you said to get clean . . .'

Mrs Young advanced with remarkable speed, seized Mina's wet hair and slapped her face, all in the same instant, with such force that her teeth seemed to rattle and her head banged against the wall, leaving her quite dizzy. 'You'll replace it,' Mrs Young said. 'Oh, yes. We'll have none of your thieving ways here. That'll come out of your wages. And you'll call me *ma'am*.'

Mina's head was spinning, and she was aware of a tremendous anger. She had never been hit like that before. Indeed, she had never been hit at all before, anywhere; Papa had not believed in corporal punishment. And to have this great hulk . . . but this great hulk was going to give her food, and money, and shelter her from the authorities – and perhaps even Charlie Stark – and thus set her feet upon the road to wealth and fame. She could not let Papa down.

She pushed herself away from the wall, and drew a long breath. 'I'm sorry . . . ma'am,' she said. 'Of course I shall pay for your shampoo.' Carefully she stepped from the shower stall; she did not feel very steady on her feet. 'May I *rent* a towel?'

Mrs Young glared at her. 'Quite the little miss,' she said. 'We'll see about that, *miss*.' Her hand came out, again far faster than Mina would have imagined possible. She put up her own hands to attempt to break the force of the slap she thought was coming, and was totally confounded when Mrs Young's fingers and thumb instead closed on her left nipple, and in no caress, but squeezing and pulling as hard as they could. Mina gave a scream, half of outrage and half of pain, but the pain was uppermost. She thought the teat was going to be pulled right off, and the agony of it took her breath away, as her legs collapsed and she knelt, the scream dwindling into a whimper. 'We'll teach you a thing or two,' Mrs Young remarked, sinisterly. 'Charlie Stark's niece, indeed. If there's one thing I cannot stand, it's a stuck-up whore.'

The pain and the humiliation were forcing tears from Mina's eyes. She fought for breath as she attempted to control her temper. 'I'm not,' she cried. 'I'm not a . . .' She couldn't say it. 'Charlie never touched me.'

The fingers released her, and Mina grasped her own breast to massage the tortured flesh. Once again she knew bubbling outrage, seething anger. She felt she was going to spit, and burst into tears, and . . .

'You expect me to believe that?' demanded Mrs Young. 'You *look* like a whore. Sixteen! Come on, girl, admit it. You're twenty if you're a day.'

'I was born on 6 December 1885,' Mina declared. 'And I don't care whether you believe it or not.' The pain was starting to fade. 'It happens to be true.'

Mrs Young gazed at her. 'Well, well,' she said at last. 'It may be possible for you to be happy here, after all. The one thing I will *not* have in my establishment is loose girls. If I even think you are misbehaving, Wilhelmina, I will personally take the skin from your arse. Remember that. But if you really are innocent, well . . . you had better get dressed; it's time for your supper. I'll help you, shall I?'

Mina wanted to reject her, utterly. But she had mentioned food! And clothes! Perhaps the white dresses and stockings and caps she had seen the other girls wearing.

But mainly, food! Mina forgot about being angry.

In fact she would not have been able to dress, without Mrs Young to show her how, even if she was made to feel rather like a doll. Everything was white, and starched: drawers, two petticoats – to set up an entrancing rustle as she moved – ankle-length dress, very plain, stockings, and cap, which was the most highly starched of all. This could not be set in place until Mrs Young had brushed her still wet hair into some semblance of order, and tied it with a white ribbon in the middle of her shoulder blades. 'That is how you will always wear it from now on,' she said. 'Neatness is everything.' The cap was then emplaced, and secured with two pins; it was no more than a sort of cloth tiara, with two little tails hanging down behind. 'There,' Mrs Young said, standing back to survey her. 'Good God, those boots. By tomorrow they must be polished, understand me? Be sure you give them to the boys tonight.'

'Yes, ma'am,' Mina said, hating her own obsequiousness almost as much as she did Mrs Young – her nipple still pained her, and the whole dressing process had been accompanied by a series of intimate pats and squeezes which she had not liked at all. But she did now look utterly elegant, and besides, she reminded herself, she was now going to be fed.

The staff dining room was downstairs, next to the kitchen, which involved another fascinating ride in the elevator. It was a large room, which was very necessary, Mina realised, because she counted nearly a hundred people sitting down to this meal, and this was the second sitting, as of course half the staff had to be on duty at all times.

She was reminded of books she had read about boarding schools, for there were several long tables arranged end on to the one at the top, where sat the great people, Mrs Young, one or two of the under-managers, the accountant and the hook-nosed guardian of the rear entrance. Mina gathered that the even more important dignitaries, such as Mr Stark himself, the head chef and indeed all the kitchen staff, and the doorman had eaten earlier, as they were now on duty. The other tables were occupied by a host of loud and jolly young people, ranging from scullery maids and dishwashers and bootblacks up through chambermaids to the reserve waiters, elegant young men in tuxedos who did their best to ignore the lesser souls beside them. In any event, they had to finish their suppers in a great hurry as business in the restaurant hotted up.

Mina found herself seated at the very end of one of the tables, in the midst of several young girls, dressed in white like herself, who never questioned her unexplained presence, and indeed ignored her for the most part as they chattered away, gossiping about the various guests, sprinkling their remarks with four letter words which sounded even more obscene than the one she had learned from Captain Stark, and referring freely to the most intimate portions of the human body. Mina was totally embarrassed, but she was also wildly excited, so much so that she quite lost her appetite – but very rapidly regained it when she discovered that they were eating what had smelt so appetising when she had first entered the hotel. There was no service, of course, but huge dishes laden with slices of roast pork, and tarts, and deliciously crisp green vegetables, and wafer thin toast, and huge pots of butter, and all the beer they could drink. Mina had never tasted beer before, and did not much like it, but everyone else was drinking it and there was no water to be seen – suddenly she was quite light-headed.

'Anyone would think you'd never seen food before,' remarked the girl sitting next to her.

Well, I haven't, Mina thought; not like this. 'What do the guests eat?' she asked.

The girl raised her eyebrows. 'Same as us. But we get first pick, eh? They're only guests.'

Mina tried to calculate what a meal like this must cost – she was well acquainted with the difficulties Mama had had trying to feed a family of three on a country vicar's stipend – and wondered if there were actually a hundred guests staying in the hotel. It seemed absurd to be spending more money feeding the staff than the customers.

She looked up, and found Mrs Young standing beside her. 'Wilhelmina is joining us,' the housekeeper announced. 'She will sleep in your room, Edna. And you will show her the ropes.'

Edna leapt to her feet and gave a quick curtsy. 'Yes, ma'am,' she said. And gazed at Mina as the housekeeper walked away. 'Your name really Wilhelmina?'

'Why, yes. But you can call me Mina, if you like.'

'I knew you were foreign,' Edna complained. 'I could tell by the way you speak. Well, come along. We have to clear the tables.'

The most junior boys and girls apparently had this chore, jostling together as they carried plates and glasses and cups and saucers into the kitchen, Mina doing her best to copy everyone else but terrified someone was going to spill something on her new dress; she couldn't imagine what Mrs Young would say, or worse, do. But she was totally fascinated by the kitchen itself, where everything appeared as a sort of ordered confusion. Under-chefs stood before the great ranges, watching each dish critically, occasionally adding a spice or stirring with huge wooden spoons; waiters moved to and fro in black-clad elegance, exiting with filled trays through a pair of swing doors at the far end and entering through another pair, their trays now laden with empty crockery – the way they balanced the trays themselves, always on the palm of one upturned hand held exactly level with their shoulders, kept Mina in a state of nervous apprehension – while skivvies assembled the dirty places and cups and others washed them and yet others dried, in a constant human chain of endeavour. Every so often one of the senior waiters would bellow out a list of incomprehensible requirements which seemed perfectly clear to the chefs – once even Mr Stark himself came in to place an order, but he did not notice her or even look in her direction; while over all the head chef, huge hat perched jauntily on the back of his head, presided with large and florid confidence.

The chatter was unceasing, even amongst the skivvies and junior chambermaids, and for the first time people seemed to discover there was a new face in their midst. 'Hey, Edna, who's your friend?' asked one of the boys, who wore a black jacket and a starched collar.

'Wilhelmina,' Edna explained. 'She's foreign.'

'From England,' Mina hastened to explain, anxious that he should understand she wasn't *that* foreign.

The boy peered at her. 'My grandad came from Ireland,' he said. 'He says the British are all lousy bastards.'

Mina stared at him with her mouth open. She had been prepared to like him on sight, because he had a big, friendly face, and fascinatingly lively brown eyes.

'But she's a looker, eh?' asked another boy, pausing beside her. 'She's got big tits. Say, Mina, you can come to our room any time.'

Mina turned her back on him in confused embarrassment, seeking Edna, who was deep in whispered conversation with another boy, but who now gave her a quick smile. 'I reckon we've done our bit,' she said, and seized her arm to hurry her towards the staff elevator.

'Where are we going?' Mina gasped.

'Well, to bed. Where'd you suppose.'

'But . . . it's only eight o'clock.'

'It's lights out for us at nine,' Edna told her, while the elevator filled with more and more girls, crowding and pushing, and chattering. 'We're up again at four, and Mrs Young reckons we need seven hours sleep.'

'At four? Whatever for?'

'There's things to be done,' Edna explained. 'We're on duty at six, with tea and coffee and juices and things. Mr Morton figures the customers like to see a woman first thing in the morning. And before then we have to shower and do our laundry, and press our dresses and brush our hair . . . it all takes time. We have to have *our* breakfasts too. There's nothing else until twelve.'

'Oh, but . . . I'm not to be a chambermaid,' Mina said, and wished she hadn't.

Several heads turned.

'At least, I don't think so,' Mina said. 'I'm to be Mrs Young's assistant, in the laundry.'

'Hark at her,' said another girl. 'Mrs Young's assistant, la-di-da.'

'Her tame tail, you mean,' Edna said, with total but slightly envious contempt. 'You want to watch her, kid. She likes the pretty ones. Especially when they have tits like yours.'

If only everyone would stop referring to her breasts all the time, Mina thought. Or if only she was small for her age, instead of apparently large – it was not a matter she had ever considered before. Charlie had made her proud of her body, for the first time. But these . . .

'You're going to have fun tonight, eh, Eddie?' asked one of the other girls.

'Some,' Edna agreed. 'Like finding out if she really is Piggy's pet.'

Mina began to grow desperately afraid. She seemed to have said all the wrong things, and she seemed to have jumped with both feet into a roaring inferno of lively obscenity. While what they were suggesting about Mrs Young . . . but she had the evidence of her own eyes and her own experience this evening to suggest that they were telling her the truth.

Most frightening of all, however, was the utterly crowded world in which she had found herself. Devon had never been crowded, save for church on Sunday mornings, and in fact the little parish where Father had served had never provided more than thirty odd worshippers at any one time. In any event, they had all been quiet, and well-behaved, and reflective. She had thought the hold of the *William McKinley* as accurate a depiction of hell as anything she had ever been able to imagine, at least partly because of the crowd, but there it had still been possible to withdraw into one's self and mind one's own business. In fact, that had been encouraged.

Now she was in a world which was not only crowded, but in which everyone seemed to share everyone else's innermost thoughts and most intimate secrets, and in which apparently, she, as a new girl, was everyone's plaything. She had the wildest urge to leap out of the elevator and run out into the street and all the way back to the *William McKinley*, and curl up in Charlie Stark's bunk, and cry herself to sleep . . . but she didn't even know how to get out of the elevator. And when the car did stop, on the ninth floor, and they all scampered up the stairs to the tenth – the elevator did not go beyond the ninth – everyone seemed so jolly and cheerful that she began to wonder if she had not just been imagining things. Dismay, at finding that the room in which she was to sleep with Edna was actually a dormitory to be shared with four others, was quite thrust aside by the view from the window. She looked across roofs, down on to the avenues, glittering paths of light, and then out across the river, to the lights on the ships at anchor, the more distant lights of Ellis Island and then the Statue of Liberty . . . 'Oh, it's grand,' she whispered. 'Just grand. I've never seen such a sight.' She wondered if the view from the top floor of the Savoy would be as splendid.

'It don't change much,' Edna remarked, without interest, having presumably looked at it every day of her life. 'This here is your locker.' She had already taken off her dress, and was hanging it up, very carefully. Mina hastily followed suit, aware that the other girls were standing around her, watching her. She faced them, arranging her features into a smile. 'I'm Wilhelmina,' she said. 'But my friends call me Mina.'

'I'm Betty.'

'I'm Claudette.'

'I'm Jo.'

'I'm Lucy.'

She supposed they were all about her own age, or a little older, with cheerfully plain features but friendly enough smiles. And she had been afraid of them.

'You'll like it in the laundry,' Jo said. 'If you can stand the heat.'

'Better hours,' Betty observed.

'From England,' Claudette said. 'You gotta tell us about the Queen.'

'Say, ain't she dead or something?' Lucy asked.

'Well, then, about the King, or whatever.'

'I know about him,' Betty said. 'He has a beard. And wears pretty uniforms.'

'This will be your bed,' Edna announced. 'It's next to mine, see? Here's your nightie.' It had been folded beneath her pillow, and was certainly clean, although when she held it against herself, she found it only came to her knees.

'What's with you, then?' Edna was asking. 'Ain't it true you're old Starky's piece?'

'No, I'm not,' Mina said. 'I'm nobody's . . . piece.'

'Yeah? How come you got this job, then?'

'I . . . my parents died on the crossing from England,' Mina explained. 'And Captain Stark, Mr Stark's brother, wanted to help me.'

'Jesus Christ,' Edna commented. 'And he didn't have to get inside?'

'Well . . .' Mina decided to change the subect. 'These clothes I've been given . . .' Because there was another complete change hanging in her locker. 'Where'd they come from? Mrs Young wasn't expecting me.'

'Aw, she keeps a whole stack of them, in various sizes,' Edna told her. 'When a girl leaves, she has to turn in her stuff.' She stepped out of her drawers and dropped her nightgown over her head. 'Old Piggy keeps them locked away until someone else turns up.'

'You mean they're not new?' Mina cried in horror, gazing at the nightgown lying on her bed. Somehow wearing someone else's cast-off dress, even someone else's drawers, once they'd been laundered, was acceptable. But someone else's night-dress . . .

'Christ, no,' Edna said. 'Say, you do have some funny ideas. You coming to bed, or not?'

Mina hesitated, then turned her back on the room to finish undressing, and discovered that the other girls had again come close to watch her.

'She *has* got big tits,' Betty commented.

'And *what* a puss fur,' Claudette remarked.

43

'You saying you're sixteen?' Lucy demanded.

'I *am* sixteen,' Mina shouted. 'And I can't help the way I was born. I wish you'd all just leave me alone.' She could feel the tears lurking very close behind her eyes.

'Okay, okay,' Edna said. 'Leave her alone, you guys. Let her get to bed. But say,' she went on, 'didn't old Piggy tell you to have those boots polished?'

'Oh, lord.' Mina dropped the nightgown over her shoulders, sat on the bed in misery. 'I completely forgot.'

'No bother,' Edna told her. 'You still have time to let the boots have them.'

'Where do I go?'

'They have a room just along from ours,' Edna said. 'You give them to one of the boys in there.'

Mina stood up. 'Should I get dressed?'

'Naw,' Edna said. 'You don't want to waste time with that. You'll only be gone a minute.'

'It's the second door on the left,' Lucy told her. 'Don't forget now, the *second* door on the left.'

'Just open it and ask for Paul.'

'Don't forget,' Edna said. 'Second door, and ask for Paul.'

'Oh . . . yes,' Mina said, and looked from face to face. They all looked terribly interested. In the blacking of her boots? 'Could someone lend me a dressing gown, or something?'

'You don't need no dressing gown,' Edna declared. 'Not just for a stroll in the corridor. Remember. The second door.'

'And ask for Paul,' Claudette said.

Now she was feeling nervous. Out there seemed a totally different world.

Betty had opened the bedroom door. Mina picked up her boots and stepped through. 'Hurry back,' Betty whispered, and closed the door behind her.

Mina looked up and down the empty corridor. She could hear noise, voices, laughter, from behind several of the doors. But if she hurried there was less chance of encountering anyone. She tiptoed past the next door, reached for the second from her own, hesitated, drew a long breath, and knocked very gently. There had been voices from inside, but these now ceased, and a moment later the door was opened, and a boy gazed at her; he wore green bellhop trousers, but only a singlet above. 'Christ!' he remarked.

44

Mina licked her lips. 'I'm terribly sorry to bother you,' she said. 'But these boots . . . I was told to ask for Paul.'

'It's the new kid,' he shouted. 'The new kid, from England.' Before she could ask him to be quiet, he had seized boots and hand and jerked her into the room, pushing the door shut behind them. Mina staggered across the floor, found herself in the middle of a room very like the girls' dormitory, save that the six inmates here were all male.

She didn't like the look of *their* faces at all, and they were all in a state of undress. 'Which one of you is Paul?' she asked, making her voice sound as confident as she could.

'Oh, we're all named Paul,' said the boy who had let her in. 'Edna told us you'd be dropping by.'

'Edna?' Mina recognised him as the boy her 'friend' had been whispering to, downstairs.

'She said you wanted us to put boot polish on your tits,' said another boy.

'I just want to *feel* them,' said a third. 'Come on, kid.'

He reached for her, aiming apparently at her nightdress, and she was once again consumed with the tremendous surge of anger and outrage she had known when Mrs Young had assaulted her – but these louts weren't employing her. She slapped his hand down, turned, and threw both boots into the face of the next boy, who was also reaching for her, sending him tumbling off balance and across one of the beds.

The boy who had opened the door remained in front of her. 'Now, kid,' he said. 'Don't act up.'

Mina kicked him on the ankle, as hard as she could. The jar hurt her own bare toes as much as it probably hurt him, but she was prepared for it. He gave a howl and stooped, and she pushed him over, again with all the strength she could muster. He gave another howl and sprawled on the floor , effectively acting as a barrier to the other three boys, who were also starting forward. For the moment Mina's path was clear. She reached the door, wrenched it open, and slammed it shut again behind her. She ran along the corridor, back to her own door, hands twisting the knob, to no avail: the door was locked.

'Let me in,' she whispered. 'Please let me in.' She dared not look over her shoulder, because she was sure the bell-boys were immediately behind her. And now she heard a giggle from behind the wood; but no sound of the key turning in the lock.

Oh, the wretches, she thought. 'Let me in,' she shouted, banging on the panelling, while her anger grew, at the way she had been set up, the way Edna had let her finish undressing before reminding her about the boots at all . . .

A door had opened, and someone *was* behind her. She gasped, and turned, flattening herself against the door, gazed at the Irish-American boy who had been rude to her downstairs. 'What the Sam Hall are you doing?' he demanded. 'You want a sore arse?'

She was panting, but the corridor remained empty, apart from him. Although she could hear doors opening and shutting, somewhere. But the bell-boys had still not left their room in pursuit; she realised they were not going to.

She got her breathing under control. 'I'm locked out,' she explained. 'They've locked me out.'

'New kid,' he said, not unsympathetically. 'It's all part of the game. But making that row . . . you'd better come in here for five minutes.' He seized her wrist and dragged her to the next door.

'Where?' she asked, trying to stop herself from moving.

'My dormitory. It's where the bootblacks sleep.'

He was a bootblack. The person she had been looking for all the time. No wonder she had been told half a dozen times the *second* door; they had been afraid she'd spoil their fun.

But she had lost her boots, and under no circumstances was she entering any other bedroom filled with young men. 'No,' she said. 'No, you let me go.'

'For Pete's sake,' he cried. 'You want to get us both . . .' He stared past her, his jaw dropping, while the colour drained from his face. Mina turned, knees knocking together, and gazed at Mrs Young.

Chapter 3

Mrs Young looked extraordinarily like an avenging angel –
save that angel wasn't the word Mina would have chosen.
'Well,' she said. 'Up to your tricks already, Wilhelmina. First
night! And you swore to me . . .'

'Please, Mrs Young,' Mina said. 'You have it all wrong.
Really and truly. The . . .' She bit her lip. It was suddenly
occurring to her that, if she intended to go on working here, she
would have to go on working with Edna and the others. No
matter what dirty tricks they had played on her. As the
bootblack had said, it was all part of the game.

And remarkably, no matter what had happened, or might
yet happen, she did still want to go on working here. Quite
apart from the necessity of earning some money, and the sheer
thrill of being in such a place at all, this evening had been the
most exciting of her entire life, if only *because* of the constant
company, so young and vibrant, and alive – even if it was also
bawdy and vulgar, and more than a little cruel.

'Yes?' Mrs Young demanded.

'I . . .' Mina gave a helpless glance at the boy.

'Well, Clancy?' Mrs Young inquired, menacingly.

Clancy opened his mouth, and then closed it again. No doubt
he could understand what was passing through Mina's mind.
'New kid,' he said feebly. 'I thought . . .'

'Indeed,' Mrs Young said. 'But she led you on. She *encouraged*
you. Come on, admit it.'

'I . . .' Once again Mina started to deny it, and then changed
her mind. Because she would once again have to work with this
boy, Clancy, too.

'Yes,' Mrs Young said, drily. 'I warned you, girl. I could see
your sort the moment I laid eyes on you. I warned you. Well, I

47

shall have to teach you a lesson. You too, Clancy. You should know better by now. Downstairs.'

'Downstairs?' Mina cried. She had visions of being hauled into the lobby in her nightclothes.

'To my apartment,' Mrs Young said. 'Down you go.'

Mina hesitated, glanced at Clancy, who gave a slight shrug and then a sigh, and went towards the stairs. Mina followed, having no idea what was about to happen, aware only that Mrs Young was breathing heavily at her shoulder. They went down the stairs, and into Mrs Young's apartment. Mrs Young closed the door. Mina stood in the centre of the floor, found Clancy beside her; Mrs Young went into a sort of cupboard beside the bed.

'What's going to happen to us?' Mina whispered.

'We're going to be caned.'

'Caned?' she shouted in consternation, and inadvertently clutched his hand.

'Caned,' Mrs Young agreed, re-emerging from the cupboard and carrying a bamboo stick. 'I am going to put stripes on that pretty little backside of yours, Wilhelmina, which I hope will discourage you from baring it to anybody else while you work here.'

'You . . . you wouldn't *dare!*' Mina shouted.

'Wouldn't I?' Mrs Young asked. 'Are you going to resist me? It's bend over or the street, girl. Now!'

Mina stared at her. This can't be happening, she thought. It simply can't. But to be put out on the street, at night, with no money, no place to go, when she desperately wanted to stay . . .

'I want to see Mr Stark,' she said.

'Don't expect him to help you, girl. Besides, he put you in my charge. Now, gather up your nightgown, and bend over that chair.'

'Gather . . .' Mina shot a glance at Clancy, her cheeks burning. 'I won't. Not in front of him.'

'You're not going to pretend he doesn't know what you look like?' Mrs Young demanded, swishing the cane. 'Haste, girl, haste.'

Mina stared at Clancy, who gave another shrug of his shoulders, and pointedly looked at the other side of the room. He was on her side, now. But what difference did that make to the coming pain and humiliation? She either hauled herself off and slapped this harridan's face – oh, how she wanted to do that – and thus found herself walking the streets, or she accepted her punishment like some little girl. She thought she would choke with indignation and outrage, but she knew she was going to accept the punishment. She simply had no alternative.

She turned away from Clancy, held on to the chair with one hand, scooped her nightdress to her waist with the other, tensed herself for the blow, or blows, which were about to descend upon her, listened to a knock and gazed at the door as it opened, and found herself staring at a man.

'Mr Morton!' Mrs Young exclaimed, her voice registering both surprise and indignation.

'I heard there was a commotion up here, so I thought I'd find out what the trouble was about,' said Mr Morton.

'But really, sir,' Mrs Young protested. 'Just walking into a woman's bedroom, when I could have been undressed . . .'

Her words recalled Mina to her situation, and she hurriedly dropped the skirt of her nightgown back into place and stood up, terribly aware that she was wearing only the single garment. Because never had she seen so elegant a man. Mr Morton was not young, by her reckoning: she estimated he might be nearly thirty. Nor was he handsome. Although tall and square shouldered, he had little chin and a long nose, a thin moustache and his dark hair was already receding. But he wore a black dinner suit which fitted him like a second skin, with a spotlessly white stiff shirt and bow tie, and patent leather shoes in which she could see her face, with a knife edge crease on his trousers – and with several most expensive looking rings on his fingers, as well as, she observed on a second quick glance, diamond shirt studs and cufflinks.

He was staring at her with equal interest, and allowing his gaze to drift up and down her body; she remembered that she was standing between him and the light, and that her nightdress was made of thin cotton. It was a most disturbing gaze. People like the Stark brothers or Tommy the steward, or even most of the other male passengers on the *William McKinley*, had all been obviously mentally undressing her with their eyes every time they looked at her – she realised with a start of

49

surprise that Clancy the bootblack, was about the first man she had met since leaving Devon who had not done that, which was why she had instinctively liked him – but this man's gaze did more than merely undress, it seemed to caress her, to arouse suggestions of intimacy when they had not yet even spoken to each other. Although she knew instinctively that they soon would.

'Indeed, Mr Morton,' Mrs Young was saying. 'This girl, taken in only today as an act of charity, would you believe it, to help in the laundry, has turned out to be a proper slut. Her first night, and she tried to seduce poor Clancy here.'

'Nonsense,' Mr Morton declared. 'That is nonsense, isn't it, girl?'

Mina stared at him with her mouth open.

'She's tongue-tied,' Mr Morton remarked. 'You'd best tell her who I am, Mrs Young.'

'Mr Morton is the Assistant Manager.' Mrs Young pronounced the words as the devil might have announced the appearance of the Holy Grail.

'Ahem,' Mr Morton said, clearly not satisfied.

'He is also the son of the proprietor,' Mrs Young went on, more bitterly yet.

Mina could only goggle at him.

'Come along,' Mr Morton said. 'Speak up, girl. Are you guilty?' He smiled, deprecatingly. 'Of, ah, seducing this lad?'

'I . . . I became lost in the corridors, sir,' Mina said, very carefully, 'while attempting to find the bootblacks. And then Mr Clancy . . .'

'Good God!' Mr Morton commented. 'Where are you from, girl?'

'She's from England,' Mrs Young told him, as if that accounted for everything.

'I see,' Mr Morton said. 'But . . . you do not speak like a chambermaid. What is your name?'

'She isn't a chambermaid,' Mrs Young pointed out. 'She's a laundrymaid.'

'My name is Wilhelmina Doberley,' Mina said. And with a flash of inspiration she added. 'But my friends call me Mina, sir.'

He continued to gaze at her.

'She is a common slut who must be taught how to behave herself, sir,' Mrs Young said.

'I am sure a young lady like Miss Doberley knows how to behave herself, Mrs Young,' Mr Morton said. 'There is some mystery here. Yes, indeed. You will come with me, Miss Doberley, Mina, is it? Yes, you will come with me, and tell me how you happen to be here at all.'

Mina glanced at Mrs Young.

'And what of the disturbance?' Mrs Young demanded. 'What of the discipline? Without discipline, Mr Morton . . .'

'I know, I know,' Mr Morton said. 'You have told me all this before, Mrs Young. Of course discipline must be maintained. But in this case, why, it's as plain as the nose on your face.' Which was a considerable assertion, Mina thought with some pleasure. 'This lad found Mina lost, and attempted to take advantage of her. Don't attempt to deny it, Clancy,' he said, although Clancy had actually not said a word.

'No,' Mina cried. 'That's not true.'

Clancy gave another of his sighs. 'Lying isn't going to help, Mina,' he said. 'I'm sorry for what I did.'

'But . . .'

'Quite,' Mr Morton went on. 'There is no point in trying to protect him, Mina. Be sure you make him suffer, Mrs Young.'

Mrs Young appeared to be speechless.

'While I,' Mr Morton announced grandly, 'will investigate this poor child further. I doubt she belongs in an establishment like this. Indeed I do. Come along, Mina, come along.' He held the door for her.

'But . . . I'm only wearing a nightgown,' Mina protested.

Mr Morton smiled. 'Really, child, I have seen young women in their nightgowns before, I do assure you.'

Mina gazed from Clancy to Mrs Young, suddenly almost wishing to stay and be caned, and then at least released to the security of her bed. But it was too late, now. She tried to convey her gratitude to the boy with a quick smile, and then stepped through the door.

Mr Morton led Mina down the corridor away from the staff elevator and the senior staff quarters, while she became increasingly aware of how little she had on. They turned a corner, and suddenly entered a different world, where the carpet was twice as thick and there were murals on the walls, while at the far end she could see another elevator with a much more ornate door.

'This one is empty, I think,' Mr Morton said, stopping outside the door of Number 903, and taking a bunch of keys from his pocket. He unlocked the door, switched on the electric light. 'Come in here, Mina.'

Mina hesitated in the doorway. Once again she was totally unsure as to what was likely to happen next. She knew she had no business at all entering an empty bedroom, or even a full one, for that matter, with a man, especially when dressed only in her nightgown – but then, she had no business *being* in a man's company at all, dressed only in her nightgown. But this was not a *man*; rather he was the supreme arbiter of her fate. If he was indeed not only the assistant manager, but also the son of the proprietor, then he would even be able to tell Joe Stark where to get off. And she could not believe that so elegant a man could possibly wish any sort of relationship with her.

Yet to go with him into a bedroom . . . she found herself inside before she meant to. Because, as with everything in this hotel, her breath was again swept away by the splendour of the place. She had thought Mrs Young's apartment elegant, but this . . . and Mrs Young had told her these were the cheaper rooms. She gazed at the huge double bed, the polished dressing table, the three mirrors, the gilt handles on the door to the closet, the china ewer and basin, the carpet on the floor, the pictures on the wall . . . and, above all, at the view out over the city, and found she was holding her breath.

Mr Morton did not seem the least impressed by his surroundings, but threw himself into the easy chair by the bed, draping one knee over the other, and stared at her. 'Wilhelmina Doberley,' he remarked. 'I suppose the girls were hazing you.'

'Sir?' She stood in the deepest shade she could find, her hands clasped in front of her.

'Oh, I understand your motives in wishing to protect them,' he said. 'And I shall respect those motives. I shall do nothing about this evening, not to *them*. But you really are a little special, you know. Come here, Mina.'

Slowly Mina took two steps forward.

'Stark told me you were a trifle different to the usual girl he takes on, and I didn't altogether believe him. Although I'm certainly glad I came to have a look for myself. A parson's daughter, eh?'

'Yes, sir.'

'Thrown out into the great wild world, courtesy of Charlie Stark. The man is an utter scoundrel.'

'He . . . he was only trying to help, sir.'

'Help, you call it. Well, I suppose he did, without perhaps knowing it. Because *I* shall help you, Mina. Indeed I shall, if you will allow me. It will be my great pleasure. Now, come over here, and lie on this bed beside me, and we shall decide what's best to be done.'

Mina gazed at him. Not even Charlie Stark had been quite so brutally frank about his intentions, at least not until they had got to know each other better. She was surprised to find that she was not angry, rather breathless. Because the possibility of accepting his invitation – with all the benefits she might therefore receive – really did not enter her mind at all. It was less a matter of her upbringing and very nature, or even the fact that she did not really like this man, as a human being, than that she just did not feel like it. Indeed, after the past month, and even more the past six hours, she did not suppose she would ever feel like it again.

So this was it, then, she thought. The shortest career in history. This man would not be fobbed off like Charlie Stark, because he was not in the least afraid of her. Charlie had known she came from several classes above him. This man knew she came from at least a class *below* him. There was all the difference in the world. She could only try to treat him as an equal, at least in intelligence and breeding.

She drew a long breath. 'No, sir.'

Mr Morton's brows slowly drew together into a frown. 'No? You find Charlie Stark more attractive than me?'

'I don't find any man attractive, right this minute, sir,' Mina said.

'Good God,' Morton replied. 'You're not one of *those*. Well, then, you'd better run along back to Mrs Young.' He was clearly becoming annoyed.

'I'm not one of anything,' Mina said. 'Why do I have to be? Everyone in this whole building seems to think of nothing else but sex.'

She paused in alarm, not having intended to say so much, but he merely gazed at her, and this time *he* was looking utterly bewildered. 'I don't suppose the average person has a lot else to think about,' he suggested.

'Well, I have,' she said. 'I'm an orphan, Mr Morton. I saw my mother and my father die of cholera. It was horrible. I don't have anything. I don't have a hotel, and I don't have any money. I want to *earn* some money. I want to make my own way in the world. Just that. I think your hotel is absolutely marvellous. I'd like to go on working here, really and truly. But I want to *work*. I'd have thought that if your father really owns the place you'd appreciate that. But I don't want to be caned by Mrs Young, or assaulted by Mr Stark, or . . . or raped by you,' she panted.

'Great Scott,' Mr Morton remarked. 'You'd rather save it all for Captain Charlie, eh? I must say, that man must have points I've never noticed.'

'Charlie Stark is never going to touch me again,' Mina shouted. 'No one is ever going to touch me again, until I want him to. Please, Mr Morton, can't you get that into your head? I'm *not* a slut, no matter what Mrs Young or Joe Stark or his brother may think. I'm just a girl who wants to work.'

Now she supposed she had finally done it, as Mr Morton continued to gaze at her for several seconds. Then he said, 'Would you like to sleep in here for tonight? Alone. I'll give you the key.' Since she obviously did not understand what he meant, he added, 'If you go back to the dormitory, the girls may well haze you again.'

'I don't mind being hazed,' Mina said. 'But . . . you mean I'm not fired?'

'Of course you're not fired, Mina,' Mr Morton said. 'I think you could be the best thing that has happened to this hotel for a long time. You want to work. You do understand that we expect our girls to work very hard?'

'I realise that, sir.'

'Well, then . . . what job had you been given?'

'I was to help in the laundry, sir.'

'Fiddlesticks. You need to be seen, and appreciated. You'll be a chambermaid, starting tomorrow. You'll spend the first week with Edna . . . it is Edna, isn't it?'

'Yes, sir. But . . .'

'After that you'll be on your own. I'm going to let you work, Mina, and settle down, and think about things.' He stood beside her, looking down at her. 'I promise you that from this moment no one, not Mrs Young, not Mr Stark, and not any of the boys in this establishment, *is* going to lay a finger on you. I can't answer for the girls. But if you don't work hard and well, Mrs Young will send you to answer to me. Do you understand that?'

'Oh, yes, Mr Morton,' she said, not actually understanding him at all.

'By the same token, if anyone treads on you again, you come to me. Understood?'

'Yes, Mr Morton.'

He opened the door for her. 'Then run along, Wilhelmina Doberley. Lights will be out in fifteen minutes. And you have a busy day tomorrow.'

'He's a deep one, that Jimmy Morton,' Claudette remarked.

Edna had a candle, so it didn't really matter that the electric light had been turned off – Mrs Young apparently had a switch which controlled the tenth floor – because the girls could still sit on their beds to talk.

'Deep?' Lucy scoffed. 'He's as shallow as a saucer. He's had me in that same 903.'

'He didn't,' Mina protested.

'He sure did. I reckon I didn't think as fast as you. Although I reckoned some good might come of it. Nothing ever did, save I skipped a jump and thought I was pregnant. And I wasn't even that. I'd watch him, if I were you.'

'Good lord,' Mina muttered. She had almost been prepared to like Mr Morton, after all, in view of the gentlemanly way he had behaved.

'He can't keep his hands off nothing in skirts,' Betty told her. 'And if he asks you to go screwing . . . , he calls it crewing . . . on that yacht of his . . . watch out.'

'You mean, he asked you?'

'Sure, I went once. Boss's son, and all. Let me tell you all about it.'

'No,' Mina said, lying down and pulling up her blanket. 'I don't want to hear.'

'Like I said,' Claudette repeated, 'he's deep. He'll get you, Mina, when he's good and ready.'

No, Mina thought. He'll never get me. Never, never, never. But bang went another dream, that he could actually be decent. There was nobody in this entire establishment that was at all decent . . . save for the bootblack, Clancy. She sat up in consternation. Because of her he had received a caning from that ogre of a woman.

'Mina,' Edna whispered, blowing out the candle, 'that was real good of you, not letting on about what happened to Morton. It was only . . . well, a sort of initiation, you know.'

'I know,' Mina said.

'We had no idea you'd go and start a fight,' Edna explained.

'You mean you expected me just to stand there and let them put boot polish on my . . .'

'I did,' Edna said. 'When *I* was new here. Gee, that was something. It took me *days* to get all of it off. And I felt so randy . . . but I guess everyone's right, and you *are* different. Maybe you don't belong here, at that.'

'I do belong here,' Mina declared. 'I'll show you I do. But . . . what about Clancy? I got him in an awful mess.'

'He'll survive,' Edna said. 'Clancy's a toughie. Don't you worry none about him. In this place you have to worry about number one. So get some sleep. Tomorrow you start work, remember?'

To Mina's surprise, she actually did sleep very soundly; she was utterly exhausted. It was incredible to suppose that she had begun the day on Ellis Island. But now . . . five minutes after she had closed her eyes, it seemed, she was awakened by a shake from Edna, to find the electric light glaring, and to begin a day of frenzied activity.

Edna had herself already been along and retrieved Mina's boots from the bell-boys, and then had had them polished. 'By Clancy,' she said, with a sly grin. 'He didn't sleep too good.'

Mina felt she should see him, and apologise, and thank him . . . but she couldn't bring herself to do it. He might have been almost a hero the way he had accepted punishment for both of them, but he had still looked at her bare bottom as she had bent over the chair. Anyway, there wasn't time. The girls scurried to the bathroom, having to fight off the boys with a tremendous amount of shouting and laughter, hair pulling and surreptitious cuddling and squeezing, showered and cleaned their teeth, hurried back to dress, and took their yesterday's clothes down to the laundry, because they had to wear clean clothes every day, and they each only possessed two sets. Here they encountered Mrs Young, already up and about, although it was still dark outside. Mina tensed herself for an explosion, but Mrs Young merely regarded her with savage contempt. The same thing happened when she met Mr Stark, a little while later, when she and Edna and the other girls went down to collect their trolleys and trays. Joe Stark gave her a similar look. 'They all think I'm . . .' She bit her lip.

Edna giggled. 'That you're Jimmy Morton's new girl. But that's all to the good, don't you see, Mina? No one is going to touch you while they think that.'

'Sixth floor for you today,' the duty chef said, reading from a huge sheet of paper. 'That's Numbers 602, 612 and 616 for early call. 616 wants coffee, not tea, and grapefruit juice. Very important. She's allergic to oranges. No juice at all for 602.'

'Papers,' came the cry from outside, and two of the bell-boys staggered in beneath huge parcels of newspapers. The parcels were slit open by the waiting under-doorman and then the various dailies apportioned to the requisite trays.

'Boots,' came another cry, and several of the bootblacks hurried in, carrying armfuls of freshly polished boots and shoes, all tagged with their room numbers. Clancy was one of them, and Mina tried to catch his eye and smile, but he ignored her.

Then she and Edna were away, pushing their trolley on to the staff elevator, jostling with the other girls; the elevator only held three trolleys, with their attendant girls, at a time, so those who were late had to wait for it to come back down. But Edna was first, as was apparently expected, with Mina panting at her heels, gazing at the trolley laden with an indescribable mishmash of cups, saucers, pots, toast racks, newspapers . . . Edna, being Edna, had even placed the various boots and shoes

57

assigned to her numbers on the trays; one set of boots rested against a slice of toast, a shoe was dipping into a butter bowl.

'Don't *worry*,' she said when Mina pointed this out. 'I've a cloth here to wipe them with.'

'How did the chef know which guests wanted what?' Mina asked. She didn't dare ask how *they* were going to remember which guest got what.

'That big chart of his,' Edna explained. 'The concierge keeps it, and the guests tell him what they want in the evenings. He sends it down to the kitchen.'

'Do the guests ever take other meals in their rooms?'

'Sure they do. But that's Room Service. Nothing to do with us, thank the Lord. That's proper service, that is.'

And this was most definitely not proper service. Edna wiped the shoe clean and placed the pair on the floor outside 602, arranged cups and saucers on one of the trays, together with the tea pot and the glass of juice, the toast rack and the slightly dented butter, knocked and, as there was no reply, unlocked the door with her passkey.

'Shouldn't we wait for him to say "come in"?' Mina whispered.

'We'd wait forever. Naw, if they puts in for a six o'clock call, they *want* to be wakened up.'

The door was open. But the curtains were drawn and the room was utterly dark. Mina inhaled stale tobacco smoke and a tremendous scent of masculinity. She stood absolutely still, afraid to move in case she knocked something over. But Edna placed the tray on the bedside table with the utmost certainty. 'Morning!' she shouted, cheerfully.

'Eh? Oh, my God!' A man, from his voice, sat bolt upright. 'Where am I? What's happening?'

'Morning tea, sir,' Edna announced, still speaking at the top of her voice. 'Shall I draw your blinds, sir?'

'No, no. Go away.' The man lay down again and buried his head in the pillow.

'*He* didn't want to be woken up,' Mina observed, as the door closed behind them.

'Course he did. He'll be grateful in a little while,' Edna declared. 'Shouldn't have drunk so much last night, the swine.'

The procedure was repeated in 612, except that the man in there was awake. There was no light on, but when Edna placed

58

the tray beside the bed with another bawled 'Good morning', his hand shot and seized her thigh.

'Got you, my darling,' he said.

'Is it me or my friend that you want?' Edna asked, without appearing in the least alarmed or even hurt by his grip.

'What? What?' The man released her and also sat up, while Edna brutally switched on the light, to reveal that he had nothing on, although thankfully, Mina thought, the sheet was across his lap. 'Oh, I say . . .' he spluttered.

'Better luck next time,' Edna said, dumping his newspaper on his lap and leading Mina from the room.

'Don't tell me *that* happens very often,' Mina said.

'Often enough. That guy's new, only came in yesterday. Some guys are always trying that. What the hell, some of them are prepared to lash out a good tip.'

'You mean you'd let one of the guests . . .'

Edna winked. 'No screwing, kid. That way lies trouble. But a kiss and a cuddle, now, what the hell? Who's to know? Only if they'll pay, though. And you can always tell the ones that will. That guy . . . no dice.'

It occurred to Mina that she was going to have to accept an entirely different and new set of standards to any she had previously held, if she was going to survive here, much less prosper. And she certainly intended to prosper.

'Morning,' Edna bellowed cheerfully at 616. This was an elderly woman, already sitting up and reading a book, her hair concealed beneath a white mob cap. She regarded Edna and the tray, and Mina, with some distaste.

'That is orange juice,' she pointed out. 'I asked for grapefruit. I *wish* grapefruit.'

'Can't be done,' Edna said. 'There's no grapefruit in the hotel. There's no grapefruit in all New York,' she added, warming to her theme.

'You gave the grapefruit to 612,' Mina hissed when they got back outside.

'So? He didn't complain.'

'You didn't give him time. But it was hers. And she's allergic to orange juice. And there's lots more grapefruit downstairs. Shouldn't we go back and fetch her one? Isn't the customer always right?'

'Only if he darn well knows he is. Or she is,' Edna told her.

'Look, we have just time to get down and load the trays for our six-thirty calls. Then there's another lot at seven. You start going back to correct orders and we'll be here all day.'

She was, of course, very right, looked at from the point of view of a chambermaid. There *were* people who wanted to be awakened at six-thirty, and even more at seven, and then seven-thirty. Mina and Edna spent the next hour, together with all the other girls, scurrying up and down stairs and elevators, doing their best to smile and to cope with the various moods and idiosyncracies they encountered. After seven-thirty the guests moved on to breakfast, and were taken over by Room Service, which, as Edna had said, comprised proper waiters. Not that seven-thirty brought any relaxation of effort of pressure for the chambermaids; by then the clean linen and dusters and brooms were waiting. There were several floors of corridors to be done, as well as each room as it fell vacant, or as a resident went out for the morning. The girls, and there were some thirty of them, were kept hard at it until very nearly lunchtime, always with the risk of encountering Mrs Young, who, whatever her personal weaknesses, was a stickler for cleanliness and indeed perfection in the making of beds and the sweeping of carpets, and always carried a short cane which she was not averse to applying to knuckles or backsides when she was displeased. In fact, Mina soon realised that her reputation as a dragon was entirely undeserved; it was easy to see that she was a large, over-tense woman who was terrified of losing her position, but who could not resist striking up a personal relationship with each of the fifty odd young people, of both sexes, who were in her immediate charge, even if that relationship, in most cases, was one of physical domination.

By lunchtime, taken early for the staff, most of the morning's work was done; only those unfortunates whose allotted rooms happened to maintain a "Do Not Disturb" sign even at this late hour were kept hanging about – and Edna, for one, made a practice of ignoring such notices and just walking in, often surprising guests in the most remarkable situations, but certainly encouraging them to abandon their rooms. Those girls who managed to get finished were free for a few hours after the midday meal, to go shopping, or just to sit around and gossip, or to nap; they were all expected on duty again, properly dressed in the best of starched uniforms, freshly showered and smelling like violets, by four-thirty. The Superb catered for a good deal of foreign trade, which, in New York in 1901, meant British trade, and the British enjoyed a peculiar function called afternoon tea – a four o'clock and after event to which Mina had in her time been partial. Tea was not, however, an American pastime, and was not served in the rooms, although it was available for guests downstairs in the lounge from half past three onwards. From four o'clock onwards, therefore, all rooms, unless adorned with the dreaded "Do Not Disturb" signs, were regarded as fair game for the evening turn down of beds, or remaking altogether, where the guests had been such nuisances as to have had a siesta.

It was, Mina soon realised, a most peculiar set-up. The hotel depended upon the guests, obviously, for its custom, but as it was not in any sense a residential hotel, its trade was entirely transitory and mostly composed of those itinerant foreigners: according to Edna there was almost no one who came back more than once, except for the odd British businessman, and such rare customers were always singled out by Mr Stark and Mrs Young, and their rooms tended and serviced by specially selected staff. For the rest, the guests were regarded as fee paying enemies, to whom the minimum of service was supplied in return for the maximum of tips or payments. A guest, she came to understand, could obtain anything, even, apparently, early morning sex, if he flashed enough money in the right direction. Until he did so, the minimum was accorded.

She was equally astonished and appalled by the relationship between employees and management, which was even more minimal as regards co-operation. The girls, and the boys, and even senior staff like Mrs Young or Mr Stark, regarded people like Jimmy Morton and the manager as even more natural enemies than the guests. They had to be subservient to such eminent figures, but they had absolutely no scruples about robbing them, in any possible way. Mina was horrified one night when she was clearing up after supper and saw more than half of an enormous cooked ham being bagged and passed to Mrs Young by the head chef, for her to take with her on her evening off. At the other end of the scale the bell-boys were not above stealing whatever they could, and often enough there would be a surreptitious knock on the door of the girls' dormitory, after lights out, and the boys would sneak in with

61

quarter full bottles of champagne, and sometimes even of spirits, left by a party downstairs, with which they and the girls would proceed to make as merry as they could. These were occasions for much hugging and kissing, and possibly even more than that in the darkness. Mina could not be sure, as she always withdrew as far as possible from such goings on, less because of any priggish sense of propriety, than because of a somewhat more disturbing realisation that she did not *want* to descend to the level of just another chambermaid. That there was a good deal of mutual horseplay amongst the junior staff was certain, but she very rapidly got the reputation of being different, which apparently meant stuck-up, because she was Mr Morton's pet popsie, and was left severely alone even by her fellow workers, after one or two had had their faces slapped.

Which contented her well enough, even if in fact she saw very little of her benefactor except in passing. Whatever his alleged licentiousness, Jimmy Morton had little time for chambermaids. Mina understood that he was being groomed to take over as manager, and was learning the trade from his superior, a large and walrus-moustached man named Howwinger, who never took any notice of the staff at all, and was certainly above investigating either their morals or their honesty. As was Jimmy Morton. He was concerned with the quality of the food and drink being served, and with personally welcoming and entertaining the guests; the Superb had a reputation for bonhomie. Neither he nor Howwinger, however, was at all interested in the quality of domestic service, which was appalling, nor indeed in the domestic side of the hotel at all. Mina soon discovered that very little that glittered in the Superb was even remotely gold. Damp patches on the walls, instead of being redecorated, were hidden by carefully hung pictures; threadbare carpets were turned so that the poorer patches were under the beds; and the bed linen itself, almost all darned and mended in several places, was disguised by expert bed-making. It was obvious to her that Mrs Young *was* concerned about all this, which was her responsibility, but that she could get no response from those in authority to her pleas for action. Mina almost began to feel sorry for her.

Equally she was distressed by the total absence of hygiene in the kitchen. The Superb food might indeed taste superb, but it seemed a miracle to Mina, having watched the same plates used over and over again with just a wipe in between, and cold food reheated to the minimum possible level, that the guests, and the staff, did not come down with acute dysentery, or worse.

But whoever complained was clearly knocking his or her head against a brick wall where Mr Jimmy Morton was concerned; he was far more interested in the form than the substance. He was a well-known New York playboy, Mina learned, who sailed yachts on Long Island Sound and entertained women and even drove a motor car – the Mortons were clearly fabulously wealthy. So who was she to criticise? Or even refuse an invitation, supposing another one ever came her way? As she assumed he had fallen for her, she arrived at her first afternoon off – the girls received one a week – in a state of excited apprehension, anticipating one of those famous invitations to go on his yacht, for all that it was a blustery May day, and totally uncertain how she was going to react to whatever advances he made. But none was forthcoming, and instead she went for a walk with Edna, taking the ferry across the East River to the spreading village of Brooklyn, where Edna's parents lived. She and Edna had now become fast friends, and indeed it was Edna who enabled her to leave the hotel at all, by scrounging various articles of clothing from the other girls – the chambermaids were not allowed to wear their uniforms outside the hotel, and Mina would not again be seen in the rags she had worn from the ship.

Mina was intensely grateful, if equally embarrassed. And even more astonished when they arrived at Edna's father's barbershop – the family lived above it – less than an hour after leaving the hotel.

'But,' she said, 'if your parents live this close to the hotel, why do you board out at all?'

'Because the hotel wants us there,' Edna told her. 'And there's no ferry at four o'clock in the morning. Anyway, who'd want to live in a crummy joint like this?'

It was all utterly confusing, and not a little frightening; meeting Edna's parents and brothers and sisters, every one as lively a personality as Edna herself, brought home with terrifying force just how lonely *she* was. And was going to remain. For if she could think of nothing finer than to have a home, and brothers and sisters, and a mother and father to go to whenever she wished, she also realised after a very brief visit, that Edna was right, and she could not conceive that there was any way she would ever have anything in common with Edna's family. But then, that applied equally to Edna, really, or to any of the girls. While at the other end of the scale she was beginning to understand, whatever passing attraction she might have held for Mr Morton, that in not gratefully leaping into bed with him she had queered her pitch. He might be willing to let it be supposed that she had done so, but there was no way she could really compete with the gorgeously clad young women who were from time to time to be seen entering the hotel on his arm. And indeed, she reminded herself, she would not have had it any other way. She was going to make *her* way, and not into someone's bed. Except that she couldn't be at all sure what way was available for a chambermaid. How did one become a Mrs Young, for instance? And was it essential to have first accumulated the Mrs? Although there was never the slightest evidence of a Mr, where Mrs Young was concerned. She did not even wear a wedding ring.

Far more important was her financial position. Of course the hotel provided her with bed and board and a uniform, down to a nightdress, but she needed cash if she was going to get anywhere. She could hardly contain herself when she opened her first week's pay packet, and was horrified to discover exactly one dollar, together with a slip of paper listing the various deductions.

'It's the same for everyone,' Edna pointed out, 'when they start. You have to pay for your uniform.'

'Even if it's only hired?' Mina demanded.

'Sure. Who's to say when you're going to go and tear it? What, are you aiming to be a millionairess? You'll have to ask your Jimmy about that.'

Her Jimmy, Mina thought angrily. Because she *had* been aiming to become a millionairess. Without any idea of how to go about it. How *did* one make a lot of money, unless one was born to it? She had absolutely no talents, no assets . . . except, as the bell-boys would have it, a big pair of tits. *They* undoubtedly would command a price. But it was not a price she was prepared to pay. And it was not something she could discuss with Edna, or with any of the girls. She found herself descending into a deeper and even more miserable loneliness. Mama and Papa had gone

64

and abandoned her, taking their God with them. To begin to pray and ask for His help would be an admission of utter defeat. But *wasn't* she utterly defeated? At a dollar a week, fifty two dollars a year – and she simply had to buy some walking out clothes, the moment she could afford to – she wouldn't be able even to find the money for a passage back to England, supposing she did admit defeat, for more than a year. And what then? What did England have to offer that New York didn't?

An absence of Charlie Stark, for one thing. In the excitement and despair of her first week at the Superb, she had almost forgotten about Charlie. It was quite a shock to receive a summons to Joe Stark's office, and find him standing there, twisting his hat in his hands, as usual.

'Mina,' he said. 'Ain't you looking smart. And Joe here tells me you're doing well, too.'

Mina glanced at the maître d'hôtel, and wondered just what Joe had told his brother. 'I'm doing the best I can, Captain Stark,' she said.

'But it's hard work, eh? Sure, I know. Well . . .' He held her shoulders. 'It's all over now.' He grinned at her bewilderment. 'Remember I told you they was putting the old *McKinley* into dry dock? Well that's done. But she's going to be there a long time; the owners mean virtually to gut her to make sure there ain't none of that cholera still about. I told them what you said about the one bad water barrel, and they said I was talking nonsense. But that's by the by. The point is that they don't want *me* hanging about for three months doing nothing, so they're giving me a ship. Not the Atlantic this time, Mina. I'm to go down to Rio de Janeiro, and Buenos Aires. Down through the tropics, and the Caribbean. It's great down there. You'll like it.'

She stared at him. 'Me, Captain Stark?'

'Why else do you suppose I'm here, Mina darling. You'll come with me. No one'll know. We'll have the voyage of a lifetime.' He winked at her. 'We'll honeymoon, you and me.'

Charlie Stark, for three months? Charlie Stark for three *minutes*? Leave the Superb? Even if she was desperately lonely, desperately unhappy, desperately uncertain of what might be going to happen next, here at least was a glimpse of the life she wanted for herself.

Besides, Charlie Stark, for three *seconds?*

'I'm happy here, Captain Stark,' she said. 'I'm grateful for all you've done for me, but I'm staying at the Superb.'

Charlie Stark looked from her to his brother in total bemusement.

Joe shrugged. 'Like I told you, Charlie, since Jimmy Morton has taken to her, she's got ideas above her station.'

'And she talks about gratitude,' Charlie said. 'You don't know what gratitude is, you little slut. Suppose I was to tell your Mr Morton about you and me?'

'Tell what, precisely, Captain Stark?' Mina asked, refusing to lose her temper, 'that Mr Stark hasn't already told him?'

'What's that?' Once again Charlie's gaze swung to his younger brother.

'Well . . .' Joe flushed. 'I had to explain how she came to be here in the first place, Charlie.'

'Well, God damn,' Charlie said.

'I *am* grateful to you, Captain Stark,' Mina said, 'for bringing me here and getting me this job. But enough's enough. I'm no good for you, and you're no good for me. So I'll say thank you, again, sir.' She looked at Joe, and left the office.

But she was more affected by Charlie's reappearance than she was prepared to show either of them. Of course there could be no question of her going away with him; to become Charlie Stark's mistress would guarantee ending up even lower than she was now, quite apart from the repulsion of the man himself. But he had so obviously counted on it, been sure of it, almost built all his anticipations of the voyage on it. She remained in a sombre mood all afternoon, so much so that even Edna gave up trying to be cheerful, and was surprised to see Mr Stark, obviously neglecting his duties, appear at the second supper sitting, and engage Mrs Young in animated coversation, apparently proposing something that she found quite repugnant. But she was only the housekeeper, he was the maître d', and so she finally had to shrug and agree, whereupon Mr Stark came down to the table to where Mina was sitting, as usual, near the end.

'Well, Wilhelmina,' he said. 'I'm sorry about this afternoon. That brother of mine has always been one for organising other people's lives for them. But I think you handled the matter very tactfully. In fact, I am told by Mrs Young that you are doing very well in every way. So much so, indeed, that I think it's time you had some promotion.'

'Promotion, Mr Stark? Me?' She was instantly suspicious. Besides, for her to be bumped up again would not go down very well with the other girls, all her seniors.

'Oh, indeed,' he said. 'We believe in discovering talent at the Superb, Wilhelmina, indeed we do. As from tomorrow, I'm going to allow you to serve our special guests. Beginning with Number 317. Remember now, Mina, 317 is someone very special. Don't let me down, now.' He smiled, and patted her on the shoulder. 'But I know you won't.'

'Number 317,' Edna said. 'That's Lord Fanning.'

'*Lord* Fanning?' Mina cried in alarm. She would have been alarmed anyway; the third floor was where the luxury suites were, and she was not yet regarded as being experienced enough to service them – none of the girls in her dormitory were. She had never been inside one of them.

'You know,' Edna explained. 'One of those English lord people, who have lots of money and big moustaches.'

'I know what a lord is,' Mina told her. 'I just had no idea any of them stayed at the Superb.'

'Well, this one does,' Edna pointed out. 'Gee, old Piggy's never let *any* of our girls look after him. But you know what? I've heard it said that one time she came away from his room stuffing a hundred dollar bill into her pocket. Wonder what he wanted for that?'

Which made Mina more anxious than ever. She had no doubt at all it had to be some kind of trap for her, engineered by Joe Stark. He was giving her the plum prize in the entire hotel . . . the same day as she had slapped down his brother. Could he have been instructed to do so by Morton, as some kind of a reward? Morton might just have been waiting to learn the true relationship between Stark and herself. But that was almost certainly wishful thinking. More likely he was following some devious plan of his own. She was only sure that Mrs Young had nothing to do with it, in view of her obvious protestation when Stark had told her at supper. She almost began to feel a soft spot for Mrs Young.

But whatever was going on, she did not see that she had any choice but to do as she had been ordered, and hope that some profit rubbed off on her – without *too* much unpleasantness. She hardly slept, was downstairs as usual with the other girls before six the next morning, to be informed by the duty chef that she was excused all other early calls, until 317's, which was at seven o'clock. The intervening time was to be made up in arranging the tray, with which the duty chef himself assisted her. His lordship took coffee and not tea, prune juice instead of citrus, lightly browned toast which had to come out of the oven just seconds before she was ready to take it upstairs, marmalade and a boiled egg, which also had to be ready just as she was ready to serve.

'But this is a proper breakfast,' she protested. 'Shouldn't one of the Room Service waiters carry it up?'

The chef shook his head. 'Room Service don't start until seven-thirty, Wilhelmina. And his lordship likes to be served by females. You ain't afraid of a little blue blood, are you?'

Edna giggled. 'It ain't his blue *blood* she's afraid of.'

Mina stuck out her tongue at her. But she was growing more afraid than ever, and desperately wanted to get the ordeal over with. At five to seven the toast and the egg were ready, and she was on her way, and on her own, as well; all the other seven o'clock calls were held back to give her sole use of the elevator, to make sure she was not late.

At one minute to seven precisely she unlocked the door of 317, following the usual perfunctory knock. She stepped inside, switched on the light, having been told this was permissible, as 317 was a suite. And gazed at a splendidly furnished sitting room; it even had an upright piano in one corner, while the carpet was the newest she had seen in any of the bedrooms.

The door to the actual bedroom stood ajar, and she hesitated there for several seconds, getting her eyes accustomed to the gloom; but the glow from the sitting room enabled her to see quite clearly the huge bed, the dressing table, the chairs, the table where she would place the tray . . . and the fact that the room was empty. Because 317 was one of the very few apartments in the hotel which had its own bathroom, and Lord Fanning was presently in there; she could see the line of light below the door on the far side of the room. She heaved an enormous sigh of relief, tiptoed across the room, placed the tray

68

on the table by the bed, straightened, and said in a loud voice, 'Your breakfast, your lordship,' then ran for the sitting room door.

She did not quite make it. 'Wait!' commanded a voice, and she stopped without thinking, turning as she did so, to take in the bald head, the grey moustache, the red face . . . and the surprisingly youthful looking but naked body silhouetted against the bathroom light. '*What* a pleasant surprise,' his lordship remarked. 'Come here, girl.'

Mina hesitated, staring at him, although she didn't really want to look. The clamouring desire to continue running was however now being balanced by the thought of that hundred dollar bill, which she had quite forgotten in her haste to be away. 'If . . . if you'll put something on, sir,' she said.

'You're not American,' his lordship declared. 'Why, you're English.' He seemed delighted.

''Yes, sir, I am,' she agreed. 'Just like you,' she added, hoping that it might create some feeling of modesty. 'Now, sir . . .' She retreated towards the door.

'Oh, come now, girl, you'll not pretend you've never seen a man before?' He was slowly advancing. Modesty was obviously a feeling he did not know.

'I have not, sir,' Mina said.

He came further into the room, switching on the light as he passed it, to delineate every square inch of his body. 'Then it is time you did. Anyone can see you're ready for it.'

Not from you, Mina thought, as she watched him becoming what she could only consider grotesque. Had Charlie Stark ever looked like that? Now she almost wished she *had* looked at him. 'Your breakfast is on the table, sir,' she said, definitely abandoning all thought of the money. Not if it involved getting close to *that*. 'And I have other duties to attend to.'

'Not if you've been sent here,' he told her. 'Didn't they tell you what I would probably require?'

'Re . . . require?' Mina asked.

'I like to be touched,' he said, without the slighest embarrassment, and coming closer yet. 'And I like to touch. No more than that. And there'll be a fat tip for you, if you behave nicely.'

'Touched?' Mina asked, aware that her voice had risen, her brain seeming to freeze as she understood what he meant. Oh,

Lord, she thought, and found she was shaking her head. 'No, sir. I couldn't. I *will* not.'

'A tease, are you?' demanded his lordship, and in the same moment moved forward with surprising speed and grasped her arm. 'And a beauty. I wonder where Stark has been hiding you all of this time.'

Mina felt her temper starting to rise, mainly because now he was hurting her. She tried to think of what Edna would do, or say, faced with such a situation. But she had a terrible feeling that Edna would do anything – to get her hands on a hundred dollar bill.

'Please let me go, sir,' she said, keeping her voice even with an effort.

'Not until I see what you have inside that blouse,' he said. 'Not rolled newspaper, eh?'

He was also stronger than he looked, and was slowly pulling her closer. Now his other arm went round her shoulders, while his hand released her arm and began to pull on the straps of her apron.

'Please,' she begged, and when he continued to pluck at the apron, she kicked him on the ankle, and this time she was wearing shoes.

'You little bitch,' he snapped, and swung his hand at her. She ducked, wriggled free, but fell to her hands and knees. Lord Fanning was immediately astride her, sitting on her buttocks with his back to her, and forcing her legs down. 'Let's see now,' he grunted, pulling up her skirts.

'Get *off* me,' Mina shouted, twisting to and fro, and managing to roll beneath him as she felt his hands under her skirts and on her thighs. Desperately she swung her fists around, hitting him on the back of the head and causing him to topple forwards. She rolled on to her face again, and pushed down with her toes to slide out from beneath him, looked over her shoulder to see him turning, half smiling and half really angry, now. He rolled her on to her back again, and resumed his original assault on her bodice, now ripping the material. Desperately she flailed her hands to find some sort of a weapon, and her fingers encountered the handle of the china chamberpot which was beneath every bed in the hotel, even those with bathrooms attached. With an effort she pulled it out, while Lord Fanning continued to tear her bodice open, reaching inside almost as if about to remove plums from a pie. Mina gave a shout of anger, and swung the pot with all her force, catching his lordship on the side of the head. The pot shattered with the impact. And his lordship hit the floor with a dull thud.

Chapter 4

Mina sat up, and stared at the nobleman; blood was trickling down his face from the cut on his forehead. 'Oh, my God,' she whispered. 'Oh, my God!'

She felt sick. She turned on to her knees, rolled him on to his back, lowered her head to put her ear to his nose and mouth, discovered he was still breathing, but heavily . . . and he was certainly bleeding copiously. She fought back an overwhelming desire to scream, pushed herself up and ran through the sitting room to wrench open the door . . . and almost bring Joe Stark tumbling into the room.

'Mr Stark!' she shouted, almost glad to see him.

'Mina?' He looked her up and down, taking in her torn bodice and disarrayed skirt, looked past her. 'Where is his lordship?'

Mina pointed, too upset to cope with the implications of the maître d's presence at the door. 'In there. He . . . he's hurt.'

'Hurt?' Stark pushed her aside and ran into the bedroom. 'Jesus Christ! You . . . you *hit* him?'

Mina had followed him back inside. 'He tried to *rape* me,' she shouted. 'Oh, Lord, he's still bleeding. Can't you stop him bleeding?'

Stark knelt beside the unconscious man, pulled a handkerchief from his pocket, rolled it into a ball and held it against Fanning's temple. 'Get help,' he snapped. 'Fetch Mrs Young. Don't make a song and dance about it. Just fetch her. And pray, you silly little bitch, pray.'

Pray, Mina thought. Curse, more likely. She hurried for the elevator. Pray for what? The entire world, the entire universe, seemed determined to do her down, to turn her into a common whore, to make her the plaything of every other human being, simply because she wouldn't lie down and do what they wanted on command. Well, God *damn* them all! Even God! 'Mrs Young,' she bawled, forgetting Stark's instructions to be quiet about what had happened. 'Mr Stark wants you, in 317. There's been an accident.'

Mrs Young came at once. Mina went with her, followed in turn by several of the girls. By the time they regained the bedroom, Stark had lifted his lordship on to the bed, and there were signs of returning consciousness – which distressed Mina even more. She had no desire to have to look at an awake Lord Fanning.

'He'll live,' Joe Stark said. 'But he's going to have a gonging headache. And what's going to be the outcome when he realised what happened to him . . ?' He stared at the gaping girls, and hastily dragged the sheet over his lordship's thighs. 'What are you lot doing here? Get out, all of you. And not a word to a soul. Can you stay with him, Mrs Young? Soft talk him when he comes to.'

'We should call a doctor,' Mrs Young remarked. 'However did he hurt himself like that?'

Stark looked at Mina, then at the shattered chamberpot on the floor.

'You didn't *hit* him?' Mrs Young asked.

'What else was I to do?' Mina demanded, now really angry. She thought that with the least provocation she'd hit *her*, as well.

'Well, that's it,' Stark said, with some satisfaction. 'You've really gone and done it now, you little horror. It's gaol for you.'

'Gaol?' she shouted, her anger dissipating in sudden fear.

'At the very least. Come along, now.' He held her arm. 'You swab his brow, Mrs Young, and keep him quiet until Morton decides what to do.'

'I'll try,' Mrs Young said, doubtfully.

'Let me go,' Mina protested.

'You are coming with me,' Stark announced, pushing her to the door. The other girls stood to either side, mouths wide. Mina caught Edna's eye, but Edna clearly did not wish to be associated with her at this minute.

'All right, Mr Stark,' she said. 'All right, I'll come with you. But you will please let me go. You're hurting me.'

'You're not running off anywhere,' Stark said. 'I've got you good and proper, now.'

'You sent me to him because you *knew* this would happen,' Mina hissed.

'I handed you the chance of a lifetime, girl, and you messed it up. I can't help you now. Nobody can help you now.'

She panted, and considered fighting him, but decided against it, as they were now downstairs and there were other people about, all stopping to stare, and making her wish the floor would open and swallow her up. Then she was being taken to a part of the hotel she had not visited before, behind the reception desk, where there were corridors and offices and, after a brief knock, was thrust into a splendidly large and airy room, filled with filing cabinets and a huge oak desk, behind which sat Jimmy Morton.

'Stark? What in the name of God . . .' He stared at her. '*Mina?*'

'She assaulted Lord Fanning, Mr Morton,' Stark said. 'Laid him out cold. Well, I would have handled the matter myself, but you said she should be brought to you next time she kicked over the traces. He's hurt bad, Mr Morton. There'll be a legal action, I shouldn't doubt. But I reckoned you'd want the police to handle the matter.'

Morton gazed at him for several seconds, then looked at Mina again.

'He tried to rape me, Mr Morton,' she said, keeping her voice quiet. 'Lord Fanning, I mean.'

'I can see *someone* tried to rape you,' Morton agreed.

'That is nonsense, sir,' Stark declared. 'His lordship likes a morning kiss and cuddle. This is well known.'

'So you sent along the one girl in the hotel who doesn't go in for kissing and cuddling,' Morton observed. 'That was careless of you.'

'I was trying to give her a break.'

Once again Morton gazed at him for several seconds. Then he got up. 'I had better go along and see what's happening.' He pointed at one of the two overstuffed armchairs before his desk. 'Sit down, Mina. Will you promise me something?'

'What?' Mina asked suspiciously. Right now she distrusted all living creatures.

'Promise me that you will sit there, and not move, until I come back,' Morton said. 'I won't be long. And in return, I will promise you that nothing is going to happen to you. Right?'

74

They gazed at each other. But she was, more than ever, entirely in his power. Because only he could save her, now. No matter how great the provocation, she had assaulted a guest. And not just a guest. A lord. 'I promise, Mr Morton,' she said.

'Good girl,' Morton answered. 'Come along, Stark.'

Stark gave Mina a long look, as filled with menace as he could manage, and then followed his employer from the office. Mina tried to calm herself. She *could* have killed Fanning. That thought kept bouncing round her brain. And he was a lord, as well as a guest. Suppose he denied ever having touched her? She looked down at her dress; the bodice was ripped almost to the waist and she was in fact quite indecent. Hastily she tucked it up as well as she could. But she could have ripped that herself. Because there was no one in the hotel going to take her word against that of a lord.

Strangely, she was still more angry than afraid. She just could not think what she had done to deserve getting in such a mess. Even more strangely, she still wanted to keep her job. The Superb might have everything possible wrong with it, but it was alive, and exciting . . . if only there was someone here prepared to like her, and trust her, and give her a chance . . .

The door opened, and she sat up straight, half expecting to see a policeman. Jimmy Morton smiled at her. 'Well,' he said. 'Quite a to-do. I think you may have cost us a customer. And a good one.' He sat down behind his desk.

Mina licked her lips. 'Is he . . ?'

'Oh, he'll be all right. An inch lower, though . . .' He shook his head.

'But will he . . .?'

'He is not going to do anything. I pointed out that he is in a very compromising position, as he was naked and your dress is torn. I also told him I would not charge him for the room. So he's leaving today. But really, Mina, you shouldn't have reacted quite so violently.'

'What did you expect me to do?' she shouted. 'Lie there and let him . . . what is this place, anyway? Anyone would think it's a . . . a . . . *brothel!*' Another word she had never used before. 'It *is* a brothel. Do you know what he wanted me to do?'

Morton raised his eyebrows.

'I'm afraid men will be men, the world over, Mina. If they suppose they can get away with it. Most girls who go out to

75

work understand that. They either go along with what men want, or they don't. But most of them, thank God, know how to say no without committing mayhem. So maybe your circumstances are a little different. That don't alter the facts. Save to confirm that you just don't belong here.'

'Don't belong here?' Mina cried, sheer panic clutching at her heart. She couldn't possibly belong anywhere else.

'I think it's something we should talk about,' Jimmy Morton said, smiling at her. 'I think you should have a ride in my automobile, and then have lunch with me.'

'Automobile?' she whispered. 'Lunch?'

'Have you ever ridden in an automobile, Mina?'

Mina shook her head.

'Well, then, it will be an experience for you. Now, I don't want you to do anything else in the hotel, today. Just go and get changed into your ordinary clothes, and then return here. I should be able to get away in an hour or so. Okay?'

An automobile ride, she thought. And then lunch. This was it, then. The actual proposition. But . . . was she going to accept what Jimmy Morton wanted after having refused Lord Fanning? She did not suppose there was very much difference between *what* the two men wanted. Save that one had been a lord, and the other was no more than a playboy.

'I can't lunch with you, Mr Morton,' she said.

'Why on earth not? It will be in a public place, I do assure you.'

'I don't have any clothes.'

Morton gazed at her.

'I mean really,' she said. 'Only my uniforms, and this one is torn. Besides . . .'

'You are a little waif,' he observed. 'Well then, Mina, we shall just have to get you some clothes, right away.'

He himself took her measurements. She expected the worst when he carefully adjusted the tape measure around her bust, the back of his hand actually brushing her half exposed breast, and then her waist and hips, before measuring from her waist to her ankles, but he was entirely impersonal and correct. Because he knows that he has me in his power, she kept thinking.

'Now', he said, 'someone will be along in a little while, with something for you to try on. Just remain here until they come. And then, choose.'

'But . . .' She gazed at him. 'I can't accept clothes from you, Mr Morton.'

'Of course you can,' he said. 'They're not from me, anyway. They're from the Superb. It's the least we can do, after putting you through such an ordeal.'

He smiled at her, and was gone. Because she *had* been through an ordeal, and he knew that Joe Stark had planned the whole thing? Or because he *knew* she was absolutely in his power? She had no idea what to think, prowled the office, started every time she heard a noise in the corridor, nearly jumped out of her skin when the telephone on his desk jangled, but did not dare answer it, stood at the window and found herself looking down onto the lawn behind the hotel, and the odd guest walking or talking there, sat behind his desk and gazed at the pens and pencils and ink pots and memo pads and wondered if she dared open any of his drawers but decided against it. She knew that she had to sit down and think very seriously about what was going to happen next, about what *could* happen next, but couldn't make herself, because the future seemed more filled with brick walls than even when she had awakened in Charlie Stark's cabin, and she nearly jumped out of her skin again as there came a gentle tap on the door.

'Who is it?' she asked in alarm.

The door opened to admit a somewhat severe looking, middle-aged woman, very sombrely dressed, and carrying two boxes as well as a large bag suspended from her shoulder. She gave a surprisingly bright smile. 'You'll be Wilhelmina Doberley,' she said.

'Yes,' Mina replied, desperately trying to adjust her torn bodice. 'Yes.'

'And you would like to see some ready-to-wears.' The lady placed her boxes on Mr Morton's desk, the bag on the floor. 'I'm Mrs Ashbourne. I've done what I can, with the figures I was given. But I think . . .' she regarded Mina speculatively for several minutes, pinching her lower lip. 'Yes,' she decided at last. 'I think we can do rather well, if we try. You are an absolute clothes-horse, my dear.'

Mina was not sure whether that was intended as a compliment or not.

'Now, let me see. Mr Morton said you would need everything, from the skin out. Well . . . would you mind undressing?' She went to the window and drew the blinds.

'Here?' Mina asked.

'I was promised we wouldn't be interrupted,' Mrs Ashbourne said. 'However . . .' She went to the door, turned the key in the lock. Which made Mina, remembering Mrs Young, distinctly nervous. But the woman was clearly interested only in the clothes she was displaying. 'I have here a neat little corset, with its own suspenders . . .' She laid the garment across the back of a chair, while Mina paused in the midst of unbuttoning her dress, and stared in consternation. She had never actually seen anything like that before, had no idea women actually wore them.

'This is the very latest fashion,' Mrs Ashbourne explained. 'I do recommend it.' She glanced at Mina. 'Oh, just throw that stuff on the floor,' she said. 'It is ruined anyway. We'll burn it.'

Mina obeyed.

And Mrs Ashbourne did some more lip pinching. 'Hm,' she commented. 'Of course, at your age, you don't really need a corset. But with a bust like yours . . . well, obviously the smaller the waist the better, don't you think? My dear, those are absolutely perfect legs. A little thin . . . but they'll fill out. I think black stockings, don't you?'

Mina was running out of breath. *Black* stockings? How incredibly wicked.

'Now,' Mrs Ashbourne said, opening her boxes. 'I was told you had to have two outfits. One for driving, and . . .'

'*Two* outfits?' Mina cried.

'To begin with. Yes. And the other for ordinary walking out.' She delved into her first box and held up a navy linen costume, tailored at the waist and padded at the shoulder.

'Oh, my,' Mina said. She had never seen anything quite so lovely.

'It has a white blouse and waistcoat, you see . . .' Mrs Ashbourne continued to lay things out, 'and this matching tie. I do think young women look so *smart* in ties. And the waistcoat . . . well, you'll see it's double-breasted.' She gave a brief laugh. 'I know big busts are all the rage, my dear, but we don't want to overdo it, do we? The waistcoat will flatten you just a little.'

'Can . . . can I try it on?' Mina asked.

'Of course. But shall we start at the bottom?' She gave another of her quick smiles. 'If you *would* remove all of those rags, I have some silk drawers here which are very nice, and then, these petticoats . . . we can worry about the gowns afterwards. Boots,' she went on, thoughtfully, while Mina hastily finished undressing. 'Yes, indeed. But I think I have the very thing . . .' She was now delving into the bag on the floor, and raised her head. 'You do like feathers in your hats, don't you, my dear?'

Mina wanted to pinch herself to make sure she wasn't dreaming.

'Well,' Jimmy Morton said. 'Well, well, well, well, well.'

Mina felt rather the same way. She wore her driving outfit, which consisted of a brown tweed tunic, double-breasted and with flaring skirts which ended just above her knees, over a white blouse, and matching knickerbockers; her black boots and stockings were almost entirely concealed by her fawn gaiters which buttoned to the knee, and for which she had matching gloves. Her hat was a straw with a brown ribbon and plume, and there was a chiffon scarf to be tied over it and beneath her chin.

'You look perfectly exquisite,' Jimmy Morton said.

Once again Mina was inclined to agree with him, even if she had not yet had the opportunity of looking at herself in a full length mirror, but had had to make do with a small hand glass held from various angles by Mrs Ashbourne, who had also brushed her hair and retied her bow, and was now looking as pleased as either of them.

'I am so glad you approve, Mr Morton,' she said. 'The other outfit I have packed into this box. Perhaps you could tell me where to send it?'

Morton gave her a quick glance. 'I think it would be best to leave it in the office for the time being, Mrs Ashbourne,' he said. 'But thanks so much. You have been an absolute treasure, as always. I'll be in touch about the other items, probably this afternoon. Well, Mina, shall we go?'

Because he had also changed, from his usual morning suit into an outfit very like hers, save that his boots were brown

79

instead of black, and that he wore a flat cap and carried an enormous pair of goggles.

Mina hesitated. But it was too late for hesitation now. Those *other* items? Because she had undoubtedly sold herself to him. These clothes were his. And therefore what was in them had to be his, too. But somehow she was sure he would not want anything as disgusting as Lord Fanning. Besides, she had the strangest feeling that she could cope with Jimmy Morton, who was clearly a gentleman, however hard he might occasionally try to disguise that fact.

And at least, before the decision became irrevocable, there was the motor car. 'It's a Daimler-Benz,' he explained. 'From Germany.'

Her eyes could not possibly get any wider, and there was nothing for her to say. She had of course seen lots of automobiles from a distance, and even one or two parked on the street – she had always admired the gleaming leather and even more gleaming chrome, the obvious suggestion of latent power. But never had she actually touched one, much less sat in one. Her first reaction was total stupefaction; however could anyone possibly remember all the levers that apparently needed pushing or pulling, all the dials that needed watching. Her second reaction was stark terror, as Jimmy Morton, having cranked the engine, sat beside her and drove out of the hotel yard and into the street, faster than she had ever travelled before in her life, while the wind whistled past her ears, and, although she had tied the scarf, she still held on to her hat with both hands.

'Fifteen miles an hour,' he told her. 'Now, watch this.'

There was an acceleration which sent passersby scurrying and had a couple of horse-drawn cabs rearing and bucking to the accompaniment of a stream of curses from their drivers.

'You're going too fast,' she screamed.

'This thing will do forty,' he claimed.

'Please,' she begged.

He obligingly slowed. 'There's a little place outside of town,' he said. 'Good seafood. How about it?'

'I adore seafood,' she said, unconvincingly; she was feeling carsick, although she had never felt seasick on board the *William McKinley*. But maybe it was the unfamiliar corset.

'And then we can talk,' he suggested.

Mina tried taking deep breaths, but her stomach had not really settled down when they pulled into the little inn. 'Where are we?' she asked, dimly aware that they had crossed a bridge and had thus presumably left Manhattan.

'It's called the Bronx, actually. Quite built up, over there.' He waved his hand to the east and north. 'But out this side it's still pretty nice.'

The inn manager obviously knew him, kissed Mina's hand before she could remember to take off her gloves, and ushered them to a secluded table down a private little wing. 'The oysters,' Jimmy Morton decided, without looking at the menu. 'And a bottle of Bollinger.'

'Of course, Mr Morton.'

'Oysters?' Mina asked, uneasily.

'Have you never tasted oysters?'

As a matter of fact she had, often, in Devon. And had never particularly liked them. 'Oh, yes,' she said. 'My favourite food.'

'I'm glad of that. They're an aphrodisiac, you know.' He stared at her, and then looked embarrassed because she was obviously embarrassed. She didn't know what to say.

'Oysters,' he said, changing his stare to a smile, 'and good champagne, and beautiful company – what more could any man ask?' The champagne had already arrived, and he raised his glass. 'To the most beautiful girl in New York.'

'Oh, Mr Morton . . .'

'Fact. But probably the most unemployable girl in New York as well. Oh, Mina, Mina . . . what are we to do with you?'

'Just . . .' The gulp of champagne she had just taken was making her bold. 'Just let me get on with being a chambermaid, Mr Morton.'

'That is the one thing I cannot do,' he explained, smiling at her. 'You see, you've broken all the rules. I tried to tell you that, in the office. Chambermaids, well, they're two a penny. We pick them for their looks, and their cleanliness, but also for their attitudes – we expect them to humour our customers. We do not expect them to sleep with the guests. We are *not*, believe it or not, operating a brothel. But we do expect them to smile, and if necessary flirt, and *when* necessary run like hell – still smiling. They are *never* supposed to brain our guests with chamberpots.'

'I'm sorry about that,' she said. 'But he wanted . . . ugh.'

'You object to the male form in any shape, do you?'

'Good Lord, no, Mr Morton,' she protested. 'But there is a time and a place for everything. Although, really . . . do men really want to be . . . well . . .'

'The word is masturbated. Although Edna and her friends would probably say "frigged". Don't look so shocked. The world is full of words you just have to get used to, sooner or later. It's called growing up. Yes, Mina, many men do like to be masturbated. I'll tell you a little secret. All men like sex, and nearly all men like to have sex with women. But not all men get on with women, when it comes to sex. Especially with those they marry. I guess there are a lot of reasons. Familiarity, boredom . . . but mainly because they're afraid of each other's reactions. You know, if you ask your wife to do something she might consider outrageous, or unnatural, even if she does it, when she's finished you can't just say good night and see her again when next you feel in the mood. She's going to be there next morning at breakfast, remembering. And the next time you have a row . . . while if it ever comes to a divorce, watch out. The things she is going to remember. I'm not choosing sides, believe me. But when the chips are down men generally have more explaining to do than women, for some reason.'

'You don't sound very keen on marriage, Mr Morton,' she said. 'Have you ever been married?'

'Yes.'

'*Have* you?' She stared at him.

'I was a whole lot younger than I am now, and it didn't last very long.'

'You asked her to do something she didn't want to.'

'As a matter of fact, no,' he said. 'I've been told that I'm not very imaginative, when it comes to sex. I'm trying to explain why men take mistresses. But even a mistress, well, she's being paid, one way or the other. And the man knows this. And to lie on a girl you know doesn't really care whether you're there or not, and go wham, bang, how's your uncle in a matter of seconds isn't terribly satisfying. If you are paying, why not have something that you really want, and maybe can't get anywhere else, and something that you can watch happening as well as feel, and savour it . . . do you have any idea at all what I'm talking about?'

Mina had been drinking champagne as fast as she could; it

was unbelievable that she should be having such a conversation with a virtual stranger. 'No,' she lied. 'I don't want to. I think . . . well, that men and women should only make love when they love each other, and that it should just happen.'

'Something we all dream of, and very seldom achieve. But I understand how strange you must find this world of men, and women . . . I don't suppose it's the ideal place for the daughter of a parson.'

Mina bridled. 'I'm quite prepared to take the world as I find it, Mr Morton. And mў mother and father were very happy, thank you. And I'm sure they didn't ever . . . well . . .'

'And were probably *less* happy for it.' He reached across the table to squeeze her hand. 'I'm not criticising you, Mina, really. I'm looking for answers. Let's begin by considering the problem. Ever since you've come to work at the Superb that problem has been growing. Naturally Stark thought that as you had . . . shall we say, accommodated his brother . . .' He held up his finger as she would have protested. 'I know and understand the circumstances, Mina, and I respect your desire to get out from under them. But facts are facts. Stark formed certain opinions about you. So did Mrs Young. So did all the others, I would say. Well, they were wrong. But that doesn't alter the facts. I just cannot have a chambermaid who, every time a guest gives her a squeeze or makes an improper suggestion, is going to bat him over the head with a china pot. You were lucky, you know. You could easily have killed the old scoundrel.'

'Mr Morton,' Mina said. 'If you'd just let me explain . . .'

'You let *me*, first. I know you think that everything about the Superb is wrong, according to what you've been taught by your dad. But it's how the world works. Trouble is, I don't think you're quite ready for that world yet, Mina. On the other hand, you face the problem of having to try to live in that world. You're sixteen years of age, without, as I understand it, a friend in the world, and without two cents to rub together. And yet you're determined to live your way and no one else's. Can't be done, my gorgeous girl.'

She stared at him, almost knowing what was coming next, feeling at once angry and frustrated and at the same time, as he had said, so alone.

'But I have a possible solution,' he went on. 'I gather you've finally split with your friend Charlie?'

'There was never anything to split from,' Mina said. 'Please believe me.'

'I do. I know he took shameful advantage of you. Believe me, the only reason I haven't had the rascal horsewhipped is because I didn't know just how you really felt about him. But now . . .'

'Mr Morton,' she tried, feeling utterly desperate at his misunderstanding of the situation.

'But that's all sorted out,' he said, as if she hadn't spoken. 'And I think you are the most lovely thing I have ever seen. And the most charming, and well brought up, and well spoken and . . . just everything. Will you be my charge, Mina? Everything. Your clothes, your food, your drink, your very dreams. I'll provide you with an apartment, with pocket money, with . . . with a car, if you like. Just nod your head, Mina, there's no need to say a word. And from that moment on you'll have no problems at all.'

Just like that, she thought. No problems at all. How she wanted to have no problems at all. Supposing that could be possible. But it wasn't possible. It couldn't be possible, even if he had not referred to her as a thing.

She raised her head. 'And you'd want . . .?'

He gave a slight shrug. 'I'd want to sleep with you, Mina. I do want to sleep with you. But I promise you, I don't want to shock you or hurt you. I just want to hold you in my arms and tell you how beautiful you are, and how much I love you.' He smiled. 'Because I think I do, you know. Or I'm very rapidly getting that way.'

It did not seem to occur to him that he was behaving no differently to Charlie Stark or to anyone else. Yet her immediate revulsion was weakening – at least partly because she simply had no idea how to go about refusing him, while still keeping her job. Or even if that was possible at all.

She licked her lips, watched the oysters being placed in front of them. She was very hungry. 'Could . . . could I think about it?' At least she would then have a square meal inside her.

'Of course you may.' Perhaps he was hungry too, or he reckoned that having got her to think at all he was already the victor. There was a strange way to think of it, she supposed. But it was how she *had* to think about it. Life was a battleground, all right. Into which she had plunged with careless confidence, and been defeated. She wouldn't dare ask him what would happen if she refused him, because she could have no doubt as to the answer: he was in love with her only so long as she was available. She wondered what he would say if she told him, as she had tried to just now, that she was still a virgin. Very probably he would not believe her, and if he did, he would take it as a refusal. If she turned him down again, he would almost certainly give one of those little shrugs, and one of those little smiles, and say, 'Well, Mina, I did want to help you. But if you're so prudish that you won't be helped . . . there's nothing more I can do. And as I have told you, I can't even employ you at the Superb, any longer. So if you'd like to go back there and collect your things . . . only you don't *have* any things, do you?' She wondered if he'd even let her walk away in her new outfit?

But why should he?

They ate in silence, gazing at each other over their glasses as they sipped champagne. Once he reached out to squeeze her hand. When the meal was over, he said, 'Do you know, I have never felt so happy in my life? Now, I have somewhere to show you. Let's go.'

She wanted to run, as fast and as far as she could. But she didn't even know in which direction lay salvation. Or if there was any salvation to be found, anywhere. She found herself sitting beside him in the car, and once again driving into New York. She realised that she hadn't said a word for some time. He realised it too, gave her one of his sideways glances. 'I know it's an immense step to take,' he conceded. 'And I know that, well . . . maybe it goes against everything you've been taught. But I'm going to make you happy, Mina. I swear it.'

No, she thought. You're going to make *you* happy, Mr Morton. I'm just the one elected to help.

The sickness was growing. Oysters and corsets didn't really go together. But she knew they did, perfectly well. It was the thought of what was going to happen to her, and quite soon, unless she could summon up some courage and some resolution. Obviously he was taking her to show her the apartment he had picked out for her to live in, as his mistress. Obviously he would then want to make her his mistress as soon as possible. Right away. The thought was suddenly quite paralysing. She'd be alone with Jimmy Morton, and he'd want to strip her naked, and then he'd want . . . she did not know what he'd want. She was afraid to think of it – but her brain was filled with the obscene and excited gossiping of Edna and her friends, almost every night.

And what about afterwards? She'd be like a bird in a cage. She wouldn't even have the bawdy company *of* the other girls, much less the constant challenge of the bell-boys and the bootblacks, of the customers themselves. Oh, if only she had kept her mouth shut and done what that old satyr Fanning wanted. What harm could it have done her?

But she had made that choice, and now she had to make this one. And suddenly she knew that it had already been made. Had been made even before she had accepted the clothes.

'Hm', Mr Morton said, and pulled into the side of the road. 'We seem a little short of gas. Not to worry, I always keep a spare can in the boot.'

He got out, and went round the back of the machine. Mina got out too, and stretched. They were well into the city now, and the street was quite busy, with horse-drawn vehicles, and bicycles and even one or two other automobiles. She looked across the road, and saw Clancy and another boy, riding bicycles. Clancy! The only decent man or woman in the entire hotel. Apart from her. Up to this moment. But in a very little while she wasn't going to be decent either.

The decision had already been taken. No matter what. The sight of Clancy just reinforced it, just as the sight of Clancy suggested how it might be implemented, which up to this moment had been her biggest problem.

She glanced at Mr Morton. His head was bowed as he carefully poured petrol into the pipe leading to his fuel tank. Clancy and his companion – someone she had never seen before – had not noticed her, although they had glanced admiringly at the car. They had now passed it, however, and were about to turn left at the next intersection, only a few yards away. Mina took a long breath, and ran, heels clattering on the pavement.

'Hey!' Mr Morton shouted, looking up. But he couldn't immediately follow her, because of the petrol can he was holding. Mina reached the corner, panting, skidded round it, and found herself only a few feet behind Clancy.

'Clancy!' she shouted. 'Oh, Clancy! Please give me a ride.'

Clancy stopped pedalling, and looked over his shoulder. Mina caught him up, gasping for breath. 'Please!' she panted. 'Get me out of here.'

'Mina?' Previously he had obviously not recognised her in her new clothes. But there could be no mistaking her voice. Now he hesitated for an instant, then acted with tremendous decision, seized her round the waist and set her on the crossbar of his bicycle, and pedalled at great speed, swinging down the next intersection. She heard a single shout of 'Mina!' from behind her, and then Mr Morton was lost in the crowd.

'I don't get it,' Clancy said, again braking to a stop, and putting his foot on the ground; his companion had also stopped.

'That was Mr Morton,' Mina explained. 'He . . .' She could feel the heat in her cheeks.

'He was taking you riding in his automobile,' Clancy said. 'But you got off. Good girl.'

'And you helped her give him the slip,' Clancy's friend remarked. 'Do you reckon he recognised you?'

'Oh, Lord, do you think so?' Mina slipped from the crossbar to straighten her suit.

'I doubt it,' Clancy said. 'He may remember one or two of the girls at the Superb. But us boys don't mean a thing to him. And I wouldn't care if he did recognise me. Say, Mina, you look just great, like a million dollars.'

'Morton paid for it,' she said, miserably. 'I shouldn't have accepted it. But I did so want to look nice. And . . . oh, Clancy, what am I going to do? You heard about this morning?'

'Some,' Clancy said. 'You know what I think? I think you could do with a nice cup of tea. My old Dad drinks tea. And you'll like him, too.'

Clancy's father, reached after some vigorous bicycling, turned out to be a large policeman, presently off duty. 'Ye're the English lass,' he pronounced. 'Philip's been telling us about ye.'

Philip? Mina gazed at Clancy; it was the first time she had ever heard his Christian name.

He shrugged.

'And I told him,' Sergeant Clancy went on, 'that it takes all sorts to make a world. And if the sorts are pretty as a picture, then the world is that much prettier, too.' He squeezed Mina's hand. 'Ye're as pretty as a picture, lass. And ye can't help being English. That's just plain bad luck, and could happen to anybody.'

Mina could not help but warm to such charm, even if her brain seemed to be opening and shutting with enormous bangs, each bang reminding her that her world, small and uncertain as it had been, had suddenly come to an absolute halt. Because Jimmy Morton would never forgive her now. So she summoned a smile for Sergeant Clancy, and then for Mrs Clancy, and for Philip – was he really named Philip? – and his brothers and sisters, and Sean, his friend, and drank her tea, and then looked at him with eyes so expressive of her desperate anxiety that he soon removed her from his family's company. 'We have to get back to work,' he announced.

'Ye'll have to walk,' Sergeant Clancy observed, having watched their arrival. 'Towing on the crossbar ain't legal.'

'We'll walk, Pa,' Clancy said. 'It isn't far. He has big ideas for me,' he explained to Mina, as he pushed the bike into the afternoon, with her at his side, almost as if he was her beau. And how she wished he could be her beau. 'He thinks I have brains. He wants me to study to be an accountant.'

'I'm sure you'll do well at that,' Mina said.

'Maybe. But what about you? The girls are saying you're going to be fired. But if Morton himself likes you . . .' He paused.

'Yes,' she agreed. 'I don't think he likes me any more.' She sighed. 'I don't know, Philip. I really don't know.'

'My friends call me Phil. And that's tough enough to live with.'

She gave him a quick smile. 'My friends call me Mina.'

'That I know.'

'Only it seems I don't have too many friends.'

'I'm your friend, Mina.'

'I know you are, Phil. Only . . .'

'Only I don't amount to much, right?'

She gazed at him. They had reached the garden of the Superb, and the idyll was over. Ahead of her lay only catastrophe.

'I didn't mean that,' she said. 'It's just that . . . I don't reckon I'm that easy to help, right this minute.'

'I'll help you, Mina,' he said. 'Anywhere, any time.'

He was staring into her eyes, and she was staring into his, and a moment later they were swaying towards each other, she was in his arms, and he was kissing her on the mouth.

Mina had never been kissed before, other than by her parents; the thought had apparently never crossed Charlie Stark's mind. She became aware of a most tremendous series of feelings, spreading all the way from her tongue, which he was touching with his, down through her body to her arms and legs, while she was even more aware of *his* body, pressed against hers. She found herself remembering Lord Fanning . . . but there could be no comparison between Lord Fanning and Phil Clancy – just as she also knew what was going to happen, no matter how long she had rejected and resisted it. She wanted it to happen. Perhaps, she realised, she had wanted it since Charlie Stark had first made her aware of what men were thinking when they looked at her. But she only wanted it with someone like Phil. And now it could be some kind of hail and farewell, because afterwards . . . afterwards, the afterwards of having to exist, much less the afterwards of having ended her virginity, did not bear consideration – unless afterwards could begin with him wanting to hold her, forever and ever. And that could only come about as a result of what was about to happen now.

His mouth had left hers, and he was looking down at her. 'Mina,' he muttered. 'Oh, Mina . . .'

She licked her lips, and looked left and right, listened to sound, conversation, laughter, the bustle of the hotel, seemingly all around them. It couldn't happen here in the garden. That would be too risky. And she'd dirty her new outfit.

He held her hand, drew her further into the bushes. He didn't seem to have any doubt about what was about to happen, either. 'There's a shed over here,' he explained.

'A *shed?*'

'Today's the gardener's afternoon off. And it has a . . .' He squeezed her hand. 'There's a cot.'

Somebody else's bed, in a garden shed. And if he knew about it, how many other girls had he taken in there? She wanted to stop herself, but could not; they were already through the bushes and at the door. Phil pulled it open and she stepped inside, into gloom and silence, inhaling damp earth and herbicide, and yet, because they were so suddenly isolated from the world, feeling like it more than ever. Sufficiently to drive away her doubts. She turned, and was again in his arms. 'Oh, Mina,' he said again. He stood away from her, unbuttoned her tunic. She waited, gazing at him, not knowing what she should do, what he might want her to do. Not really wanting to do anything, at this moment, save be touched by him. Be *loved*, by him.

He took the tunic from her shoulders, hung it on a hook behind the door, then gently removed her hat. One of the pins caught and she had to help him. Their hands touched, and on an inspiration she carried his hand against her blouse. Then he was unbuttoning that as well, to no great purpose, as she was as thoroughly concealed as ever, even with the blouse open.

'Mina,' he said again, and kissed her again.

She undressed herself, desperate that he should not lose his desire. Her clothes fell away, even the corset as she tugged the ties free, and she was against him again, feeling his hands on her flesh, sliding round in front to hold her breasts, while her nipples came up as hard as she ever remembered them in Charlie Stark's cabin, and the want seemed a huge bubble within her body, which was going to burst if something wasn't done about it, quickly.

She found herself sitting on the cot; there was no mattress, merely a canvas base; it was rough, and seemed to serrate her bottom. For the first time she was truly aware of being naked, from the knees up. From the knees down she was an absolute cluster of garments, but these Phil was kneeling to remove, very gently unlacing her boots and unbuttoning her gaiters. 'Mina,' he whispered, sliding his hands over her stockings. 'You have the most beautiful legs in the world.'

She suddenly remembered that he had seen her legs before, and her bottom, when Mrs Young had made her bend over. Somehow that embarrassed her, when she knew it should have reassured her. And she was embarrassed by the closeness of his face to her thighs. His head was bowed as he tried to find his way through the bewildering assortment of underclothes. And unfastening the suspenders that Mrs Ashbourne had insisted she wear would take too long. Mina stood up, and the already released corset fell away. She sat down again to roll down the stockings, and kick them off together with her boots, before standing again, now absolutely naked, while a wave of unexpected ecstacy swept over her, only checking, and then resuming, when he threw both arms round her waist to kiss her groin, holding her tight against his face. She didn't know how to respond, or if she dared respond; she was afraid to think what he might do next. She rested her hands on his head, and was laid down, on her back. She didn't know what to do with her legs, kept them pressed together as he undressed in turn, watching him with a boldness which surprised herself, and wanting him, where she had only been afraid of Lord Fanning.

He knelt before her, and held her knees. She allowed them to fall apart and watched him come down to her, felt him against her as he kissed her again and again, mouth, eyes, nose, chin, each breast in turn, while his arms went round her and his hands gripped her buttocks to lift her from the cot and bring her against him.

There was more pain at his entry than she had expected. But it was the most satisfying pain she had ever known in her life, and seemed to project feeling in front of it, and away and away and away, until it reached her brain, and dispelled the last of the bubble.

The desire remained, but now there were other emotions as well.

Clancy pushed himself away from her, his desire suddenly swamped in embarrassment. 'Oh, Mina,' he said. 'I . . . I'm sorry.'

Mina sat up. 'Sorry? About what?'

'Well . . .' He looked at her, then down between her legs, then suddenly began to dress in great haste. 'Gee whizz, it's later than I thought. I've got to rush. You too, Mina. Gee willikins, it's half past four.'

She caught his hand. 'Phil! I don't want to be sorry. I expected to be hurt. And it was only a little.'

He hesitated, apparently afraid to look at her. 'You will be sorry,' he said. 'When you think about it, Mina. I thought . . . after what they all said, about Charlie Stark and Jimmy Morton . . . but . . . God, I'm sorry. Because I can't . . . I mean . . . But Mina, I will help you if I can. I swear it.'

Then he was finished dressing, hesitating at the door. 'Don't you need to hurry too?'

'Yes,' Mina said, her voice flat. 'Yes, I need to hurry too. I'll be right behind you.'

'Well . . .' He blew her a kiss. 'That was great, Mina. The greatest I've ever . . . well, I ain't *ever* known anything like that. And Mina . . . you *have* got the loveliest legs in the world. And the biggest tits. Mina, you're just perfect.'

But not perfect enough, she thought, less bitterly than with utter resignation. What had Jimmy Morton said? No man really enjoys lying on a girl who is obviously *not* enjoying it, and going wham, bang, how's your uncle . . . but she had enjoyed it. The point was, had he known that? Because she had never even moved, that she could remember; she hadn't known whether or not she was supposed to.

The door closed, and she was alone. Alone, she thought. Alone, alone, alone. For just a few minutes she had been part of a pair, and it had been the most glorious feeling she had ever known. It had far transcended the mere act of love, splendid as that had been. Now she was alone, and aching, and feeling so many different emotions. She was even aware that the desire bubble remained, behind the pain, unassuaged. But only the fact that she was alone mattered.

Tears began to roll down her cheeks, and she got up and began to dress. Clancy had his own life to live, his own environment in which to exist. She did not know whether he would ever manage to qualify as an accountant and thus raise himself off the ground floor he presently inhabited – she did not think that was very likely. But it would not matter, because

Clancy had Sergeant Clancy and Mrs Clancy and all the other Clancys, all the New York Police Force, in fact, to go home to and be happy with. Whatever happiness he found outside of that magic circle was simply jam. And when it was with a girl everyone had told him was a slut – even if he knew that had been wrong – well, it wasn't even jam he needed to digest.

She had no one, and nothing. Nothing, nothing, nothing, she realised as she buttoned her blouse. She had even been suspended from duty. She did not have anything to hurry to, any longer.

She could not even pray. Although she thought she might, at any moment.

Slowly she went inside, walked past the kitchen, to the staff elevator. People looked at her, one or two smiled at her . . . everyone in the hotel would know what had happened this morning. Probably they thought she had already been fired, could not believe that this elegantly clad young woman was really little orphan Mina.

She rode up to the tenth floor. This was quiet, and deserted. All the girls would be busy making beds. As she should be doing. All the girls. Her friends! Whose sole desires that morning had been to remove themselves as far as possible from her.

Then why was she here at all? Simply because she had no place else to go. So here she might as well stay until they threw her out.

And here maybe she could pray. The idea was growing on her. She was defeated. She was stupid, and sinful, ever to have supposed she could make her way entirely without religion, or belief, or support, or any of the things Papa had known were essential to success. But Papa had also said that God would always welcome a repentant sinner. Well, He would have to look very hard to find a bigger sinner than her, right this minute; she had just committed the ultimate feminine sin.

She opened the dormitory door, stepped inside, hurled her hat across the room in the general direction of her bed, and stared in total amazement as it was caught by Jimmy Morton.

He had actually been sitting on her bed. Now he stood up. He still wore his driving clothes. 'Mina? Where in God's name have you been?'

The thought passed through her mind that he had no

business to ask that. But hard on its heels there was arising a tremendous excitement, mingled with apprehension. So she said, 'Just walking, Mr Morton. But . . .' She wanted to ask him what in the name of God he was doing, sitting by himself in the girls' dormitory. But as it was his hotel, presumably he could sit in whatever part of it he chose.

Morton was taking in her dishevelled clothes. 'Mina . . ?'

'I lay down for a while,' she said. 'I got tired.'

He frowned. 'But you're all right?' Obviously it was not occurring to him that she could possibly have lain down beside somebody, much less under somebody. 'My God, I've been so worried, Mina. The way you ran off. I didn't know what to do. You're sure you're all right?'

'Sure,' she said. 'Sure I'm all right.' She sat down on Edna's bed; she didn't want to get close enough to him to be touched. 'I guess you'll want these clothes back.'

'Mina!' He came across the room.

She raised her head. 'I can't be your mistres, Mr Morton. I just can't.'

'I know that.' He sat down beside her. 'It was criminal of me even to think of it, much less suggest it. But Mina . . . I love you. I can't do without you. Mina . . ' He held her hands.

She stared at him in amazement. Couldn't he tell she'd just been . . . what would Edna say? Laid? Screwed? Fucked?

What would Mother have said? Lost her virginity. That sounded far more final, far more damning, than the obscenities.

'Mr Morton,' she protested. 'No . . .'

His grip tightened. 'I know,' he said again. 'I'm not going to louse it up again, Mina. I want you. Just you, Mina. Will you marry me?'

Chapter 5

They stared at each other in mutual consternation, as if the words had not really meant to be said. Then Morton seemed to recollect that he had actually said them. 'Will you, Mina?' he asked again, almost defiantly.

'I can't marry you, Mr Morton,' she said. She hadn't planned to say anything as blunt as that, but the words just came out.

'Why not?'

And as they were out, they made sense. 'Well . . . I'm a chambermaid, and you're the owner's son. I'm poor as a church-mouse, and you're rich. I'm . . .'

'Anyone can see that you're not meant to be either of those things, Mina. And I wouldn't care if you were. You're Mina. I've been dreaming about you since the first day I saw you. And I thought you belonged to that scoundrel Stark. But you don't. And like you said, you never did, no matter what happened. I was foolish even to think it. But I've been foolish so many times in my life, Mina. I don't want to be foolish any more. And letting you slip away would be the most foolish thing in the world.'

'But . . .' There were so many reasons, so many arguments. 'Your parents . . .'

He smiled. 'They may not go for the idea right away. But they'll just love you, Mina, when they meet you. And they've been on at me to marry again for years.'

'The daughter of one of their friends.'

'God forbid. You, Mina.'

But I don't love you, she thought. I have never even thought of loving you. I have only ever considered being loved *by* you, and been afraid of it. And . . . 'I *can't* marry you,' she insisted. 'I'm not a virgin.' She had just about forgotten that vital fact, even if he had long supposed it to be so. She had not properly considered what making love with Clancy had meant. She couldn't marry anyone, now, except Clancy. But Clancy didn't want to marry her, that was obvious. And did she want to marry him? It would mean being poor for the rest of her life; there was no way Philip Clancy was ever going to be rich.

Jimmy Morton took her hands again. 'I know that, Mina,' he said. 'I know that, and I hate him for it. But you were forced. I know that, too. And I am not going to let a virtual rape come between us, my darling girl.'

Mina opened her mouth and then closed it again. He thought it was Charlie Stark. But did that matter? To tell him the truth, now, to tell him by what a narrow time margin he had failed to be the first, would only confuse matters and hurt Clancy. Jimmy Morton might have hesitated about attempting to horsewhip a burly sea captain like Charlie Stark, but he would have no hesitation at all about firing one of his own employees.

'Will you, Mina?' he asked, his grip on her fingers tightening.

She gazed into his eyes. She didn't love him. She didn't know if she could ever love him. But then, she didn't know if she was ever going to love anyone, who would love her back. And this man was rich, and elegant, and very much in love with her. And he owned the Superb. At one step she would soar from the very lowest personage in that teeming world to the very highest. She wondered what Joe Stark and Mrs Young, and Edna, would say.

What Clancy would say.

The Superb. This man owned the Superb!

'If . . . if you really want me to, Mr Morton,' she said.

It was only after they reached the apartment that Mina realised she had, after all, done exactly what he had first wanted her to, entirely on his promise to marry her. But by then she didn't know what she could do about it, because by then she most certainly wanted to remain in the apartment.

It was situated high in a building overlooking Seventh Avenue, and had four rooms, apart from a little entry hall opposite the elevator. There was a sitting room, comfortably furnished with overstuffed armchairs and a settee, a kitchen on the left, and on the right the most luxurious bedroom she had ever been in, if rather obviously designed as a passion pit, with crimson and gold curtains at the windows and surrounding the bed itself. The quilt was also in crimson and gold, and the carpet was in a matching design. The bathroom was beyond the bedroom, and here too the taps and door handles were in gilt, while the bath was a gleam of glowing white perfection, above which there was even a shower head. Mina was speechless; she had never had a bathroom of her own in her life.

'But Mr Morton,' she said, 'this must have cost the earth. I can't possibly live here.'

'You are living here, as of now,' he pointed out. 'And I do think you should have a stab at calling me Jimmy. I took a year's lease on this place, but of course, in the present circumstances, we won't be needing it for that long. Unless you want to keep it as a pied-à-terre.'

She gazed at him, and he held her hands. 'I will come to see you, and I will take you out. I want all New York to get to know you and to love you, because they are going to love you. But from now until we're married this place will be your home. We're engaged, my darling girl. And as we are engaged, I swear not to lay a finger on you below the neck until we are married. Tomorrow I'll buy the ring, and then we'll go and call on the folks.'

'Oh, Lord,' she muttered. 'Oh, my God!'

'There's nothing to be afraid of. I'll be there. Now . . . do you think I could kiss my bride?'

She went to him, not knowing what to expect. But his kiss was very like Clancy's, only more certain, more knowledgeable. Clancy! The pain had worn off now, and she still felt the desire. It almost overwhelmed her as she was kissed, and she almost wanted him to make love to her all over again. Only it wouldn't be again, because this wasn't Clancy. She had belonged to two men all in the space of a few hours. But she didn't actually belong to Jimmy Morton, yet. Surely.

'Oh, Mina,' he said. 'My dearest, darling Mina.' He held her away from him, looked at her. 'I just can't believe it.'

I can't believe it either, she thought. But she didn't say it.

A little clock chimed on the mantelpiece. 'Damn,' he said. 'I have to go to a meeting at my club. Still . . .'

'You're leaving?' Suddenly she was afraid. She was going to be utterly alone, in a strange apartment. In a still strange city.

Her world did not really extend beyond the Superb.

'Don't worry,' he said. 'Jessie will be along in a few minutes.'
He gave a guilty smile. 'Well . . . I told her not to come before
seven-thirty. Well . . . when I arranged it I didn't know we
were going to be engaged, did I?'

'Mr Morton . . .'

'Jimmy.'

Mina took a deep breath. 'Jimmy! You . . .' She licked her
lips. 'You don't have to go through with it, if you've changed
your mind.'

'That'd be the day.' He held her shoulders, kissed her on the
forehead, then brought her close to kiss her mouth again. 'That
would be the day,' he whispered. 'I love you, Mina. Oh, how I
love you.'

The door closed, and she was alone. In her apartment. How
grand that sounded. Of course it wasn't actually her
apartment, but she was living in it. All by herself. She had never
in her life possessed so much space. She stood in the centre of
the lounge, and stretched her arms wide, and did a pirouette.
She went into the kitchen, opened the cupboards, looked at the
canned food waiting there, things she had only ever read of, like
pâté de foie gras, and Gentleman's Relish, opened the larder
and peered at the cooked ham, went back into the lounge,
discovered there was a cupboard here too, in beautifully
polished oak, with a glass top; inside it was filled with bottles,
some of wine, some of spirits. The only alcohol she had ever
tasted before arriving in America had been the communion
wine Papa had served her in Devon – the wine and beer she had
drunk at the Superb had been no better in quality or taste. But
spirits . . . had Charlie Stark served her spirits? She couldn't be
sure. The entire voyage had taken on a hazy and uncertain
quality, like a street looked at through a gauze curtain, or a
half-remembered dream.

Carefully she opened a brandy bottle, something called
Hine, poured herself a little into a tumbler, sniffed it and then
sipped, and all but choked. Hastily she put the glass down,
went into the bedroom and gazed at the bed. She should be
lying on that bed now, with Jimmy Morton. And he would be

doing what Clancy had done – whatever that had been, exactly. She wasn't even sure of that, right this minute. Would he also hurt her? But more important than that, would he also fill her with that building desire?

She wondered when he intended that they should get married?

But that would depend on his parents' reaction to meeting her. His parents! She threw herself across the bed on her stomach, buried her face in the quilt. His parents! Tomorrow, he had said, casually. But he had been nervous too. His parents! They would take one look at the errant chambermaid and order her out of their house.

She rolled on her back, gazed at the canopy. She wondered what Jimmy Morton would do then? But she would have slept one night in more luxury than she had ever supposed possible. And perhaps more than one night. Jimmy was not going to let her go until he had made love to her. She sat up, staring at the door. What a wanton she had become, at least in her thoughts. But it was true. And she had his promise that he would not do that until they were married. But it was a promise made to her alone; there were no witnesses. Would such a promise matter to him?

What a way to think of one's future husband, supposing it were actually to happen. Here was a man she was not even sure she liked, and whom she certainly did not wholly trust – and she was giving him the only thing of value she possessed, herself. In exchange for luxury, she hoped. And kindness, she hoped. And to become one of a pair, which she so desperately wanted. But in Jimmy's case there was something more, she knew. The Superb! If only he would let her help with the management of the Superb. Her brain was filled with so many ideas, dreams, thoughts . . . *if* he would let her help him. If he ever married her.

If she could ever figure out why he should want to. Quite apart from having her in his power, here in his apartment, he was Jimmy Morton, who seemed able to have the pick of virtually every girl in New York – and she was one of his employees. For him to babble on that he loved her just didn't ring true. And his decision had been so sudden.

She knew that she should sit down and very carefully

consider everything that had happened. Because today had been the most important of her life – even more important than the dreadful day when her mother and father had died, and she had awakened to find Charlie Stark holding her in a bath tub. After today, after Lord Fanning and then Clancy, and then Jimmy Morton, she could never be the same again, whether or not she married Jimmy. While after marrying him, without love, without even respect . . . there was a challenge to fate, to upbringing, to all the romantic ideals her novel reading had encouraged . . . to God Himself. But God could play no part in her life. He had turned His back on her, and she had to be prepared to accept that, and make her own way as best she could, no matter what she had to become. She had been about to surrender to Him, when she had returned to the girls' dormitory after Clancy. But she hadn't needed to. Her fate had been waiting for her. All she had to do now, having grasped it, was never let it go, never doubt where she was going, and never doubt that with sufficient determination she would reach her goal.

What she really needed to determine was what her goal was.

She left the bed, rising to her feet like a startled pheasant as she heard the outer door open. Had he come back? Was he, after all, just a cheat and a liar?

There was a gentle tap, and then the bedroom door opened. She gazed at a black woman, considerably older than herself, she estimated, without suggesting age, surprisingly small, in that she was shorter and slimmer than Mina, and dressed with a quiet elegance. 'You'll be Wilhelmina,' she said. 'I guessed that Morton had left – his car was gone. He don't go anywhere without that car. I'm Jessie.'

'Jessie?' Mina asked weakly. And remembered that Jimmy Morton had mentioned the name.

'I'm to look after you,' Jessie explained. She came closer, and frowned at her. 'You meaning to leave?'

'To leave?' Mina looked down at herself, realised that if circumstances were as Jessie had obviously been told they would be, she should have been undressed. 'No,' she said. 'No, I'm not meaning to leave.' She lifted her head. 'Mr Morton and I are going to be married.'

Jessie raised her eyebrows. 'You have got to be joking.'

'I am not,' Mina declared, ready to take offence.

To her surprise, Jessie came right up to her, and embraced her. 'Then you have got *something*, child. And I am so happy for you.'

'Are you, Jessie? Are you?'

'He don't make a habit of marrying,' Jessie observed, releasing her. 'He don't *ever* marry. Not since the first one.'

'Did you know her?' Mina asked, suddenly consumed by curiosity, and apprehension. The first Mrs Morton must have been some utterly glamorous creature.

'Sure,' Jessie said. She went to the table, picked up the glass of brandy, sniffed it, and then emptied it into the slop bucket. 'She drank. Nothing wrong with drink, child. A glass of wine, maybe. But when a woman starts falling over she ain't no lady. You don't want to do that, child. Not you. A gentleman, now, every time *he* falls over he becomes more of a gentleman. But then, whoever said it was a fair world? You want me to help you undress?'

'No,' Mina said. 'No. But . . . why should I undress?'

'Because you ain't driving in a car right this minute,' Jessie pointed out. 'You undress and I going run your bath. You ain't got much time.'

'Much . . .' Mina frowned at her. 'Much time before what?'

'Before he comes back, child.'

'He's not going to come back.' Now it was Jessie's turn to stare, and Mina flushed. 'Not until after we're married. He said so.'

'And you believe that?'

'He said so,' Mina repeated. 'Because I said . . . not until we're married.'

'You really must have something,' Jessie observed, and peered at her again. 'Maybe I can see what it is.' She shrugged. 'You don't want to bathe?'

'I'd love a bath,' Mina said. And she knew she certainly needed one, after Clancy and the potting shed. A bath might even help her to wash him, and what had happened, out of her system. 'And something to eat. I'm so tired.' She clasped both hands to her throat in consternation. 'He's taking me to meet his parents, tomorrow.'

Jessie raised her eyebrows again. 'Then he is serious. So

maybe he ain't coming back, after all.'

'But . . . What am I to do, Jessie? What am I to say? What am I to wear?'

'You just be what you are, Wilhelmina. That's who he's marrying. And you just say what comes naturally. Anyone can tell you're a lady the moment you open your mouth. As for what you're going to wear . . .' She went to the wardrobe, threw the doors open. Mina had not thought to look in there before. Now she saw that it was absolutely filled with clothes. 'I guess they're all your size, too,' Jessie pointed out. 'That man sure does know the way to a girl's heart.'

Mina felt she should be angry at the way he had so taken her for granted. Jessie reckoned he would have got the sizes from Mrs Young. Which meant that the charade with Mrs Ashbourne had been just a charade, intended to overwhelm her with his careless, all-embracing generosity. 'Seduction is his big hobby,' Jessie told her. 'He ain't much good at anything else. So why get fussed about it? He's marrying you. Like I said, that ain't in character. Maybe he's turning over a new leaf.'

Mina reminded herself that she had nothing to lose. That every night she lived in this apartment, every day she wore these clothes, every meal that Jessie prepared for her, she was one hundred per cent ahead of anything she had ever known. He *did* apparently mean to marry her. As she didn't actually love him, what right did she have to cavil at his peccadilloes, especially if they were in the past?

But she decided to wear the navy blue costume that Mrs Ashbourne had shown her; she could not feel the other clothes belonged to her, and no matter what was going to happen she wanted to wear this one at least once. But actually, by morning, she was much more relaxed. It was difficult to be angry or even tense in Jessie's company, and Jessie, realising that her charge was in an extremely nervous and upset state, had offered to spend the night. Mina wanted her to share the bed, but Jessie chose to sleep on the settee in the lounge. 'You're getting all set to move into high society,' she explained. 'Don't you know that? You can't go sleeping with any old black woman.'

Mina, who had never seen a black person until after landing

in New York, had not considered the matter before. There were no black employees at the Superb, but until now that had not struck her as strange, either. 'Why not?' she asked.

Jessie gazed at her for several seconds. 'You have got a lot to learn, child,' she said. 'And I don't know that I'm the best one to teach you. Let's say that in this city there's Us and there's Them. Us are people like the Mortons and their friends. Them is everybody else. With a white skin, it's just possible for a Them to become an Us. With a black skin, it ain't. You're about to take that step up. I ain't. You have to remember that, now and always.'

'But you're my friend,' Mina said. 'Aren't you?' She so desperately wanted a friend, and while her instincts told her that Jimmy Morton would never actually be a friend, any more than Edna had ever been a friend, this woman *would* be, faithful and loyal and yet protective. Clancy might have been those things, had he been a woman, or she a man. But sex had got between them, and their relationship could never be the same again.

Once again Jessie allowed her an appraising gaze. Then she smiled, her rather solemn face lighting up as if someone had turned on a light behind her eyes. 'That would be my pleasure, Wilhelmina. But we'll talk about that later. Now you get to bed and get some sleep. Tomorrow's your big day.'

And she had slept, very soundly. More soundly than on any occasion since leaving Devon. Because she was utterly alone in her huge bed in her huge bedroom, yet knew that Jessie was but a call away. She even felt she could face Jimmy Morton, as well as his parents, and had only a momentary pang of fear that he might not turn up.

'Well, I sure hope he does,' Jessie said, pinning a watch to Mina's lapel and standing back to inspect the finished product. 'I got a home to go to.'

'Oh, Jessie!' Mina was utterly contrite. 'I kept you here all night.'

Jessie shrugged. 'It ain't what *you* would call a home, Mina. But it has a man in it. You know what I mean?'

'Yes,' Mina said, but could not prevent herself from giving a quick glance at Jessie's left hand; she wore no ring.

'I told you, I'm not so lucky as you,' Jessie agreed. 'That's the problem with the Thems. They just ain't lucky. Now, you know what? I think we should start again and put your hair up. You're a big girl, but that hair lying down your back and that bow makes you look like a sixteen-year-old girl.'

'But . . . I am a sixteen-year-old girl,' Mina told her.

'You're joking.'

'No, I'm not. I won't be seventeen until December.'

'Great Walls of Jericho,' Jessie remarked. 'That Morton . . . he should be horsewhipped.'

'He's going to marry me,' Mina said, more to remind herself of that fact than in an attempt to convince the maid.

'Sure he is, honey,' Jessie agreed. 'But I still think we'll put your hair up, or when he starts showing you off he might just get arrested for statutory rape or something.'

Mina had never had her hair up before in her life. But Jessie was obviously an expert lady's maid. From one of the drawers in the dressing table she produced a small pad and a variety of hairpins; the pad was pinned into position on the crown of Mina's head, following which the deep yellow hair was rolled up around it, and then somehow loosened again, to form a gentle pompadour, sufficiently free at the back and sides almost to obscure her ears, while looming over her forehead in front. 'There,' Jessie said. 'That's the latest fashion amongst the swells. Just keep out of any strong winds,' she recommended, carefully pinning a straw boater with a blue ribbon into place. 'And if you take off the hat, do it real careful and slow.' She stood back, pinching her lip. 'Now you look twenty. Maybe he'll reckon you're too old.'

He didn't, apparently. He arrived only a few minutes afterwards, wearing a carnation in his buttonhole, and looking as immaculately dashing as ever – and as much in love as ever. 'Mina!' he cried, holding her shoulders and bringing her forward for a kiss on the forehead. 'Oh, Mina! How beautiful you are.'

'Jessie did it,' Mina explained.

'Of course she did. Jessie is a treasure. But she had to have something to work on. Now, I have something for you.'

Mina took the little box, her heart pounding. She knew what had to be inside it, and yet she had no idea what to expect. She lifted the lid, and stared at the solitaire diamond, which seemed to wink at her. 'Oh,' she said. 'Oh, Lord. But Mr Morton . . . it must have cost the earth.'

'Jimmy,' he reminded her. 'And it didn't cost half enough.'

'Jimmy,' she said. 'Oh, Jimmy!' She had no idea what it *had* cost, but she knew it was the most valuable single article she had ever seen, much less possessed. For the first time she began to feel that it was really going to happen.

Jessie was clearly experiencing the same emotion. 'Now it's official, Mina,' she said. 'Man, that is one big stone.'

'Now,' Jimmy Morton said. 'We can go and tell the folks.' He held Mina's hand as he saw the expression on her face. 'They can't say no, Mina, my darling girl. I'm over twenty-one.'

But they *could* say no, Mina knew. Simply by threatening to remove Jimmy from the assistant managership of the Superb. She wondered how he would react to that?

Even more disturbing, she wondered how she would react – supposing he still wanted to go through with it – to marrying a man who *didn't* own the Superb?

But there was surprisingly little time to worry about it; the senior Mortons lived only a block away from the apartment, and in fact only a block away from the hotel itself. The old brownstone was large and elegant, although already beginning to be dwarfed by the rising architecture to either side. There was a butler to hand Jimmy's hat and cane to a second footman, before escorting them towards a huge pair of double doors. Mina was so lost in admiration of the high ceilinged hallway, with the curving staircase to the upper floor, and the paintings, some of horses but most of people, clearly Morton ancestors, that the doors were opened before she was ready.

'Mr James,' the butler announced. 'And, ah . . . Miss Doberley.'

Mina blinked, because the room was enormous, and very light and airy, with french windows leading on to a croquet lawn beyond. It was a place of vast overstuffed furniture, and more paintings, and an enormous fireplace, presently empty, and two huge dogs, Great Danes she thought, which arose silently from the hearth rug and came forwards to sniff her.

'They won't harm you,' Jimmy said. 'They know a friend when they see one.'

But they were certainly distracting, because Mina knew she should be concentrating on the people. There were only two of them. A woman, at once tall and thin and elegant in her clothes and her movements, now raising a lorgnette to gaze at the intruders, and a man, somewhat shorter than his wife, wearing a smoking jacket over baggy trousers, and heavy spectacles, through which he was also peering at her.

'Mina,' Jimmy said. 'I would like you to meet my mother and father.'

Mina went forward, propelled by his hand under her elbow. Her knees banged against each other and she could feel the heat in her cheeks. Should she curtsy? She decided against it – mainly because she wasn't sure she would be able to straighten again.

'She doesn't look like a chambermaid,' Mrs Morton observed.

'I keep telling you that she isn't, really,' Jimmy pointed out. 'Do say hello, Mina,' he whispered desperately; obviously he was counting on her voice to sway them in her favour.

'This is a great pleasure, Mrs Morton,' Mina said.

'She's *English!*' Elizabeth Morton exclaimed.

'I told you that too, Mother,' Jimmy reminded her, severely. 'Now come and meet Father, Mina.'

Mina felt herself becoming angry. How dare these people behave as if she wasn't really there?

'English,' observed Mr Morton Senior. 'I knew an Englishman once, with the same name as you. Used to buy liquor from him when I was managing an hotel in London. Yes, sir, I remember him well. Crusty old coot. But very top drawer. Eton and Oxford and all that.'

'You are speaking of my grandfather, Mr Morton,' Mina remarked.

'Your . . .' Morton stared at her.

'Your grandfather?' Jimmy cried, in a mixture of consternation and delight. 'John Doberley, Doberley and Sons, is your grandfather?'

'Yes,' Mina said. 'My father also went to Eton and Oxford. But Grandfather disowned him for becoming a parson.' Which was of course a lie; but she did not feel she owed these people the truth – not any of them.

'Good heavens!' commented Mr Morton.

'Good God!' Jimmy remarked.

Mrs Morton dropped her lorgnette.

'I knew it the moment you walked through that door,' Mr Morton said, and held her hands to draw her forward for a kiss and a hug, which nearly displaced her hat. 'Class will tell, eh? Yes, sir, class will tell.'

'My dear girl,' Elizabeth Morton said, having recovered her glasses and her composure. 'You must come and sit beside me and tell me about it.'

'All about what?' Mina asked.

'All about . . . well, everything. And then we have to plan the wedding. You'll have to tell me to whom we must write for permission for you to marry – your grandfather, I presume – and which members of your family need be invited, and . . . oh, there are so many things.' She dragged Mina down to the cushion beside her, holding her hand. 'But mainly we must get to know one another. Because I know that we are going to be the best of friends, just as I know you are going to be the best thing that has ever happened to James. Oh, indeed. My dear, I am so happy I could cry.'

'Well,' Jessie Dobret observed, closing the door of the apartment behind Jimmy Morton. 'There goes one happy man.'

'Yes.' Mina pulled off her gloves and then took off her hat and let her hair collapse; her blouse was soaked with sweat, and so was her underwear.

'But you ain't? After winning those people over, like he said?'

'I'm just wondering whether I truly want to be their daughter-in-law,' Mina said. 'Whether I want to be an Us, and not a Them.' Or if she was going to make it at all, she thought, now, with Elizabeth Morton apparently determined to write to Grandfather and ask for his blessing on his granddaughter's marriage – Mina just could not imagine what reply would arrive. If any.

'Don't say that, child,' Jessie recommended. 'Being an Us has got to be better than being a Them. No matter what.'

'Oh, Jessie, they remind me of . . . of my father's family. Really they do. Ghastly people.'

'The important thing,' Jessie pointed out, 'is that they ain't going to be ghastly to you. Not now they know you're one of them.' She smiled. 'I mean, Us.'

And this was the path she had chosen, Mina reminded herself. She did not suppose that Mr and Mrs Morton were any worse than Joe Stark or Mrs Young; they simply possessed the money to make their unpleasantness more effective. And the same went for their friends, to whom Mina found herself being introduced at a succession of dinner parties and soirées. It was in fact a most peculiar existence, for, in strong contrast to life at the Superb, her day did not now actually begin until three o'clock in the afternoon. Before then she was left strictly to herself. Jimmy told her to buy whatever she liked, and he had opened accounts for her at places like Saks and B. Altman, but he and Mrs Ashbourne had fitted her out so completely that she didn't really need to buy anything save her food, and the odd handkerchief or perfume. Often he came round to lunch with her – which was really breakfast, as she seldom rose before noon – at which times she wanted to talk about the hotel, but he would never discuss what he called 'shop'.

'The news sure put the staff into a tizz,' he admitted. 'Stark and Mrs Young actually offered their resignations. Do you want me to accept them?'

'Of course not,' she cried. 'I'm sure they're both very good at their jobs.'

'As a matter of fact, they are,' he agreed, and leaned across the table to squeeze her hand. 'I'm so glad that's your attitude. Not that I expected anything different from my darling Mina.'

She decided there could not be a better time to launch her great plan. 'I want everything to be just right with the Superb, Jimmy,' she said. 'I did love that place. I do love that place. In fact . . . I'd adore to be allowed to go on working there, after we're married.'

'Working there?' He was obviously totally astonished.

'Well . . . I could help Mrs Young . . . or plan menus . . . or . . .' She watched his expression in dismay.

Then he smiled, and squeezed her hand again. 'Those days are behind you, darling Mina. Forever and ever. In a couple of weeks' time you are going to be Mrs James Morton.'

Because that was how soon it was going to be. And meanwhile, and after they were married, she was very much afraid she was going to be merely his darling Mina, as she was Elizabeth Morton's darling Mina, and Mr Morton's darling Mina, and soon, all of New York's darling Mina. At three o'clock every afternoon Jessie drew her bath, and then dressed her in some brand new outfit, and a cab called to take her to the Morton household, either for a reception there, or for herself and Elizabeth to visit some other prominent New York household, where, in a gathering entirely female, she would be introduced and told how beautiful she was, and how tastefully she dressed, and how good she would be for poor James – it was always 'poor James', presumably because his first wife had been an alcoholic – while all the time she was aware that once she had passed on to the next group, the last were whispering behind their fans, tearing her to pieces, waiting for her to make some social or feminine gaffe, discussing – often audibly – the extreme oddness of the fact that she should have actually *worked* at the Superb, and that she should now be living in an apartment leased by Jimmy, and that she should be so young. Clearly she was a looming scandal. Equally surely she was already Jimmy's mistress, and thus no better than she should be. 'Poor' Jimmy certainly had no luck when it came to choosing women. And thus, most obviously of all, she could be expected at any moment to make a slip and reveal what she truly was – a slut – however much the Mortons kept harping on her wealthy grandfather.

But they waited in vain. Mina had attended sufficient tea parties thrown by her mother in the Devon vicarage, at which people like the wife of the Squire and even, occasionally, of the bishop, had been guests, to ride serenely through any traps in conversation or etiquette which might be laid for her, to do no more than nibble at her cream buns and seed cakes, and to satisfy herself with sipping a single glass of sherry. But one day, she thought to herself, one day, when I am really and truly Mrs James Morton, and I can let my hair down and say what I think, and do what I like . . . one day . . .

Only thoughts like that could preserve her self-respect, her determination to go through with it, no matter what. Because even with Jimmy she was afraid to relax. He took over as soon as his mother was finished with her for the day; every evening they would either dine tête-à-tête in the apartment, served by Jessie, before going to the opera or the theatre, or he would take her to dinner at a friend's house – it was apparently not done for 'ladies' to eat in restaurants, except in places like the Plaza, which, as a rival establishment, he refused to patronise. This was a disappointment; even more disappointingly, he never took her back to the Superb for any reason at all – no doubt, she reasoned, he was afraid she might be too familiar with the staff.

On Sundays, he would either take her driving in his automobile – with a picnic lunch – or sailing in his yacht on Long Island Sound. But this last was soon abandoned because, to her disgust, after the way she had coped with the Atlantic crossing, the motion of the sailing boat made her seasick, and Jimmy was too enthusiastic a racing yachtsman to want to have a complete passenger cluttering up the deck. In some respects this was reassuring; she had gathered that in the cases of the girls he took out for non-racing purposes, he merely sailed to some secluded bay and dropped anchor. On the other hand, she was concerned that her weakness might somehow diminish his adoration of her, but apparently sea sickness was regarded as an entirely normal feminine affliction – amongst ladies.

She was in fact equally uncomfortable when driving in his automobile, because he insisted on going so very fast, but at least, however terrified, she was never actually carsick.

Jimmy's enthusiasm for every aspect of life was by far the best thing about him, and promised indeed much enjoyment after their marriage, presuming it extended beyond cars and boats. She could only hope it did. The private parties they attended were very restrained affairs, but she could not escape the suspicion that the restraint was for her benefit; there were numerous allusions to wild occasions. But, of course, these could also be traps, to be listened to with a disapproving, and disbelieving smile, just as it was necessary always to be on her guard against the insinuations and downright propositions whispered to her – clearly Jimmy's male friends also felt that she was no better than she should be. She hated both the suggestions and the people who made them, considered saying as much to Jimmy – and didn't, because he so obviously enjoyed showing her off, and, like his parents, reminding people that she was John Doberley's granddaughter. However reassuring he found that fact, she found it necessary often to remind herself that he had proposed before he knew of it.

While his goodnight kisses were always passionate, he sometimes clearly had difficulty in restraining his hands from roaming to her breasts and hips. Just as sometimes she wished he wouldn't be quite so restrained, again without any decision as to how she would, or more importantly, should, respond. She only knew that somehow he had to create the same bubble of desire that Clancy had done – or she didn't know she would be able to go through with it.

But Jimmy was good manners personified, content to wait for the great day, because the great day was now only a few days off; his mother had protested against the unseemly haste, and dropped heavy hints that all the world supposed it had to be caused by Mina's pregnancy, but Jimmy was revealing a very pleasant, and reassuring, streak of determination himself. This was very necessary for Mina, because nearly every night she would awaken at about two in the morning, and find herself in a cold sweat at the thought of marrying a man who never excited her, and a deep gloom at the thought of all the things that might have been, and thus would need to exert all her own determination to stop herself from bursting into tears.

Because enthusiasm and determination apart, and allowing that sexual love would have to wait on marriage, there was not a great deal to her future husband. She had never really considered what a man should actually be like, and thus judged them all by her father, who had appeared as the ideal blend of masculinity, thoughtfulness, and learning. Jimmy never seemed to read a book, and was openly bored by the plays they saw; again, they were merely occasions for displaying his beautiful fiancée. He was not interested in politics and dismissed philosophy as bunkum, while she knew just how disinterested he was in the actual running of the hotel.

So what *was* he interested in? Cars, and boats. And women! Of whom she was currently the favourite. But, unlike the other favourites who had occupied his time since his divorce, she was going to be his wife, even if Elizabeth Morton's letter to John Doberley had elicited a very brief reply to the effect that, while he regretted the unfortunate death of his son – he made no reference whatsoever to William Doberley's wife – such a catastrophe was nothing more than the family had been expecting for years, and stating that he did not regard himself as having, now, or at any time in the future, any responsibility for Mina, or for any other offspring William might have produced, and that she could marry whomever she chose.

Rather to her surprise, and to her relief, Elizabeth Morton had been just as angry as herself. 'Wretched old man,' she had declared. 'Well, we can certainly take this as permission for your marriage. And as of this moment, my dear, you are no longer a Doberley. You are a Morton!'

The important point was that Grandfather's letter had confirmed everything Mina had claimed.

So she could at last allow herself to anticipate the day itself, wanted it to hurry towards her, as it was in fact doing – once the introductions were completed, her days suddenly became filled with activity, as she was delivered to Mrs Ashbourne for measuring and then fitting her wedding gown. This again was reassuring, combining with Jimmy's smiling confidence to keep her mind fixed on the glittering prize which lay in front of her, to the exclusion of all else.

But all else was not to be so easily excluded. Mina was sitting in her bath one morning, this event having been brought forward to allow for the arrival of Mrs Ashbourne and her minions at eleven o'clock, when there was a tap on the door, and Jessie looked in, her face unusually anxious. 'There's some lad here wanting to speak with you,' she said.

Mina frowned. 'Some lad?'

'Some Irish layabout,' Jessie explained. 'I told him to get off, but he wouldn't go. Says you'll see him. Says to tell you his name is Clancy.'

'Clancy!' Mina screamed, and leapt out of the bath, scattering water.

'You know him?'

'Oh, yes.' Mina ran for the door.

'You must know him very well,' Jessie observed.

Mina checked, and looked down at her nude body. 'Oh, Lord!'

'I told him to take a seat,' Jessie said, wrapping her in a towel. 'You have time.'

And what was he doing here, in the middle of the morning, when he should be working? He'd get into the most awful trouble.

But Clancy, coming to see her . . . it had not occurred to her before, but Clancy could make a lot of trouble for her. But surely not Clancy.

'I guess that'll have to do,' Jessie said, removing the towel and wrapping her in a dressing-gown instead. 'Now you mind how you sit, and remember, I'll be in the kitchen if you need me.'

'Yes,' Mina said. 'Oh, yes.' She opened the bedroom door, and Clancy hastily got to his feet. Mina found it strange how young he looked, and how ill-fitting his clothes appeared – he was not in his hotel uniform, but in a suit which seemed several sizes too small for him.

He was equally surprised by her appearance in a brocade dressing-gown. 'Mina?' he asked incredulously. 'Is it really you?'

'Of course it's me, silly,' she said, and held out her hand. 'It's good to see you.'

He didn't take it. 'They told us . . . well . . . I couldn't believe it.'

Mina realised it was going to be more difficult than she had even anticipated. She sat down on a straight chair, knees primly together, back straight. 'Mr Morton and I are to be married.'

'You mean you love him?'

'Doesn't one usually love the man one is going to marry?' Mina asked, carefully.

'But . . . you went with me . . .'

Mina said nothing. This was the moment she had most dreaded. Her brain seemed turned to stone.

'I . . .' Clancy bit his lip. 'I didn't believe it,' he said again. 'Then I wanted to come to see you, but I didn't. I guess I was angry. But now . . . Mina . . .'

'Yes?' she asked, suddenly breathless.

'Don't do it, Mina. Please don't do it.'

Mina gazed at him; he couldn't just stop there.

'I . . .' Once again he chewed his lip. 'I love you Mina. Really I do. I . . .'

Then ask, she said to herself. Just ask, you numbskull.

'I can't ask you to marry me, Mina. Not right now.'

Mina leaned back. She had indigestion. And she wanted to cry.

'I don't have any money, you see. I don't have anything. I've quit my job.'

Mina sat up again. 'You've done *what*?'

'Well . . . I couldn't stay at the Superb. Not with . . . well . . .'

'Don't be foolish,' Mina shouted. 'Quit your job? Whyever should you do that? Don't you see, I'll be able to help you, once I'm Mrs Morton.'

'To help me? You? Mrs Morton? You mean you'll still go with me?'

'No,' Mina said. 'I didn't mean that.' Because she most certainly didn't. She might be prepared to marry without love in the hopes of advancement – but a marriage was a marriage. That was one thing Papa had always hammered into her. Besides, the very idea of cheating precluded the dream she had of becoming entirely one of a pair, who trusted and respected and counted on each other – whether or not they loved. Perhaps she would rather 'go' with Clancy, as he put it, than with any other man in the world; but she was marrying Jimmy Morton. 'No, no, no,' she said, more to convince herself than him. 'But we're friends, Phil. I owe you a lot. And . . . I do like you, so very much. I will help you, if you'll stay on. I'll see you get promoted.' Would she be able to do that? Would Jimmy let her? Or would he immediately suspect? But she could get round that, she was sure; Jimmy would remember that Clancy was the boy who had tried to help her on her first night in the hotel.

'Promoted,' Clancy said, bitterly. 'And I'd see you, every day, and know where you were going that night, and what you were doing. Mr Jimmy Morton.'

'You had me,' Mina said. 'You had all of me, Phil. And you didn't want me.'

'You never gave me the chance. And anyway . . . oh, Mina, I didn't know . . . I didn't know how much I loved you. I didn't know so many things. Mina . . .' To her consternation he knelt on the floor at her feet, and held her hands. 'Will you come away with me, Mina?'

'Come away with you?'

'I'm going west. That's where the future is. Everybody says so. You and me, Mina. Will you? We're young, and we're strong. We can do things, together.'

'What things?' Her heart was pounding, and she was aware of a gathering excitement.

'Well, maybe . . . we could farm. Or, if we didn't have the

money for that, I can always black boots. And you can always be a chambermaid.' His grip tightened. 'We'd be together, always. And I would marry you, Mina, just as soon as I could afford it.'

And we'd be poor, she thought. Always. Even poorer than at the Superb, where at least we had beds and were fed. So maybe we'd love. In a way she could never love Jimmy Morton. And in a way she did not think someone as shallow as Jimmy could ever love her. But could even she and Phil stay loving, while they were poor?

'I went west, once before, Phil,' she said. 'With my mother and father. They died. It was horrible. And then I had to work in the Superb, like you say, as a chambermaid, because I didn't have any money. I'm done with that, Phil. I'm never going to be a chambermaid again, not ever. I want you to understand that. How I feel.'

He gazed at her, and then slowly pushed himself to his feet.

'But if . . .' Her turn to bite her lip. Because she didn't know how to say what was in her mind. Or even if it was possible to say it.

It wasn't possible. 'I can't ask you to wait for me, Mina,' he said. 'I don't reckon you can wait that long.'

He closed the front door behind him, very softly.

Mina stared at it, did not even turn her head when Jessie came in.

'He the one what took your cherry?'

Mina's head jerked.

'I know it wasn't Morton,' Jessie said. 'And I washed your clothes the day you came here, so it was sure somebody that day. That lets out Charlie Stark.'

'Oh, Jessie . . .'

Jessie smiled. 'I won't tell anybody, child. But . . . I reckon you could just have made a mistake. A big one. That boy loves you. To Morton you're a late model toy, like his automobile or his yacht.'

'Oh, Jessie,' Mina said again. And started to cry.

Chapter 6

People! So many people. Perhaps all of New York. But no church. Because Jimmy was divorced. But Mina was actually glad about that, when she thought about it. Church had no place in her life.

The wedding and reception were, naturally, held at the Superb, and this delighted her. It was the first time she had entered the hotel since leaving it with Jimmy two months before, and it was the first time she had *ever* entered by the great revolving doors to the lobby, being turned for her, very carefully, by Joe Stark, wearing his frock-coat, who anxiously kissed her hand.

While inside, lined up to greet their employer's bride, were most of the staff. For the first time she was actually glad Clancy had quit. She shook hands with Mrs Young, who was sweating with nervousness, looked her in the eye and allowed her a cold smile, and then proceeded down the line of bell-boys and chambermaids until she reached Edna and the others. They all looked as if they were seeing a ghost. Because while they were in their starched bests, it was cotton, and, as they knew she knew, mended hand-me-downs into the bargain, while she was in satin over taffeta, with long satin gloves and her hair piled on her head, and a pearl necklace Jimmy had given her as a wedding present – and most important of all, she had Jimmy Morton at her side.

Strangely, she felt humble rather than proud, wanted to explain to them that she hadn't really changed, was still Mina Doberley rather than about to become Mrs James Morton . . . but she had no time to speak with any of them, because the guests and the judge were already waiting in the ballroom. The service was mercifully short. Then the afternoon became a kaleidoscope of faces and names, and glasses of champagne, and more faces and names, and more glasses of champagne, then endless speeches, with her sitting beside Jimmy at the head of the long table in the restaurant – another room she had never entered before today – and more faces and names, and more champagne. Following which, head whirling and feet unsteady, she was taken upstairs by Elizabeth Morton and Mrs Ashbourne, into one of the best suites – shades of Lord Fanning, she thought, expecting him to emerge from the bathroom at any moment – where to her great relief Jessie was waiting for her, to help her change into her going away outfit, which consisted of a pale blue tunic and skirt, trimmed with dark blue, and a magnificent pale blue felt hat with enormous dark blue ostrich plumes – Mrs Ashbourne had decided, correctly, that blue was Mina's best colour.

She could not believe it had really happened, perhaps *because* there had been no church and no parson – but in every way the noise, the excitement, the very obvious tipsyness of many of the guests, and the equally enormous cost of the whole event bore very little relationship to the quiet, dignified and carefully budgeted weddings her father had conducted in Devon, and at which she had often been a bridesmaid or a flower girl. For *her* wedding she did not have a bridesmaid at all, merely a matron of honour, one of the detestable young women, daughters of Elizabeth Morton's friends, to whom she had been introduced during the social whirl.

Yet it had happened, and here she was, sitting in a railway carriage opposite her husband, still hearing the cheers that had filled the station as the train pulled out. She had, she reminded herself, finally got her feet on to the ladder she had chosen, the ladder which was going to take her forever out of the reach of the company of the Clancys and the Starks, the Mrs Youngs and the Ednas, of this world, which was going to take her to the ownership of the Superb – at least at second hand.

They were actually only riding as far as Atlantic City. 'We're to honeymoon,' Jimmy told her, 'not sightsee. But Atlantic City in September can be fun.' He smiled at her across the compartment. 'You're so lovely, Mina. So . . . so just *right*. Those bitches . . .'

She was shocked, because she did not associate foul language

117

with Jimmy Morton. But she was also secretly pleased. Did he dislike the New York society in which he lived as much as she did? And was then frightened. Because, had he thus married her out of some feeling of defiance, even of spite, for his friends, and their male friends?

Once again she had to remind herself that his motives for marrying her could never be as sordid as hers for marrying him, and that as he was prepared to accept her – he must know she wasn't madly in love with him – she had no right to criticise him. She told herself that even if it had been a straightforward auction, she would still consider that she had obtained the best of the bargain. She had to keep reminding herself of these things – there was too much fear and apprehension, and misery and uncertainty, lurking just beneath her consciousness. Too much awareness that her life was all wrong. And had been from the very beginning. Mother and Father had counted on her birth to bring about a reconciliation with grandfather. Mama had told her how they had taken the babe up to London, to call on the old man – and been refused admittance. And the pattern had merely been repeating itself ever since. She supposed that after one's own birth, and before one's own death, the three most important events in a human's being life would have to be the death of one's parents, the loss of one's virginity, and one's marriage – these were certainly the big events in the novels she had read. So in the space of six months her parents had died in the most ghastly possible manner, she had surrendered her virginity without actually knowing what she was doing, and now she was married, to a man she did not love and after a ceremony which was an unchristian and certainly unromantic and unlovable blur.

All the while telling herself that she was following a plan!

But, however it had happened, she was married, and if she expected anything at all from him, she had first to give him what he wanted from her. If she could. She could feel his excitement growing as the train pulled into the station, and as they disembarked and got into a cab. She had actually braced herself to be kissed and fondled on the train, and he had just sat and stared at her, and occasionally smiled, more to himself than at her. Because, she realised, that was his way. She did not suppose Jimmy Morton ever denied himself much. But, as he had denied himself her until they were married, he intended to carry the denial to logical lengths, so that the enjoyment of her, when it came, would be the greater. He was the complete sensualist. which, she reminded herself, was no reason to be afraid of him.

Until they were alone in their hotel suite, overlooking the beach and the Atlantic rollers. Perhaps it was the sea which upset her. She had not seen the sea since leaving the *William McKinley*. But there it was, a reminder of everything she had once been. And here she was, alone in a bedroom with a man, knowing that in a few seconds she must *be* everything she had become.

All in six months.

'Mina!' Jimmy exclaimed. 'You're crying.'

'Am I?' She sniffed, and forced a smile. 'I suppose the sea reminded me of Mama and Papa.'

'Of course,' he said sympathetically, and took her into his arms. 'I should have realised that. What a fool I am to have brought you here.'

'I want to be here, with you,' she whispered. Because suddenly she did. This was what she wanted. Perhaps, she thought, this was all she really wanted, to be held and loved. To belong. She turned her face up for his kiss, and her hat fell off, allowing her hair to cascade past her shoulders.

'Such beauty,' he said. 'Such beauty.' He kissed away her tears. 'Mina . . . will you undress for me?'

Because they had a bargain. Her body in exchange for his wealth. 'Of course,' she said. 'Shall I . . .' She looked left and right, seeking another room.

'Right here,' he said. 'I want to watch. May I watch you, Mina?'

'Of course you may,' she said again. 'I'm yours, now, Jimmy.'

She hoped he wouldn't misinterpret that, by understanding exactly what she meant. But he merely seemed delighted, threw himself on the bed, his hands beneath his head, while she slowly stripped. She might have been on a stage, she supposed. Although she did not know of any stage where the end result was so preordained.

'You are gorgeous,' he said. 'Gorgeous!'

And she felt gorgeous, standing before him, stretching her arms above her head and extending her body to follow it. She

119

had felt this way in the potting shed. She liked being naked. And if it would bring on the passion bubble . . . but suddenly she was apprehensive again. Would he want to kiss her the way Clancy had done? She hoped not. That was a special memory, to Clancy and herself. Besides, she had been sufficiently embarrassed when Clancy had done it. If Mr Morton . . . she just could not think of him as Jimmy, at this moment.

'Those fellows,' he muttered. 'Those fellows . . .'

What fellows? she wanted to ask. What did they say? But he had left the bed, to hold her, and feel her, and explore her with his fingers. This came as a surprise, and a shock, more even than if he had kissed her. She had expected him to wish to play with her breasts, had even braced herself *for* that kiss. But her bottom was surely forbidden ground. Clancy had held it to bring her against him; that had been functional, and in any event, it had been when passion had already been peaking. Mr Morton wanted to part her buttocks and put his fingers between.

'No!' she protested, and he raised his head in alarm.

Oh, lord, she thought. She didn't dare anger him. Not yet. She had to pretend, to distract him . . . 'Don't you undress too?' she asked.

His head went back as he looked down at her in surprise. Then he gave a brief laugh. But certainly he was delighted, tore the clothes from his body. To do that he had to let her go, and she went to the bed, lay down, as she had before Clancy, legs together. But now she was prepared to watch, and take in what she saw. Jimmy Morton was a splendid specimen of manhood. He made her wish she had looked more closely at Clancy. But he frightened her as well. Not the size of him, but the desire in his eyes as he knelt beside her. 'Mina,' he said. 'There are so many things I wish to do to you. But only if you want me to. I won't ever hurt you, Mina.'

Mina licked her lips. She did not wish to reject him, but she did not wish to be explored, either. There was a passion bubble inside her – nothing like the day with Clancy, but still there – and she wanted him in her and on her, so that maybe she could feel some of the sharing she had with Clancy.

'That Stark,' he muttered. 'By God, I'll kill the swine if I ever see him again.'

Mina held his shoulders to bring him down on top of her.

'Forget Stark, Jimmy,' she begged. 'Forget Stark, and love me. Love *me*, Jimmy.'

Perhaps he was too quick. Or perhaps the passion bubble had not had the time to grow as it should have done. Perhaps so many things.

But at least, she thought, as he lay on her, crushing the breath from her lungs, gasping into her ear, he owns the Superb!

'You know what, child,' Jessie remarked. 'You ain't even looking any older.'

She sounded both surprised and a trifle disappointed. Which Mina could understand. She had gathered that in Jessie's world, a sexual relationship invariably left scars – and some of them were very physical. Was she then blessed? Not blessed. Never blessed. But maybe, she thought, she was tougher than most.

Yet not tough enough. She could not be disappointed in what she saw. She stood in a hallway, and looked up a flight of stairs. To the right was a spacious drawing room, and beyond the french windows a still tangled garden; to the left was an equally spacious dining room, and down the hall there was a study-cum-library before one reached the pantry and then the kitchens. Standing before her were several very anxious domestics, and if *she* knew she was more in awe of them than they of her, with Jessie at her side she could project a massive and almost disdainful confidence. Upstairs were six bedrooms and two bathrooms. It was a magnificent house, and on Upper Fifth Avenue it could not really be improved on for position; from the bedroom windows she could make out the Plaza itself, blocking out the view of Central Park – but she would far rather look at the Plaza, the most famous of all New York hotels, than at Central Park.

What was disappointing was the way it had all been done. Another of Jimmy's eternal surprises. She would have supposed their home would at least be something for them to plan together. If he had had the time to choose it and buy it between their engagement and their marriage, he had certainly had the time to show it to her. But apparently he had not even shown it to Jessie, had merely left instructions for her to move herself and her mistress in during the fortnight he and his bride spent in Atlantic City. That was Jimmy's way. Because for all the thirty-one love-makings they had indulged in during their two weeks in Atlantic City, they had not yet become the pair she sought. Now she knew they never would, barring a miracle. She would not have supposed it possible for two people to perform the act of love thirty-one times in fourteen days without achieving something together. But they had done so. Or rather, *she* had. Jimmy Morton always managed to accomplish quite a lot, for himself. But after that first time, even her passion bubble had disappeared.

What was so crushing was that she knew it was her fault. Mr Morton would no doubt have accomplished quite a lot for her as well, had she let him make love to her the way he seemed to want – but he wanted things she would not even have been prepared to grant Clancy, and with Clancy it would have been a boy and a girl mutually finding out about lust, together. With Morton she was too aware that he had done these instinctively disgusting – to her entirely unsophisticated mind – things before, too often, with other women. Perhaps even with his first wife. But even more than that, even had he been as truly virginal as herself, she was aware of the damning knowledge that she did not *want* a man's hand between her legs. Nature had given the male sex an entirely adequate means of procreation as well as, apparently, enjoyment. Surely that was sufficient.

That Jimmy Morton seemed unable to provide any pleasure for her as well as himself, she put down entirely to the fact that she did not love him. And that was something she had gone into with her eyes open. So she really had no cause for complaint. She had been a little worried that her prudishness – as he undoubtedly considered it – might offend him. But, on the contrary, he continued to adore her. This was at least gratifying, if mystifying, and it left her with a terrible feeling of guilt. He liked nothing better than to look at her, to touch her, to hold her in his arms, and to lie on top of her. Whenever he looked at her, he seemed to want sex. And this was certainly reassuring. If only she could want sex every time she looked at him. But every time she looked at him in the nude she found herself thinking of Clancy. This was criminal of her, she knew. She was not married to Clancy, and she would never see Clancy again. He had disappeared from New York, so far as she could tell, and she was not about to go and visit Sergeant Clancy to find out where he now was. Her mistake had been in assuming that the passion bubble she had felt with him could be transferred to any other man as the occasion arose. Now she knew better. But in fact she wasn't sure she would be able to let even Clancy make love to her with his hands.

'So Morton don't make you jump for joy,' Jessie remarked, having elicited at least a part of the truth. 'That ain't something I would worry about, child. Men don't understand women, and that is a fact. So that Irish layabout stirred you up. You know what? You are just lucky he is the only one. Husbands . . . they don't *ever* stir you up.'

'Is that why you never got married, Jessie?'

'I ain't never got married, child, because nobody ain't ever asked me, that's why. Maybe husbands don't ever stir you up. But they is still the most important thing a woman can have. Without a husband, you ain't got no rights. With a husband you got plenty. And soon enough you going to be pregnant, and then again and again and again, and you going to be happy. Not wild, mind. But happy.'

'Oh, Lord,' Mina said. She was going to be a mother. Well, that was inevitable, she supposed. Motherhood went with marriage. Until she had gone to work at the Superb and started listening to Edna and the girls, she had presumed that it was an inevitable comcomitant of having a gold band placed on one's finger. Certainly it had to be a concomitant of being made love to at least once every day – for Jimmy's passion did not diminish one iota on their return to New York. But she, a mother! It was unbelievable.

'And that going to give you even more rights,' Jessie pointed out.

Rights, Mina thought. Rights, to share. To share, perhaps, even in the Superb.

'But first, there's one or two things you got to straighten out,' Jessie went on. 'Like this man Stark.'

'Stark?' Mina screamed.

'The sea captain,' Jessie explained, with massive calm. 'He's been here, twice.'

'Oh, Lord,' Mina said. 'Oh, my God!' But He wasn't her God. He had never been her God. He spent His time tormenting her.

'So I reckon you just have to see him off,' Jessie said. 'I told him to come back this morning, at eleven o'clock. I reckoned Morton would be gone by then. And he is.'

The clock was chiming eleven.

'But . . . I don't want to see Charlie Stark,' Mina shouted. 'He has nothing to do with me, any more.'

'Now that's a fact,' Jessie said. 'But he reckons he does. You just have to tell him different. I reckon he's here now.'

The door bell was ringing.

'What you have to do,' Jessie said, 'is walk down those stairs, nice and slow and regal like, and look him in the eye, and say, "Git!". Remember that I'm right behind you, and that Dutton, the butler, is there too, and that you are Mrs James Morton, and that there ain't nobody, nobody on this earth, can trouble you.' She winked. 'Charlie Stark may be a sea captain, but he's still a Them. You're an Us. And all of the people in this house are going to keep you up there. You're our bread and butter.'

Sometimes, Mina wished Jessie was not quite so frank. She would have liked to feel her maid would stand behind her no matter whether she was paying her or not. But that was a quibble. Just to feel Jessie *was* behind her was enough. She went down the stairs, taking each step in time to Chopin's Funeral March, which she kept humming, gazing at Charlie Stark, who had been stalled in the hallway by Dutton the butler, and was twisting his cap in his hands. He wore seagoing clothes, and looked at once weather-beaten and immensely strong. And also immensely masculine. Now that she understood more of what he would have wanted, had she surrendered in the cabin of the *William McKinley*, she could not look at him without a shudder, and had to grit her teeth to keep her expression coldly polite.

He looked equally embarrassed. 'Mina?' he asked. 'Is it really you?'

'It is I, Captain Stark,' she said, having reached the foot of the stairs. 'How good it is to see you.' She extended her hand, as regally as she could, and, after a brief hesitation, he took it.

'I got in a week ago,' he said.

Mina freed her hand. 'From Buenos Aires.'

'Why, that's right,' he agreed, obviously pleased that she should have remembered. 'It was a great trip.'

'I'm glad.'

'You'd have enjoyed it, Mina.' He looked towards the drawing room door, but she ignored his hint; Dutton had tactfully withdrawn, but she knew he was lurking right behind the pantry curtain, just as she knew Jessie was at the top of the stairs, although also out of sight. 'And the first thing I hear is how you're married,' Stark went on. 'And on your honeymoon.'

'That's right, Captain Stark. I'm married to Mr Morton.'

'Well, by Christ! I didn't expect that, Mina. I really didn't.'

'Were you expecting me to wait for your return, Captain?' she asked. 'Do you suppose you have some sort of right to me?'

'Wouldn't you say I did? For Christ's sake, I just about saved your life. And I found you a job. If I hadn't taken you to the Superb, you'd never even have met Morton.'

'You did those things, Captain Stark,' Mina agreed, keeping her voice cool and her face stiff, although now she had butterflies in her stomach. 'But you did not do it for Christ's sake. You did it for your own sake. However, as I told you two months ago, I'm not for you. Then, or ever. I am grateful to you, Captain Stark. I would like you to know that. But now I shall bid you good day.'

He stared at her with his mouth open.

'Will you show Captain Stark out, Dutton,' Mina said, still without raising her voice. Dutton immediately appeared.

'By God, you little tart,' Stark said. 'You're all set to climb, eh? But you'll come a cropper, one of these days. Oh, yes, you will. Then you'll be praying for me to come and pick you up off the floor.'

'I won't be praying to you, Captain Stark. Or to anyone. And if you come to this house again I will summon a policeman.'

She turned away from him and climbed the stairs, without looking back, while her heart pounded and she could feel sweat rolling down her shoulders; before she had reached the landing the front door banged shut.

'Well, glory be,' Jessis commented. 'You know, I keep thinking you going to need help, Mina. I figured, well, you might be able to handle that Irish boy, but a big sea captain, now . . . and you cut him down like a weed, that you did.' She peered at Mina. 'And you know what, child? This time you ain't even crying.'

'I have a firm of jobbing gardeners coming in tomorrow,' Jimmy said over breakfast. 'That place out there is like a jungle. But of course you must tell them exactly what you want done. I thought we might have a lawn, bordered with flowerbeds, and a little orchard down at the bottom. You know, the sort of thing.'

Exactly what his parents had, she thought, but on a suitably smaller scale. He was smiling at her, so she smiled back, with an effort. Gardening, even in a supervisory capacity, had never held any attraction for her.

And right now she had too much on her mind. She was not concerned that soon she would have to tell him about Stark's visit – he would be certain to find out, one way or the other, but he could only be proud of the way she had handled it. Nor was she prepared to let her conscience badger her about that; however much she owed the wretched man in sheer survival, he *had* done it with his own gratification in view rather than any advantage for her. But what he had said kept roaming through her mind. Because she knew just how insecure was her foothold on the ladder she had so precariously erected. It consisted entirely of Jimmy's desire for her.

'And then we shall have to sit down and make up lists,' he went on, 'of the people we need to entertain, and when. It's very important to get the right mixes for each party, you know, just as it's important to get in on the ground floor with one's invitations. Now the nights are drawing in, the party season will be beginning, and we want to be invited to all the best places, don't we?'

'These people . . . will they be the same I've already met?'

'Well . . . mostly, of course. They're my friends. You could try looking a little more enthusiastic about them. I know they're all delighted with you.'

Oh, yes, she thought. 'I suppose I was just shy,' she said contritely.

'Of course you were. You'll find them all the very best of chums. Besides, entertaining, and being entertained, will give you something to do.' Another bright smile. 'We don't want you getting bored, my darling Mina.'

Bored, she thought. But it seemed to her that her situation was becoming more precarious by the moment, if he was aware how much she disliked his friends. Somehow she had to make herself more valuable to him than just a toy – and the only way she could think of achieving that was the way she in any event wanted more than anything else. 'How are things at the hotel?' she asked.

He shrugged. 'Same as usual. People don't change.'

'I'd love to talk about it with you.'

'God forbid! What's there to talk about? You've been there. You know the score. So-and-so hates his or her room mate. So-and-so has been caught pinching. So-and-so was rude to a guest. It's eternally tiresome.'

Mina frowned at him. 'You mean you know about the pinching?'

'Of course I do.'

'But you don't do anything about it?'

'Sure I do, when it's as blatant as this case. I mean, a bit of food and drink is one thing. Every hotelier expects that. But two silver spoons . . .'

'A bit of food and drink?' Mina cried. 'Jimmy, half the kitchen goes home every night.'

Was she betraying her friends? But they had never been her friends. And it was *her* future that mattered to her. Not theirs.

'Oh, come now.'

'It does. I've seen it.'

He grinned. 'They're a clever lot. So what did you pinch when you were there?'

'I didn't.' She bridled, then realised he was joking. 'Of course I didn't.'

'Because you always knew that one day you'd be management rather than staff.'

An opening? 'Maybe I did dream a bit. Jimmy . . .' She leaned across the table. 'There's so much . . .' She held his hand. 'Those rooms that need redecorating. I've so many ideas for them.'

'Which rooms?'

'Well . . . just about all of them, surely.'

127

'Nonsense. They'll do.'

'But some of those carpets, and the linen . . .'

'They'll do,' he said again. 'For our clientele, anyway. We're not the Plaza, you know. There's no money for that sort of thing. And I can tell you that the Plaza is losing money hand over fist. The word on Wall Street is that it isn't going to last too much longer.'

But for the moment Mina was not even interested in the Plaza. 'But . . . if you kept a check on the pinching,' she urged, 'and used the money you saved there to redecorate and refurbish, then you could raise your prices, and . . .' She gazed at his expression.

'Darling, delightful Mina,' he said. 'I love your enthusiasm. Really I do. But you simply have to get your facts straight before lecturing me. Now then, we charge one dollar fifty per night for a room. Without bath, of course. With bath, it goes up to one dollar seventy-five. Now, that's in line with all the main New York hotels, save the Plaza, of course.'

'What does the Plaza charge?' she asked.

'The Plaza charges two,' he told her, 'and is losing money.'

'Suppose,' she said excitedly, 'we put in a bathroom for every bedroom? That way we could charge more, with a perfectly good excuse.'

'A bathroom for every bedroom?' He was aghast. 'Have you any idea? We have one hundred and eighty rooms, twenty to a floor. And we have nine bathrooms, one to a floor. That's not including the third floor suites, either. Think of that. Better than one bathroom to twenty rooms. Do you know what the average ratio is in England? In London? No better than that.'

'I'll bet it's better at the Savoy.'

'We're not discussing the Savoy, any more than we're really discussing the Plaza. Those places try to maintain absurd standards. We're an ordinary hotel. That's a place where people stay when they're away from home. They don't want a bathroom. They want to be able to have a bath when they want one, and they can do that. We don't cater for royalty or for millionaires, simply because there aren't enough kings and princes and millionaires to go round. So Mrs Vanderbilt maintains a suite at the Plaza. I can't imagine why, as her house is hardly across the street. But she does, and if there were a hundred Mrs Vanderbilts in New York, we'd all be rich in the hotel business too. But there's only one, unfortunately. That means that, while you have to maintain your carpets and your décor and your public rooms to *her* requirements, for fear she'll move, there's nobody else occupying those rooms on a permanent basis, so you're losing money five days out of seven. I'll settle for Lord Fanning, who's after paying as little as possible and enjoying life.'

'He was a horrible man,' Mina declared.

'Granted. But if it wasn't for him, you and I might not be sitting here smiling at each other. That's where I want you to be, my darling girl, sitting there smiling at me. Now and always. Forget the Superb. It earns us our bread and butter, and that's all there is to it. You know what you have to do? Get pregnant.' He got up, holding her hand, and drew her behind him. 'Let's send the servants home and see what we can do about that number one priority.'

Pregnancy! The very thought filled her with horror. It was more than the thought of the discomfort and the very real dangers of childbearing. It would also mean an utter incapacitation for months on end, and it would mean that she would grow fat and unattractive. But it was an inevitable development, when Jimmy Morton demanded sex almost every night; she had no choice but to accept him, having already limited the *sort* of sex he could have.

And of course, as Jessie kept reminding her, pregnancy, and even more, motherhood, was the best of all securities for a marriage. And if she was now no longer certain she wanted an absolutely secure marriage, if she was never going to be allowed to involve herself in the Superb in any way, that was surely muddled thinking. What alternatives did she have?

The result was actually only half as bad as she had feared. Pregnancy certainly meant a limitation on their social activities, as a pair – but this she did not object to in the slightest, as she still could not bring herself to like any of Jimmy's friends. But it brought her much closer to Elizabeth, who was delighted at the prospect of becoming a grandmother: Mina gathered that the principal fault of the first Mrs Morton –

at least in Elizabeth's eyes – had been that she had never conceived. It also clearly delighted Jimmy himself, as much as it delighted Jessie.

On the other hand, the following March she lost her figure, and with it her energy and the feeling of physical well-being she had always enjoyed. By then, Jimmy had long ceased to have sex with her. This too would have been very acceptable, indeed, a relief – except for the certain knowledge that he was having sex elsewhere, and probably again every night, for he was seldom home before midnight. He accepted without argument her decision not to attend any more parties . . . but he insisted on going himself. 'My darling Mina,' he explained, 'we cannot just totally disappear from sight. No one expects *you* to appear in public any more, but they will when you are yourself again. Meanwhile, I have to keep your seat hot, eh?'

She gazed at him, wondering just what he meant by that remark. But he merely smiled, and bustled off. Enthusiastically. Jimmy Morton was never bored; he had too much to do. Too many toys to play with – the yachting season was about to start and from then on his weekends were totally occupied. Mina now knew that Jessie's remarks the day Clancy had left had been absolutely true; she was nothing more than a toy herself, to her husband, like his car and his yacht and his other lady friends. In fact, she was at last beginning to understand the great mystery of her life – why he had married her at all. Jimmy liked owning things, including women. Or especially women. But women, not being inanimate objects, did not always like to be owned. His first wife certainly hadn't. Nor had most of his lady friends been enthusiastic about belonging to Jimmy Morton. Thus he had been driven to looking amongst his own staff, composed of girls so far socially beneath him there could be no question that they would not gratefully accept whatever he chose to bestow. Of course, having abandoned the search for social requirements, he had sought beauty and sexuality instead – without a great deal of success, until her appearance, and then he realised he had fallen on his feet, because in addition to beauty, she actually possessed breeding as well, no matter how thoroughly it might have been concealed when he had first met her. And when he had discovered that she also came from a good family, he had been over the moon.

Yet he still intended to own, had been disappointed in her

obvious lack of the sexuality he sought, and appalled by her wish to take even the smallest share in the running of the hotel. Her business was to be his wife, and line up alongside his car and his yacht when required. And just as he laid up his yacht every winter, so this summer he was laying up his wife. That did not mean he wasn't going to find something else, or somebody else, to occupy his time. A pair, she thought bitterly. She was more lonely than ever before in her life. She was beginning to accept that she might never *be* paired. She mistrusted people too much. No doubt Jimmy was as disappointed in her as she in him . . . but he had ways of relieving his disappointment. She had nothing to do, except sit in the garden, and go for carriage rides, at a very sedate pace, with Jessie, and endure the cloying company of Elizabeth. Elizabeth's enthusiasm for what would be her first grandchild was unbounded. Indeed, it might have been her child instead of Mina's, the way she planned and organised, bought baby clothes and powders and lotions, gave Mina books to read on child upbringing . . . and selected names.

'He will be called James, of course, if it is a boy,' she announced. 'James Junior. James Morton the Fourth, do you know. All our first-born sons are named James.' For a moment she was pensive, as if recalling that she had only had the one. 'And if it is a girl . . .' She gazed at Mina, her eyebrows arched. 'Would you like to name her after your mother, my dear?'

Mama had been named Harriet. But Mina had never been terribly fond of Harriet, and she understood what Elizabeth wanted. 'I think we should call her Elizabeth,' she said. 'After all, Mother, you say I'm a Morton now, and not a Doberley.'

'You are such a dear, sweet girl,' Mina,' Elizabeth said, while Mina hated herself for a hypocritical sycophant. But why should she hold out against Elizabeth's wishes? She didn't want the beastly child; Elizabeth did. She wanted . . . what did she want? She wanted love – but only from someone she herself could love, without reservation. And he had to be wealthy. Because she also wanted wealth, limitless wealth. Marriage to Jimmy had made her realise that there were degrees of riches. To a chambermaid, or a failed parson, the Mortons were very rich indeed. But the Mortons did not consider themselves very rich at all, because above them were people like the Vanderbilts. Far above.

And in fact their lack of wealth was not merely relative, she began to understand. She had no idea of their actual financial position, as Jimmy never discussed his personal affairs with her, and in any event she found financial matters difficult to grasp, never having possessed any money herself; she left the housekeeping to Jessie and Dutton, merely telling them what food she wanted served and what household items she wished bought, and they never seemed short of the necessary funds or credit – presumably they obtained what they needed from Jimmy. But there were obvious inconsistencies in the Mortons' way of life, and these did worry her.

The Mortons owned the Superb, and seemed content with the return they were getting, however much of it was wasted by the staff – but there was apparently no money to rebuild or even refurbish. Jimmy spent money like water on his yacht and his car, and he had bought her a house, and had spent a fortune on clothes for her – but when she suggested that she would like a carriage of her very own, instead of having to hire a cab whenever she wished to go out, he had said, 'Can't be done, my darling girl. We just can't afford it, right this minute.' She thought she could understand this: Jimmy didn't own the hotel, his father did, and no doubt he was paid a salary, with an allowance on top. Thus she accepted his decision without demur, and was indeed embarrassed to have asked. And was even more embarrassed when, having refused the carriage, which would have been most useful, he presented her with a piano; piano playing had never been one of her best accomplishments, and she was sadly out of practice.

But having started to consider things in this logical manner, and having little else to do but think, Mina even began to arrive at solutions. Clearly Jimmy could not be expected to do anything about the hotel, because of his subordinate position. No doubt he had discussed the matter with his father, and been snubbed, just as he in turn had snubbed her. In the circumstances, this was perfectly reasonable. She had been trying to hurry too fast. After all, she was only seventeen. She had her entire life in front of her, and a large part of that life would be lived after James Morton Senior was dead, and when Jimmy was in sole control. Then would be the time to push for everything she wanted done, everything she knew had to be done, to make the Superb better even than the Plaza, and more than that . . . she had not forgotten her argument with Charlie Stark in the cabin of the *William McKinley*. Just owning the best hotel in New York was nothing. She wanted to own the best hotel in London, too. She wanted to go back there and sneer at Grandfather, and all her uncles and aunts and cousins, who had for so long sneered at her. When her conscience threatened a revolt, she could subdue it with total ease. Consciences were for Christians, for good people, for secure people – for people whose parents hadn't rotted away before their eyes, for people whose families wanted to look after them, for people who could love, and be loved.

Not for Mina Doberley – she could never bring herself to think of herself as Mina Morton. She had a life to live, which she planned. And which she was actually carrying out, step to step, with no help from anyone, God or man. Or devil! But she *was* carrying it out. All she required was patience. So, she would have her baby, and make everyone happy, and then sit back and be a dutiful wife, and wait for James Morton Senior to die.

She was horrified when her father-in-law died first.

'Just like that,' Jimmy explained. 'A heart attack, and he was apparently dead before he hit the floor. At least you have to agree that's the way to go.'

Mina could think of nothing to say. She had wanted James Morton to die, simply so that he would no longer stand in Jimmy's way – and, therefore, in her way. She had *wanted* it, without any idea that it could really happen, as Jimmy had said, just like that.

As she was more than eight months pregnant, Jimmy decided that she should not attend the funeral, which in June was certain to be a hot, as well as long drawn-out affair. She was also forbidden to call on her mother-in-law, who was in a state of collapse, so she wrote Elizabeth a note of condolence, to which she did not receive a reply. And in fact, although she endeavoured to remain calm and rationalise what had happened, reminding herself that James Morton had been quite old and somewhat overweight, and had therefore been likely to die at any moment, she was more agitated than she knew at the thought that she might somehow have *wished* him to death, and as a result James Junior was a week premature.

Not that there were any complications. It was over very quickly, because, as Dr Munnings constantly reminded her during the cramps, she was a big, strong girl made for childbearing. But it was distressing to be utterly incapacitated when she felt there was so much she should be doing, and she was doubly upset when Elizabeth came to see her – obviously it should have been the other way round in the circumstances.

Elizabeth did not stay long, and would not even kiss the baby, but gazed at it with intent misery, and remarked, 'James. One comes, another goes. James would have liked to see his grandson.'

'Almost as if she feels little James was responsible for your father's death,' Mina told Jimmy. 'I feel so wretched. Perhaps she's right.'

'What on earth for? I doubt the old man ever actually realised you were pregnant.' Jimmy pushed the hair from her forehead, regarded the baby sucking noisily at her breast with a speculative expression. 'Anyway, this way you've missed all the comings and goings, and all the lawyers. You don't know how lucky you are.'

'What's going to happen?' She had been dying to ask this, to *know*, ever since the funeral, but hadn't wanted to appear over-eager.

'Oh, there are no problems,' he promised her. 'I'm the only son and heir, so I own the Superb. Would you believe it? I own the Superb.'

He did not sound as pleased as he should. She could only think, at last! 'But . . . what about your mother?'

We own the Superb, she thought. After all this waiting, we actually own it. But if Elizabeth could interfere with their plans . . .

'Oh, Mother isn't interested,' Jimmy said. 'She's always felt owning a hotel was a little infra dig. Her father was a Boston Woodley, you know. If he wasn't the chap who sighted Plymouth Rock, he was the first to trip over it, or something. He thought she was marrying beneath her, a hotelier, even if we've had the Superb for three generations, so when *he* died he set up an independent trust fund for her which the old man could never touch. She's rolling in it, and Dad left her all his outside stock as well, and his savings. All he left me was the hotel.' His tone was bitter. 'That great ugly white elephant is what I have to live on. Jesus Christ!'

'Jimmy!' she cried in consternation. 'The Superb isn't a white elephant. Or it shouldn't be.'

'I just cannot imagine why you are so fond of the dump. For God's sake, you can't have very many pleasant memories of it. It *is* a white elephant, my darling. Do you know what would be the best possible thing that could happen to us? If some lunatic were to come along and make us a reasonable offer. I'd jump at that.'

'Jimmy!' she cried again. 'You wouldn't ever sell the Superb?'

'Watch me.'

'Jimmy!' She clutched his hand, and her nipple slipped from James' mouth. He promptly started to cry, but fortunately Jessie hurried into the bedroom to remove him and allow her to concentrate. 'Jimmy! Now that your dad is dead, we can change everything. Don't you see? Do you know what's wrong with the Superb? The *only* thing that's wrong with it? It's been standing still, for years. Things don't stand still in this world. They either move ahead, or they fall back. So the Superb has been falling back, little by little, oh, I don't know for how long. But now . . .' He was staring at her with his mouth open, and she hurried on, the words tumbling over each other in their haste to get out. 'So we'll have to spend a little money on it. Let's do that, Jimmy. I don't mind pulling in my horns for a while, having a few less parties, perhaps. I don't have to have new gowns every year.' She hesitated, wondering if she dared suggest he might do without his yacht for a while – and decided against it for the moment. 'We can do it, Jimmy. We can get rid of Howwinger, for a start – I'm sure he's a colossal waste of money – and you can take over managing. And then let's strip the place down, redecorate, and refurbish.'

'Get rid of Howwinger? My God, the place would fall apart. You think *I* want to manage that dump? Strip the place down? Redecorate? Refurbish? Oh, don't start playing that cracked record again. My dear girl, you don't know what you're talking about. A million, at the very least.'

'Is that so very much?' She genuinely didn't know.

'So very much,' he mocked. 'No, my darling girl, it's not so very much – if you happen to have it lying around. Shall I tell you something? The Plaza has been sold, because it can't make a profit. Even the Hammond brothers, mind, can't make a profit, and what they don't know about running a hotel, nobody knows. And shall I tell you something else? When the lease is up, in a couple of years' time, the whole buidling is coming down.'

'Coming down?' Mina couldn't believe her ears.

'Coming down, Mina. It is going to be a pile of rubble on the pavement. Oh, there's talk about a consortium – people like Harry Black and that German fellow Beinicke – getting set to rebuild, a new hotel. Now those boys do have a million or two lying around. But, build a new luxury hotel, right now . . . I'll believe that when I see it.'

The Plaza, being pulled down. The Plaza, disappearing from the Manhattan skyline. Mina still couldn't believe it. She refused to believe it. But in any event, it wasn't relevant to her plans, except maybe in the shape of the removal of her most powerful competitor. 'So forget about the Plaza,' she said. 'You told me it was going to go bust last year. Let's worry about us. Keep Howwinger, if you think he's so good. But you take control, at least of overall policy. You have to, now, Jimmy. You own the place. And your policy has got to be to expand and to keep on expanding. Maybe the Plaza people made the same mistake as your dad did, and just tried to stand still. Jimmy, if we borrowed what we needed, and redecorated from start to finish, and really tidied the Superb up, made it *the* place to stay in New York – and we can do it, especially if the Plaza is coming down – then maybe we could buy another hotel somewhere else, like London. We'd call that the Superb, too, and make it the best there. People would want to stay at the London Superb, because they'd have heard how grand the New York Superb was, and vice versa. Okay, so we'd be competing with the Savoy, and this new place that's being built, the Ritz. But we could do it, Jimmy, because I have an even bigger idea. Suppose . . .'

He pulled his hand free and stood up. 'Competing with the Savoy,' he sneered. 'Big ideas. Oh, you're full of big ideas, Mina. But what the hell do you really know about it?'

'Jimmy!'

'You don't know one goddamned thing about the hotel

business, Mina,' he declared. 'Not a single goddamned thing. Look at you, some orphan from the storm, whose sole working experience is as a chambermaid, trying to teach me my business.'

She lost her temper at his contempt. 'Well, somebody has to,' she shouted.

He pointed. 'You just keep your nose out of my affairs, Mina. Now and always. You're my wife. And you're making a pretty goddamned poor job of that. Like you say, life don't stand still. So I suggest you start moving, forward. As my wife. Try enjoying my company, the company of my friends, the hobbies *I* enjoy. That's what a wife is all about. Try *being* a wife for a change, instead of a prudish little girl. I thought you were a woman. *Be* a woman. And stop badgering me about the hotel.' He went to the door, looked over his shoulder. 'Who the hell did you marry, anyway? Me, or the Superb?'

Chapter 7

It was the first time they had ever quarrelled. 'Which can't be no bad thing,' Jessie pointed out, 'seeing as how you've been married near a year. I guess Morton has a lot on his mind right now.'

Jessie just did not understand. No one would understand, Mina thought bitterly. She didn't want to be just a wife and a mother, even of Mr Jimmy Morton the Third. She wanted to do something with her life – and there was only one thing she wanted to do. But that was the one thing that was barred to her. Well, she thought, prepared to turn the anger she felt against fate, and life, and God Himself, against her husband as well, if he wants me to change, I will damned well change. I'll change so much he'll have the shock of his life, and maybe *beg* me to help in the hotel.

She could not immediately put her resolve into effect, as she was feeding James and, remarkably, Jimmy did not wish to make love to her during this period, despite the fact that he had been necessarily chaste – as regards her – for several months already. Undoubtedly he had accumulated a mistress. She reminded herself that she should be more relieved than jealous, but as soon as she was able she began to present a different picture of herself, by dressing as provocatively as possible, and by taking a drink with him in the evenings. He was immediately pleased and re-aroused. Their quarrel might never have been.

'When are you going to take me out again?' she asked.

'Why, my darling girl, this very evening if you wish. And if you'll promise not to leak milk all over the place.'

'I'll wear pads,' she said. They went to a party and for the first time in her life she drank enough to make herself tipsy. Once again James seemed delighted, and being very nearly as tipsy as herself made love to her when they got home. Indeed, he might have done anything he liked, because she could remember nothing of it the next day. And suddenly she realised that there was the answer to her problem. Get drunk every night, and then she could be as willingly lascivious as he could wish.

But strangely, in the cold light of day, Jimmy did not seem quite so pleased as the previous night. 'I've never seen you like that before,' he remarked at breakfast.

'I'm going to be a woman,' she reminded him. 'And not a girl. At your request.'

He gazed at her for some seconds, but she refused to lower her eyes. So he gave a smile, and said quietly, 'There's a school of thought says that drinking while feeding might have a bad effect on the baby.'

'Nonsense,' she said. 'He likes my milk more than ever. And it'll probably do him good.'

He changed the subject. Because he was, Mina was starting to realise, an oddly timid man, especially where women were concerned. Outbursts like the other night were very rare, and undoubtedly Jessie had been right in concluding that he had then been upset by his father's death. Normally he would do anything to avoid a quarrel, or even a difference of opinion. Which was why he had married a chambermaid, she supposed. That she happened to be a chambermaid with a good background had been a bonus, but only up to a point. Now that she was his wife, she was proving as recalcitrant as all the society women he knew, and whom he had been afraid to marry just because he had known he would not be able to dominate them.

That night she got tight again, just to show him that she meant what she had said, and from then on made a habit of it. Nor did he again raise the subject – certainly she could not see anything wrong with young James, who appeared as healthy as a horse, and as messy and noisy; in any event, a couple of months later she weaned him to a bottle.

From being a wallflower she became the life and soul of the parties they went to, at least among the male guests – the females regarded her with some distaste – and this certainly pleased Jimmy, although he took to watching over her very closely – which pleased *her*, as he had never taken that much interest in her public image before. But he needn't have bothered. She had no intention of having a flirtation with anyone, much less an affair; she had had just about all of the masculine sex that she could stand, for the moment, and she knew that Jimmy was always there to take her home when she got really tight. More important, the young men who clustered round her rapidly developing beauty soon learned the score; she was a tease, but not a serious proposition. They treated her accordingly, cracked jokes and gave her affectionate hugs, and regarded her with a mixture of uncertainty and apprehension – which she enjoyed. She was thus the more taken by surprise when towards the end of the year, at a Christmas party, she was introduced to a surprisingly good-looking man who was obviously several years older than most of the guests, and at least twice *her* age. He was tall, and strongly built, with quite beautifully cut clothes. His face was aquiline, his hair black, with just the slightest suggestion of grey at the temples, and worn very short, so that it stood straight away from his scalp. His eyes were black also, in keeping with his somewhat swarthy complexion, and seemed to gloom at her. She instinctively disliked him, but allowed him to take her hand and kiss it, while she felt herself being mentally undressed. But she was still totally unprepared for what came next. He straightened, and smiled. 'The famous Mina Morton,' he remarked. 'I have heard so much about you, Mrs Morton, and even seen you from a distance. I have thus far counted it my misfortune never to have met you, because I have always thought, that of all the women in New York, you are the one I would most like to bugger.' His arm went round her and his hand slid down her back to give her satin-clad bottom a gentle squeeze. 'Shall we go upstairs?'

Mina's consternation lasted only a split second. Then she stepped away from him, turned to face him, closing her fist as she did so, and hit him with all the force she could muster.

'My God, my God, my *God!*' Jimmy sat on the edge of the bed, his hands drooping between his knees, his head almost as low. 'Felix Petersen! The man is a multi-millionaire. Railways. And a silver mine. And a shipping line. And God alone knows what else.'

'And that gives him the right to be obscene to your wife?' Mina demanded. She was still furious. Her hand was sheer agony; the knuckles were split, and her nails had driven a good quarter inch into her palm before they had snapped, while her arm and shoulder were just a dull throb. She had had another drink after coming home, but with no useful anaesthetic effect.

'He was joking,' Jimmy wailed. 'Can't you understand that? That's his way.'

'I don't think he was joking at all,' Mina said. 'And even if he was, I don't think much of his sense of humour. He was about as deliberately, viciously rude as it is possible for a human being to be. I suppose you would have preferred me to go upstairs with him rather than offend him?'

'Of course not, Mina. But . . .'

'Well, I don't care how wealthy he is. I don't care if I never see him again as long as I live.'

'Oh, don't bother, you're not likely to,' Jimmy moaned. 'We're not likely to see *anybody* again. To go to a party and knock out a fellow's tooth . . . a woman . . . my wife . . . and what a fellow . . . oh, Jesus, what are we to do? You'll have to apologise. You'll have to grovel.'

'I'll see him, and you, damned first,' Mina said. 'I think the best thing we can do is go to bed and sleep on it. Or would you rather do something else first?' She was realising she had to try to reassure him.

He raised his head. 'Is that all you can think about?' he demanded.

She was so surprised she couldn't think of a reply. And in fact five minutes later he was on top of her. It was the first time they had had intercourse without her being drunk since James Junior's birth, and she discovered that he was indeed taking increased liberties. But she gritted her teeth and said nothing, and after a while he subsided and went to sleep, clearly certain that he was forever socially damned by marrying a woman who couldn't take a dirty joke and knocked out men's teeth.

In the event he could hardly have been more wrong. They awoke to a perfect barrage of invitations, which Jimmy opened with the air of a man handling a live shell. Mina regarded them all with contempt – come to the peepshow that is Mina Morton, she thought; you won't know what she may do tonight! But she

141

was totally surprised, to receive, three days later, a note written on headed notepaper, and in a huge, scrawling hand.

> *My Dear Wilhelmina,*
> *No man has ever hit me so hard. My congratulations. Perhaps one day I shall be able to repay the compliment. Meanwhile, be assured that I am ever your most devoted admirer, and, given the opportunity, your servant,*
>
> *Felix Petersen*

Mina gazed at the letter for several minutes. Was he laughing at her, or apologising in his own way? Or was he deadly serious? Repay the compliment! Her fingers crumpled the letter into a ball, and she threw it into the wastebasket. But instantly retrieved it, smoothing it and then folding it into the pages of a book.

She did not tell Jimmy about it. And a week later, when she again encountered Felix at a party, with her host and hostess, Jimmy, and all the guests clearly in a state of highly anticipatory excitement, they smiled at each other, and he kissed her hand, and then insisted on showing her his gold replacement tooth. Everyone seemed at once disappointed and relieved; the episode was over, and Mina had gained a new niche for herself in Manhattan society. Jimmy was enormously pleased, as she became the most sought-after woman guest in the city. But before the summer of 1903 arrived it was all irrelevant, as she was once again pregnant.

Mina was furious. Young James was actually beginning to grow on her, as he started to walk and talk, and reveal a certain amount of intelligence – although she saw as little as possible of him as she employed a nurse, a severe-looking lady named Agatha – but she had not intended to get pregnant again so soon. She was at last beginning to enjoy herself – and now another year was being removed from her life. Then she'd be nineteen, and already twice a mother. She dared not suppose how many children she might have by the time she was thirty.

'Surely one can do something about it?' she asked Jessie.

'About this one?' Jessie raised her eyebrows. 'That ain't good, Mina. And it can be dangerous.'

'Oh, of course I don't mean an abortion, silly,' Mina snapped. 'I mean, afterwards. Surely there is some way of preventing babies. You've never had a baby.'

'Once,' Jessie said. 'But she died.'

'Oh, Jessie!' Mina was instantly contrite.

'I ain't never had the time to have any more.'

'But you've, well . . . you say you have a man at home?'

'Sure. I make him wear a sheath. That is the only sure way.'

'A sheath?' She just could not imagine.

'They makes them of all kind of things,' Jessie explained. 'But nowadays they got one made of rubber. That is the best.'

'But . . . is it the same?'

'I ain't knowing about for him, child. But for us, it's better. He's that bigger, see. And there ain't no risk of pregnancy. Or disease, for that matter. It's all a matter of persuading the man to use it.'

'Um,' Mina said, thoughtfully.

'But girl,' Jessie went on, 'why don't you want a lot of children? It must be better than drinking and fornicating.'

'I do not . . . fornicate,' Mina said. 'Except with my husband.'

'But you sure do drink. And smoking . . . that ain't right for any woman, much less a lady.'

'How do you know I smoke?'

Jessie took her right hand and turned it over to show her the yellow stained fingertips.

'Oh . . .' Mina snatched the hand back again. 'It was a party. Everyone was doing it. All the girls. I had to.'

'You only got one life,' Jessie pointed out. 'It ain't worth wasting. Looking after children is better than drinking and smoking.'

Only one life, Mina thought. She hadn't meant to waste it, in any way. But then, she had only envisaged marriage as a stepping stone to greater things. Her dream had simply been to make the Superb the finest hotel in the world, and have everyone know that *she* had done it. That marriage could become such a dead end had never occurred to her. Now she realised that it was the biggest trap that existed, for a woman. Because marriage meant children, and children meant an end to freedom. No matter what happened now, she couldn't ever walk away from Jimmy Morton, even if she accepted the fact

143

that her life was a totally empty shell, that she was *never* going to be allowed to do anything with the hotel – that she could not even stop Jimmy from selling it, were he to receive that 'reasonable' offer he was dreaming of. Because of James Junior. And soon, because of Harrison – the name, after Elizabeth Morton's grandfather, had been selected following the most perfunctory of inquiries as to whether or not Mina wanted to use William. But they could use what they liked. Harrison was just another millstone to hang around her neck.

'Oh, but he's a real sweetie,' Elizabeth declared, holding the baby in her arms for a moment before restoring him to the waiting Agatha. 'Every inch a Morton. I really am proud of you, Mina. Do you know, that dreadful girl Jimmy took up with first had the impertinence to suggest that he wasn't capable? I hope she reads the newspapers.'

And probably says a prayer of thanks every time she does so, Mina thought. 'As a matter of fact, Mother,' she said, 'it's a subject I would like to discuss with you.' Elizabeth was clearly the best person to talk to James about the folly of having too many children.

'Now isn't that strange,' Elizabeth said. 'There is a very important matter I wish to discuss with *you*.'

Mina sighed; she knew that her problem would have to wait.

'The subject,' Elizabeth said, portentously, 'is Jimmy and yourself.'

'Why,' Mina cried in delight. 'That's exactly . . .'

'Jimmy's way of life,' Elizabeth went on, ignoring the attempted interruption, 'has long been a source of concern, both to his dear father and to myself. We had supposed that it was a result of that terribly unhappy first marriage of his, and thus we were overjoyed when he told us he was to wed again. Unfortunately, well . . . my dear, I know you are so much younger than he is, and I know that on the surface you have been an absolutely model wife. And of course motherhood is an important part of being a wife. Yes, indeed. We should all be delighted if you were to have a child every year for the rest of your . . . ah, childbearing life.'

'Really,' Mina remarked.

'Of course. But you must realise that your responsibilities

144

extend beyond mere motherhood and looking decorative.'

'I have no idea what you are talking about,' Mina said, beginning to get angry.

'I am talking, my dear girl, about Jimmy's mode of existence, as I have just told you.' Elizabeth held up her hand and ticked off the fingers. 'He is too extravagant. He drinks too much. He smokes too much. He spends too much time at parties. He drives too fast. It is possible to say that he is living too fast.'

'And I am supposed to do something about all that?'

'You're his wife, my dear girl. You could at least attempt to set him some kind of an example, instead of being just *as* extravagant. It's your duty.'

'To tell a man thirteen years older than myself how to live his life?' Mina demanded. 'You have got to be joking. *You* tell him how to live his life, Mother. You're his mother.'

Elizabeth stared at her for several seconds, and then changed the subject.

She was obviously very angry, but really, Mina thought, my duty! Her sole desire was to get *back* to that extravagant and careless life she had been just coming to enjoy when Harrison had made his unwelcome appearance. As for living extravagantly herself . . . Jimmy expected her to give lavish parties – she couldn't do that on air. But the thought that they might be living above their means did disturb her, and she mentioned the conversation to her husband.

'Dear old Mum,' he said. 'The Woodleys got their wealth by *care*, my love. And a more dried-up looking lot of prunes you never did see. Mother doesn't realise she would have been like them too, if it hadn't been for Dad's influence.'

'But what about the money?'

'Money's tight. There's a recession on, didn't you know? Business is slack. That means people aren't travelling, and that means the hotel is only half full. All hotels are only half full. Consequently, profits are down. I've had to let some of the staff go.'

'But . . . what are we going to do?' Suddenly she was terrified. 'Shouldn't we economise, or something?'

'Economise? What on earth for? So some of our bills may go unpaid for the moment. Everyone knows I'm good for the money. I own the Superb, don't I? Even more important, everyone knows that Mother is good for the money. She has millions, and she never spends a bean. And I'm her only son. When she pops off, we'll be rolling in it, Mina my love. I shall be a millionaire, at least twice over. So quit worrying, and relax.'

It was not possible to argue with that and, besides, it was what she wanted to hear. Of course they would inherit Elizabeth's money. So what *was* there to worry about? She could have wished he would condescend to discuss actual amounts, like just how much they owed, and how much he thought the Superb might fetch if placed on the market – but she didn't want to raise that subject again. No one had apparently hurried forward with an offer, and he had allowed the matter to slide.

Besides, a millionaire twice over! Now there was wealth, beyond her wildest dreams, even if it was in dollars and therefore some distance short of a million pounds. But for the time being it was Elizabeth's, and Elizabeth was tight-fisted. Now everything fell into place.

She was very careful not to consider Elizabeth's death at all. But one day it would all be theirs, and then . . . just another exercise in patience.

Yet she could still suggest that it might be an idea not to produce too many children, too quickly – and to her pleasure and relief found him perfectly agreeable. 'I think two children is quite sufficient to go on with,' he acknowledged. 'We can't have our Mina getting fat and frumpy.'

And whatever his views on the economy, there were not lacking those in the hotel business with complete confidence in the future. Exactly as Jimmy had predicted, the Plaza was torn down the moment the lease expired, in 1905. But immediately work was under way building a new Plaza, and this, it was freely claimed, was going to be the greatest hotel of all time. To Mina this was as infuriating as it was frustrating; she did not even enjoy her twenty-first birthday party the next December. Time was again passing her by. It might have been possible to build something bigger and better than the old Plaza, but if someone was now doing just that . . . but when she was told that the new building was going to cost upwards of ten million dollars, she realised what a pipe-dream hers had always been. She had married into the second rank of hoteliers, and, sadly, she understood that she would have to be content with that.

Which did not mean, she thought fiercely, that she was not, one day, going to make the Superb the very best *second-rate* hotel in the world.

The building of the new Plaza was the only topic of conversation in New York for the next two years; Mina took James Junior and Harrison – being pushed in his pram by Agatha – along almost every day to watch it slowly rising above Fifth Avenue and Fifty-Ninth Street. The construction plans had called for twenty-eight months, which had had everyone laughing; the hotel was actually completed in September 1907, which was only twenty-seven months from commencement. It was an event which had everyone waiting and watching; even the new petrol-driven taxi cabs, ready to go into service at the end of 1906, were kept back so that they could take to the streets on the same day as the opening of the Plaza – 1 October, a Tuesday.

'We simply have to go,' Mina said.

'For God's sake, why?' Jimmy demanded. 'It's just an hotel.'

'It's not. It's a happening,' she insisted. 'Anyway, everyone else is going.'

As indeed Jimmy soon found out. So they made up their own party, which included people like Felix Petersen, because it really was necessary to have a millionaire in tow if one was going to the Plaza, and Felix had always been the soul of politeness to Mina ever since their fight – and found that even with Felix along they were very irrelevant indeed, although Jimmy refused to use one of the new cabs and drove up to the hotel entrance in his own automobile, Mina disagreeably windswept beside him. But Alfred Gwynne Vanderbilt had already been the first to sign the guest register, and the first to reserve a suite of rooms; lesser millionaires were two a penny.

Mina could understand why. Here were all of her impossible dreams come together under a single roof, and what a roof. She could feel, as Jimmy scornfully remarked, that creating the exterior appearance of a French château overlooking Central Park was the height of retrograde thinking, when New York was supposed to be the home of progress, but once inside the building her breath was swept away by the crystal chandeliers, the gold leaf which had been used so lavishly that the effect was positively eye-watering, the apparent acres of leaded glass, on ceilings as well as doors and windows and just *there*, the superb caryatids which appeared to support the roof of the lobby – 'imported direct from Italy,' someone whispered, which was in fact untrue, as they had been made in New York itself – the opulence of the curtains and carpets, and of the waiters' uniforms.

She also, for the first time since leaving the Superb, felt like a poor orphan again when she compared herself with the women around her. She did not suppose they were better dressed than herself, and in her pale blue satin evening gown with its white ribbon embroidery and lace bodice with white chiffon sleeves, and her engagement ring and pearl necklace were probably as good as any jewellery in the room, but she could not escape the feeling that these people had hardly troubled to dress in their best, while *she* could not improve her appearance no matter how hard she tried. At least she was gratified to observe that she was herself being remarked on for her youthful and yet, as twice a mother, mature beauty.

The food was as superb as the décor, but for the first time Mina was a little disappointed. It was possible to have just about anything under the sun, according to the menu, but the menu itself was presented with a strange lack of enthusiasm; each dish was listed with a baldness and absence of description which made selection difficult unless one was very knowledge-able about food, and somehow detracted from the quality of the dishes themselves. Or was it, she wondered, that she just had to find something to criticise?

Jimmy found a great deal, being openly and jealously contemptuous of the luxury which surrounded him. His mood was not improved by Felix, who was in one of *his* most provocative moods, and got one of the under-managers, who happened to be an acquaintance of his, to join them in the Champagne Porch for coffee and cigars after dinner. 'How many bathrooms do you have in a place like this?' he asked.

'Why . . . three hundred, of course, Mr Petersen.'

'Three hundred bathrooms?' Jimmy demanded.

'Well, sir, we have three hundred bedrooms,' the under-manager explained.

Jimmy was speechless.

'And how many elevators?' Felix asked.

148

'Ten.'

'*Ten* elevators?' Jimmy finished his port, noisily.

'It is not our intention to keep anyone waiting, sir,' the under-manager pointed out.

'You're goddamned well keeping me waiting for my port,' Jimmy told him, loudly.

'Jimmy!' Mina remonstrated. She had remained absolutely sober all night, so dazzled was she by her surroundings. While he was distinctly drunk.

'Forgive me, madam,' the under-manager said. 'But sir is quite right, of course.' He snapped his fingers, and a port decanter appeared.

'Forget it,' Jimmy said, and stood up, swaying slightly. 'This place is claustrophobic. Come along, Min.'

'You're not going so soon?' Felix demanded, raising his eyebrows. 'The night has not yet begun.'

'Of course we're not going,' Mina said. 'He's just in a bad mood. Jimmy . . .'

'*I* am going,' Jimmy said. 'If you wish to stay, stay. Felix can drive you home. Or somewhere else and feel your backside for all I care.' He walked from the room, leaving Mina staring after him in consternation; he had never been so rude to her before, and certainly not in public.

'The devil', Felix remarked. 'I've never seen him so far gone before.'

'He's just green,' giggled one of the other girls.

'I'd take him up on that, Mina,' smirked another.

Mina looked at Felix, knowing she was blushing. Felix gave the slightest of shrugs. But she knew that *he* would accept the invitation.

As if it was something she would ever consider doing.

'I must go with him,' she said. 'I am sorry about this,' she told the under-manager, who bowed. It was not part of the Plaza's intention to criticise the guests, either.

Mina satched her fox fur wrap from the waiting attendant, ran outside, found that Jimmy had already cranked the engine and was behind the wheel; the car had been left parked outside the main entrance in a most ostentatious position.

'Jimmy!' she shouted.

He had been just moving off. Now he braked, and turned his head.

'Jimmy,' she said more quietly, climbing in beside him. 'I'm sorry you got so upset. But you behaved very badly. Even Felix was shocked.'

'Felix,' he said, mockingly. 'I am not the least upset.' He gunned the engine as he swung on to the brilliantly lit, overcrowded amphitheatre of Fifth Avenue. 'I am merely disgusted by such an exhibition of shocking vulgarity. That place lowers the tone of the whole city. Felix, of course, likes it. Because he is totally vulgar himself. Oops.'

The car lurched across the road and lurched back again, to the accompaniment of blaring horns and shouted curses.

Mina realised he was at least as drunk with envy as with liquor. But she said, 'Yes, Jimmy. Do you think you could slow down a bit? We only live in the next block.'

'Bah,' Jimmy said, weaving in and out between two drays and sending pedestrians scurrying for shelter.

'You'll be arrested,' Mina cried as he increased speed.

'Bah!' he declared again.

'Oh, my God!' She groaned, because the night was suddenly cut in two by the blast of a whistle, as he half mounted the pavement, then slid off again as he regained control. And their turning was next. 'Slow down,' she shrieked. 'You'll kill somebody. And there's a police whistle.'

'Where?' Jimmy demanded, and turned his head to the left while turning the car to the right.

Mina kept staring straight ahead, and saw the lampost rushing at her. She couldn't even scream, any more.

The pain seemed very far away, at first. But as the room itself swam into focus, the pain came closer and closer, until it completely enveloped her; breathing was agonising as well as difficult – she kept wanting to fill her lungs but was afraid to, and in any event knew that she couldn't, because her lungs were being compressed.

She tried to move, and the pain increased. A hand was placed on her forehead. 'Now, Mrs Morton,' a soft voice said, 'you must lie still.'

Mina obeyed, because now her head was hurting as well, since it had been touched. While her brain seemed sandbagged. She just could not imagine what had happened to her.

She had no idea of time. There was electric light in the room, and it seemed permanently on. Once she thought she saw Elizabeth's face, but she knew she was mistaken, because this was a hard and angry face, and Elizabeth's had never been that. But at least the pain was subsiding. Her principal problem was thirst. Every so often one of the soft arms encircled her head and liquid was brought to her lips, a few drops at a time . . . sheer nectar . . . but never enough. 'Water,' she kept saying. 'I must have water.' And the liquid would be brought back.

'And how are we today?' asked a male voice, with brusque jocularity. Jimmy! It had to be Jimmy. He would tell her exactly what was happening and where she was. And what she was doing here.

Amazingly, when she opened her eyes, she found she could focus. And it wasn't Jimmy, but a man she had never seen before, wearing a white coat and benevolent smile. 'Where's Jimmy?' she asked.

'Ah . . .' Some of the benevolence left the man's face. 'You've been very ill, Mrs Morton,' he said. 'Very ill indeed. Do you know, you broke three ribs? On the dashboard of the car when you were thrown forward. And nearly split your skull open on the windshield. You were really very fortunate, I suppose. But very ill.'

The dashboard of the car. Memory flooded back. Those last terrifying split seconds as she had watched the lamp-post coming towards them, as she had listened to the shrill of the police whistle. 'Jimmy!' she gasped. 'Where's Jimmy?'

'Soon,' the doctor said. 'Soon.'

Three broken ribs, and a split skull. 'I would like a mirror,' she told the nurse.

'Soon,' the girl said. 'Soon, Mrs Morton.'

Was that the only language they spoke in this God-forsaken place?

'My children,' she said. 'I must see my children.'

'They're fine, Mrs Morton,' the nurse said. 'They're being looked after by Mrs Morton. They're fine. You'll see them soon.'

There was so much to be asked, so much to be understood, so much to be done – and nothing she could do. Soon, they said. Soon. And soon there was Jessie, standing by the bed and looking down at her, tears streaming down her cheeks. 'Jessie!' The pain was much less, now, and she could even cry out without wincing. 'Oh, Jessie.'

'Mina.' Jessie held her hand.

Mina squeezed the fingers tight. 'How's Jimmy?'

Jessie raised her head, and Mina realised the doctor was standing at the bottom of the bed. And nodding, almost imperceptibly, but sadly.

Jessie sighed. 'Morton is dead, Mina,' she said. 'He hit that lamp-post so hard he went clean through the windshield and broke his neck. But you're going to be all right, Mina. They say that, once your hair grows back, you won't even have a scar that'll show. You're going to be all right.'

Mina was surprised to discover that the house had not changed. Because it seemed that everything else had, so completely. But the house was the same as on the evening she had left it, with Jimmy, to go to the opening of the Plaza, save that the hall was filled with flowers. Flowers from just about everyone they knew.

The remarkable thing was that she had not changed either, in essentials. They had given her a mirror after she had finished dressing this morning, and she had found herself looking at Mina. True, a Mina whose hair was still short, because they had had to shave her scalp to get at her wound – but the scar was now concealed, as they had promised. And a Mina whose face seemed unusually gaunt, but perhaps the more beautiful for that. And a Mina whose eyes had looked on death once too often. But only she seemed able to see that.

She moved slowly and cautiously. Dr Bedford had said she was completely recovered, and she no longer suffered any pain – but the three weeks in bed had left her very thin and even more weak. 'Mama?' James Junior asked, not entirely sure. 'Is it really you?'

Harry just jumped up and down, shouting, 'Mama! Mama! Mama!'

She hugged them, and didn't want to let them go. It was the first time she had ever felt that way about them. Jessie had told her they had been told of their father's death. But did they understand? Could they possibly understand?

There were several other people waiting to see her. The Reverend Mobsley, to offer his condolences, because she hadn't been able to attend her husband's funeral. She had never attended a funeral in her life. Not even her parents'.

And then Mr Howwinger, accompanied by Joe Stark and Mrs Young, wearing black and watching her intently. Because she was at least partly their employer, now. She wondered what they thought about that. 'There are things we must discuss,' she said. 'But not here. I'll come down to the hotel tomorrow.'

'Of course, Mrs Morton,' Howwinger said.

Mina went towards the drawing room. The thought, the realisation, had been slowly gaining momentum in her brain during the past weeks, even if she was reluctant to let herself believe it. And even if she had no doubt it was very wrong to feel the least ecstatic when she had just been widowed. But . . . she owned the Superb! She presumed that in all the circumstances Jimmy had probably left the hotel jointly to his mother and herself, no doubt in trust for James Junior and Harrison. But she didn't foresee any problems there – Elizabeth would be only too happy to hand over the running of the Superb to her.

Was that more important than Jimmy's death? She didn't want to think about that. She didn't want to think about anything, right now. She had already been thinking too much without meaning to. She had never loved her husband, but she had given herself to him, and by him she had borne two children. All for the Superb. And now it was to be hers. Surely.

She was about to find out, she knew, as she gazed at the two tall, thin men waiting for her. Jessie had warned her they were here.

'Mrs Morton!' said the first man. 'I cannot tell you how sorry we are. I'm Marshall, of Marshall, Surple, Brent and Partners.'

'And I'm Surple,' said the other man, kissing her gloved hand. 'What a tragedy, if I may say so.'

'Yes,' she said. 'Dutton, these gentlemen would appreciate something to drink, I'm sure.'

'Well . . . a glass of sherry would be very nice,' Marshall said. 'But you'll join us, I hope, Mrs Morton?'

Mina raised her eyebrows. The tone of his voice suggested she might need to. Her heart began to pound. But she did feel like a drink. 'I shall have a brandy and soda, Dutton.' She sat down in the centre of the settee, forcing the lawyers to use the armchairs opposite her.

Marshall opened his briefcase, took out a sheaf of papers. 'You will forgive us for appearing to press you on these matters, Mrs Morton,' he said. 'But you were in hospital for a very long time, and, well, there were things which needed attending to.'

'Of course,' Mina said. Dutton arrived with the drinks, and she sipped, and felt better. Her stomach remained full of butterflies, however. Was it possible that Jimmy had left the hotel solely to his mother? She wouldn't put it past the swine.

'In your absence,' Marshall went on, 'the will was read, in the presence of Mrs Morton. Mrs Morton Senior, of course. She was, if you like, acting for you, because it was really a very straightforward document. Mr Morton merely left everything he possessed to his wife, Wilhelmina.'

Mina stared at him. Her mouth opened, and then shut again. Then she opened it again, to finish her drink, and hand the glass to Dutton for a refill. 'Everything?' she whispered. Her heart seemed to be dancing a fandango, while her brain refused to accept what she had just been told. 'No conditions?'

'No conditions, Mrs Morton. You are Mr Morton's sole heir. Now, as to the estate itself, there are some small items, but the bulk consists of the Superb Hotel, which we have valued at one million dollars – it is a little run-down, as I am sure you know – Mr Morton's yacht, which we have valued at fifteen thousand dollars, and this house, which is valued by the estate agents at thirty-five thousand dollars. Mr Morton's automobile is subject to an insurance claim, which will certainly be met, but is only in the amount of a thousand dollars. Fortunately, there are no third-party claims as the only damage caused by the accident, apart from to Mr Morton and yourself, of course, was to the car and the lamp-post.'

Mina's brain whirred as she kept adding. She had just inherited one million and fifty thousand dollars. Certainly a quarter of a million pounds. She wanted to scream her joy. But only the hotel mattered. Dear old Jimmy? She was even prepared to forgive him for everything, not least for nearly killing her. But he had left her all he owned. He had truly loved her, after all.

Marshall was watching her closely. Now he glanced at

Surple, who cleared his throat. 'Unfortunately, Mrs Morton, in the circumstances, the creditors have made representation to Mr Marshall and myself, as Mr Morton's, the late Mr Morton's, attorneys, for settlement in full of their accounts. We have of course pointed out your delicate state of health, and told them how inconvenient this would be right this minute, and I am happy to say that they have been most co-operative. However, within the next six months they will have to be satisfied.'

'The creditors?'

'Those persons or companies to whom your husband owed money, Mrs Morton,' Marshall explained.

'I know what a creditor is, Mr Marshall,' Mina said. 'So Jimmy had some debts. Perhaps you will tell me what they amount to.'

'Well . . .' Marshall glanced at Surple again.

Surple took a sheet of paper from his briefcase. 'Only the two large items really matter – the Hanson and Westerley Banking Corporation, to which the Superb Hotel is mortgaged for seven hundred and fifty thousand dollars, and the Seventh Avenue Banking Corporation, to which this house is mortgaged for twenty-five thousand dollars. There are in addition a large number of unpaid bills, which all together come to something like twenty-five thousand, so we can round out the total debt at approximately eight hundred thousand dollars.'

Slowly Mina put down her glass. 'Eight hundred *thousand* dollars?'

'There is absolutely no reason to be alarmed, Mrs Morton,' Marshall said hurriedly. 'You are absolutely solvent. There is no question of bankruptcy. No indeed. However, my colleague and I would strongly recommend that you act now, rather than await the consequences of a forced sale. When that happens, you know, word gets around, and people expect to find bargains. But if you were to place the Superb on the market now, for no other known reason than that owning a hotel is not exactly the occupation for a lady, you might well realise that million of which we spoke. That would liquidate your debts and leave you with two hundred thousand clear. And that, suitably invested . . . well, I am not sure you would be able to maintain an establishment quite as large as this, requiring so many domestics, and of course we assume that you would wish to sell Mr Morton's yacht, but having done that you would certainly be able to live very comfortably.' He gazed at her. 'So . . . that is what my colleague and I would recommend you do, Mrs Morton.'

'Sell the hotel,' she said, quietly. 'You want me to sell the Superb.'

'I'm afraid you have absolutely no choice about that, Mrs Morton,' Surple told her.

'Thank you, gentlemen,' Mina said. 'I am sure you do not require my answer right this minute.'

'Your answer?' Surple asked in surprise. Clearly he did not suppose they needed an answer.

'I have just returned from hospital,' Mina pointed out. 'I need a little time to become acquainted with the situation. I shall be in touch with you in a few days.'

Marshall and Surple exchanged glances, and then seemed mentally to shrug at each other. 'Of course, Mrs Morton. We will await your instructions.'

Dutton saw them out, while Mina finished her second brandy. She felt sick. They wanted her to sell the Superb. After everything she had endured to obtain it. And not a thought for Jimmy? Jimmy, she thought angrily, had all but killed her in his drunken jealousy. Not even over a man. Over an hotel. An hotel which he could have matched, had he possessed the slightest spark of ambition, or even guts. And now she discovered he had so mismanaged his affairs that he did not even really own his hotel. Instead of a fortune, he had left her a fortune in debts. Sell the Superb, they said. The answer to all her problems. So that she could become a fading widow with two little orphan sons. Well, that was not how she saw her future at all. Throughout the long weeks of lying in that hospital bed, coming to terms with the fact of Jimmy's death, with the certainty that she now at least part-owned the Superb, she had been aware of only one thing. She did not know who or what had removed James Morton the Second so suddenly, and then James Morton the Third even more suddenly. Those were some of the things she was afraid to think about, too closely. But they were connected with her dream. It was possible to say they were connected with her destiny. A destiny she was going to realise, come hell or high water.

Anyway, Marshall and Surple were showing a lamentable lack of knowledge of her affairs, of Morton affairs. Eight hundred thousand dollars might be a huge percentage of one million; it was less than a third of three million, and that was an entirely different matter.

'You'll call a cab,' she told Dutton, who raised his eyebrows and hurried off to tell Jessie.

'Now, you know that Dr Bedford did say you got to rest, and take it easy,' Jessie remonstrated. 'Where you going in a cab?'

'I am going to see my mother-in-law,' Mina told her. 'Don't you think I should? After all, she never came to see me, in hospital.'

'I'm sorry I only got to see you once or twice while you were ill,' Elizabeth Morton said. 'But I was so very busy. There was so very much to be done. And you were incapable.'

She made it sound as if it was all her fault, Mina thought. So it *had* been Elizabeth's face she had seen when semi-conscious. And come to think of it, she realised, it was just as hard and angry now as she remembered it being then.

'But it is gratifying to see that you seem to have made a full recovery,' Elizabeth went on. 'I hope you are pleased with the children. I kept them here, you know.'

'I know,' Mina said. 'And I am most awfully grateful.' She certainly had not come here to quarrel.

'Yes. Well, their future is something we will have to discuss. There are several things we shall have to discuss. When you've rested up and feel stronger.'

'I think we should discuss them now,' Mina said, wishing Elizabeth would offer her a drink; the two brandies she had had at home had left her feeling quite exhausted. 'I really am quite well again,' she lied. 'I received a visit this morning from Messrs Marshall and Surple. A visit! They were waiting for me when I got home from the hospital.'

'They are Jimmy's solicitors. Were, Jimmy's solicitors,' Elizabeth corrected herself. 'Good men, I understand.'

'I'm sure they are,' Mina agreed. 'They brought me up to date with my financial position, very succinctly. It seems that Jimmy was a trifle in debt.'

'Jimmy has always been in debt,' Elizabeth said. 'As I am sure you knew. However, I understand that he has not left you unprovided for. I believe you will inherit something in the nature of a quarter of a million dollars. Regarding the boys, of course . . .'

'I may clear a quarter of a million, providing I place the Superb on the market,' Mina said, speaking very carefully. 'And supposing I obtain the best possible price. But that would be criminal.'

Elizabeth raised her eyebrows and her lorgnette together.

'That hotel has belonged to the Mortons for three generations,' Mina said. 'Jimmy was very proud of it. He dreamed of it belonging to James Junior.' Which was not exactly true. But it should have been true, she reminded herself.

'That hotel has never been anything other than a disaster,' Elizabeth stated. 'If you knew the number of times I tried to get Jimmy's father to sell it, and invest the money in something worthwhile . . . but he always carried on about it being in the family for so long.'

'Exactly,' Mina said, triumphantly.

'Well, now is the time for you to get out while you can, my dear. Call it an act of God. James Junior can never blame you.'

'I don't mean to sell,' Mina said.

Elizabeth gazed at her.

'I think it's possible to make the Superb once again just that, superb,' Mina said. 'I've always thought so, but Jimmy wouldn't spend any money on it. Well, I think he was wrong.'

'Indeed? Jimmy didn't spend any money on it because he didn't have any money to spend. Whose money are *you* planning to spend on it?'

'My own.'

'You have two million dollars? It will cost that to liquidate the mortgage *and* renovate.'

'Of course I haven't two million dollars,' Mina said. 'Not in cash. But I have assets worth half that.'

'Not once your debts are paid,' Elizabeth said. 'Messrs Marshall and Surple gave me to understand the creditors were asking for their money now.'

158

'Well, they are, Jimmy being dead,' Mina said. 'And everyone knowing that I don't have any ready money. But between us, you and me, we have assets worth more than three million. Don't we? Jimmy always said so. If you were to step in, Mother, and guarantee Jimmy's debts, and guarantee me the necessary loans from the banks as well, then . . .'

Elizabeth Morton laid down her lorgnette. 'You wish *me* to guarantee you?'

'Well . . .' Mina gazed at her, the butterflies back in her stomach. 'You are my mother . . . my mother-in-law,' she added hastily.

'That is my misfortune,' Elizabeth said. 'Your effrontery is absolutely amazing. Almost as amazing, and as distasteful, as your total lack of concern for your poor dead husband. My son.'

'He killed himself,' Mina snapped, losing her temper despite her resolution that she wouldn't, no matter what the provocation. 'And he damned near killed me too.'

'Yes,' Elizabeth remarked, conveying very clearly that she regarded the word "near" as a stroke of ill fortune to the world at large.

'And they're *his* debts,' Mina shouted. 'Not mine.'

'They were mainly incurred keeping you in the style to which you so rapidly became accustomed,' Elizabeth observed.

'Why, you . . .' Mina checked herself before she said something she might regret. 'That is simply not true. The money went on his boat and his car and his parties. And his mistresses.'

Elizabeth's face froze. 'You little slut,' she said. 'I think you had better listen to me, very carefully. My son chose to marry you, a chambermaid, for some reason of his own. Don't talk to me about your grandfather. He disowned you, no doubt for some very good reason of *his* own. I was prepared to accept you, even if I knew Jimmy was marrying beneath him, because I thought you were a nice quiet girl, and I hoped you might be a good influence on Jimmy. I asked you to be such an influence, remember? Instead of which you became one of the fastest young women in New York. It isn't as if you ever loved Jimmy. Don't you suppose he talked to me about you? He would sometimes come here almost in tears that you never showed him the slightest affection. That you never showed your children the slightest affection. Can you deny that?'

Mina stared at her. Because she couldn't deny that.

'In all the circumstances,' Elizabeth went on, 'I think you are an extremely fortunate young woman. Presumably you married my son in search of wealth. Well, you have obtained a very reasonable fortune. You should clear a quarter of a million from selling everything up. This will enable you to live in a very reasonable fashion for the rest of your life, if you invest it carefully. It is certainly far more than you deserve. I suggest you go back to England and see if you cannot discover some other rich husband. I know that you are the mother of my grandsons. I do not desire that they should ever suffer, and to that effect I am altering my will to leave my entire fortune in trust for them. But the trust will be exercised by trustees, and not by you, Mina. I'm afraid I do not have any faith in your . . . ambitions. As for backing any of those ambitions, I would not do so if you went down on your knees.' She rang the little silver bell at her elbow. 'Will you call Mrs Morton a cab, please, Hardy; she is just leaving.'

Chapter 8

Mina took the cab direct to the Superb. She knew that if she went home she would merely burst into tears. She felt absolutely exhausted. Perhaps she should have waited until she was stronger – supposing she had had the time. Now she did not dare go home to bed. She had to keep moving, keep doing something, until the mood of despair passed off. Because it was the despair of guilt. Every word Elizabeth Morton had said had been quite true.

But Jimmy Morton had known that when he had married her. She had never pretended she loved him. He had wanted the use of her body and she had granted him that. It had been a bargain. Perhaps she had not granted him as much use of it as he might have liked – but then, in return, he had not granted her quite the wealth she would have liked. Or allowed her to help him make something of the hotel. So why *should* she feel guilty? He *had* damned near killed her as well in his drunken, jealous anger.

All of which did not alter the fact that she had failed, and that she now had to sell the Superb.

The Superb! The cab stopped, and immediately the doorman was there to assist her down. Joe Stark was there to hold the door for her, and Howwinger was inside to greet her. Such guests as happened to be in the lobby stared at her in humble surprise, while the bell-boys whispered to them just who she was. The Owner! She wondered if any of those little twerps had been in that dormitory the night they had wanted to put boot polish on her nipples.

Now all of her ambitions had come together in a single climactic peak. For at least a few hours, she thought bitterly.

Because she was the owner of . . . what? She looked around her, comparing what she saw with the last hotel she had been

161

in, marking the damp patches in the ceilings and the worn patches in the carpets – and this was in the lobby, the very best the hotel had to offer. It was nearly one in the afternoon, and she went to the restaurant doorway, but only half a dozen of the tables were occupied. 'We used to do better than this, surely, Mr Howwinger,' she said.

'Ah . . . not recently, Mrs Morton. Not since the scandal.'

She raised her eyebrows, and he looked embarrassed.

'I thought perhaps Mr Morton might have told you about it. There was an entire party taken sick after eating a meat pie . . . well, word got about.'

'Yes,' she said, and went upstairs. They were fortunate no one had died, she supposed, remembering the filth of the kitchen. The elevator creaked and groaned. 'How old is this elevator, Mr Howwinger?' she asked.

'I have no idea, Mrs Morton. I imagine it has been here just about since the hotel was built. It's quite safe,' he added hastily. 'We have it serviced every year. It's just not very fast.'

'Or very smooth,' Mina observed.

Mrs Young was waiting for her. 'Mrs Morton,' she said, 'I had no idea you were coming down today. Girls . . .'

The chambermaids stood to attention. Mina recognised none of their faces; presumably six years was a long time in the life of a chambermaid. But she thought she could recognise their dresses and caps and aprons.

'It has been so difficult,' Mrs Young began.

'I think you have done wonders, Mrs Young,' Mina said, and she meant every word of it, even if the old dragoness was still given to tanning pretty backsides, from the way the girls watched her.

'Is it true that you intend to sell, Mrs Morton?' Mrs Young asked. Together with Howwinger she hurried at Mina's shoulder as they went from room to room.

'Obviously that depends on a great number of things,' Mina said. What a brilliant actress she would have made, she thought. 'My backers will have to determine whether it is worthwhile pouring money into this place. How much do you suppose it would take completely to renovate the hotel, Mr Howwinger?'

'Completely?'

'Everything that needs doing. Including the elevator.'

'My word, Mrs Morton. I wouldn't like to say.'

'I would like you to try.'

'Well . . . two million dollars. Maybe. It would be cheaper in the long run to tear it down and rebuild.'

'Indeed? How much would that cost?'

'Well . . . if you didn't try to match the Plaza, you might do it for five million, Mrs Morton. But you'd have something new, something modern.'

'Do people want something modern, Mr Howwinger?'

'I think they do, Mrs Morton. Our sort of clientele certainly. That's the travelling public. Businessmen and the like. It would have to be run on modern lines, too, mind. You should hear some of our guests carrying on when they can't get a telephone line.'

'I see. Well, I shall have to give it some thought.'

She wept all the way home, in the cab.

'You looking ill, all over again,' Jessie remonstrated. 'What, you aiming to wind up back in hospital? I don't understand you at all, Mina.'

'Just get me a glass of sherry,' Mina said.

'No food?'

'I don't think I could eat a thing.'

'And what about him?' Jessie lowered her voice.

Mina raised her eyebrows.

'That Irish layabout?' Jessie said.

Mina stared at her, her jaw slowly dropping. Then she pushed Jessie aside and ran to the drawing room door. 'Phil?'

He had been standing before the french windows, looking out at the garden. Now he turned, slowly. He wore a good suit, with a watch chain. His collar was clean and starched. His hair was carefully cut, and he even sported a little moustache. He looked gravely prosperous. 'Mina!'

They moved towards each other, checked when within a few inches of each other.

'I read about the accident,' he said. 'I came to see you, but they wouldn't let me in. Only family, they said.'

'Oh, Phil.' She held out her hands, and was in his arms, held

163

close, tenderly, without excessive passion. But the passion was there; she could feel it.

'I read about Morton, too,' he said in her ear.

She stood back from him, and then sat on the settee, drawing him down beside her. Dutton came in with two sherries. 'Have you ever forgiven me for that?' she asked.

'Forgiven you? What did I have to forgive you for? I couldn't marry you, then.' He gave a half smile. 'And I didn't offer you much else, did I? But, Mina . . . now . . .' He looked into her eyes.

She returned his gaze. Then smiled. 'Now . . . you look so good. So . . . well, so prosperous.'

'I'm qualified, now,' he said, with conscious pride.

'Qualified?'

'As an accountant.'

'Oh. Oh, yes. Oh, Phil, I am so proud of you.'

'Mina . . .' His hands were tight on hers. 'If you knew how I've missed you. How I've dreamed of you. Mina . . . I know this isn't the time, with Morton only dead three weeks, but Mina . . . listen. I have a job. I'm with Rigby and Smith. They're big. And they say I have a future. I'm on twenty dollars a month now. Can you believe that, Mina? Twenty dollars a month. That's more than enough for two.'

Twenty dollars a month. She continued to gaze at him, and slowly the animation left his expression. 'That's great, Phil,' she said. 'I'm so happy for you.'

'But . . . it's not your kind of money, eh?'

'I . . .' She bit her lip. 'Like you said, Phil, it's too soon after Jimmy's death.' She forced a smile. 'I never loved him, you know. I . . . but I was his wife.'

He nodded, and released her. 'I understand.' He stood up. 'I shouldn't have come.'

'But I'm glad you did. Really I am. So glad. So very glad, Phil. Please say you'll come again, in a day or two? Please?'

He hesitated, then smiled. 'I'll do that. In a day or two, Mina.'

The door closed, and she fell back against the cushions. There was happiness. Contentment. Even sexual passion which could be shared. On twenty dollars a month. To which she could add a quarter of a million. If he'd accept it. But they'd both be total fools to look any further.

She glared at Jessie. 'If you say a word . . .'

'I am all done talking,' Jessie said, and placed a pile of visiting cards on the coffee table.

'What're those?' Mina asked, suspiciously.

'The people who wrote, and the people who sent flowers,' Jessie said. 'You really should reply to them.'

'Um,' Mina said, and flicked the cards, carelessly. People she loathed. People she would cheerfully turn her back on. To marry Phil Clancy, and be an accountant's wife? How New York society would laugh. People . . . she turned over a larger card than average – Felix Petersen's card.

'Mina!' Felix said, and kissed both her hands. 'I had intended to call, of course, but I felt now was not quite the time. I had no idea you would recover from your grief so soon.'

Mina understood that, being Felix, he had to make some such remark, took pleasure in watching him look past her down the hallway, at the waiting Dutton . . . but not at the other hats and coats, because there weren't any. Then he looked at her again, took in the plunging décolletage of her pale blue silk rep evening gown, the fact that she was wearing no rings. Jessie had not been pleased with that idea, especially entertaining a man like Felix Petersen, who apparently had more of a reputation than Mina knew. But then, Jessie did not know the stakes for which she was playing.

Did she know herself? Did she really understand what she was risking? She was quite sure that she did. However attractive a business proposition she put to Felix, he would eventually wish for more. But then, she would have to hold out the promise of more, eventually, for him to be interested at all. What would happen then? Because she had no intention of giving him any part of herself. Jimmy had suggested that Felix was hardly a gentleman, and she knew that he could be unspeakably vulgar. But he could hardly present any serious physical threat to a woman who had once coped with Charlie Stark, with total success. She felt quite confident there.

Phil Clancy would of course say that she was being at once ruthless and dishonest. But it had been a week now, and Phil had not returned. He had no doubt been able to discern the truth of what she wanted. But that *was* what she wanted. What she was determined to have. What she had to have, if she was not going to write off her entire life as a failure.

'They were lovely flowers,' she said.

'Roses are my favourite,' he agreed, and walked beside her into the drawing room, again hesitating as he understood that this was, indeed, going to be a tête-à-tête. 'I keep remembering that night,' he said, obviously fishing for reasons.

Mina smiled, and took a glass of champagne from Dutton's tray. 'I keep trying to forget it.'

'Of course. How silly of me.'

They dined, gazing at each other down the length of the table. She could feel his excitement growing, but equally his mystification. Not even Felix Petersen could imagine what she had in mind. She hoped he was big enough to cope with it – but if he wasn't, then she would at least have the pleasure of reducing him to his proper size.

But her own excitement was growing as well. She might have been the heroine of one of the novels she had read as a girl. Except that no novel she had read as a girl had had a heroine prepared to assault life the way she intended to. 'Thank you, Dutton,' she said, when they returned to the drawing room. 'You may leave the port.'

Dutton bowed, and withdrew.

'That was a magnificent meal,' Felix said.

Her cue. 'Annie is a good cook,' Mina agreed. 'It is such a shame I shall have to let her go.'

'Must you?'

Mina filled his glass; to her pleasure, she did not spill a drop, so steady was her hand. 'I'm afraid so. Didn't you know? They mean to sell me up. Jimmy was somewhat careless with money.'

'Good Lord!' Felix commented, with not altogether convincing surprise. 'We can't have that. My dear Mina, if it's a loan you wish, you have but to ask.'

'And you would lend it to me?' She smiled, even as she took a long breath, and felt her heart skip a beat. 'Twenty million dollars?'

Felix spilled the port instead; it splashed on to his stiff white shirt front. 'Jimmy Morton owed twenty million dollars?'

His consternation was just the fillip she needed to regain her confidence. 'Good Lord, no. The idea of such a sum would have given him a nervous breakdown. No, no, he owes just enough to make it imperative for me to sell the Superb unless I can raise twenty million dollars.'

'That is an enormous sum of money,' Felix remarked.

'But you could raise it?' She almost hoped he would have to admit defeat.

'Oh, indeed I could. With no difficulty at all. However, I must admit I don't quite understand how you arrive at such a figure.'

'Then I shall tell you. I do not wish to sell the Superb. Indeed, I wish to expand, rather than contract. I have been putting together some facts and figures. Right now, the Superb is a dump, with a bad reputation for food and service. It will have to come down and be rebuilt if I am ever going to take any profit from it. Oh, don't worry, I'm not going to build a second Plaza. I would build a modern hotel, with modern services, for the travelling public. I think that will cost in the region of five million dollars. What I would then like to do is to buy or build a similar establishment in London. I would call it the London Superb. I think we would have to allow about ten million for that. But I also intend to link the two in more than just name. It's an idea I've had for years. Travel, completely trouble free. Travel is the thing, nowadays. Every year the passenger traffic across the Atlantic, both ways, goes up and up. I'm talking about first and cabin class, not steerage. Yet the same problems and irritations with luggage and schedules remain. Don't you see . . .' She was becoming enthusiastic, despite her determination to remain perfectly calm and composed, and businesslike.

'You must have done a lot of travelling, Felix. You know the problems. We would take care of all those to the last detail. Suppose you were intending to visit London, from, say, Chicago. You would travel to New York to catch your ship, and you would check in at the Superb. From that moment all your travel arrangements and accommodation requirements would be the Superb's responsibility. My staff would see to the transportation of your baggage to the ship – we would already have booked the cabins when you gave us your required dates.

When the ship reached London, or Southampton, or wherever, you would leave the ship and be taken straight by our transport to your room or your suite at the London Superb. Everything would be our concern. You wouldn't have to think of a thing save your business, or your pleasure if you happened to be on holiday. And when you were ready to come back, the same thing.'

'It's ambitious,' Felix said. 'And it'll take some organising.'

'I'm prepared to do that.'

'You might upset one or two travel agents. Not to mention a whole lot of rival hoteliers.'

'So they get upset. I won't be breaking any laws. I've thought it all out, Felix. As I said, I'm aiming at modern hotels. Not too large, but with every possible convenience. And the very best food. That's essential. And well presented, too.'

He stroked his chin. 'And the missing five million is to buy yourself a transatlantic liner?'

'Oh, of course not. The missing five million is partly to book up blocks of accommodation on existing transatlantic liners, so we always have the very best to offer our clientele. But I will need nearly a million to settle all of Jimmy's debts.'

'You *have* thought it all out, Mina. Twenty million dollars. What exactly are you offering, as security?'

'The hotels, naturally.'

'When they are purchased or built,' Felix pointed out. 'But you would need a large proportion of the money right away, wouldn't you?'

'Agreed. So I am offering you a partnership.'

'What sort of a partnership?'

'A full partnership, Felix. I am offering you fifty per cent of the business. Providing that I manage it. And I would like the right to buy you out, if I ever can.' She drew a long breath. 'I think you and I would make good partners, Felix. We both know what we want.'

Felix studied her for several seconds, while she felt her cheeks filling with colour. Almost she felt he could see into her brain, could tell just how dishonest she had just been. Then he said, 'And you consider yourself as being worth twenty million dollars?'

'Me?' she asked in mock surprise. 'My dear Felix, all I am offering is a share in the success I know is going to be mine. There is no way my plan can fail.'

'There is every way your plan can fail, Mina. It depends entirely upon your talent and your experience. You may have some of the former, but none at all of the latter. And if it does fail, I will have laid out twenty million dollars and be left with just you.'

She gazed at him, realising for the first time what an immensely strong face he had. And a cruel one? 'The plan will not fail, Felix.'

'Nothing is certain in this life, Mina. It is an interesting plan, certainly. An intriguing one. I am tempted. But I will have to have more security than you are offering.'

Her head came up.

'I do not think,' Felix went on, 'that I could consider such an outlay for anyone less than my wife.'

'Your *wife?*'

'You sound appalled. Am I that much of an ogre?'

Mina found herself breathing heavily. And getting annoyed into the bargain, as usual despite her resolutions. But the conversation was taking a course she had not planned at all, and she was in danger of losing control of the situation.

Felix smiled. 'I assure you, my dear, that while I may be a few years older than you, I am absolutely fit. I do not have a single physical ailment. I would say, in fact, that it is I who am taking all the risk, quite apart from paying you an enormous compliment in valuing you at twenty million dollars. For example, I know for certain that you are not only another man's widow, who has also twice been a mother, but that you have also been knocked to pieces in a car smash, according to the newspapers.' He pointed. 'You might have a wooden leg under there, for all I know.'

Mina stood up. 'I think you had better leave.' She knew that if he did not, she was liable to burst into tears. The effrontery of the man.

Felix never moved. 'Why do you not consider my offer? I am asking you to marry me, Mina. Of course, I understand that you have only recently been widowed. And yet, somehow, I do not truly feel that you are overcome by grief. So let us stop sparring, and look at the situation like sensible adults.'

Suddenly his voice was crisp. 'You are in dire financial straits at the moment. You are all but bankrupt. But you are a courageous and ambitious woman. Instead of merely surrendering to the inevitable, as so many women would do, you have devised a remarkable plan for reinstating at once your fortune and your position. Its only flaw is that, like most plans, it depends upon money. In your case, a quite preposterous amount of money. But . . . money which I happen to possess. I do not think it unreasonable that, if I provide the financing you require, you in return should provide me with the only thing you possess which is of any value to me. I am not interested in hotels and ships, Mina. I have sufficient physical assets. I am interested in you.'

She stared at him. Because put like that it *was* quite a reasonable proposal. As it was, in fact, an honourable one. A proposal of marriage. A promise of a lifetime beneath the umbrella of the Petersen millions. So she did not love him. She had not loved Jimmy Morton. Was she then utterly mercenary?

She could at least be honest. 'You do know that I am not in love with you, Felix? That I shall never be in love with you?'

He shrugged. 'I would hardly expect it, as I'm very nearly old enough to be your father. But I am sure you will make me a good wife.'

What did she have to lose, if she was going to reach for those stars of which she had always dreamed? As he had just reminded her, he *was* twenty years older than she. She had everything on her side. 'If I married you,' she said, 'I would not wish for any more children.' At least by you, she thought, wondering if she was again deliberately trying to antagonise him, so as to retain at least a glimmer of self-respect.

In any event, he did not seem prepared to take offence. 'I would not dream of inflicting such a misfortune on you, my dear. All I ask is that you will give me the use and comfort of your body.'

'Jimmy did warn me that you could be inexpressibly vulgar, Felix,' she said. 'But then, I have observed that for myself.' It was her turn to shrug. 'If you wish it so badly, it is yours.'

'My dear, I am overwhelmed. Am I allowed to kiss my fiancée?'

She presented her face, but he merely brushed her forehead

with his lips. She felt quite weak at what she had just done – but she would triumph, because she was the stronger. She did not doubt that.

'Now,' he said, suddenly businesslike. 'As there is no love involved, I think we should draw up a contract. I will undertake to finance you to the extent of twenty million dollars,' Felix said. 'However, I do not want a business partnership. I suspect you and I would go about things too differently for that to be a success. I will advance you the money on a permanent, interest-free loan. Whatever profits you manage to make from this enterprise are yours. Would that suit you?'

'Oh, Felix!' Her knees felt weak. Perhaps she had misjudged him after all.

'But this is on condition you fulfil your side of the bargain,' Felix went on.

'To be your wife.'

'Why, yes. To be *mine*, when and how I require you.' He held up his finger as she opened her mouth to protest. 'I really am an entirely reasonable man, Mina. I thought you would have gathered that. I do want to possess that body of yours, very badly. I think I have wanted that more than anything else in the world, for five years. I have even been confident enough to feel that I would do so, in the course of time, although never so soon or so completely. But I will confess to you that I also never supposed you would be quite so expensive. No wonder poor Jimmy died virtually a bankrupt. However, I am not complaining. But I am sure you will agree that twenty million dollars is an enormous sum of money. I am happy to agree to your proposition, providing I feel I am going to get twenty million dollars worth of pleasure from such an investment.'

Mina found herself panting; but he was only a man. 'By possessing me,' she said. 'You will have to explain exactly what that means, Felix.'

'In the first place, my dear girl, it does not mean that we spend every day for the rest of our lives rubbing elbows. Or every night sleeping thigh to thigh. We both have our own lives to live, and as I have said, I think we should make it perfectly plain in the contract what our obligations are to each other. I have outlined what I will consider to be mine to you. And you accept them.'

171

'Of course.' She could not believe her ears. He could be arguing for her side.

'Then in return, I shall, of course, wish you to sell this house and move in with me. I'm afraid I'm not quite so far uptown as this, Forty-Fourth Street, but it is a large and comfortable house, and I am not asking you to be friends with any of your neighbours.'

'The boys?'

'Oh, they will come with you, of course. There are bedrooms for all. Even for such of your servants as you choose to bring. And you will have a private suite of your very own. Will that be satisfactory?'

'Entirely. I hadn't . . . well, did you say a suite of my own?'

Felix smiled. 'Your very own. Everyone needs complete privacy from time to time. I have a suite of *my* very own. I would not be without it. But you are worried about our connubial bliss. Well, I would expect you to come to visit me, and spend some time, shall we say, four nights out of every seven?'

'Four nights?' Once again she could not believe her ears. The evening was taking on a dreamlike quality in which her every prayer or ambition was being granted.

'I think that will be sufficient,' Felix said. 'And that will give us each sufficient time to pursue our own interests, will it not? Of course, when you do come to me, you will allow me total possession.'

Even through the waves of euphoria which were sweeping across her brain, Mina seemed to hear warning bells jangling. '*Total* possession?'

Felix continued to smile. 'I mean to love you, my dear. That is what this contract is about, is it not? There is no need to look quite so alarmed. I have promised not to make you pregnant. I will also undertake to cause you no lasting bodily harm, not even to knock out one of your teeth.' He laughed gently. 'I am sure you can put up with the odd bite. I am a passionate man. But I do require total possession.'

She stared at him. It occurred to her that she could be selling her soul to the devil. But it was not her soul, only her body. And he was a devil who had promised not to harm her, who wanted her only four nights a week, who would provide her with her every dream, and who was, in addition, more than twice her age. So what did he intend? His humour was spiced with a subtle malice. No *lasting* harm. No doubt he meant to beat her, from time to time, because of the time she had hit him. But he was nearly fifty. She could outlast him, any time. She had no doubt about that. And no doubt she could out-think him as well, as she had out-thought Charlie Stark.

Felix had been studying her, attempting to read her expression. 'Of course, my dear Mina, should you at any time decide *not* to put up with my whims, you may at such time end our relationship. I shall write into our contract that, should you make such a decision, or decide to withhold the total possession which I desire, then I shall without argument or hesitation grant you a divorce. Of course, in such circumstances, I am sure you will agree that the twenty million loan will then have to be repaid in full. Immediately.'

She gazed at him. He wants me, she thought. Oh, how he wants me. Because surely that was all that truly mattered.

'That seems a very fair arrangement, Felix,' she said.

'Well?' Mina demanded, parading to and fro before her mirror.

'You look just great,' Jessie observed, without enthusiasm. Jessie was dead against what she was proposing to do, Mina knew, even if she had no idea what she was really doing, supposed only that the beautiful young widow who was her mistress was quite unnecessarily snatching at the first offer of remarriage to come her way. But Jessie would come round. And Mina knew that she did look splendid. She and Felix had decided that, as they were both in some haste to be wed – if she would not let him make love to her before then, he would not advance any money, either – they should be married both quickly and quietly at City Hall before just witnesses. There was going to be a scandal anyway when the news became public – there was no point in making it any worse. Thus she had given considerable thought to her costume. Obviously she could not wear white, and she had no desire to wear any bright colours, because it was winter, because she did not wish Felix to think she was over-anxious, and most of all because she was very conscious of how soon it was after Jimmy's death. So she had selected a grey woollen coat trimmed with squirrel fur, worn over a white lace blouse and a grey skirt; toque, gloves and boots were all black, but as a touch of defiance to the world, and indeed to herself, she had added scarlet ribbons to the hat.

'Well,' she said. 'It's not until tomorrow. Help me off with it.'

'I thought maybe you'd want to show it to the boy,' Jessie said.

Mina raised her eyebrows.

'He's downstairs,' Jessie continued. 'While you're trying on all this rubbish, he's waiting. And you know something, Mina? If you let him go this time, then you're all kinds of a fool.'

Mina frowned at her, then ran down the stairs. 'Phil?'

His smile was shy. 'I said I'd give you a week or so to think about things.' His expression slowly faded into disappointment as he took in her appearance. 'But you're going out.'

'No,' she said. 'No.' She held his hands, and he kissed her forehead. 'A week or two? I thought you said a day or two. Phil . . . where have you *been?*'

'Nowhere in particular. But you said . . .'

'Phil!' She drew him into the drawing room, herself poured the sherry. 'Oh, Phil.' She opened her mouth, closed it again as the doors opened. 'What *is* it, Dutton?'

'Ah . . . Mrs Morton, madam.'

Mina stared at her mother-in-law. 'What on earth . . .?'

Elizabeth entered the room like a battleship under full steam. She allowed Phil no more than a glance. 'Wilhelmina,' she said, 'I have heard the most ridiculous rumour, that you are to marry Felix Petersen.'

Mina glared at her, and then looked at Phil, who had put down his glass with a thump. She had intended to break the news to him in her own way and her own time. Now she could show her anger. 'It is not a rumour,' she said. 'Felix and I are to be married tomorrow morning.'

'I absolutely forbid it,' Elizabeth declared.

'You absolutely forbid it? What do you suppose it has to do with you?' Mina demanded.

'You are the widow of my son. Whose poor bones are hardly cold yet, and you are proposing to marry a well-known rake, a man old enough to be your father, a scoundrel, a . . .'

'I am sorry, Elizabeth,' Mina said. 'I cannot permit you to speak of my fiancé in such terms. I understand that I am marrying Felix rather soon after Jimmy's death. However, I find myself quite alone in the world, without protection or even the friends I thought I had, save for Felix himself. He has offered me his protection and his friendship, and his support for my future plans.'

'You mean he has offered you money.' Elizabeth's tone was filled with contempt.

'Exactly what he has offered me is my concern,' Mina pointed out.

'And what about my grandsons? Do you suppose I am going to stand idly by and watch them brought up by a rogue?'

'I doubt that Felix intends to have anything to do with *my* sons, save when it is absolutely necessary,' Mina said. 'But even if he does, how James and Harry will be brought up is my concern, not yours.'

'Why, you little minx. You . . . I shall take you to court.'

Mina raised her eyebrows. 'They are my children, Elizabeth. And your son was not some Indian prince who could require me to commit suttee or never marry again because I had once known his bed. By all means take me to court.'

Elizabeth stared at her, cheeks pink with anger.

Mina smiled, and rang her bell. 'You'll show Mrs Morton to her carriage, please, Dutton,' she said. 'She is just leaving.'

'I suppose,' Mina said, when the doors had been closed, 'that you think that was beastly of me. It was. But then, she was even more beastly to me, only a couple of weeks ago. I suppose I don't have a very forgiving nature.'

Clancy was on his feet. 'I must be going too,' he said.

"Because I'm going to marry Felix Petersen?"

'I have never heard of Mr Petersen before today,' he said. 'But I am leaving because you are going to marry, yes. I have no right being here.'

'Phil,' she said. 'You have every right to be here. Please sit down again, just for one minute. I want you to understand. I *have* to marry Felix. If I don't, I'm bankrupt. It's a business deal. He will finance me in what I want to do, in return for . . . well, for having me as his wife. Nothing more than that. He knows there is no love involved.' She forced a smile. 'He's even drawn up a contract. I only have to spend four nights out of every seven with him. Phil . . .'

'You'd like to spend the other three with me.'

She flushed. 'I wouldn't have put it quite so baldly. But I don't see why we cannot remain close friends, and see each other as often as we wish.'

'Because I want to marry you myself, Mina. I want you to be mine. Not to be shared with somebody else, half and half. My God, the thought would drive me mad.'

'Isn't that a rather old-fashioned point of view?' she asked – and immediately wished she hadn't.

'Not to me, Mina.' He stood up again. 'I wish you every success in your marriage.'

'Phil!' She caught his hand. 'Can't we just be friends? I was telling Elizabeth the truth, just now. I don't have any friends. Felix is a business partner. I'd so like to have a friend, Phil. A friend like you.'

He looked down on her, then very gently pulled his hand free. 'I don't think you need friends, Mina. You have dreams, instead. And you make them all come true.'

'James, and . . . ah, Harrison, is it? You see, I remembered.' Felix Petersen gravely shook hands with the two little boys, who were clearly overawed by their surroundings. 'An instant family. Do you know, I have always wanted a son. Now I have two. I am delighted. Now, Mina, if we could be on our way . . .'

Mina kissed the boys, hugged Jessie, embraced the two witnesses, friends produced by Felix. 'You be good,' she told James. 'And look after your brother. And do what Jessie tells you.'

'You're not going to be away all that long,' Felix pointed out. 'Only four days.'

'Four days?' Mina had been looking forward to a trip into the country, although he had consistently refused to tell her where they would honeymoon.

Felix laughed, and tucked her arm under his and they went down the City Hall steps. 'Isn't that all I'm entitled to?'

'Oh, Felix! I didn't mean on a week in, week out basis.'

He helped her into the waiting carriage. 'I didn't suppose you did, my dear. But four days is quite sufficient for a honeymoon. We both have a great deal to do.'

Mina blew kisses to the boys as they drove away. She felt truly happy. However suspicious she might have been of Felix, he was the most perfect gentleman in every way, even down to pretending he liked his new stepsons, when he obviously couldn't care less about them. Perhaps he was overly concerned with business, but that, she supposed, was how one got to be a millionaire in the first place – it was a habit she would have to cultivate. 'Where are we going?' she asked, squeezing his arm.

'Just down the road.'

'Down the . . .' She gazed at the Superb.

'Don't you want to honeymoon in your own hotel? It won't be here very much longer, will it?'

'Felix!' But she was secretly delighted, once again to be pelted with confetti by the bell-boys and the chambermaids, once again to see the beaming faces of Stark and Howwinger and Mrs Young – word had of course spread that the hotel was not, after all, going to be sold, although they did not as yet know her plans.

And as Felix had said, it would be the last time; she intended to start the ball rolling the moment they finished their honeymoon, and he gave her his cheque.

Was she the greatest prostitute in all history? But it was going to happen . . . why, in four days' time.

'My God,' Felix said, as they travelled upwards, to the accompaniment of a cacophony of groans and shudders. 'Is this lift safe?'

'I am assured it is,' Mina said. 'I'm not so sure I can guarantee the food. Although I imagine they've made a special effort for us.'

'I should hope so. You go in first,' he told the bell-boy. 'I have to carry my bride across the threshold.'

'Felix!' she squealed in happy embarrassment as he swept her from her feet, carried her inside, and threw her on to the bed, so that she landed with legs and skirts scattered. The bellhop tactfully averted his eyes, and Felix gave him a note.

'Shall I open the champagne, sir?'

'No,' Felix said. 'I will do that. You just get out.'

'Yes, sir.' The boy ran for the door, and Felix locked it behind him.

Mina sat up. 'Aren't we going to have a celebration supper?'

'Of course. I've ordered it for midnight.'

'Midnight? But it's only six o'clock. What do we do for the next six hours?'

He gazed at her, and she flushed. Then he removed his jacket and tie.

'I've never done it before dinner,' Mina muttered.

'You amaze me. I have never been able to understand the custom of sending a bride and groom off to bed stuffed to the eyeballs with food and drink. To be appreciated, sex needs to be undertaken on an empty stomach, fortified with perhaps one glass of wine.' He opend the champagne bottle with consummate dexterity, poured, 'Now remember, nurse it.' He brought the glass to her, put it on the bedside table, sat beside her, and then, for the first time in their relationship, kissed her, while his hands slid over her gown, lightly, just stroking across her nipples. But it was the kiss that was sending her mind whirling. No one had ever kissed her like that before, at once tenderly and possessively, and so totally sexually.

Mina was suddenly breathless. 'You want sex, now?'

'That's why we're here.'

She made herself speak in a quiet, unconcerned voice. 'It's just that . . . well, I thought we would sort of sit, and drink champagne, and maybe talk. Let a little romance come into it.'

'Romance has got nothing to do with sex, Mina,' he told her. 'Even if the one sometimes leads to the other. And just what were you proposing to talk about?'

She gazed at him, and sighed. 'Nothing, I suppose.' She sipped some champagne, felt better, and got up. 'Do you wish me to undress?'

'It's customary.'

She ripped off her clothes as fast as she could. If he was that anxious, the thing to do was to get it over with as rapidly as possible; besides, in a strangely repulsive fashion he had made her want it too. But to her surprise and disappointment, he didn't watch her, as had done Jimmy Morton on their first night; instead he rummaged through his suitcase, and finally found a small tube of ointment.

'What's that for?' she asked.

'To coat you with. I don't mean to hurt you, Mina. That's a part of our contract.'

'To . . . *coat* me?' She was suddenly terrified; could he be abnormally large?

'When I bugger you, my darling. I've waited five years for this moment. I really am quite impatient.'

'When you . . .' She could not believe her ears. 'You have got to be crazy.'

'Just passionate. You may remember I told you what I wanted to do to you, the first time we met.'

'That was a *joke*,' she shouted, 'Wasn't it?'

'My darling Mina, I never joke.'

'You . . .' She shook her head. 'No, sir. No way. Just forget it.'

He sat at the desk, began writing out a cheque. 'We have a contract.'

'Which I can break, any time I like,' Mina said. 'You agreed to that. I'm sorry, Felix, but this is going to be the shortest marriage in history. Sodomy is out. Out, out, out.' She began to dress herself again. 'I really am sorry, Felix. But there are some things . . .' She felt if she stopped talking she would burst into tears.

'Five million, wasn't it, as a down payment?' he said, apparently to himself. And looked up to smile at her. 'I'm sure you'll enjoy it, Mina. And there are so many others things I want to do to you. And with you, of course. You'll enjoy them all, if you'll let yourself. But if you really do feel so strongly about it . . .' He tore the cheque into little strips, dropped them into the wastebasket. 'I suppose I should say, goodbye.'

Mina, dragging her corset up her thighs, stared at him, the sickening awareness of total defeat creeping over her.

He gave her another smile. 'I can, of course, always write another cheque,' he said. 'I have a whole book of them.'

Mina looked at the door, and then down at herself. The corset began to slide back down her thighs. But she couldn't just surrender. To *that*.

'Shouldn't you ring for a bell-boy?' she asked, as scathingly as she could. 'I'm sure if you wrote him a cheque as well, he'd be happy to oblige.'

Felix shrugged. 'Perhaps the next time. Then he can have you while I have him. Or vice versa. But tonight I wish you all to myself. Just kneel on the bed, my darling. You don't have to do a thing.'

She glared at him, in total outrage, and he blew her a kiss, and poured champagne. 'But I think, in the circumstances, that we can allow you *two* glasses of wine, tonight.'

Chapter 9

'So,' Mina said, 'you will take no bookings for any day after 30 November, and you will terminate all existing occupancies by that time.'

'30 November,' Howwinger said, writing busily on his pad. 'And then . . .?'

'It will take approximately two years for the new Superb to be ready,' Mina told him, looking from face to face down the table. 'As I have said, Mr Howwinger, during that period you will remain on the payroll, together with Mrs Young and Mr Stark . . .' again she looked from face to face, 'and anyone else that you firmly recommend. I am thinking of people like the head doorman.'

'And the chefs?' Joe Stark asked.

'No, Mr Stark,' Mina said. 'I do not think we will retain the chefs. I am sorry if they are friends of yours, but I do not think they will fit into the new set-up, and even more into the new ambiance I intend to give the Superb.'

Stark gazed at her, and she returned his gaze. He was concerned about his thieving friends. She wondered why he could not see what she was concerned about.

But what was she concerned about? That these people might somehow learn the truth, of how she spent her nights? How she had spent the past four nights, certainly. How her husband had made her pander to every obscene craving he possessed; how he had used his hands in a way poor Jimmy could only ever have dreamed of – how he had made her belong, to him, and understand that she no longer belonged to herself. Poor Jimmy, indeed, if he had dreamed so much, and been able to persuade her to so little.

And poor Phil Clancy, who had perhaps not dreamed at all,

save of having her in his arms.

And most of all, poor Mina Doberley. Not Mina Petersen. Never Mina Petersen. That way lay her only salvation, the only way she could look these people in the eye, even if she wondered if they ever thought the thoughts of Felix Petersen – or more, ever dared have the courage to share such thoughts with their loved ones. Their possessed ones.

She smiled at them. 'I thank you,' she said. 'I shall be holding meetings with each of you, over the next few days, to discuss things like staff requirements, uniforms, kitchen practice, and the like. Now I must see my architects. You'll excuse me.'

She got up as they rose respectfully, found herself next to Mrs Young. 'We are all so happy for you, Mrs Morton,' Mrs Young said, and flushed crimson. 'Oops. I meant Mrs Petersen. So happy for you. We have never seen you looking so well. So radiant. We are so happy for you, Mrs Petersen.'

'A telephone in every room, as well as a bathroom.' Felix leaned back in his huge swivel chair, turned the pages of the specification for the new Superb. 'That's going it a bit.'

'It's what people want,' Mina told him.

'Tailor-made uniforms for the bell-boys, individual dresses for the chambermaids. Two chambermaids to a room . . .?' He raised his eyebrows.

'The uniforms are for their morale,' Mina explained. 'We won't get good service from them unless they're proud to be working at the Superb. Doubling up when they enter a guest's bedroom is for their own protection.'

'And you've costed this?'

'Yes. If you look further down you'll see there will be no free accommodation for any staff who actually live in New York, and right here is where I mean to do most of my recruiting. Stark and Mrs Young know this. You will also see that I am ending the practice of free meals for all staff. Meals, at a very reasonable cost, will be deducted from staff wages.'

'The union will agree to this?'

Mina gazed at him. 'I do not intend to employ union labour, Felix.'

181

'You sure mean to take on the world,' he agreed. 'Well, you're the boss. Very much so.' He winked at her. 'I'm glad I'm just a hanger-on.'

Sometimes, often indeed, when she sat in his spacious office with him, high in the huge Petersen Building overlooking the Hudson, she found it difficult to believe this was the same man with whom she shared her nights. It was more than his good humour. In business matters he was so calmly impersonal – he never touched her in public – and at the same time so dynamic; she loved to watch him making instant decisions which might involve millions, without so much as a flicker of an eyelid.

But wasn't that the real Felix? The man who had accepted her proposal, which had involved millions, with no more hesitation than had been required to make sure he knew what he was getting?

And wasn't that also the Felix she knew in bed?

She thought she now understood why he only required her attendance four nights out of seven; it was all an aspect of his total self-control, his total will, his total understanding of the needs, as well as the necessities, of humanity. She did not know how capable *he* was on his other nights, or what he did with them, but she knew that on her off days she collapsed every evening in a state of total exhaustion, mental as well as physical – and she was only twenty-three years old. It was not even, now, the things he wanted – she was becoming used to those. It was the sheer energy he put into everything, and required of her as well. Just lying on her back, as she had done for so long with Jimmy, was no pleasure for Felix Petersen. She knelt, or she sat, or she stood, or she rolled to and fro, or she pushed herself upwards on her shoulders and feet, supporting his weight, or from time to time she even ran, round and round the room, so that he could watch her, as he put it, 'jounce', a word which had no place in a dictionary, but conveyed exactly what her hair and breasts and belly were doing as they moved, and what he felt about them.

To all of which she acceded, without demur. Because they had a contract. Easy to say. Because it was no longer true. Felix had reached into her soul with those long, prying fingers of his which could so easily reach into her body, and he had dragged up every secret and obscene longing she had never even known she possessed. She supposed possessed was as good a word as

182

any to describe her present state. She was possessed by the devil.

Which made her life outside of his bedroom the more exciting. Because nobody knew. Not quite true. Jessie knew. She had never told her, but Jessie could tell from her mistress's often puffed and bruised lips, the bite marks on her body, the shaven groin, that she and her husband could have no conventional relationship. But Jessie never commented. And Jessie was alone in her knowledge. To the building contractors, the architects, to Howwinger and Stark and Mrs Young, she was always superbly dressed, superbly poised, and superbly rich, as fitted the owner of the Superb hotel. Because she was superbly rich; she merely informed Felix of what she needed, and the money was deposited in her account the next day. As now, having finished reading the latest order list, and made his comments, he was writing a cheque.

With a smile. Because he was a happy man, with all the money he could possibly want, and a beautiful, superbly groomed wife who was his sexual slave. Because she wanted to be? Or needed to be? Or because she hated herself for what she had become? There was the problem; she did not know which of those was the truth.

She hardly dared consider the future. But she had to. If she went to his bedchamber every other night, like a drunk reaching for the bottle he loathed and feared but had to have, she knew, like a drunk, that it could not endure. She had supposed that she could outlast and outmanoeuvre a forty-eight-year-old man, no matter what he wanted. Now she was no longer sure of accomplishing that. She was no longer sure of anything when in his presence, and she was too exhausted when away from him to think coherently, at least about herself. She needed to get away from him, for a while, to find herself, to plan, once again. How strange to be thinking that, when her every dream was falling into place like perfectly pocketed billiard balls. But the dream was meaningless, unless she was in control, of it as well as of herself.

So now was the time. They had been married two months, and they had a contract. Which she had fulfilled to the last crossed t and dotted i. Now it was his turn. And her salvation.

She took the cheque and folded it into her handbag. 'Thank you, Felix,' she said and drew a long breath. 'I think I have done all that can be done here for the time being. Perkins is a good man. He will oversee the details of the actual building. I would like to move on to Stage Two.'

'The London Superb?'

'Yes.' She gazed at him.

He nodded, as usual taking her by surprise. 'Of course. I'm afraid I will not be able to accompany you.'

'Oh. Won't you?' Even if she had relied on that, still her heart burst into song.

'I have some business commitments here.' He smiled at her. 'I think you are actually trying to get away from me. However, I will give you letters to some contacts in London who may be useful to you.' His smile widened. 'Business contacts, my dear. And I will be here when you get back. You have made arrangements for the children?'

She nodded. 'Agatha and Jessie will look after them. But it would be nice if you could, well, pat them on the head, occasionally.'

'It will be my pleasure.' He leaned across the desk and picked up her hand to kiss the knuckles. 'Don't stay away too long, my dear Mina. And do remember to come back.'

They walked on the sand, Jimmy holding her right hand, Harry her left; Jessie had thoughtfully remained with the pony and trap, out of earshot. They gazed at the huge rollers, pounding out of the Atlantic, encountering Long Island as their first obstacle after three thousand miles, resentfully eating at the beach and tossing spray high into the air.

'Mummy has to go away, for a while,' Mina said.

Jimmy's lower lip began to tremble. 'To hospital, Mummy? Like the last time?'

He was the most sensitive six-year-old she had ever known. And for all the lies she had told him, told them both, she had a feeling that he knew his Daddy wasn't ever coming back, from that visit to the hospital.

'No,' she said. 'I'm not going back to hospital.' She pointed. 'I'm going across the sea.'

'The sea,' little five-year-old Harry shouted. 'The sea. I want to go to sea, Mummy.'

'And so you shall,' Mina promised. 'When you're a little

older. I'm going on business. You wouldn't enjoy it. And I may be gone a little while. But I'll be back. Will you miss me?'

'Oh, yes, Mummy,' Jimmy said. Now his eyes were full of tears. 'Uncle Felix isn't going to look after us, is he?'

'Well, only in a manner of speaking. Agatha and Jessie will actually be looking after you, same as now.'

'Jimmy doesn't like Uncle Felix,' Harry confided.

'Don't you, Jimmy?'

Jimmy flushed through his tears. 'He frightens me. He frightens Harry too,' he added. 'Harry has nightmares about Uncle Felix.'

'Oh, my darling,'she cried, and knelt to embrace them both.

'I wouldn't have nightmares, if Daddy were to come home,' Harry said.

'I know, my darling, I know. But . . .' The truth was beyond her. Certainly just before leaving them. 'Daddy can't come home right this minute. But there is nothing for you to be afraid of. Uncle Felix can never harm you.'

Not you, she thought. Because of Uncle Felix, one day you are going to be rich, and happy, and do all the things you have ever dreamed of. If she did not believe that, believe that everything she had done and was doing and would do was for them, then was she damned indeed.

'No one is ever going to harm you,' she promised, and kissed them both.

As she leaned on the rail of the first-class promenade deck and watched the chimneys of Southampton rising out of the mist, while the bulk of the Isle of Wight, also mist-shrouded, faded to the south as the *Lusitania* slowly made its way from the Solent into Southampton Water, already surrounded by a fussing crowd of tugs, Mina thought that perhaps it had all been worth it, even for her. Because this was what she had truly dreamed of – travelling across the Atlantic in a first-class suite, with eager stewards and stewardesses waiting upon her every whim, returning to England, in total triumph, and only eight years after she and Mother and Father had crawled away from the painful memories of which this land was composed, in search of a new land, and a new life.

Tears sprang to her eyes, quickly dried by the icy April wind.

She was no longer as prone to tears as once she had been. For where Mother and Father had fallen by the wayside, she had triumphed, as she had determined she would.

At what cost? Only of some damage to her moral character. Having been away from Felix for five nights, and with the prospect of at least another month of freedom in front of her, it suddenly seemed very little. The fingermarks had all but faded now, and even the bites were nothing more than hardly noticeable blue stains on the white flesh. Even her pubic hair was beginning to grow out again, and she could take a bath without feeling embarrassed. Even so, as she had left Jessie in charge of the children, she was travelling without a ladies' maid, and never allowed any of the stewardesses to help her, or to see her undressed. No doubt she was as fruitful a source of gossip on board this ship as she was in New York.

And he would be there, in New York, waiting for her to return. But that was a long way in the future. Ahead of her lay England, and her ultimate triumph. She had so much to do. She was not only in the market for a hotel, but she was also studying first-class travel at first hand. The *Lusitania* was the finest liner afloat – apart from her sister ship the *Mauretania* – and since they had left New York everything had gone perfectly. But before departure there had been the inevitable problems of baggage and timing. And these would recommence, once the liner tied up. She would have to find a train to London, instead of having a uniformed flunkey to escort her to her private compartment and provide her with anything she wished. But those things would be there, in the future. Right now, she had something even more important that she wished to accomplish, more important even than buying her hotel. To reach this moment she had dared all, and suffered all. And would now triumph, over all.

The butler held up the gold embossed card, peered at it. 'Mrs Felix Petersen,' he said, 'to see Mr Doberley.'

Mina blinked into the gloom. The room was a library, and therefore dark in any event; even at eleven o'clock in the morning there were lights burning, because outside was a dank and dripping April day. But not even the gloom which hung over London could compare with the gloom, of spirit and decoration – or lack of it – as much as an absence of natural light, which haunted this ancient mansion of which she had only heard – and of which she had formed such extravagant ideas.

'You have business with my father, I believe?' The woman was in her forties, and clearly a Doberley, even if her tight features and dowdy clothes suggested someone who had allowed life to pass her by; but she could also recognise a Doberley when she saw one – her brows drew together in a frown as she gazed at Mina.

'It is a social call,' Mina said. 'You'll be Aunt Bettina.' Papa's youngest sister.

'Betty? What is it, girl? Who's there?'

The voice was thin and high, and issued from a far corner of the room. While Bettina Doberley stared at her niece in consternation, Mina stepped past her and stood above the man in the armchair, gazing in equal consternation at the tortured figure, the twisted lips, the mottled complexion. Her triumph, she thought.

'William's girl?' Bettina was still trying to get her bearings. 'Wilhelmina? We had heard of your marriage, of course . . . but the name was Morton.' She gazed at the fur coat Mina had refused to remove, at the rings on her fingers, and the pigeon's blood ruby given her by Felix to wear on her left hand far surpassed even Jimmy's diamond solitaire.

'My first husband died,' Mina said. 'And I have married again. Do you not remember me, Grandfather?' She stooped beside the old man.

The tired eyes narrowed, the mouth trembled.

'He's had a stroke,' Bettina said. 'It is not too severe. But it limits him.'

'I'm Mina,' Mina said. 'Wilhelmina. William's daughter. Do you remember William, Grandfather?'

'Wilhelmina?' The word seeped through the tight lips. 'You've come home? You need help, no doubt. Aye, you'll need help.'

Mina raised her head to glance at her aunt; Bettina's face remained as tight as her father's. A triumph over these people was no triumph at all. Yet had she come three thousand miles and endured much to arrive at this moment. She straightened. 'No, Grandfather. I have not come for help.'

'Then why *have* you come?' Bettina demanded.

'To call upon my family,' Mina said. 'I considered it my duty, as I happened to be in England. As to why I am in London, why, I am here to purchase a hotel.'

She stayed at the Savoy, of course. This was all part of her triumph. Her triumph, she thought bitterly. She had been going to have her grandfather to dinner here, and dazzle him with her elegance as much as her wealth. Of course, were she to buy the Savoy . . . but she had never allowed her dreams to become unreal. She was here to translate ambitions into realities.

She had no wish to attract any attention, public or private, took her meals in her suite, and when she went out to look at London, that most famous of cities, of which up to now she had only read, she went by herself, to the alarm and concern of the doormen. But there was a coldness in her eyes, an assurance in her walk, an almost conscious challenge in her demeanour, which frightened off any would-be dandies, much less pickpockets. And which, she could tell, disconcerted even the people to whom Felix had given her letters of introduction.

She had them to lunch in her suite, John Drummond the solicitor, Peter Humphrey the architect, and Donald Burns the estate agent. She fed them smoked salmon and steak, Pouilly-Fumé and Château Margaux, finished with Cock-burns. And watched their uncertainty grow. They had never been entertained by a beautiful, unattached woman before, much less in this style – and much less a beautiful woman who was young enough to be the daughter of any of them. They could only take refuge in the knowledge that she was Felix Petersen's wife; she wondered if any of them understood what that meant? If they did, they gave no sign of it. Because they dared not. She had not realised before how powerful abroad is the international entrepreneur who is also an enormously wealthy man, where in his native city he is so often merely an object of critical comment, only slightly envious.

But he was her passport to a similar eminence.

'What I have to tell you is in the most complete confidence,' she said, after inviting them to light their cigars. 'But Felix, my husband, assures me that you are all to be trusted. And of course, gentlemen, as my plan develops there will be a great deal of work and profit for each of you; as my home is in New York, I shall require reliable people here in London.'

Once again they exchanged glances. She was being deliberately arrogant, and here also they were undergoing a new experience.

'So this is my plan,' Mina said, and outlined it. The men listened in silence.

'It's ambitious,' Drummond said, when she had finished.

'An international hotel business,' Humphrey commented.

'It's never been done,' Burns pointed out. 'I'm not sure it's legal.'

'What can be illegal about it?' Mina asked. 'Mr Drummond?'

'Why . . . nothing that cannot be overcome, I'm sure, Mrs Petersen. I take it you're a British citizen?'

'I was.'

'Ah. You are now an American?'

'That is correct. Is it important?'

'Only in that you'd have to have a mainly English board of directors, of course. But I would be happy to handle that for you.'

'Board of directors?' Mina asked.

'To manage your company for you. It would have to be an English company, don't you see.'

'I am not forming a company, Mr Drummond.'

'Not . . . my dear Mrs Petersen, the risk involved . . .'

'I am perfectly used to taking risks. This enterprise is going to belong to me, and nobody else.'

'Mr Petersen . . .'

'To me, Mr Drummond. And nobody else. Mr Petersen is merely providing me with whatever financial backing I require to get started. Is it against British law for an American to own property?'

'Of course not.'

'Not even commercial property? I do intend to employ an English manager.'

'There is nothing illegal in your owning any property in England, Mrs Petersen, whatever your nationality,' Drummond said, a trifle stiffly. 'I was thinking of the liability risks in not being limited.'

'I will accept the liability, Mr Drummond. Now, the first thing we need is an hotel. It need not be a large hotel, to begin with. But it must be in a very good area. I propose to gut it in any event and rebuild, so that it will have an almost identical interior to the New York Superb. My guests must feel that they are going from home to home. Mr Burns?'

Like his companions, the estate agent was clearly in a state of shock. 'Ah . . . there's the Marchmount. Just off Park Lane. That's a very good area. A hundred bedrooms and a solid reputation . . . but I have heard it might be for sale.'

'You would recommend it?'

'Well . . . it's in good shape. To gut it . . .'

'Will it serve my purpose, Mr Burns? Yes, or no.'

'Well . . . yes, it would, Mrs Petersen.'

'And what would the present owners want for it?'

'Ah . . . well, it's owned by Lord Wallsea. The rumour is that he's in some financial difficulties, and I know he's not too well, either . . . I would say you might get it for two million pounds.'

'Which is?'

'Well, just short of ten million dollars.'

'That is too much. I am prepared to offer one and a quarter million pounds.'

'My dear lady, that is absurd. The Marchmount is worth much more than that.'

'Not to me. And not to this Lord Wallsea, if he is as ill as you say, and has financial problems. You may use that telephone and call him now, and tell him you have a buyer who will write him a cheque for one and a quarter million pounds sterling, this instant, if he will accept it.'

It came as something of a surprise to Mina to realise that she felt she was coming home as the *Mauretania* nosed its way past the Statue of Liberty. Devon had always been her home, and she had not expected ever to transfer her allegiance. But Devon was a long time ago. And the girl who had walked the moors and dreamed there bore no relationship to the woman who now stood on the first-class promenade deck, gazing at the approaching skyscrapers. This woman no longer dreamed; she made things happen. One of those skyscrapers would soon belong to her.

Felix was there to greet her. 'My darling Mina,' he said, holding her close. 'Six weeks. My God, it's seemed like an eternity.'

Mina smiled at him. When he talked like this, whenever they were in public, indeed, he made her proud to be married to him. If only . . . she had done a great deal of thinking about their situation. It had begun as a cold, almost vicious bargain, undertaken in mutual dislike, and he had used her accordingly. But they had now been married for six months, and it had been a successful and prosperous six months. Even in many ways, a happy six months. Felix was a reasonable man. No doubt he had been annoyed by her denial of the total love he had first asked for. She thought that if she was prepared to offer him that now, then surely he could cease to treat her as a toy, even more than Jimmy had ever done, but rather as a human being who would grow in stature along with him. Surely.

'I've missed you too,' she confessed. 'And I've so much to tell you.'

'The Marchmount?'

'How did you know?' she cried.

'Drummond wired me. He was quite worried about it. And about you. He thinks you have a heart of flint, and a manner to match. But I think you got a most splendid bargain. One point five million, was it?'

'I let them push me up a quarter of a million,' she confessed.

'Still a bargain. Now come along, darling. Do you know, I reckon you owe me twenty-eight consecutive nights?'

'Felix,' she said. 'I want to talk to you about that. Felix . . .'

He looked down at her as they walked towards the waiting car. 'We have a contract, darling Mina.'

'You ain't getting up?' Jessie asked. 'I know it was your first night back, and I guess that man has rights, but the boys was kind of hoping you'd breakfast with them, seeing as how it's been six weeks. Now they've done gone to school.'

Mina refused to raise her head. She lay on her stomach, her face buried in her pillow, and no matter what happened she was not going to look up. After six weeks, Jessie had suddenly become as much a stranger as Felix had been.

'You feeling sick, Mina?' Jessie asked, and touched her shoulder.

As what Felix had wanted had been as strange, and frightening, and horrifying, and disgusting as that first night. Only even more impersonally brutal and humiliating, as if he had been punishing her for going away at all. And she had twenty-seven more consecutive nights ahead of her.

Yet she was sure he was proud of her business acumen. If only she could make him proud of her as well.

'I going call the doctor,' Jessie decided.

'No.' Mina rolled over and sat up, clutching the pillow to her chest.

Jessie frowned at her. 'That man shave you again?' It was the first time she had ever directly referred to anything Felix had done, although certainly she had always known how deeply humiliated Mina had been by that particular quirk of her husband's. 'Putting my mark on you, my dear,' he would say with that terrifying smile of his. 'He is one sex maniac in truth,' Jessie remarked. 'You know what they calls a man like him? A satyr. Yes, sir. A satyr. I think one of these days he's going to do you an injury.'

Mina drew a long breath. 'Mr Petersen did not . . . shave me again,' she said. At least, not last night, she thought; he had been too busy doing other things. 'And he didn't hurt me. Is he still in the house?'

'I believe so.'

'Then will you ask to come to me? I wish to speak with him. And fetch me a jug of black coffee.'

Jessie surveyed her for a moment, and then left the room.

Mina lay down again. She had thought she could make it all right. She had come home *wanting* to make it all right, prepared to act . . . she could never love Felix. She wasn't sure she could ever even like him. But they were partners, and together they were going to prosper. Surely they could be friends. She gazed at him, standing by the bed.

'No ill effects, I hope?' he asked.

She sat up. 'No. And you can just stand there . . . Felix, you have made me into a prostitute.'

'Oh, come now. You're being as hysterical as you were that

192

first night, when you were practically half a virgin.'

'Felix . . .' She knelt on the bed. 'Felix, let's call it quits. The desire to score off each other, I mean. I . . . you have certain tastes that I do not share. It is unreasonable of you to force me, time and again. We are married. We are man and wife. Let's try to respect each other, even if we can't love each other. Surely that's possible.'

He was smiling at her, contemptuously, and she could feel her desire for reason dissolving into anger. 'I don't know whether it's possible or not, my dear Mina,' he said. 'But *I* am quite happy with the way things are. Force you? Don't make me laugh. You may not like what we do in the abstract, but when we're doing it you love it. Do you know how many orgasms you had last night? Seven. I counted.'

'You . . .' Mina leapt out of bed. 'You are the most horrible creature I have ever encountered in my life. You . . ' She gazed at the door as Jessie came in with the tray of coffee, on which she had thoughtfully put two cups. Jessie regarded her naked mistress with a quizzical expression, and then left.

'Your familiar,' Felix observed. 'She really is fond of you.'

'Can you imagine what she would say, or do, if she found out how we made love?'

'I have no intention of trying, my dear girl. What someone like Jessie says, or does, means absolutely nothing to me.'

'Felix . . .' She knelt at his feet. 'Listen to me. Last night you took me by surprise.'

'Because you were out of practice. You mean you didn't have a single man all the time you were in London? I thought you were going in search of a change. I assure you, I had a change. But none so good as you, Mina.'

'You . . . you are unspeakable.' But losing her temper could only be a waste of time, she knew. 'Listen to me, Felix. I am your wife. I accept that. I am prepared to be your wife, in everything. But I am your *wife*. Not some . . . some obscene plaything.'

He chucked her under the chin. 'But you are my favourite plaything, my dear girl. I paid a fortune for you, and I mean to enjoy you.'

'And if I refuse, from this moment? Absolutely and finally refuse?'

Felix sighed, and poured the coffee. 'The decision is yours, alas. I should regret it very deeply. But I never welsh on a contract. You're free to do anything you wish, Mina. And do you know something, because you have made me so happy these last few months, I am going to be generous.'

She stared at him, unable to believe her ears.

'At this moment I calculate that you owe me fourteen million dollars. Well, you got the Marchmount at a bargain price, and I suspect you could probably raise ten million on that. The Superb, well, right now it's just a heap of rubble, isn't it? But I would say the site alone is worth half a million. That's ten point five million, leaving you owing me two point five. But as I say, I'll write that off, Mina, to show my generosity. Just turn over all your property to me, and we will call it quits. I will even let you keep your clothes and jewellery. Providing you take your brats with you, of course.' He handed her a cup of coffee. 'If you leave, that is.'

'Ladies and gentlemen,' Mina shouted, teetering precariously on the table as one high-heeled shoe became entangled in a shattering fruit bowl, although there were sufficient male hands seeking to hold her up, 'I give you, the Superb Hotel!'

Applause swept through the dining room, out through the double doors into the lobby, crashed on to Seventh Avenue itself. The nosie was deafening, as people clapped and cheered, champagne corks popped, and the band struck up. 'For She's a Jolly Good Fellow!' If every second of the evening was costing a minor fortune – because she had determined to upstage the Plaza for this one evening in her life, and all the guests here tonight were invited at the hotel's expense – this had to be the pinnacle of all her ambitions.

And at least she could be sure of the quality of the banquet. Together with the French wines brought in by the case, she had imported Anatole Dubois himself from Monte Carlo to take sole charge of her kitchens, as indeed he had immediately taken charge of them like a drill sergeant. No speck of dust was permitted down there, and although he had installed the very latest in refrigerators, at extraordinary expense, every scrap of leftover food was discarded, so much so that Mina had hastily reinstated meals, or at least suppers, for the staff so that some of the waste could be consumed. But Anatole – the Superb

Anatole, he had taken to calling himself – had the ability to make food sound extraordinary as well as taste extraordinary. Instead of such cold and unembellished dishes as English Sole Meunière, or Chicken Sauté, or Ribs of Beef, as listed on the menu Mina remembered from the Plaza, here were Sole Anglaise Marie Walewska, or Poulet Sauté Grimaldi, or Roast Beef Superb, his speciality. Mina did not suppose the food tasted any better than that served by her rival, but it *seemed* to do so.

If Anatole was her great coup, the entire setting matched the occasion, not least in that it was a glorious June evening, and that somewhere up there Halley's Comet could be seen tearing through the skies, an event to make the most blasé New Yorker feel that somehow this year of 1910 had to be different to any other. The Superb, with its suggestion of the future, no less than its indication of what could be done in the present, in the young present, as typified by the twenty-five-year-old girl who had just climbed on to the table to give the toast – 'the youngest major hotelier in the world' the *New York Times* had called her – belonged to such a year.

As it equally belonged to the future, in its somewhat stark, but superefficient furnishing, the greys and blues of the paint on the walls – no wallpaper, because paper was an accumulator of dust and grime and was more difficult to clean. There were none of the usual overstuffed armchairs in the lounges, but severely functional leather furniture, guaranteed, it was claimed, never to cause backache, just as there were no large areas either of glass or gilt, and the electric light bulbs in the chandeliers were tinted with a very soft blue – no guest at the Superb was going to get either eyestrain or a headache.

There was the same carpeting, a soft royal blue, throughout the entire ten floors. The pictures on the walls were all watercolours, and all by various so far unknown New York artists – if the result would never send a connoisseur wild with excitement, here was surely tremendous patriotism, and again, faith in the future, when compared with the multi-million dollar foreign art collection housed at the Plaza. And so onwards and upwards. The elevators, all four of them, whirred noiselessly from floor to floor. The bedrooms were eye-openers, not large, but made to seem so by the cunning use of mirrors, and by the furniture; no fourposters, but severely functional

195

sleeping couches, again supported by the magic hint of being good for you, in their firm mattresses and low height from the floor. And each bedroom had its adjacent bathroom, in which, again with daring simplicity, there was no partition between toilet and bath. While opposite each bedroom there were two small singles, one for valet and one for ladies' maid, an essential in England, but a less common convenience in the democratic United States.

One critic might already have written that Mrs Petersen's dream seemed to have emerged from the pages of Jules Verne and Mr H. G. Wells. Another, less kindly, might have suggested that she had created less a luxury hotel than a luxury hospital. Mina preferred the third, who had said that 'Mrs Petersen has boldly created a vision of the hotel of the future; if style is truly the maximum of effect with the minimum of effort – or in this case, expenditure – then the Superb has more style than any other establishment in this city.' She could ask for nothing more than that.

People had come tonight to look at that style, as they had come to eat Anatole's food, and as they had come to be served, not only by the eager young waiters in sky blue tuxedos, but also by the charming young waitresses in sky blue evening gowns. Having girls wait on table was the final suggestion of the twenty-first century, the final touch of splendour, or vulgarity, according to taste. Certainly of titillation. But Mina was quite sure no critic would dare print what must have crossed their minds, without proof. And proof they were not going to get. Mrs Young patrolled the upstairs corridors, making sure that no bedroom was ever entered by a single chambermaid . . . and the girls had all been warned that the slightest suggestion of familiarity with a guest meant instant dismissal. Mina had already confronted the various unions with her arbitrary requirements and challenged them to do their worst – up to now they had not been able to decide what their worst might be.

But more even than the pleasure of being served by pretty girls, the guests had come for the feeling of being part of a gigantic international movement. For, opposite the reception desk in the lobby, and dominating the room, was the Superb Travel reception, where eager frock-coated young men waited with ready pens to answer any query, and satisfy every requirement – providing one was travelling the Superb way.

And a great many people were. Of the three hundred guests invited to dinner, one hundred and seventy were staying the night – the hotel capacity was two hundred beds – and fifty of those were booked in at the London Superb off Park Lane, due to arrive there in five nights' time, after departing New York tomorrow night on the *Mauretania*. Even better, forty of those fifty were spending only two nights in London, and then were coming straight back again by the *Lusitania* at the end of the week. It was a send-off beyond Mina's wildest hopes.

She was assisted down from the table, found herself in Felix's arms. 'My congratulations, my darling,' he said, and kissed her, while people cheered and slapped both of them on the back.

'Secure in the love and support of one of the world's richest men,' one of the columnists had written, 'Mina Petersen is able to indulge her dreams of what transatlantic living should be like. May some of her success rub off on us.'

Love and support, she thought, as she clung to him. Oh, indeed. She thought he did love her now, after two years, as much as he was capable of loving anything. Because in those two years she had filled his every obscene requirement. And he certainly was happy to support her. She wore the aura of success.

And she? She actually seldom dared to allow her own feelings to form coherent thoughts, much less words. Hate, and fear, and loathing came high on the list. But those were passive things, mere emotions. There were occasions when her brain, merely to retain its independence of him, considered deeper and darker concepts.

But the mainspring of all her feelings was a continuing anger. Because she had actually offered to be his wife, in spirit as well as physical being. And had been told that was not necessary, as long as she fulfilled their contract. Yet she no longer demurred, whatever his suggestion. Hating Felix, putting him into the class of dreams for the future, as she had once put Grandfather Doberley, was part of her nature, now – and she was never going to feel any pity for Felix, as she had for Grandfather. One day Felix would grow old, and decrepit, and become only half a man, like John Doberley. And then he would be at her mercy. And when she was finished with him, he would die. And that would be the answer to all of her

197

misfortunes, that precious moment; she did not doubt that Felix Petersen would be afraid of death. The devil! Whom she would eventually conquer.

Such anger she could justify. Where she knew her personality was changing, from good to evil, was in realising that hatred, a continuing anger against fate, and God, and humanity, was the mainspring of her success. She even hated all of the people here tonight, wished only to take their money, to glory in their envy, just as she hated her own staff, wished only to enjoy their obsequious adoration, from Joe Stark and Mrs Young down. She wondered what Charlie Stark would make of her now. He would be afraid to touch her with a bargepole, because she was at least as diseased at this moment as anyone on board the *William McKinley* those long ten years ago.

But she was what God had made her, she told herself angrily. And she would be, just that, and rise above them all, on evenings like this. If she allowed herself moments of special softness, such as when she could picnic with Jessie and the boys, the only three people in all the world she had allowed herself to love, these were merely to renew her strength, and her hatred. Just as her trips to London, however strenuous they might be in a business sense, were blessed weeks when she could be utterly alone, and thus utterly herself. Such a period was commencing tomorrow. Because she intended to supervise this first Superb Travel venture herself; she could not afford to have anything go wrong. And then, a whole month, away from Felix.

But Felix had read that article too. Now he kissed her again. 'I think this party is liable to continue all the way to England,' he said. 'I'd hate to miss any of it. I shall come with you. I don't have that much on at the moment, here.' He smiled at the look on her face, held her close again. 'I know you were seeking to escape me, my darling girl,' he whispered in her ear. 'So I promise, I shall not touch you throughout the voyage. I shall only observe. Because you will be working, will you not?'

The band played, streamers flew to and fro, people hugged each other and wept, the vast crowd on the deck oohed and aahed. Mina hugged and kissed the boys, embraced Jessie, and saw them to the gangplank; it was way past their bedtime, but she always allowed them to come to the ship to see her off – they loved exploring the huge liners. Then she joined Felix at the rail to wave. 'Quite an occasion,' he remarked, putting his arm round her waist. 'And it happens every week when one of these ships sail. Isn't that remarkable?'

'It's exciting,' Mina said. Because it was. She had now made the crossing by either the *Mauretania* or the *Lusitania* several times in the past few years – she would not consider travelling by any other line, and not only because she was virtually in business with Cunard, although she was realising that she might have to go into business with White Star as well if their new flagship *Titanic*, was as magnificent as she was supposed to be. But that decision was two years in the future. And White Star would have to go some to match Cunard, at least as regards her. She had long been one of the most pampered of passengers, because of her looks as much as her wealth. Tonight she had been made to feel like a queen, by the captain and officers, even upstaging Felix – and why not, as she had brought them fifty first-class passengers, with the promise of a whole lot more.

She smiled at Mr Howwinger, puffing through the throng towards her. 'Well, that's that, Mrs Petersen. Everyone's aboard, with all their gear, and not a hitch. So I'll wish you bon voyage. Mr Petersen.'

'Thank you, Mr Howwinger,' Mina said, squeezing his hand. Amazing how she had once hated him, and wished Jimmy to fire him. He had proved a tower of strength in seeing to all the last details. 'I'll wire you from London with names and numbers.'

'And I'll have everything waiting for you when you come back,' Howwinger promised. 'So . . .' He turned, as a woman hurried across the first-class promenade towards them.

'Mrs Petersen,' she was shouting. 'Mrs Petersen. My bag.'

Mina identified her as Laura Freindship, the wife of the copper millionaire, and just about her most important customer, on this voyage. And looking very upset. Mina's stomach did a lurch and seemed to land upside down. 'Your bag, Mrs Freindship?'

'My blue bag. A valise. It has all my cosmetics in it. And it is not in my cabin.'

Mina looked at Howwinger. 'I'll see to it right away,' the

manager said. 'Although I checked every label personally.'

'It's still at the hotel,' Mrs Freindship declared. 'I know it is.'

'That's not possible, Mrs Freindship,' Mina said. 'All the luggage was checked out, and every bedroom was checked out too. I did *that* personally.'

'Well, you must have missed it. I remember now, I stuck it down behind the bed.'

Mina stared at her in amazement, while Felix coughed into his handkerchief to avoid laughing. 'Behind the bed? Why?'

Laura Freindship waved her arm. 'How do I know, why? I just did. I do things like that. Walter shouts at me and I get upset. Now it isn't here. All my cosmetics. I don't know what I'm going to do. I just don't. It isn't here.'

Mina looked at Felix, whose eyes were dancing. Her dream, about to be busted wide open, because of the totally irrational act of a totally irrational woman. Like hell it will be, she thought. 'Felix, my dear,' she said, 'I wonder if you'd be so good as to take Mrs Freindship to the lounge and get her a drink.'

He raised his eyebrows.

'But my cosmetic bag,' Mrs Freindship wailed. 'I must have my cosmetic bag. My God, I knew this trip was going to turn out to be a disaster. I told Walter. I just knew it. And the expense . . .'

Mina squeezed her hand, when she would dearly have liked to slap her face. 'Don't *worry*,' she said. 'My husband will look after you for an hour, while I fetch your bag. Please, Felix,' she said.

He stepped forward, put his arm round the stricken woman's shoulders. 'I know everything will be all right, Mrs Freindship,' he said. 'Because Wilhelmina says it will be. She always keeps her word.'

Mina resisted the temptation to stick out her tongue at him, and ran along the deck, suddenly aware that the engines were rumbling beneath her. She reached the gangway at the same moment as Howwinger. 'Silly old bag,' the hotel manager grumbled. 'Don't they sell cosmetics on board this ship?'

'That's not the point,' Mina said, and stepped on to the gangway.

'There's no time to go ashore now, Mrs Petersen,' said the

officer in charge. 'We're just casting off. I'm about to send the gangway down.'

'Can't you delay?'

He looked shocked. 'Delay?'

'For . . . not more than an hour.'

'An *hour?* My dear Mrs Petersen, the engines are ready. The tugs are standing by. The orders have been given . . .' He hesitated, remembering that this *was* Mrs Felix Petersen. 'I could try to contact the Captain . . .'

'Forget it,' Mina said. 'But keep a look-out for me. I'll catch you up.' She pushed him aside, and hurried down the gangway, people parting before her as she reached the dock, Howwinger panting at her heels.

'What are we going to do?' he gasped. 'You'll miss the voyage.'

'Like hell I will. You,' she told him, 'are going to charter the fastest launch they have around here. It must be ready in forty minutes. Telephone the hotel in fifteen minutes and tell me which pier.'

'Fifteen minutes? But, Mrs Petersen . . .?'

'Just do it.' She summoned a taxi cab, got in. 'The Superb. And hurry.' She gave him a fifty dollar bill.

'Yes, *ma'am.*' They were there in ten minutes.

'There's another fifty if you wait and take me back,' Mina told him, and went inside. Staff and late guests stared at her in amazement as she ran through the lobby for the reception desk to grab the keys to Mrs Freindship's suite before dashing into the elevator; a message was clearly sent up to Mrs Young, for by the time Mina reached the third floor the housekeeper was waiting for her, hair in curlers. 'Mrs Petersen?'

Mina led her along the corridor, opened Suite 302, ran across the sitting room and into the bedroom, pulled the bed from the wall . . . and saw nothing. 'There was a valise behind that bed,' she said. 'A blue one.'

'Oh, yes, Mrs Petersen. The girls found it when they were tidying up, this evening. It's gone down to reception. Well, I know the Freindships are coming back to this apartment next week, but I felt it would be safer down there.' She peered at her employer. 'Aren't you sailing tonight, Mrs Petersen?'

'Yes, Mrs Young,' Mina said wearily, and regained the lobby, and the bag.

'A message for you, Mrs Petersen,' said the duty clerk. 'Mr Howwinger is on the line. He says to tell you Pier Thirty-Seven. Do you know what that means?'

'Yes,' Mina said, and ran back out to the waiting cab. Forty minutes after leaving the *Mauretania* she was being helped into the already puffing steam launch, while the uniformed crew peered at her fur coat and high heels and jewellery. 'But . . . this is a police boat.' Mina gasped.

'That's right, ma'am,' the sergeant said. 'Mr Howwinger here told us you'd missed the sailing, and that your father is seriously ill in England. Well, that's what we're here for, ma'am.'

'My . . .' Mina gazed at Howwinger, who raised his eyebrows. 'How fast can this thing go?'

'Thirty knots, ma'am,' the sergeant said proudly. 'We have turbines. Cast off there.'

'The *Mauretania* does twenty-five,' Howwinger pointed out.

'Not until she's reached the Ambrose Light and dropped her pilot,' the sergeant reminded him. 'It's a calm night. We'll catch her by then.' He pointed, and Mina stared into the darkness to see a huge, brilliantly lit city apparently slipping through the water, only a few miles away. Now the throttles on the police launch were wide open, and the pinnace was racing through the seas, siren blaring, spray flying to either side. Blood pumped through her own veins in total exhilaration. She was Mina Doberley. Mina Doberley! As Clancy had once said, she made dreams come true.

And she kept to her contracts. She went into the cabin, sat down at the table, opened her handbag, and began to write, as best she could in the constant movement.

The pinnace screamed up to the liner, and nosed alongside. Mina returned on deck, guarded by Howwinger and the sergeant himself. The accommodation ladder was down, but out here there was already a swell, and the launch bobbed up and down, while the combined washes of the two ships sent water sloshing over the platform at the foot of the ladder. And above the ladder the sides of the ship seemed to stretch forever. Fortunately sailors were now coming down to help her but, even so, the gap she had to cross kept opening and closing.

'Think you can make it, ma'am?' asked the sergeant.

'Watch me,' Mina said. She took off her shoes, and gave

them and her mink to Howwinger. 'Put them in my room, will you?' Then she gritted her teeth, drew a long breath, and stepped across the heaving water, a seaman's hand closing reassuringly on her arm; as she attempted to catch her breath, a wave surged over the bottom of the ladder, soaking her and the sailor to their waists.

'Mrs Petersen!' Howwinger gasped in horror.

'Nice work, ma'am,' the sergeant called, as the launch fell away into the darkness.

It was still a long, squelching climb up to the deck; soaking wet and without her mink she was freezing – but the sailor had relieved her of the valise, and there were others to help her up, until she arrived at the deck, panting, surrounded by eager passengers, by Felix, and by Mrs Freindship.

'My cosmetic bag,' Mrs Freindship screamed. 'Oh Mrs Petersen, you went and got it. Just like Mr Petersen said you would. Oh, Mrs Petersen, I didn't mean you to go to all that trouble. My dear, your feet are all wet. So is your dress. And you've no *shoes*.'

'It's a warm night,' Mina told her. 'The sea is absolutely delightful.' She tried to stop her teeth chattering, opened her handbag, and took out the cheque she had written on board the launch. 'This is yours, Mrs Freindship.'

'A cheque? Whatever for?'

'It is the cost of your trip, madam, there and back,' Mina said. 'When the Superb guarantees trouble-free travel or your money back, it means what it says.

Laura Freindship burst into tears, and threw both arms round Mina's neck. The onlookers started to clap. Mina looked past the woman at Felix, who was staring at her. For the first time since she had met him, she thought she saw admiration in his eyes.

Chapter 10

'Can you tell us how many Superb Travel clients were on board the *Titanic*, Mrs Petersen?' asked the reporter from *The Times* of London.

'Seventy-four,' Mina said. She spoke in a low voice, and wore black; her entire office in the London Superb had been draped in black.

'And how many of those survived, Mrs Petersen?' asked the reporter from the *Daily Telegraph*.

'As far as I am aware, forty-three,' Mina replied. 'You must know, gentlemen, that reports are still very sketchy. The *Carpathia* only docked in New York four days ago. But I can tell you that *none* of the male passengers travelling with Superb, over the age of ten, survived.' This was very important at a moment when the courage of the male upper classes was being suddenly called into question.

'May we have a comment from you on the tragedy, Mrs Petersen?' asked the reporter from the *Daily Mail*.

His colleagues looked at him with faint distaste.

'I am shocked and horrified,' Mina said. 'I cannot believe it has really happened. Of course the loss of so many valued clients affects me more deeply than anything else. Not because they were clients, but because they were my friends. Mrs Freindship and her husband, General Warlott, Mr and Mrs Brewster . . . I have known them all for years.'

'Mrs Freindship is amongst the few ladies missing, I believe?' asked the reporter from the *Daily Sketch*.

Presumably, Mina thought bitterly, the hundreds of *women*, as opposed to ladies, who had failed to reach the lifeboats were not relevant; she wondered which class she would have fallen into, in the eyes of the press? 'I believe that is correct,' she said.

'But that is Laura Freindship all over. She would never dream of leaving her husband's side.'

No doubt the silly woman had gone back to fetch her cosmetic bag. Because did Mina mean any of the nice things she was saying? Of course she was sorry to have lost so many valued clients. But they had never been her friends, however much they might have been faithful to Superb Travel; Mina Doberley did not have any friends, no matter how completely she might be trusted by those who put their affairs in her hands – she had earned that trust by hard work and determination. The loss of the ship itself, the finest vessel ever put to sea, everyone had said, and unsinkable, the experts had said, was actually far more unthinkable. That, and something else, which she hoped had not come to the notice of these eager young men.

But it had. 'Is it true, Mrs Petersen, that you were to sail on the *Titanic* and cancelled your passage at the last moment?' asked the reporter from the *Manchester Guardian*.

Mina gazed at him, her face cold. 'Yes,' she said. 'That is perfectly true.'

Because it was, and that was the most frightening, inexplicable thing of all. In the four years since 1908 she had crossed the Atlantic not less than sixteen times, each way; she had never cancelled a passage before. Last week she had done so, at the last moment, to attend a trade union meeting. Something else she had never done before. She had always told the New York union to do its damnedest, and had got away with it. She had wanted to adopt the same attitude to the English. But both Drummond and Pierre Raizman, the manager of the London Superb, had been concerned; it seemed that trade unionism in England was even more militant than in America, and England was so much smaller a country that it could flex proportionately more muscle. Recently there had been a wave of strikes, affecting even such vital industries as the coal-mines and the railways – the unrest could easily have spread to the hotel industry as well. There had also been a request from her London bankers for a conference. Both problems had in fact easily been resolved. She had made a few concessions to the trade union, and they had seemed content; the bank problem had not yet actually been solved, but she had an idea how it could be done – she intended to discuss it with Felix as soon as she returned to New York. Felix! Because the cancellation of her passage, and her consequent survival when so many others had died, had to be linked with the fact that she was Mrs Felix Petersen. Her devil! The thought gave her goose pimples.

As usual, he greeted her with a quite overwhelming display of solicitude. 'My dear Mina,' he said, holding her close, while the photographers snapped away, for prints of this so happy and successful – if so ill-matched as regards age and background – couple, were always good for a front page slot. 'If you knew how worried I was, until your wire arrived. It was an act of God. An absolute act of God!'

She gazed at him, and raised one eyebrow. 'An act of *God?*'

For a moment he frowned, and then smiled. 'Well, perhaps not. But I was still very worried. And about possible repercussions.'

'The tragedy may lead to a reduction in transatlantic passenger traffic,' Mina told him. 'But most people think it will only be temporary. In any event, there is no reflection whatsoever on Superb Travel. We chose what was reputedly the finest and safest ship ever to go to sea.'

As if any of that mattered, she thought, when compared with the more than one thousand dead in this most unexpected, and therefore tragic, of tragedies. But that was how Felix thought, and that was how she had to think too. From her point of view, only the Superb Travel and Hotel Business could ever matter – it was her life.

'So you will as usual come up smiling,' Felix observed. 'And now . . '

'I've kept count,' she said. 'I owe you twenty-two nights, consecutively.'

He laughed, and tucked her arm under his as they went towards the waiting Rolls Royce, cameras still exploding around them. 'I do adore your sense of humour, Mina. And I have so much to tell you. I have guests coming to supper tonight. Just the four of us. They're the most charming young couple, about your age, whose acquaintance I made about a year ago. Very well-bred very accommodating, absolutely determined to please. I just know you'll adore them, Mina. But

I thought I would get to know them better before introducing you to them. Now, I have no doubts at all that you are going to have the time of your life.'

Mina gazed at him. He must take me for a total fool, she thought. But she was past being disturbed, or angry, or even frightened. 'If they are so pleasant,' she said, 'then surely you do not need me at all.'

'But I do,' he insisted. 'Nothing is really worthwhile, without you. Besides, I want to watch, you see. You. When one is the sole actor in a drama, one never really has a chance to watch.'

And you expect me to say yes, she thought. To that. No, no; you *know* I'll say yes. To a further progression down the ladder of vice and lust. Could he possibly be getting bored with her? The suggestion of sharing her with another man, and also with a woman, while her husband watched, did not even shock her, any more. She was impervious to shock. She sometimes thought she was impervious to feeling. Physical feeling, anyway. Felix had made her so.

The odd thing was that she did not really have to agree, any more. Her Superb Travel had been so successful that she had nearly two million dollars already invested. And both hotels were now worth far more than she had paid for them. She was a multi-millionairess in her own right. She could sell both Superbs and thus repay Felix his twenty million and still clear about three, on which she and boys and Jessie could live in total comfort for the rest of their lives. So, here was the moment to spit in his eye, and pick up the pieces of her character, and attempt to regain her self-respect.

Except that her ambition was already soaring, in the direction of other plans, other ideas . . . and not only the banking idea, either. And here, she realised, was a means to make that expansion at his expense. Because she had almost known what he was eventually going to suggest, as a broadening of their sexual scope, and had taken certain precautions.

And did it matter who did what to her body? She *would* probably even enjoy it, when it happened. 'Well, then,' she said. 'Let us hope you enjoy what you see.'

'You look absolutely beautiful, as usual. Especially after . . .

how shall I put it? An energetic night?' Felix smiled across his desk at his wife. 'What do they say? A thing of beauty is a joy forever? Now come along, admit you enjoyed it.'

'It was the most disgusting experience I have ever had,' Mina said, evenly, pulling off her gloves.

'But you did enjoy it.'

She gazed at him. 'I came here to talk business. Not to reminisce.'

'So shoot.'

'One day I may do just that,' she agreed.

'At least we'd both go out in style,' he said. 'Me by a bullet, you by the noose. Or the chair. That would be a genuine sensation, the beautiful Mina Petersen executed for murder. They'd line up for miles.'

'I'm sure they would,' she said. 'Business, Felix, business. Coutts are a little disturbed. You know a part of the Superb service has always been to cash whatever cheques may be presented to us, either at hotels, or indeed on board the ships.'

'And you've been had. It was always on the cards.'

'Yes,' she said. 'I have been had. But by only a few bad pennies. And I have no intention of upsetting my regulars for the sake of one or two crooks. So I have thought of a solution. Superb traveller's cheques, which will be bought in whatever amount each customer considers necessary, before the commencement of each trip. This will give the customer's cheque time to clear, of course. The traveller's cheques would be cashable at any establishment owned by me, and on board the Cunard ships, and in time, I would hope, with Coutts' backing, to have them accepted elsewhere as well. However, Coutts themselves would of course need certain guarantees.'

'How much?'

'They estimate two million. Pounds, that is, of course.'

Felix raised his eyebrows. 'I reckon you could just swing that.'

'Perhaps I could, Felix. But I think the time has come to do some more expanding.'

'Oh, yes? That Chicago fellow, Statler, has got the idea. He's setting up a chain across the States.'

'I know that, and I have no intention of competing with Mr Statler. I wish to expand into Europe.'

'Now that I do not recommend at all,' Felix said. 'There is

208

going to be a lot of trouble over there one of these fine days. France and Germany are just straining to be at each other's throats, and now that France has an alliance with Russia, and Germany with Austria-Hungary . . . whereabouts in Europe were you thinking of?'

'Berlin,' Mina said. 'And Ostend in Belgium.'

'I don't get the link.'

'A large number of people from America, and from England, Felix, are visiting Berlin nowadays. And an even larger number of Germans are leaving Berlin for trips to England and America, either for pleasure or on business. The way Germany has been expanding, Berlin is rapidly overtaking Paris as the Capital of Europe, London excepted, of course. And Ostend is a famous, and European favourite seaside resort in virtually a straight line between Berlin and London. I have been doing some investigating. Ostend is served by a daily ferry service from Dover. That fits exactly into the pattern of services already being offered by Superb Travel. And then it is linked, through Brussels, with the east-bound transcontinental railway. Which eventually reaches Berlin.'

'It eventually reaches Moscow,' Felix pointed out.

'All in good time,' Mina said.

'Well, well,' Felix commented. 'You are even more ambitious than I had supposed, my dear girl. You realise these people speak either French or German?'

'I have been taking lessons,' Mina said.

'Fait accompli and all that, eh? How much is this expansion going to cost?'

'I am reliably informed that I can get what I want in Berlin for two million dollars, and for even less in Ostend; prices over there are not yet as inflated as in London or New York.'

'So it will be that or your private banking scheme. I would recommend the banking, and forget Europe.'

'I would like to do both, Felix.'

'Oh, yes?'

'I can finance one half of the expansion,' Mina went on, gazing at him. 'I need backing for the other.'

'Form a company and sell shares. In my opinion you should have done that years ago.'

'I shall never do that,' Mina said. 'I will never share one brick or one cent of my business. I would like you to put up the money for one or the other. You may take your choice. As you say, I can finance either.'

'You mean you wish a loan.'

'No, Felix. I wish a gift.'

He raised his eyebrows to their highest possible point. 'Now, tell me why I should do that?'

'Because you have broken our contract. I sold myself to you, as you would put it, from tit to toe, and with lips and hair thrown in. But only to you, Felix. Last night, by making me . . . perform with those people, commit adultery with that detestable young man, you exceeded your rights.'

'You really are the most absurd of women. Are you trying to tell me that on all those trips to London you don't commit adultery, time and again?'

'I have never committed adultery, Felix. Before last night, that is. Which was in your presence. And if you live to be a hundred you will never procure any evidence against me of betraying my marriage in any shape or form. However, I *have* taken legal advice regarding the obscenities to which I have been forced by you throughout our marriage.'

He stared at her. 'You have discussed our contract with a lawyer?'

'With John Drummond.'

'Jesus Christ! But . . .'

'Oh, indeed,' Mina said. 'And that was before you decided to farm me out. But I suspected it was something you had in mind; you've been dropping sufficient hints for the past year.'

Felix gave a brief laugh. 'And Drummond reckons you have a case to take to court? He's mad as a March hare. Or his brain was turned by listening to your titillating tale. You sold yourself to me, Mina. For a vast sum of money.'

'I'm not denying that, Felix. But what I sold myself to do is also there in the contract.'

'And you'd stand up in court and admit that, and then claim you're now calling a halt because we finally got four in a bed? Have you any idea of the scandal? Of the effect it will have on your high-falutin friends?'

Mina pulled on her gloves again. 'Would you care to put me to the test, Felix?' She smiled at him. 'I think that would be a mistake, for you, whatever it might cost me in reputation.' She stood up. 'I also think, after all your comments, that you would prefer to back Coutts than any European expansion. I shall write them to tell them so. It will not actually cost you a penny, Felix. You will merely place two million pounds on deposit with their bank. You will get the interest.' She leaned across the desk and kissed him on the nose. 'And a reputation as the most generous husband in all the world.'

'Ah, Frau Petersen, but this is truly Superb!' General Freilinghausen was tall and thin, dignified and urbane, magnificently uniformed in black and red. But also enthusiastic, although Mina suspected he was at least as enthusiastic about the beautiful American lady beside him as he was about the hotel itself, the opening celebrations going on all around him. 'So . . . so grand! I drink to you.'

'Why, thank you, Herr General,' she said in German; over the past year she had become quite proficient in both German and French, as she had spent so much time on the Continent. They had, in fact, been the two happiest years of her life. The Berlin Superb, the old Reinhold Hotel on the lower Wilhelmstrasse, had actually required very little doing to it; the Ostend Superb had been a more difficult proposition, because Ostend was strictly a resort town and a port, and had no distinguished small hotel for sale; it had been necessary to build, which had been more costly than she had originally estimated and had absorbed all of her spare capital. But she had enjoyed the challenge, and it would all be worth it when she finally got the doors open; certainly no one could doubt the success of her internal financing system for Superb travellers. She had even gone in for a little private banking of her own, by advancing selected customers their requirements in traveller's cheques several months before they were in a position to pay for them, or allowing them to pay over a period of several months – for a considerable fee as well as interest, of course. Whenever someone accused her of being somewhat mercenary, for so lovely and wealthy a woman, she would give a little smile and remind her client that her business was entirely separated from her husband's, and must stand or fall on its own feet.

Which was not absolutely true, but she was in no hurry to have to blackmail Felix again, simply because she was not sure it would work again. And this was because, when she had almost given up hope, the signs of her ultimate victory had suddenly become apparent. Felix was, she reminded herself, twenty-five years older than her, and thus fifty-four. But he was still a splendidly fit man, to the casual observer, and in his mind, at least, still as much of a satyr as he had ever been – but without warning he had been overtaken by that most dreadful of masculine misfortunes, a creeping impotence. Initially she had supposed him ill – but he was obviously perfectly healthy. Only afraid. This in itself had been an enormous victory, even if a precarious one. Two or three nights of almost frenzied frustration would be followed by an enormous explosion of sexual energy which would leave her as battered and as exhausted as ever in the past. But now she knew the end was in sight. Even more important, she had been spared any more of those dreadful orgies he had experimented with briefly in 1912. She knew these had not been ended out of any concern for her feelings, or even out of any fear of further blackmail on Felix's part – he simply could not stand the thought of being seen in his growing weakness by anyone else.

This lack of confidence had slowly spread even to his relations with herself. The old rigid insistence upon four nights out of seven had long been abandoned, by him; if she often insisted upon carrying out the terms of their contract to the letter, it was merely to taunt him, to lie naked beside him, to be caressed by him, and know that there was nothing else he could now do to her. To know that, at last, she was the stronger. A strength which gave her the power to order her own life as she chose, at last, knowing that she could be away from him as often and for as long as she chose; if he fell upon her like a hungry bear when she returned, he could never sustain the energy of his passion for more than a single night, and was then left to the mercy of her fingers. Truly, she thought, the wages of sin.

Thus, two happy, vigorous, consuming years. James and Harry were at high school now – her memory of what her father had told her of his miserable youth had decided her against sending them to an English public school such as Eton, although she could well afford it – and thus she endeavoured to time her long stays in America to coincide with their holidays, when they would take trips together into the mountains, always accompanied by Jessie of course, or go skiing in Vermont, where she had bought a small house. When they were at school was the time for business, and increasingly this was comprising foreign business. The New York Superb ran as smoothly as she could wish, under the meticulous care of Howwinger, and Raizman kept things on as even a plane in London, while her business affairs were increasingly being handled by John Drummond, in whom she had the utmost confidence. But new business was her province, and thus this summer had been the first exception she had had to make to the holiday rule. She had toyed with the idea of bringing the boys and Jessie to Europe, and had decided against it, knowing that she simply would not be able to spare them the time to entertain them or even to be with them. Because this summer, with the Berlin Superb ready and the Ostend Superb at least nearing completion, the third stage of her great plan was about to happen.

It had not been accomplished without a great deal of effort and determination. The cross-Channel ferries were not Cunard liners, and did not employ the same devoted crews. But ship travel, at whatever level, was from the point of view of an organiser a bed of roses when compared with rail travel, simply because when the passangers and their luggage and their idiosyncracies were finally installed upon a ship which had sailed, it was possible to relax for the duration of the voyage. Trains had a habit of stopping in stations, at which time people who had not previously wanted to do so suddenly wanted to get off, and there were borders to be crossed and delays to be encountered. Mina had had to make all the first six trips herself, and wondered at the absence of grey hair at the end of it. But now everything was under control, and her clients were in the hands of reliable couriers, prepared to cope with anything. Thus had her reputation grown. Superb Travel was the only way to go anywhere, in the eyes of the wealthy. Once again a victory, somehow epitomised by dining at the Berlin Superb, with a handsome general beside her, looking at a crowded dining room filled with happy travellers. Superb travellers. It was marvellously exciting to watch her empire growing, to know that she was getting richer by the day, almost by the minute – and thus to know that she was growing stronger by the day, while Felix was growing weaker. The day of reckoning might not yet actually have arrived, she would think as she lay in bed waiting for slumber, but it was at hand; the thought never failed to send her into a deep sleep.

And meanwhile she was the toast of two continents. And already making plans to invade a third. As Felix had reminded her, one did not have to leave the train in Berlin; it was possible to go all the way, via Moscow, to Vladivostock or Port Arthur in Manchuria. Which was only a short sea trip from Yokohama. And then . . . because surely that had to be the ultimate dream, passengers who would travel the Superb way, right round the world.

And if that might have to remain a dream for a few years yet, until she had accumulated a little more capital of her own – she thought of it as Plan Five, where Berlin and Ostend were Plan Three .and London had been Plan Two – she had a more attainable objective closer at hand, in yet another continent. More and more Americans were seeking instant culture by means of visits to the Mediterranean. And at the far end of the Mediterranean lay the centre of the most ancient culture of them all – Cairo. Somewhere she had always meant to visit. The ascent of the Nile, the Superb way. Plan Four.

She blew a gentle kiss at the general. Like every man who sat beside her at dinner, he could not understand why so beautiful a woman, separated by several thousand miles from her husband, would never do more than flirt; she wondered what he would say if he knew that the very thought of sex filled her with revulsion.

'It has turned out well,' she said. 'I really am very pleased.'

'And you are going to stay in Berlin for some time?'

'Good heavens, no, Herr General. There are so many other things I have to do. Now that the Berlin Superb appears to be going as planned, I am leaving tomorrow, for Ostend. There is a lot of work to be done there.'

'Ostend,' he said thoughtfully. 'The Ostend Superb. When do you open there?'

'Oh, God knows,' she said. 'It's already the end of July. There's no hope of being ready before October. I am missing the entire season. Do you know, I am having to board out my guests at the Splendide, which is not only tiresome but costing me money. It is all very disappointing.'

'If you cannot open before October,' Freilinghausen pointed out, 'you will in any event also miss the end of the season. Nobody travels in October unless they have to. So why do

214

you not just leave the opening until next year. The Spring, perhaps.'

Mina raised her eyebrows. 'I will have *some* custom, Herr General.'

'I wonder, Frau Petersen. I wonder. There is an air of crisis in Europe. Perhaps you have not noticed this.'

'There is always an air of crisis in Europe, Herr General.'

'Some crises are, how shall I put it, more critical than others, perhaps. I am thinking of the murder of the Archduke Ferdinand, last month.'

'Oh, that,' Mina said. 'As I understand it, Austrian royalty are always being murdered, or committing suicide with their mistresses – it's the only way they ever die off.'

Freilinghausen did not respond to her attempt at humour. 'Nevertheless, my dear Frau Petersen, I would recommend that you leave the opening of the Ostend Superb until next year. And perhaps, for the time being, go back to America yourself, eh?'

It was almost as if the general was one of Felix's agents, Mina thought. Or had been trying to tell her something. Perhaps he was both. Did he think there was going to be a war over the Archduke's death? Felix certainly thought so. Felix held the opinion that only good fortune and fast talking had averted a European war on more than one occasion in the recent past. But she did not really see how it could affect her plans in any major way. Wars were fought along frontiers; Berlin was an enormous distance from any frontier, except perhaps that with Russian Poland – and not only were the Germans utterly contemptuous of Russian military ability, but even if the Russians were to win they were hardly likely to wish to damage a major city: the Germans hadn't destroyed Paris in 1871, indeed most of the damage had been caused by the Parisian mob. There was no such thing as a Berlin mob. While Belgium was perpetually neutral. All the Great Powers had agreed to that. So there was no danger to the Ostend Superb. And she was an American citizen. A war might be bad for business, but it could hardly pose any danger to Mina Petersen. It might even be exciting.

And even a business sag was not likely to last more than a few months, because no modern war could possibly last longer than that, according to the pundits. The war of 1870-71 had been over in six months, virtually, and had affected business not at all, except in Paris. Paris, she mused. Supposing the Germans were to beat the French with the same ease this time, there might be some property going cheaply in Paris. She had deliberately stayed away from the French capital so far, because of its expense. But if the opportunity was to be presented to her . . .

Meanwhile, there was still a great deal to be done. She had had to start from scratch in Ostend, buying two seafront houses, knocking them down, and building on the sites. It had been a long two years; work had commenced before Christmas 1912, and as she had told the general, there was no hope of opening much before Christmas 1914. But at least it was nearly done; only the interior decorating remained, and this she wished to see at least under way before she returned home, despite the wires waiting for her from Felix, some plaintive, some angry, some demanding, some begging. Well, he would just have to wait. When she returned, she would, as usual, throw his forty days or whatever he claimed in his face – and then tell him that she would in any event be returning to Belgium for the opening. The wages of sin, she thought, with grim satisfaction. And did she have no wage bill to meet? If she did, it was a long way in the future; she had never been healthier. Or more confident.

But she certainly wanted to be home for Thanksgiving, however temporarily, and if that was still a long way off, the work at least had to start. She stood in the huge empty lobby and tapped her boot on the parquet floor, anxiously watched by the cleaning women; Monsieur Pleydel, the interior decorator, was late. What was even more irritating, Monsieur Castenau, the architect, was also late. She knew he liked to return to his Brussels home every night, but really, he should be able to get down to Ostend by ten o'clock in the morning.

'Mrs Petersen?' The uniformed boy was breathless.

'Yes,' Mina asked.

'I am from the Splendide across the way, madame. There is a telephone call for you. Most urgent. From Brussels.'

The Superb's telephones had not yet been connected. Mina

followed the boy across to the rival establishment, wondering what on earth could be the matter; no one seemed to be doing any work, and people were gathered in anxious huddles on the street – while she could see the Dover ferry steaming out of the harbour, at least three hours before schedule. Things like that, with her life built around timetables, bothered her.

'Mrs Petersen.' The Splendide's manager was waiting for her. 'What terrible news. My dear Mrs Petersen . . .'

'There was a telephone call for me,' Mina said. Definitely something had happened. To Felix? Her heart bounded. Or to the children? Her heart lurched.

'In here.' He hurried her into his office, and she seized the receiver.

'Hello?'

'Madame? Madame?' The woman's voice spluttered down the line. 'It is I, Madame Petersen, Madame Castenau. Philippe asked me to call to tell you that he cannot come to Ostend this morning. He has been called to the colours.'

'To the colours?'

'The army, madame. The army. He is a reservist. It is the Boche. They have crossed the frontier. Of Belgium, madame. We are invaded.'

'A telegram, Madame Petersen,' said M. Chaffaux, panting as usual. He had panted almost every day since the Germans had crossed the frontier, and that was some two months ago.

But in that time she and he had become very good friends. Mina had had to move into the Splendide herself, and now she was the only remaining guest; M. Chaffaux was obviously not sure that she was any longer worth the trouble when there were safer places to be – were there safer places to be, for a Belgian? – but the presence of the redoubtable Mrs Petersen provided a certain reassurance, even while sheltering in a cellar during a bombardment. There had been several bombardments, to Mina's concern. She had not personally been frightened – it was unthinkable that a German could aim a shell at Mina Doberley – but the Superb could very easily have been hit. As it happened only the odd pane of glass had so far been shattered, and the Splendide had also escaped serious damage, for which good fortune M. Chaffaux was clearly prepared to thank the presence of his distinguished guest. So she smiled at him as she slit open the envelope. She had a very good idea of what she was going to read. And she was right.

'ARE YOU MAD QUESTION ARE YOU ALIVE QUESTION INSIST YOU RETURN IMMEDIATELY STOP FELIX.'

'What will you reply?' Chaffaux inquired. 'Or will you go? Madame, I truly feel that you should go. The Boche will soon be here.'

Mina could no longer argue with that. Belgium had actually been defeated, as a military force, within the first week of the war. Ostend had become a pitiful depot for the arrival of the wounded, waiting to be shipped out to hospitals in France and England, men utterly shattered by their exposure to the horrors of twentieth-century firepower. Yet the arrival of the Germans had been delayed for week after week, and month after month, because they had been concentrating on their main objective, the capture of Paris. Throughout September the battle had raged the length and breadth of Flanders, the sound of gunfire clearly audible even on the coast. Throughout the month the wounded had trailed through the port, and British reinforcements had from time to time landed; like everyone else she had lined the street to cheer them on, quite why she did not know, apart from the fact that they were her kith and kin, even if once removed. She certainly had no positive ideas as to the rights and wrongs of this conflict, and like most impartial observers, if she had been prepared to condemn the Germans for violating Belgian neutrality in the first place, she was also inclined to discount the tales of rape and pillage which had seeped in from refugees before the German advance.

Thus she had stayed, trying to carry on as if there was no war at all, as if completing the Superb was still only a matter of weeks, even if all work had come to a standstill – there were neither men nor materials to be spared.

She had also stayed because she was an American, and therefore felt she should be above the fears and the passions, or even the disruptions, of a European war, and because now she had a stake in this country, and she knew that were she not here, and should Ostend become the centre of a battle, her hotel would probably be left a heap of rubble. She was not at all sure

218

how she was going to prevent that happening, even by standing in front of it with her arms folded – but she certainly meant to try. The Ostend Superb represented her money, not Felix's. It was the first of her investments to be financed entirely by her.

And finally, she had stayed because she was Mina Doberley. She was internationally famous, internationally acclaimed. Last month she had even made a return journey to Berlin, travelling north to Holland, and taking the train from Rotterdam. And had been welcomed as enthusiastically as ever in the past by a German society confident of an early victory, eager to explain that so widespread a conflict had been provoked by the British joining in, to nobody's advantage, and that swinging through Belgium had been essential to bring about a speedy end to the conflict, and thus less bloodshed. Well, she did not see that they had been thinking very accurately there. Paris had not been taken, and the French and British armies had not been defeated, whatever had happened to the Belgians. While nobody knew whether or not to believe the extravagant claims of victory over the Russians coming out of Poland.

Of more immediate concern to her, she had found the Berlin Superb almost empty – her fellow Americans had all left for home. But this had to be a temporary setback; the very size of the casualties reported by both sides meant that the conflict could hardly last very much longer.

She thus had no intention of going anywhere until it was resolved, so that she could get her project restarted with the minimum of delay. Her reply to Felix's telegram was merely a variation on the theme she had been using for two months. 'BATTLE APPROACHING CRUCIAL MOMENT STOP HOSTILITIES WILL SOON CEASE STOP CANNOT ABANDON HOTEL STOP HOME FOR CHRISTMAS STOP MINA.'

M. Chaffaux counted the words lugubriously. 'You may be home for Christmas, madame,' he said. 'Few Belgians will be.'

Mina squeezed his arm. 'Even the Germans will be tired of fighting by Christmas,' she said. 'Then we will all be going home.'

Mina stood beside M. Chaffaux and his staff to watch the

Germans enter the city. The previous day the last Belgian soldiers had departed, and with them many of the residents; nearly all the fishing boats had left the harbour, and of course the ferries had long ceased to run. Ostend was like a ghost town, with just the grey waves of the North Sea beating against the piers and the promenade, their own unceasing rumbling lost in the greater rumbling that came from the east and south. But now the greyness had reached the very streets.

She was, however, impressed with the smartness and discipline of the German soldiers, even if their brusqueness as they checked houses for snipers and shouted at those people who had turned out to watch their entry was rather disconcerting. But no doubt, she reflected, they had been sniped at in other cities. Certainly she had to suppose, whatever the uncertain news from further south, that as the invaders held Brussels and Antwerp, and had now reached the sea within a few miles of the French frontier, they were the victors as regards Belgium. What would happen next was impossible to say. But surely, if Belgium was definitely out of the war, she should be able to get on with her hotel.

But first she had to get on with the conquerors. General von der Goltz came up the steps of the Splendide, uniform freshly pressed and moustached face severely composed, followed by his staff, peeling off his gloves as he approached the reception committee, his sword slapping his thigh and his spurs jingling. He had entered the city at the head of his troops, and for the occasion had worn the pickelhaube; this he now removed, and one of his aides stepped forward with a peaked cap, heavily decorated with gold braid. 'M. Chaffaux?' he demanded.

The hotelier advanced and bowed; he was very nervous.

'This hotel will be our military headquarters for this city,' the general said. 'It is a pleasant spot, overlooking the sea. We will be able to watch the English navy, eh? Your staff will prepare the rooms.' He gazed at Mina, and the stern lines of his face dissolved into a smile. 'You will be Frau Petersen.'

'Why, yes,' Mina said, deciding against curtsying; *she* was not one of the conquered people.

'My dear lady.' Goltz kissed her hands. 'General Freilinghausen sends his warmest regards. But also, alas, a message. It was received at the Berlin Superb just three days ago, and he sent it on to me, to deliver personally.' He snapped his fingers and an aide hurried forward with the envelope.

'It will be from my husband,' Mina said. 'He wishes me to return to America.'

'And you do not wish to go?'

'I wish to know what is to happen to my hotel. It is not yet complete.'

'Ah.' Goltz turned to look across the street at the Superb. 'It looks complete.'

'The building is finished, but the interior is not yet decorated, and it is not yet fully furnished. I must point out, Herr General, that that hotel is American property.'

'Of course. And will be treated as such, I promise you. Why do you not read your message?'

Clearly he knew what was in it. Mina slit the envelope. 'ESSENTIAL YOU RETURN IMMEDIATELY JAMES SERIOUSLY ILL DO NOT DELAY FELIX.' Mina's heart gave a great lurch. James? But . . . he had seemed perfectly well the last time she had seen him. But that had been four months ago. On the other hand, it would not be beyond Felix to tell a lie to draw her back. But how could she risk that it might not be a lie? She raised her head.

General von der Goltz was looking suitably compassionate. 'I have already arranged transport for you, Frau Petersen, from here to Holland. To Scheveningen. From there you can obtain a passage to England, and thence across the Atlantic. You will be home in seven days.'

'I am most grateful, Herr General,' she said, but she was still gazing at the hotel.

'And I shall place guards on your property, Frau Petersen,' Goltz said reassuringly. 'I will give you my word, as a German officer, that not one iota of damage will be done to your hotel, at least by any German, however long this war may last.'

'James,' Mina said. 'Oh, James.' She held his hand between both of hers as she sat on his bed, gazed into his eyes.

'I am all right now, Mother,' he assured her. 'Just a little stiff. But Dr Chalmers says I'll soon be all right again'.

He actually looked all right; thinner than usual, but that was no bad thing. But the stiffness . . . every movement seemed to take him an eternity and apparently it was still too painful for him to move his legs at all.

'What on earth *was* it?' she demanded in the privacy of the doctor's office. 'He's only eleven years old.' She frowned as a dreadful thought crossed her mind. 'It's not something hereditary, is it?' Because Jimmy had certainly lived a very irregular life, both before and during his marriage to her. There could be no saying what disease he might have picked up.

Dr Chalmers smiled, as reassuringly as he could. 'Good heavens, no, Mrs Petersen. James caught an infection.'

'An infection?' The only infections she knew about were things like measles and mumps – and cholera.

'It's actually a more common illness than is generally realised,' Chalmers said. 'But we're only just beginning to understand anything about it. The medical term is poliomyelitis.'

'Poliomyelitis? My God!' It sounded dreadful.

'It's a disease which attacks the spinal cord,' Chalmers explained. 'Young James has had a fairly typical illness. Rapid onset, high fever, total paralysis for a day or two, because, as you know, most of your movements are connected with the spinal column. I should tell you that there is a high incidence of fatality from this disease, especially in young people. Indeed, many doctors call it infantile paralysis.'

'Fatality?' Mina shouted.

'In its early stages, yes. Obviously, if the paralysis becomes so complete that breathing is affected, then the patient will die. Of course James,' he added hastily, 'had no such complications. But we were naturally concerned that such a development could take place, as soon as we had actually diagnosed polio, which is why we asked your husband to send you an urgent cable. But I do assure you that at no time was James' life in any danger, nor is it now.'

Something in his tone made Mina suspicious. 'But? There is a but?'

'Well . . .' Chalmers chewed his lip. 'As I have said, the disease attacks the spine. With varying intensity. At one end of the spectrum, death from respiratory paralysis. At the other, no after-effects at all. In the centre, the vast majority of cases, there is usually . . . well . . . perhaps some lingering difficulty as regards movement.'

Mina stared at him. 'Are you trying to tell me that my son has become a cripple?'

'A cripple is too all-embracing a word, Mrs Petersen,' Chalmers said, his embarrassment obvious. 'It is too early to say for sure. He has problems in moving his legs and arms, certainly. But with proper exercise, and given time . . .'

'A cripple,' Mina said. 'Oh, my God, James . . . he's just a *boy*, doctor. Can't something be done?'

Chalmers sighed. 'I'm afraid there is no known cure for polio, Mrs Petersen. We must pray that James will be able to live a normal life.'

'Pray,' Mina said bitterly. 'Fifty per cent. I have fifty per cent of a son.'

'For God's sake, Mina,' Felix begged. 'Will you stop that pacing and come to bed. That's all I ask tonight, that you come to bed.'

Mina gazed at him. He lay on his back, naked – a repulsive sight. But also an impotent one, at this moment, and probably for the entire night. That was all he could ask, nowadays, to be able to lie on her belly and hope that something might develop. How are the mighty fallen.

And how tasteless the victory. Because it had come too late. She had known Felix was going to be brought low, one day, and had waited with a deadly patience for the revenge that would then be hers. Because she was immortal. Strong in her physical health and strength, her indomitable spirit, her certainty as to her goals and how to reach them – and in her complete severance from the cloying weaknesses of religion, of sentiment, of all human fallibility, she had never doubted that nobody and nothing could harm Mina Doberley.

But Fate, or a vengeful deity, could still reach out with icy fingers and tap those dear to her on the shoulder. Pray, Chalmers had suggested. He did not know the impossibility of that. But just down the corridor James would be lying, probably awake, staring at the ceiling, knowing he would not be able to leave his bed unaided, unable to understand why.

And still hoping that his condition might be temporary.

He had lain like that for six months. She had not celebrated her birthday, and it had been the most miserable Christmas she had ever known. James' arms were now as strong as they ever had been, but all her efforts, whether by encouragement or massage, or by long hours spent with him in a heated swimming pool, as recommended by Dr Chalmers, had failed to enable him to use his legs with any degree of certainty. These had been the longest six months of her life; she could almost be grateful that because of the war there was so little business to impinge upon her time.

But what had they been like for him?

'It isn't as if he's your only son,' Felix grumbled, catching her hand and drawing her down to him. 'You have two, you know. Harrison is perfectly fit. And James isn't even going to die. So maybe he won't ever be a baseball star. Neither was I, even with two good legs.'

One day, Mina thought, I am going to take your neck and squeeze all the breath from your lungs, you lousy, superannuated lecher. One day. But not now. She still needed his backing, and besides, as he had laughingly told her once, she would be electrocuted for it. When he went, she wanted to laugh at his grave.

Besides, he was the cross she had to bear. She had always supposed that, and as she had gone from strength to strength had been content with it. As long as she had to suffer Felix, she would succeed – he was a sort of human *Picture of Dorian Gray*. But recently she had even been mastering him, as now, when only she could bring him relief, let alone satisfaction, and when she alone was in possession of the secret of his impotence, to a man like Felix a far more devastating potential skeleton in his closet even than if he had been an escaped convict. She had enjoyed that; she enjoyed it still. Only that had not pleased God at all. That was making her life too easy. Every man, and every woman, especially a Mina Doberley, had to have their cross to bear. Escape the burden of Felix, and be prepared to watch James suffer for the rest of his life.

What absolute nonsense, and defeatist thinking. She lay on her back, her husband now sleeping peacefully, and stared at the ceiling. God had nothing at all to do with it, as perhaps He had had nothing at all to do with the deaths of Mama and Papa.

James, like them, had caught a germ. Even guilt had nothing to do with it. She had to remember that. She did not deal in dreams, or in superstitions. Mina Doberley dealt in realities. Her only guilt was in leaving her sons for too long while she pursued her continental ambitions. She had opted to remain in Belgium, protecting her hotel, protecting her investment, to the exclusion of every other consideration – while all the time her son had been getting ready to die.

But he had not died. Because he was *her* son. And if he could not walk, well, he could still live. She would see to that. And she would never leave his side again. She felt suddenly more relaxed, and more determined, than she had at any time since returning to America last October. Then the world seemed to have suddenly come to a full stop, leaving her in a gigantic limbo, suspended in mid air, with the collapse of everything she held dear apparently imminent. But six months had passed, and nothing had actually collapsed. Nothing had even happened in the war. It had settled down into a long and meaningless winter stalemate, all hopes of an early victory, or of a victory at all, apparently vanished for either side, as the massive armies glared at each other across a thousand miles of mud and barbed wire. If these six months had proved anything, it was the utter futility of war, in modern conditions and with modern weaponry. Now it was just a case of which side would make the first overture for peace; all the political commentators were confident this would be done by summer – President Wilson, for all his determination not to allow America to become involved, was apparently standing by to act as mediator, as Theodore Roosevelt had done between Russia and Japan in 1905 – and then the armies would be disbanded and the whole absurd fiasco would be relegated to history. And then life could begin again. And profits would begin again. And her onward march could begin again.

'Letters,' Jessie announced at breakfast, in her usual cheery way. Jessie was in fact far more cheerful nowadays than she had been for a long time. She had been shattered by James' illness, having been left in charge of the boys. But Mina had refused to allow her to accept any blame whatsoever, had convinced her that it was, as Dr Chalmers had described, a bacteria which she could not have prevented even had she known about it. Added to that relief was the pleasure of having her mistress home for an entire winter, and also of observing, in her quiet but watchful manner, that relations between Mina and her husband were definitely changing, in Mina's favour. Gone were the bites and the bruises, the utter exhaustion. Gone too were the often desperate moods of despair, of shame and revulsion. Jessie of course knew nothing of their true relationship, or their contract, had no idea that Mina might still have to perform acts which would be deeply shaming to other women just to keep Felix sane – and even more, to keep him dependent on her. Because this was a new and unexpected aspect of the victory she was slowly gaining. Felix at last needed her more than he wanted her, because he dared not turn to anyone else. But Mina never confided in Jessie, for fear the older woman might not understand the true depths of her mistress's mind, or agree with everything she might discover there.

But she remained the best of friends, fussing over the boys as she placed their cereal before them, pouring the coffee, sidling round Felix as if he were still the devil. It was actually, Mina thought, a happy domestic scene, father, mother, and two sons with their old family retainer – only it was one and a half sons, for James sat in his wheelchair.

'Damned prices are slipping again,' Felix grumbled, looking through his latest stock market returns. 'One would have supposed they'd have got used to the idea of a war being on by now. We're not involved.'

Mina hardly heard him. She had opened the letter from John Drummond. 'It is just a suggestion,' the solicitor had written, 'but my information is that there are several very promising hotels lying empty and idle, Paris being still virtually under siege. A positive offer might well secure one well below the true market price. I have taken the liberty of consulting with Coutts on your behalf, and although of course they are not in a position to advance any large sums while the present crisis continues, they advise me that their American correspondents might well be willing to help; you could offer various other of your properties as collateral. I appreciate that this will involve long-term borrowing, something you have up to now managed to avoid, and I am of course assuming that you have not changed your mind as you outlined it to me when last we spoke about approaching Mr Petersen for further financing. I am sure you are right there, in all the circumstances. But I strongly recommend that you give the Paris project some consideration, believing, as I do, that I understand your long-term aims. Of course I realise that the investment will have to, as it were, lie fallow for the duration of the war, but that cannot be very much longer, and . . .'

Mina allowed the letter to rest beside her coffee cup, and gazed at the wall. Some consideration. What consideration did she need? 'Paris,' she said, half to herself. Linked, when the war ended, with London and Berlin, and Ostend, of course. The whole to be linked with New York. And with Cairo? And Moscow? And Tokyo? More important, just planning it meant that she would be living again. Expanding. Making dreams into realities.

'Paris?' Felix inquired. 'Jesus Christ! Don't start that again.'

'I have often asked you not to blaspheme in front of the children, Felix,' Mina said. But his comment merely concluded her decision. 'John Drummond informs me there may be some bargains there. I shall have to go and see.'

'Paris?' Felix shouted. 'Paris, France? Has no one told you there's a war on?'

'The war is not being fought in Paris, Felix,' Mina pointed out, as she might have remonstrated with a small child. 'You seem to forget that I was in Ostend throughout the battle for Belgium, much closer to the front line than Paris is, and was in no danger at all. I shall go and look, and make a decision, and then come home again.'

'Take me with you, Mama,' James said. 'Don't leave me behind.'

Mina's head turned, sharply. But she had just resolved, last night, that she would never leave him again. And why not take him? An ocean voyage might be just the thing to lift his spirits for a fresh effort. Of course she could not take him to France. She had no intention of taking any personal risk, and she knew that the English Channel and the Bay of Biscay were infested with German submarines prepared to shoot at any English vessel on sight. The only safe way to get to Paris was to take a Dutch ship to Rotterdam, thence travel through Germany, neutral Switzerland, and thence into France well south of any fighting. There would be stoppages and delays, and the whole journey would be quite unthinkably arduous. But how her

227

blood tingled at the thought of such an adventure. She would be able to visit the Berlin Superb and make sure that all was well. She might even be able to fit in a trip to Ostend. James could never cope with all of that. But if she took him as far as England, and left him there with Jessie to look after him for the fortnight or so she would be away . . . that would be very different to abandoning him on the far side of the Atlantic.

She gazed at Harry, who gazed back at her, his lower lip trembling, afraid to ask.

'I shall take you both,' she decided. 'And Jessie. We'll have a holiday.'

'Mama!' Harry screamed, springing up and throwing both arms round her neck.

'Mama!' James shouted, heaving in his wheelchair and bringing tears to her eyes.

'You are quite crazy,' Felix said. 'I absolutely forbid it.'

Mina raised her eyebrows. 'You forbid it, Felix? It is a business trip.'

'Taking the boys?'

'The boys are no concern of yours,' she reminded him, quoting their contract for the second successive sentence.

'They have schools to attend, haven't they?'

'James is not going to school for a while,' Mina told him. 'And if I decide to give Harry an extra holiday, that is my business. Nobody else's.'

'Yippee!' Harry shouted.

Felix glared at her. 'Have you no sense of responsibility? And what *about* the war? There are submarines out there in the Atlantic, waiting to attack merchantmen, certainly those flying the British flag.'

'There are no submarines in the Atlantic, Felix, and you know that. There may be one or two around Britain itself, but none of them has yet been able to attack either the *Mauretania* or the *Lusitania*, for the simple reason that there is no submarine afloat that can catch them and force them to stop.'

'And suppose they just shoot, without warning?'

'Oh, really, Felix, you do dream up the most horrific absurdities. The ship we sail on won't be carrying troops, or guns. Or even much cargo. She'll be a passenger liner. Have you ever heard of anyone attacking a passenger liner without warning? Particularly the Germans. You seem to forget that I know them very well. They are the most perfect gentlemen. And obviously Cunard think so too, or they wouldn't have restarted their service, week in and week out.' She got up to consult a catalogue.

Felix also rose. 'Nevertheless, I absolutely forbid it. And that is my last word on the matter.'

Mina turned to face him, the catalogue in her hands. 'Your last word? Do you seriously suppose you can stop me going?'

'I do.'

'And I say you can't, Felix,' Mina said, speaking very evenly. 'Our contract says that I am entitled to depart the United States whenever it is required by my business activities, and for as long as I deem necessary, providing only that I make it up to you on my return. I promise you, I will make up every second, on my return.'

The boys looked from one to the other, not understanding a word that was being said.

'I know you,' Felix shouted, for the first time that Mina had ever known quite losing his temper. 'I know you for a skiving bitch. You think you can play some game with me, out for everything you can get, while giving as little as possible in return. By God . . .'

'Would you *mind* controlling your language in front of the boys?' Mina asked, coldly.

'I'll control my language when I wish to,' Felix shouted. 'And let me tell you this: you go off to Europe now and you'll be in a divorce court before you know it. With repayment of all my loans to face.'

Mina gazed at him contemptuously. 'You do that, Felix,' she said. 'You just do that. And watch me *destroy* you.' She glanced down at the page open in her hand. 'The *Lusitania* sails for Liverpool on 3 May. That will be ideal.' She looked at Felix. 'And you may do your damnedest.'

Chapter 11

He had never before threatened her with divorce. But then, they had never before had such a quarrel, simply because she had never been able to anger him before; he had always been far too confident, too sure of his power over her, of his power as a man. Now the boot was on the other foot.

And Mina knew that she was actually in a very strong position, legally as well as sexually, providing she maintained certain safeguards, and even supposing Felix was angry enough to lose her, and attempt to find someone else. If John Drummond had been appalled at what she had confided to him, back in 1912, and even more appalled when he had read the contract, he had also been intensely reassuring. 'This document is, of course, a travesty of human relations,' he had said. 'Yet you did sign it, and you have, ah . . . carried out your share of the bargain, as I understand it. It is therefore likely that, were you to leave Mr Petersen, while I have no doubt that any court, and all public opinion, would condemn him out of hand for forcing you to agree to such a vicious document, they might also, I feel, require you to repay at least part of the very large sums of money loaned to you by your husband, and clearly set out here as being payment for services to be rendered, an agreement into which you entered of your own free will, and being of sound mind as they say. Actually, you know, it could be a most interesting test case. In this country, for example, one cannot legally enforce a gambling debt. Nor can a prostitute legally collect money from a client, as she is performing an illegal act – which is why they normally do so in advance. Not,' he added hastily, 'that I am implying . . . well, Mrs Petersen, in this case we have an agreement between husband and wife to commit an illegal act. Because sodomy is an illegal act, and so are, ah . . . some of the other duties he has made you perform. Yet you performed them, if not willingly, certainly in return for monetary payment. It *would* be an interesting case.'

'But not one you would recommend I took to court,' Mina had remarked.

'Well, no. I cannot recommend it. You might win, you might lose; but the effect on your reputation would be frightening. But of course, the more illegal acts he forces you to perform, the stronger is your eventual position, supposing you can stand it.'

'Oh, I can stand it,' she said. 'But supposing he gets tired of me and wants a change? In a couple of years' time, don't forget, I am going to be thirty.'

'Is that a fact?' Drummond, who was clearly twice that, did not seem to find the prospect as alarming as she did. 'I really don't think you have anything to worry about there.'

'It's very nice of you to be complimentary, Mr Drummond, but you don't know Felix.'

'I was speaking legally, Mrs Petersen. Because there is a flaw in this contract, which can only work to your advantage. It sets out very clearly the penalties to which you are liable should you ever refuse your husband his every demand, and thus, in effect, terminate the marriage by default. However, no mention is made of *his* terminating the marriage, therefore, as that is outside the contract, that falls under what we might call a normal relationship. As I see it, should he ever seek to divorce you for nothing else than a desire for change, or for some domestic misunderstanding which has nothing to do with your, ah, sexual duties, I do not see there is any way in which he can reclaim his twenty million dollars, providing only that you remain at least apparently willing to fulfil your part of the bargain to the bitter end. And also providing,' he added, regretfully, for she was one of the most attractive women he had ever known, and over the years they had worked together in considerable intimacy, which had just been brought to a new mental height, 'that you are never proven to have committed any offence against the marriage bed.'

'There is absolutely no risk of that, John,' Mina had asserted. 'You may believe that after five years with Felix I don't really enjoy even shaking a man by the hand.' She had smiled at him. 'With one or two exceptions, of course.'

Which had brought another sigh from the solicitor; he had

never been permitted to do more *than* shake her hand throughout their acquaintance. The important point was that Felix would almost certainly obtain a similar opinion from his lawyers. Therefore he was powerless to harm her, save by dragging her reputation through the courts – and she could do the same for him, and still retain her financial empire. The boot was indeed on the other foot, years before she had really supposed it could happen.

So on this occasion it had merely been important to establish that she was not walking out on him. She *was* entitled, by the terms of their contract, to pursue her business ambitions whenever and wherever she needed to do so, providing only that she made up the time in his bed when she returned – and that was nowadays nothing more than a chore. And she was certainly entitled to do what she chose with her own children. Thus she had carefully left her wardrobe full of clothes, and even left some of her best jewellery in the safe – taking Jessie was obviously necessary because she could not be expected to cope with the boys herself. And she had told everyone she was only going away for a month.

It was up to Felix to make the next move. If he apologised and invited her back, she would have to go, after the month had been stretched into two or even three by circumstances entirely beyond her control – there was, after all, a war on. And when she did return, it would be to another victory, over him and his body. But for the moment at least he had shown no sign of apologising, had behaved like the average angered husband and moved out of the house himself to his club, from where he was no doubt frantically consulting his lawyers – to be told that *he* had committed the breach of contract. She found that rather amusing. No doubt he would then hastily move back in, but it would do him no good. And for the moment she was free. Free! She stood on the first-class promenade deck of the *Lusitania* and filled her lungs with air, holding James' hand tightly; the poor little mite, seated in his chair and watching Harry running up and down, was close to tears – the *Lusitania* might be a second home to their mother, but it was their first ocean voyage.

'Mina Petersen.' Alfred Gwynne Vanderbilt, handsome, debonair, and perfectly groomed, as Mina had always known him, raised his hat. 'I had no idea you were travelling.'

He was the great-great-grandson of the famous commodore,

and was personally more famous as a sportsman than a businessman; he had brothers to attend to the family fortune. Mina had met him several times before, mainly on transatlantic voyages, for he was always moving to and from England, although he had never availed himself of the services of Superb Travel; some people were rich enough to organise their own superb travel. But he was a bachelor, and a charmer; they had even indulged in the occasional mild flirtation, rapidly abandoned as he had recognised that she was quite disinterested in extramarital sex.

But she was always glad to see him. 'I love travelling, Alfred,' she said. 'But I'm so glad you're going to be along.'

'Nervous?'

'No,' she said, honestly. 'I suspect this famous war is dead on its feet.'

'Ah, I believe things are actually stirring again,' he said, seriously. 'There is some big offensive being launched in Flanders right this minute. And the British are bombarding Constantinople, would you believe it? I suspect they'll be fighting for some time yet.'

'They're mad,' Mina declared. 'Absolutely mad. I saw some of it, you know. I was in Ostend when it began. It was quite horrifying.'

'Yet you're going back? Or are you stopping in England?'

'Oh, no,' she said. 'I'm going to the Continent. Business, Alfred. Business. And you?'

'A little bit of each, you could say. I'm going to make sure a stud I'm interested in hasn't been requisitioned by the British Army. Can you imagine a thoroughbred worth perhaps a million galloping across a Flanders mudfield filled with potholes?'

'No, I can't,' she smiled. 'Or what you would say if you saw it.'

'But seriously,' Vanderbilt went on, 'you're not at all upset by this advertisement the Germany Embassy has been running, that passengers on the *Lusitania* travel at their own risk?'

'Propaganda,' Mina said. 'I'm not sure it isn't being paid for by the British, to make the Huns seem more Hunnish than ever. Even if I thought any German would do something like that, I don't see how they can. They'd need half their High Seas Fleet to catch this ship, and I suspect the Royal Navy would have something to say about that. Are *you* worried by it?'

Vanderbilt smiled in turn. 'No. But there are some others who are a little nervous. Will you join my party for dinner? You can reassure Mrs Frohman.'

It was the first time in four years that Mina had crossed the Atlantic, east-bound, without being responsible for the comfort and welfare of most of the first-class passengers. The feeling of relaxation and well-being was enormous. She was able to devote all of her time to the boys, would push James in his chair round and round the promenade deck, Harry skipping at their side, while telling them both about the beauties of England they were going to visit – never had she felt so close to the boys; obviously this was something she should have done long ago. In the evenings, when they had been sent to bed, she played whist and chatted with Alfred Vanderbilt and the Frohman – Charles Frohman was a theatrical producer, full of interesting anecdotes about the famous players with whom he had been associated, and his wife, if distinctly nervous at the start of the voyage, became visibly less so as day succeeded day, and in Mina's reassuringly confident company.

The ship was indeed surprisingly full, with everyone in a state of some excitement. In the first few months of the war, with so much talk about submarines and torpedoes and various other modern methods of destruction, Cunard had suspended the service. But it had soon become apparent that had been an overreaction. In the first place, there was no submarine in the world with the range to cross the Atlantic, or even to operate very far beyond the Irish coast. And in the second place, the great speed of the Cunard flagships, better than twenty-five knots, made nonsense of the nine knots possible to the average submarine. Surface raiders were a different matter, but it had taken a very short time for the Royal Navy to drive every German warship either back to the safety of Wilhelmshaven, or to the bottom of the sea; the destruction of Admiral von Spee's squadron off the Falkland Islands that February had completed the clearing of the oceans except for one lone raider, the *Emden*, reported to be in the Pacific. Certainly the North Atlantic was as safe as a lake, in most experts' opinions. The boys, indeed, were disappointed that they had not seen a warship of any size or description on the whole crossing.

Nonetheless, as Captain Smith was happy to explain to his favourite passengers, the company, in conjunction with the Admiralty, had drawn up an impressive list of safety precautions to be carried out when the ship entered home waters, the most important of which was to steam to an irregular zigzag pattern, that is to say following one course for perhaps half an hour, and then altering to another compass heading for fifteen minutes, and so on and so forth. This was to prevent any German submarine from having the time to aim a torpedo, which apparently took some time and required the intended victim to be steering a steady course. For, unbelievable as it appeared, a U-boat had actually torpedoed a merchantman without warning, quite recently, although this was not yet common knowledge, and while everyone supposed it had been a mistake or an aberration very unlikely to be tried on a ship like the *Lusitania*, even if, with all her watertight compartments, she *could* be sunk by a single torpedo, it was not worth taking the risk. But zigzagging, the captain explained, even if the course alterations were slight and always in the general direction in which they were travelling, did not make navigation any easier.

'You mean we might miss England altogether, and wind up in Germany instead?' Alfred Vanderbilt asked with his usual easy humour, as they lunched at the captain's table on the fourth day out.

'Not exactly, Mr Vanderbilt,' the captain replied. 'But no skipper wants to be even a mile off course, especially when navigating the Irish Sea, and we'll be entering that tonight. We shall soon know for certain. I estimate that this afternoon we'll sight the Old Head of Kinsale. That's a headland on the coast of southern Ireland, you know. That will give us an exact fix, and from then on we should be all right.'

'You mean we're about to sight land?' Mrs Frohman cried. 'Oh, I shall be so glad to see it.'

'Then come up to the bridge when you've finished your meal,' Smith invited.

Mina and Harry went up as well; getting James up the ladders was not an easy task, and Jessie took him for a constitutional instead. But it was fascinating to stand on the

235

bridge and watch the low green hills appearing in the distance. 'How far off are we?' Mina asked.

'That we shall have to discover, exactly,' the captain told her. 'So we will take what we call a running fix. That is, we take a bearing on a known point, in this case that headland, and then, maintaining course and speed for an hour, take another bearing and lay that off on the chart. Where the two bearings cross is our exact position.'

'Oh,' Mina said. He made it all seem so very simple, and she had always thought navigation the most complicated of arts. 'But you'll have to stop zigzagging while you do it.'

'Just for the hour required. There's hardly likely to be a submarine in this exact position, my dear Mrs Petersen. It's too close to the land. Why, do you know, there are only three hundred feet of water under us now? Besides, those fellows track their intended victims for some time before attacking, and we'd have seen him before now; we keep a very careful lookout. Steady as she goes, now, cox. Steady.' He and his officers used their sextants and hand-bearing compasses to take their bearings of height and position of the headland. 'Now we wait an hour,' he said, 'on this same course and speed, and then we'll know where we are to within fifty feet. That's what it's all about.' He winked at Harry and rumpled his hair. 'You come back just after two, and I'll show you how we enter it on the chart.'

'I think I'm going to be a sea captain when I grow up, Mother,' Harry confided as they went down to the first-class promenade. 'It's so much fun.'

'I think that's a splendid idea,' Mina agreed. 'Then you can take me wherever I want to go.' It was such a fine afternoon, the deck was crowded with passengers, all delighted and, Mina suspected, intensely relieved to have sighted land at last. She spent some time searching for James, but could not find him. Jessie must have taken him to his cabin for a nap; he was still prone to tiredness after the slightest exertion. She leaned on the rail, Harry at her side, waiting until it was time to return to the bridge, looking down at the heaving, grey-green sea, itself an indication of the shallowness of the water after the deep blue of the ocean, and noticed a most peculiar phenomenon, a sort of frothing white line in the water, just beneath the surface, and coming closer, and then, with total unexpectedness, found herself lying on the deck.

'Mummy,' Harry was shouting. 'Mummy, you must get up.'

He also had been thrown to the deck by the force of the explosion, but had regained his hands and knees. It occurred to Mina that he must have been shouting for some time, because his face was quite red, but her ears were still ringing – her head had struck the deck as she fell and she must have been unconscious for a few seconds. She still felt too surprised, and too winded, to move, however she knew it was both ridiculous and unladylike to be stretched on the deck at two o'clock in the afternoon. Then she saw Alfred Vanderbilt, reaching down for her. 'Mina?' he asked. 'Are you hurt?'

She stared at him in amazement, because he was accompanied by his valet, who had never before appeared on the first-class promenade, and they were both wearing life-jackets.

Vanderbilt held her arm and assisted her up. 'We must find you a lifeboat,' he said. 'Have you no jacket?'

'Jacket?' Mina was too confused to understand what was going on. It seemed as if the world had gone quite mad, with people shouting and screaming from all about her, and with the deck suddenly seeming to have developed a tilt, not sideways, as if the shop was rolling, but forward. As if she was . . . she turned round, and looked at the bows; the seas were choppy, but not enormous, and yet the bows were dipping under water, and not coming up. 'Oh, my God!' she gasped.

'Yes,' Vanderbilt agreed. 'I think Smith should stop her. However . . . now, a lifeboat. And a jacket.' He took his off, draped it around her shoulders, tied the strap. 'Higgins, the boy.'

'Of course, Mr Vanderbilt.' The valet did the same with his, for Harry.

'But . . . we can't take your life-jackets,' Mina protested.

'Of course you can, my dear girl. Higgins will find us others, I have no doubt. Come along, now.'

His tone was quite brusque, because the slope of the deck was increasing. The boats were already being swung out, filled with women and the few children on board. Many of the women were crying, others were shouting out to their husbands who had remained on board, but there was actually no panic. Harry was pulled aboard and given a seat, and Vanderbilt himself lifted Mina, when the concussion wore off and her brain started to work again. 'James,' she screamed. 'Jessie! Where are they?'

'I'll find them for you,' Vanderbilt said. 'And get them into a boat. There's a promise. But you really can't keep these good people waiting, Mina.' He placed her in the boat, gazed at her for a moment, and then, to her total consternation, kissed her on the forehead. 'God help you and keep you,' he said. 'God help us all, my dearest Mina.'

'But . . . James . . .' she protested feebly. Yet Alfred Vanderbilt would find him, she had no doubt, and get him and Jessie into a boat, as he had promised to do; she thought that of all the men in the world, she would trust this magnificent millionaire more than any.

A lifeboat. She looked left and right at the other women, all first-class passengers, as the boat was swung out from the side of the ship, which was now listing as well as sinking by the bow. Some just gazed at her, others attempted to smile, and one put her arm round her shoulders. Another was hugging Harry.

Harry! But not James!

'James,' she screamed, her brain regaining full control of her senses for the first time since the numbing blow on the head. 'James!' She stood up, and grasped at the rail to pull herself back out of the boat. Harry was clearly safe. But James, poor little crippled James, she could never desert him, even if Alfred Vanderbilt had promised to fetch him to safety.

But the lifeboat was already being lowered. As she caught hold of the rail she felt it drop away beneath her, and people started to shout at her, while someone, a sailor on the deck of the ship, started to prise her fingers loose.

'You don't understand,' she screamed. 'I must get up. My son is up there. My son!' she shrieked, as the man freed one finger and then the next, and she felt herself starting to slip. A moment later she had collapsed again into the bottom of the lifeboat, and the deck was a good six feet above her head.

'My son!' she screamed, trying to get up again, and being restrained by two of the women. 'My son!'

'Jesus Christ,' muttered the sailor on the tiller. 'Why doesn't the old man reduce speed. Jesus Christ!'

Mina turned her head to look forward, and wanted to scream again, but now she couldn't utter a sound. For the ship was still plunging onwards, at a good fifteen knots; her bows had completely disappeared, but were setting up a tremendous disturbance, racing away from the sides of the hull, a series of high and sharp waves, into which the lifeboat was about to plunge.

'Jesus Christ,' the sailor said again, and Mina felt herself flying through the air. Then she was in the water, going down, down, down, so deep into the green. Desperately she tried to kick, and couldn't; she was wearing one of the new fashioned hobble skirts designed to keep her ankles close to each other. Her lungs started to burst, and lights shot across her brain, then she suddenly broke the surface, gasped for air and swallowed water, vomited and gasped again, kept afloat by the life-jacket which had already saved her life.

'Harry!' she screamed. 'Harry!'

'Mother!' He was only six feet away.

'Oh, thank God, thank God,' she wept, and swam to him. The upturned lifeboat was only a few feet further, and they struggled towards it, and the women holding on to the safety lines – about half the women who had originally been in the boat. But the sailor was there too, and he caught her arm to bring her to this temporary refuge, and then stared past her. 'Jesus Christ!' he repeated, as if those were the only words he knew. Mina turned her head, and felt like echoing him as she looked at a sight she would never be able to forget. The *Lusitania* was sticking out of the water at an angle of some sixty degrees, bows and foredeck and forward superstructure having disappeared beneath the waves, the stern high in the air, and crowded with people, beneath whom the huge propellers were still turning. The ship itself was absolutely motionless for the moment, and she understood why. As the captain had told her, there were only three hundred feet of water here; thus the bows had hit the bottom, while the stern was still above the surface, because the ship was eight hundred feet long. Somehow that seemed the most incredible aspect of the entire incredible afternoon. It was simply not possible that a ship could be resting on the bottom, and still also be above the surface – and that her passengers and crew should be drowning. If only it could stay like that, an island, until rescue came. But even as she watched, the stern began to sink, slowly at first, and then with increasing speed, while people threw themselves into the already crowded sea around the ship. Then the stern disappeared, and there was only bubbling water, surging about them, and the sailor began to weep.

The crowded sea. Suddenly, mysteriously quiet, after the tumult of only a little while before. But still crowded. People moaned, and sighed, and occasionally cried out, their voices immediately lost in the slurping of the waters, the wails of the sea birds. But enormous numbers of people made no sound at all, and just floated by, face down or face up, staring lifelessly at the heavens. It was not comprehensible to Mina to suppose that *she* was floating in the midst of so many people, in sight of land, and that so many were dead.

And they? She would not have cared, would happily have gone floating sightlessly off herself, if only to stop herself from thinking, but for Harry. 'I'm so cold, Mother,' he said. 'So cold.'

She could take one hand from the rope she held and put the arm around his shoulders, but to what avail? She was as cold as he. One or two of the women were actually trying to sing; others preferred to shout at the few lifeboats which had reached the sea right side up; but they were all crowded and would not approach anyone in the water for fear of being swamped.

'Why didn't he reduce speed?' the sailor asked. 'Why didn't he reduce speed?'

'Obviously he couldn't,' Mina told him. 'The engine room telegraph must have jammed.'

'Ah,' the sailor said, 'That must have been it.' And as if he had just been waiting for an explanation, he released the rope and drifted away into the afternoon. Mina felt she should try to stop him, but if it was something he wanted to do . . . because that was the most incredible thing of all. Whenever she had thought of shipwreck, it had always been at night. Ships were always wrecked at night. The *Titanic*, on which she had so miraculously missed sailing, had gone down at night. But this was a balmy May afternoon, with the sun peering through the fleecy white clouds and green hills only a few miles away. Only there wasn't sufficient sun to warm the sea.

Strangely, she felt no anger. Whoever had done this, whoever had lined up his submarine and pulled the lever to release the torpedo, had just committed murder on a scale which made Attila the Hun seem one of humanity's great benefactors. But it didn't seem to matter at this moment, because soon she also would be dead. She had no feelings from the waist down, and now her fingers were going numb. She would die, and Harry would die, as James had already died, unless Alfred Vanderbilt had got him into a lifeboat. Oh, but surely Alfred would have done that. Alfred was so confident, so reliable . . . she almost expected to see him in the bows of a lifeboat, rowing towards her, calling out to her that everything was going to be all right.

And Jessie? She hadn't given a thought to Jessie. But surely, as Jessie had been with James, when Alfred had rescued James he would also have rescued Jessie.

If he had managed to do it. He would have had to go to the cabin, and get the door open, while the ship had been listing and tilting more and more, and faster and faster . . . tears started to roll down her cheeks, and Harry squeezed her shoulder. 'We'll be all right, Mother,' he said. 'We'll be all right.'

Mina rested her head on her arm, her face dipping in and out of the sea, and wept, while she shuddered with the cold.

Summer in London. Soft sunshine and balmy breezes. But it was never going to be summer again. It was never going to be warm again. It was as if the icy water off the Old Head of Kinsale had entered Mina's blood.

Clarity was missing. Which was the most terrifying thing she had ever known, because clarity, coherent, consistent thought, had nothing to do with memory. Memory was as vivid as day, and twice as bright, and twice as horrible. Memory of being dragged from the water by the fishermen whose trawlers had come to their rescue, of screaming for Harry until reassured that he was at her side. Memory of lying on the deck, wrapped in a blanket, and drinking hot soup. Memory of Queenstown, where they had sat around a church hall, still wrapped in blankets, stared at by officials and voluntary workers, begging for news of those they could not see. And most terrible memory of all, over the next few days, of being taken to look at the pitiful, horrible, mucous-stained faces of those bodies retrieved. Jessie's face, surprisingly calm. But then, Jessie had been a calm person.

There had been no other face she had recognised, save for that of the nameless sailor who for a while had shared her rope beside the upturned lifeboat. No other face. She had refused to leave Queenstown, even when the other women, those strange intimates who had shared so much without even knowing each other's names, had departed in silent grief. Because where there was no body, there had still to be hope. But there were lots of bodies still missing. No trace had been found of Alfred Vanderbilt, or his valet, or Mrs and Mrs Frohman. She had no doubt they would have been together at the end, because they were friends. Would Alfred have had James with him? He would have lifted the boy from his wheelchair, and held him close as the grey water had rushed over the deck and lapped at their ankles, and being Alfred Vanderbilt, he would have laughed at approaching death, and shouted, 'Look at that, James. Isn't that a sight to remember?'

A last sight to remember.

Eventually John Drummond had come for her, to save her sanity. But had he done that? Was she sane, just to sit here at her window, and stare out at the sky, and remember? No doubt it was not positive madness. Because she was sane enough to know that when she stopped remembering, and started to think . . . 'Are you mad?' Felix had demanded. 'Have you no sense of responsibility?'

And she had replied, at least in her mind, I am Mina Doberley. I *make* the rules. Just as Alfred Gwynne Vanderbilt and Charles Frohman had always made their rules for living, as they were successful men. And now, out of the only three people she had allowed herself to love since the death of her father, she had managed to drown two. She should have gone for James herself. But she knew that was not true. Alfred Vanderbilt had been far more capable than her of getting James into a lifeboat – had he ever even reached the cabin? – just as she knew that, even had James been with her and Harry in their lifeboat, his weakened constitution would not have stood the several hours

242

they had spent in the near freezing water after capsizing. Yet once again she was overwhelmed with the sensation of aloneness, as distinct to loneliness, of being totally isolated from the rest of humanity.

Drummond had persuaded her that there was no more hope, had made her leave Queenstown, and go to England. He had instinctively taken her to the Superb – and she had burst into tears at the sight of it. So he had established her in this apartment – the English called it a flat – found her a ladies' maid, a girl named Alice, young and pretty and excited to be working for the famous Mrs Petersen, but definitely no Jessie. Drummond had also found her a nurse for Harry, and a cook, and a butler, and had bought clothes for Harry and herself. So she had nothing to do but stare out of her window. He was relying on time, left the specifications for various Paris possibilities on the table, reminded her that whenever she felt like it Coutts were looking forward to a chat. He had brought her all the gossip, and rumour, and legend, about the *Lusitania* that he could discover. How Mrs Frohman had refused to leave her husband. How Alfred Vanderbilt had been seen smoking a cigar just before the final plunge of the ship. And holding a little boy in his arms? That too. But which was fact and which was legend?

He had also discussed the technical side of the tragedy. 'Undoubtedly the torpedo damaged the engine room telegraph system,' he said. 'That's why the captain couldn't stop the ship. And of course that's why she sank so fast. She literally drove herself under.'

'But the explosion,' Mina muttered. 'It was so tremendous. It knocked us off our feet on the very top deck. Could one torpedo have done that?'

'Well . . . some people are claiming they saw two torpedo wakes. And the Germans are claiming, as you know, that the *Lusitania* was carrying munitions, and that the torpedo ignited them.'

The Germans, she thought. The Germans had, in the beginning, denied all knowledge of the incident. Now they were claiming it as a victory, and also claiming that the *Lusitania* had in fact not only been armed with concealed guns, for possible use as an armed merchant cruiser, but had also been carrying a vast store of arms and munitions for the British Army, and that it was the greatest coup of the war so far; that one of their submarines, taking a tremendous risk, had waited off the South Irish coast for several days, knowing that had to be the liner's landfall, and determined to destroy this floating munitions factory. No one believed such claims. The British Government had hardly troubled to deny them. And the American press and public were clamouring for action. Sometimes she thought like that as well. And then she would think, what can we do? Declare war on Germany, and kill some more people? And suppose, just suppose, the German claims were true?

But could that even justify sending over a thousand innocent men, women, and children to their deaths?

She wondered what Felix was clamouring for. Because she had heard not a word from him, not of sympathy, nor of reproach. Not even of interest. He had to be the most hateful man she had ever encountered. And she had sought him out, to make her dream come true. Another example of Mina Doberley making the rules. At times she felt so desperately miserable and uncertain, and so utterly a failure, that had it not been for Harry she would have committed suicide.

A fact of which Drummond was certainly aware. Hence his unending solicitude, his frequent unannounced calls. She could hear him now, talking with Jennings, the butler, and with someone else . . . she got up and faced the door, feeling a spasm of anger that her private grief should have been so invaded. Drummond entered the room, and smiled at her, while she looked past him at the wheelchair, pushed by the woman, and sending goosepimples up and down her spine.

'I've some visitors to see you, Mina,' he said. 'Your grandfather, and your aunt.'

Mina went forward, slowly. 'Grandfather? Aunt Betty?'

'Oh, my dear girl,' Bettina Doberley said. 'My dear, dear girl.' She held Mina close.

'We would have come before,' John Doberley said. 'But we didn't know you were in London.'

Mina looked above his head at Drummond. Who returned her gaze without a change of expression. The decision had clearly been his, and he stood by it.

She sat between her aunt and the wheelchair, gazed into her

244

grandfather's face. For all the tortured pain it had endured for several years, the frustrations of being a cripple, it remained both a strong face and a calm face. Perhaps James would have looked like that, had he lived. Tears ran down her face, and increased when Alice, alerted by Drummond, no doubt, brought Harry into the room.

'Harry,' John Doberley said. 'You're a strapping boy. Do you know, he is my first great-grandson?'

'Harry,' Bettina said. 'Come and sit here beside me.'

'What are you going to do?' Doberley asked.

Mina's head jerked. No one, not even John Drummond, had dared ask her that question before.

'Are you going home?' John Doberley asked.

Mina stared at him. Go back to sea? Cross that ocean again, every waking moment expecting another explosion, another crash to the deck, another ghastly immersion in freezing water, surrounded by dead bodies?

Perhaps he could read her mind. 'I suppose not, right away,' he observed. 'Mr Drummond tells us that you actually came over on business. Something to do with an hotel in Paris, was it? Of course you haven't felt much like that recently, for obvious reasons. But now I imagine you're anxious to get on with it.'

'Business?' she repeated. The thought was incomprehensible.

'Paris,' he said, gently. 'Hotels. You're a famous woman now, Mina. You're the most famous Doberley there ever was, now. I was once.' He smiled. 'Now it's you.'

Paris, she thought. To get there she had been going to Berlin. A city filled with Germans.

'How can I go to Paris?' she asked.

'I would have thought that you, as an American citizen, and more important, as Mina Doberley, can go anywhere,' John Doberley said, gazing at her.

Mina returned his gaze for several moments, and then got up, to stand at the window once again, and stare at that so familiar view. He was right, of course. She was Mina Doberley. And she was still unharmed and healthy, as healthy as ever in her life. Once before God had waved His hand, and swept away her family, left her alone. Now He had done so again, but He had failed to complete the act of destruction. He had not taken

Harry, because Harry had been at her side. And, so strangely, He had even made it possible for her to have a family, outside of her own children, for the first time in her life. Could it be possible that she was earning His respect?

Or was it not more possible that there was no God, no anything out there, that life was merely composed of a series of incidents which could either be catastrophes or accidents, depending upon one's character? She had survived the deaths of her parents, simply because it had never occurred to her not to. Was she not also going to survive James' death? She was Mina Doberley. She had things to do. Oh, she had things to do. Such as punishing the Germans for James' death. She did not know how she would, or could, do that, but she could certainly make them understand that they could not defeat *her*, with all their guns and their torpedoes.

'We would be happy to have Harry stay with us,' Bettina Doberley said, quietly. 'We'd take him to our home down in Surrey. We have ponies, and dogs down there. And the loveliest countryside. He'd be safe, while you . . . attended to your business.'

Mina turned and gazed at them, and at John Drummond most of all. He had engineered this. And just in time, or she would have allowed herself to become a cabbage. After all, she had friends, and she had a family. And she still had a son. 'I thank you,' she said. 'I thank you all. Well, John, do you think you can arrange that meeting for me, with Coutts? And then get me a passage to Rotterdam?'

'Right away,' Drummond said.

While John Doberley smiled. 'Mina Doberley,' he said. 'I like that better than Mina Petersen. By God, I do.'

'But first,' Mina said, 'you must all come to lunch with me, at the Superb. Poor Pierre Raizman will wonder what is happening, the way I haven't been to see him.'

Chapter 12

'My dear Frau Petersen,' said General Freilinghausen. 'My dear, dear Frau Petersen! How very good to see you again. Do you know, when I heard you were in Berlin I could hardly believe my ears?'

'Because of all the other things you had heard?' Mina asked.

'Well . . .' Freilinghausen flushed, and sighed. 'It was terrible. Quite terrible. I'm afraid . . . but you do not wish to speak of it, I am sure.'

'I do wish to speak of it, Herr General.'

He shrugged. 'It is simply that one's leaders are not always the men you suppose, and hope, they are. Tirpitz . . . but you must understand that this war is developing into the most frightful struggle in all history. There is an enormous battle now going on in Flanders. Millions of men. And it is costing tens of thousands of casualties. This is war to the death, between the German Reich and those who would strangle us. Now, there are some of us, myself included, who would wish to preserve certain illusions, that even wars can be fought in a spirit of chivalry. There are others, Admiral von Tirpitz amongst them, who are only certain that victory must be secured, at whatever the cost. No doubt, when victory has been secured, we shall be grateful to such men. But you, the thought of you on that ship . . . and then, in the water . . .'

'Not the thought of my son drowning?' Mina asked.

'I know. I was most distressed. My dear Frau Petersen . . . may I call you Wilhelmina?'

'No,' Mina said. 'You may call me Mina, if you wish.' Because she believed his protestations of abhorrence for the deed. That did not mean she would ever forgive him, simply for being a German. But, because he was a German, and because she had trusted his people and his government, and even defended them, to such great personal cost, she was determined to use him, to use them all, as ruthlessly as she had used Felix. And that meant encouraging him to fall in love with her, as he was so obviously anxious to do. 'As you say, Herr General, terrible things happen in wartime. Your nation stands condemned before world opinion, there can be no doubt about that.'

'I must argue with that, Mina,' Freilinghausen protested. 'The *Lusitania* was both armed and carrying munitions, and passengers were warned against sailing in her.'

'And you have struck a medal, have you not, celebrating their deaths? But I did not come to Berlin to quarrel with you. I am here on business.'

'Business?' The general mopped his brow. He was not enjoying his dinner at all. 'Can there be any business in wartime? Except the business of war?'

'There can,' Mina said, 'for those of us sane enough not to wish any part of your quarrel. You tell me there is a battle raging in Flanders. Is Ostend involved?'

'My dear Mina, Ostend is virtually in the front line. The British hold Nieuport, and that is only six or seven miles down the coast.'

'You mean they are actually fighting in Ostend?'

'Oh, no, no. The British offensive has been launched further to the eas. But I can assure you that Ostend is no place to be. Why, every so often the Royal Navy brings up monitors and bombards it. Our U-boats use it as a base, you see.'

'They do?' Mina asked. 'How interesting.' She wondered if the U-boat which had sunk the *Lusitania* was based at Ostend. 'I wish to go to Ostend, Herr General.'

'To Ostend? My dear lady, that is quite impossible.'

'I have an hotel there,' Mina reminded him. 'American property.'

'Which has been under German guard since we occupied the port,' Freilinghausen declared. 'If there has been any damage whatsoever to your property, it has been caused by the British.'

'Well, then, I would like to discover if the British methods of making war are as frightful as yours. I am sure they are, Herr General. In any event, as I am here, I wish to go and make sure everything is all right. I would be grateful if you would make the necessary arrangements, obtain the passes I shall require, and so on and so forth.'

'My dear Mina . . .'

'I should be *very* grateful, Claus,' Mina said, gazing into his eyes and for the first time using his Christian name.

'Well . . .' He pulled his nose. 'I think it can probably be done. But the danger . . . I will have to accompany you.'

Another meaningful stare.

'If you wish.' Mina returned his gaze. 'Provided you always remember that I am a happily married woman.' She was willing to let the future take care of itself, but she had no doubt she could hoodwink poor Claus Freilinghausen – yet she wanted him to remember that she had not been dishonest. 'Now, how soon will the arrangements be made?'

'In a few days.' Very obviously, he was also content to let the future take care of itself. The immediate future. 'I will get to work immediately. Alas, I have an appointment tonight – your arrival was so unexpected, my dear Mina – but if you were to dine with me tomorrow night, at my apartment . . .'

'Alas, dear Claus, I am leaving Berlin tomorrow morning.'

'Leaving? Tomorrow?'

'Well, yes.' Mina looked around her. She actually was very pleased with what she saw; at least the Superb restaurant was doing a roaring trade, mainly in young German officers and their lady friends. Adolf Braun, her manager, had of course pointed out that a good restaurant trade was not sufficient to stop them losing money hand over fist, but she had told him not to worry – the war would soon be over. And he was certainly keeping the hotel ready to move into higher gear the moment people started to travel again. 'Now that I have ascertained all is well here, I have business to attend to. In Paris.'

'Paris?' He was aghast. 'You cannot go from Berlin to Paris, in time of war.'

'Of course I can, Claus. I am going from Berlin to Vienna, and from Vienna to Geneva, and from Geneva to Paris. I can go where I choose, because I am an American citizen, and because I am Mina Doberley. I shall return, via the same route, probably within a week. It would be good of you to have the arrangements made by then.'

'Madame Petersen!' M. Chaffaux looked a trifle thinner, and

certainly greyer, than when last Mina had seen him – was it less than a year ago? – but certainly pleased to see her. 'Herr General!' He bowed to Freilinghausen.

It occurred to Mina that actually very little had changed. The staff of the Splendide seemed the same, if, like their manager, somewhat shabbier than in the past, as the hotel certainly seemed shabbier; the guns still growled in the distance – they had had to make a detour right round by the Dutch frontier to be sure they were not fired upon; and across the road a sentry still patrolled outside the shuttered and derelict Superb. But at least the scope of the battle had saved her from having to make any decisions regarding the general's amorous intentions – they had both had to sleep sitting up in a crowded train compartment since leaving Berlin, and in the circumstances, with the dignity of the General Staff to be preserved, he had not even got around to kissing her.

While, at least externally, the hotel seemed undamaged.

'We Germans keep our word, you see,' Freilinghausen remarked. 'You have rooms for us, Chaffaux?'

'Of course, Herr General. Ah . . .' He gazed inquiringly at Mina.

'Two rooms, M. Chaffaux,' she said, while Freilinghausen went very red in the face.

'And one for your . . .' Chaffaux looked past her, expectantly.

An orderly was carrying her bag. 'I have no maid, M. Chaffaux,' she explained. 'My American maid was drowned . . .' she gazed at Freilinghausen and he flushed again – she was coming to the opinion that if she could keep this up he would even lose interest in getting her between the sheets '. . . and her replacement is English. So I considered it best to leave her behind.'

'Of course,' Chaffaux said. 'I quite understand. I will appoint one of my girls . . .'

'That would be very kind of you,' Mina said. 'Now, I simply must look at my hotel. You have the keys?'

Chaffaux obtained them from his office.

'You will have to be quick,' Freilinghausen told her. 'I have accepted an invitation for us to lunch with General von der Goltz.'

Mina ignored him as they crossed the street, nodded to the salute from the sentry, and after some wrestling with the rusted lock, opened the door and went inside. To stand in the lobby, aghast. It was incredible how much deterioration had taken place in less than a year; she realised that it had probably been a blessing in disguise that she had not been able to complete the furnishing and decorating. Rain had got in even through the shutters, hardly a window having any glass left in it, and was gathered in pools on the parquet floor, while there were damp patches in the ceiling from which the plaster hung in great swathes to indicate that the same thing must have happened on the upper floors. Cobwebs gathered in the corners, and a rat scurried across the floor in front of her as she went past the silent, powerless elevators towards the stairs.

'This was a brand new building,' she said over her shoulder.

The general stood in the street doorway, sniffing the musty air in distaste. 'It can be saved, if it is structurally sound.'

'Supposing I do something about it right away.'

'I do not think that will be possible, in present circumstances, and having regard to the danger of its situation. It is a miracle the British have not yet blown it up.'

'Perhaps they know it is mine,' she said, wickedly, and after a brief hesitation, opted to descend to the basement first; it was the foundations which really mattered – holes in the roof could always be mended. Chaffaux had loaned her a lantern and this she held above her head as she made her way down the stone steps to the first cellar, and peered left and right. In front of her were the doors to what had been going to be the wine store, to her right were the doors to the future cold room, to the left miscellaneous storage. She went in there first, the lantern held high, and sighed with relief. For all the shell blasts which had shattered the windows, there were no visible cracks in the walls, and there was probably less water down here than in the lobby itself. It *could* be saved. And it would be saved. She turned, her confidence returning . . . and listened to a noise in the far corner. She frowned, while her blood tingled; that had been no rat.

Then what could it have been? She opened her mouth to call for Freilinghausen, whose boots she could hear stamping about the lobby, and then some instinct made her change her mind, and she took a few steps towards the noise, holding the lantern above her head again, and gazing at a pair of frightened eyes, emerging from an unshaven face, haggard with exhaustion and lack of food, the whole resting on top of what was clearly the uniform of a pilot in the Royal Flying Corps.

He stared at her, his expression eloquent of his fear and his necessities and his hunger. She stared back, her brain for a moment totally blank. He could be no danger to her, with a German general within earshot. But she realised he had no intention of being a danger to her; she was the danger to him. And he was English. He might even have come from Devon. Certainly he was fighting against the ruthless machine which had commanded the sinking of the *Lusitania*.

'Yes,' she said, in English. 'We will have to see what can be done, about you.' She turned and hurried for the steps.

'What is that?' Freilinghausen asked from above her, in German.

'I was talking to myself,' Mina said, climbed the stairs before he could come down. 'I am afraid this place is a wreck, Claus. I shall have to skip lunch, I think, and spend the afternoon making detailed notes.'

'But my dear Mina, General von der Goltz, an old friend . . .'

'Of mine, also, Claus,' she agreed, hurrying him across the lobby and on to the steps. 'You will have to make my apologies. I'm afraid I never let pleasure interfere with business. You know that, Claus. Perhaps the general could join us for dinner.'

'I had looked forward to *supper*,' he said meaningfully.

Mina shrugged. 'I leave it to you to sort things out. Monsier Chaffaux,' she called, bustling into the Splendide, 'A word with you, please.'

'Madame?' Chaffaux scampered behind her into his office, which she had already entered.

'The Superb is more of a mess than I feared,' Mina said loudly. 'Perhaps you would be good enough to close your door, that we may discuss the situation.'

Chaffaux raised his eyebrows, but had no objection to being closeted with a beautiful and extraordinarily wealthy young woman. He obeyed.

'Chaffaux,' Mina said, lowering her voice and leaning across his desk; she had taken his chair. 'Do you believe that the Boche will win this war?'

'Madame . . .?' Chaffaux cast an anxious glance at the door.

Mina leaned back. 'Because I do not.'

'Well, of course they cannot, madame. Not against the British and the French. And the Belgians. But . . .'

'Therefore,' Mina said, leaning forward again, 'as you are a patriotic Belgian, you believe that Belgium will one day be freed.'

'Well, of course, madame.' Chaffaux sat in the straight chair opposite her, and began to wipe sweat from his neck.

'Therefore,' Mina continued relentlessly, 'you will do everything in your power to bring that day about, will you not? Now, listen to me, very carefully. There is a British flying officer in the cellar of the Superb.'

'The British? My God!' Chaffaux clapped his hand to his forehead. 'Four days ago, there was a plane crashed into the sea, just off the beach, at night. No trace was ever found of the pilot. Everyone supposed he had drowned.'

'Four days,' Mina repeated. 'The poor man must truly be starving. Very well, Chaffaux. First of all, you and I are going to take some food across to that man. A loaf of bread, a big sausage, some cheese, and a bottle of wine. He could probably do with some decent drinking water as well. Oh, and a razor. He looks dreadful.'

Chaffaux stared at her. 'Are you mad, madame? There is a sentry.'

Mina opened one of the drawers of his desk, and into it emptied the contents of the large handbag she used for travelling. 'This will do very nicely,' she said. 'Now, M. Chaffaux, the next thing we have to decide is how we get him out of Ostend, and either down the coast to Nieuport, or up the coast to Holland.'

'Madame?'

'It can be done, can't it? You must have some contact with Holland, certainly.'

'Well . . . indirectly, madame. But . . .'

'Tell me about it.'

'Well, madame . . .' Chaffaux wiped his brow. 'We do not

have any contact, but . . . this hotel is very popular with the German officers, you see. They come here regularly, and they require good service, clean linen, good wine and food . . . Ostend was badly damaged during the fighting, as you know, madame. We do not even have a proper laundry here any more. So twice a week I send our laundry up to Antwerp. But also, there is no good wine, and little enough food, left in Belgium, so my chef goes with the laundry, and is allowed to cross to Holland and buy. Holland is just across the river from Antwerp. But madame . . .'

'That sounds absolutely ideal,' Mina agreed.

'But madame,' Chaffaux protested. 'To help an English soldier escape, it is very dangerous. Nurse Cavell did it, and . . .'

Mina raised her eyebrows. 'Nurse Cavell?' The name was certainly familiar.

'An English nurse in Brussels, madame. She helped English soldiers to escape, and the Boche caught her at it. They have put her under arrest, madame, and have charged her with espionage. Her trial is soon to be held. They are saying that if she is found guilty she will be shot.'

'That has to be nonsense,' Mina declared. 'How can they possibly shoot a woman for helping her own people? How can that possibly be espionage? Anyway, I am not an English nurse, Chaffaux. I am an American hotelier. They would not dare put me under arrest. Now fetch me a basket with that food and wine I requested.'

'Madame,' said the flying officer, tearing at the loaf of bread as if he had never eaten before in his life. 'You are too kind. But the risk . . . and you do not even know my name. I am . . .'

Mina shook her head. 'I do not wish to know your name, monsieur. I will call you James.' She poured a glass of wine for him. 'Now listen to me, very carefully. We are going to get you out of here, and into Holland.' She glanced at Chaffaux, standing shivering by the door as he listened to the pounding of the boots of the German sentry outside the hotel. 'When?'

'The next laundry load leaves at dawn tomorrow morning, madame. As that is obviously too soon to make any arrangements we must plan for the next, at the end of the week.'

'Tomorrow morning,' Mina told the Englishman.

'Madame!' Chaffaux objected. 'That is too soon. I must protest . . .'

'The sooner the better,' Mina pointed out. 'Surely you can see James cannot remain here for another four days? And do not tell me you cannot trust your own staff?'

'Well . . .' Chaffaux sighed.

'Your husband?' James asked in English.

'Of course not.'

'But you own this place?'

'Yes,' she said, and poured herself a glass of wine as well. 'I am an American. My name is Mina Petersen.'

It didn't register. Obviously he was not a Superb Travel class of man.

'An American,' he remarked. And smiled. 'My lucky day. Although I would never have thought that. I always understood you people wanted us to stew in our own juice.'

'Not all of us,' she said, and finished her wine. 'I must go now, and I'm afraid I cannot leave you the lantern. But remember, somebody will be along for you just before dawn, tomorrow.' She glanced at Chaffaux. 'No, it would be best if he was taken across to the Splendide and placed in the laundry basket at the very earliest moment, tonight. As soon as everyone is in bed.'

'Madame . .' Chaffaux rolled his eyes. 'This is quite impossible. He will certainly be arrested the moment he reaches Antwerp, and then . . .'

'Why should he be arrested in Antwerp?' Mina demanded.

'Because no one in the laundry there will know he is coming, madame. They will be surprised, and frightened, and . . . *voila!*' He threw his hands into the air.

'They will not be frightened,' Mina explained, patiently, 'because I will tell them who he is and what they must do.'

'You, madame?'

'I intend to accompany your laundry, M. Chaffaux.'

'I think you're taking a darn sight too many risks for me, Mrs Petersen,' James said. 'I mean to say . . .'

'Well, don't,' Mina continued. 'I will tell you what to do, and what to say. And when to say it. Just sit tight, and finish your meal. We will come for you.'

She climbed the stairs, Chaffaux at her elbow. 'It is

impossible, madame,' the manager said again. 'We will not even get him out of the building. There is a sentry on duty, all night. At your request, madame. And General Freilinghausen . . .'

'Ssssh,' Mina said, because the general was waiting on the front steps. 'Claus! I have great news.'

'Indeed!' Freilinghausen had clearly not enjoyed his lunch, with General von der Goltz but without her.

'I have discovered that there is a builder in Antwerp who is still in business, and even has some materials. I must get up there to see him as soon as possible. Chaffaux tells me there is a laundry load going up by truck at dawn tomorrow. I will ride with that. Would you write me out a pass, please?'

'Antwerp? A laundry load? At dawn? My dear Mina, I have just learned that I must return to Berlin tomorrow. Antwerp . . .'

Mina sighed, to herself. It was necessary to take a distasteful decision; the only time in her life she had broken her marriage vows was when Felix had forced her to it. But here was a much more worthy cause. She almost thought she could enjoy this, because holding her in his arms, he would be helping an English officer to escape. And one day she would be able to tell him that. But to sleep with him, a man, voluntarily . . . and she would have to be at her very best. She gazed at him, perhaps truly saw him for the first time. Always before he had merely seemed the epitome of a German soldier, with his height, and his close-shaven head, and his scar on the cheek, and his monocle, and his big features – but there was kindness in the often cold blue eyes, of a sort at least, and certainly there was desire for her.

'Well, then,' she said. 'As I am determined to go to Antwerp tomorrow morning, and you have to return to Berlin as well, I suggest we do not waste any more time. I am sure M. Chaffaux has a room waiting for us, where, in due course, we may have that supper you were looking forward to.'

'Mina!' the general cried in delight.

'Madame?' M. Chaffaux asked in consternation.

'But there is one thing I insist on, Claus,' Mina said. 'It is a complete waste of time maintaining a sentry on a derelict building, and I am sure it is harming your war effort. Please remove him, this very minute.' She squeezed his hand. 'As I intend to come to Germany regularly from now on, my love, I am sure I can take care of my hotel myself.'

'One million dollars,' Mina told the astonished Drummond. 'And in a very good area, only a hundred yards from the Champs-Élysées. I think that is an absolute bargain. Of course, as you say, the money will have to lie fallow until the end of the war, and frankly I do not any longer believe that is about to happen, but I have no doubt it will be worth it in the long run. Can you raise the money?'

'I have no doubt of that,' Drummond said. 'And it will be a good investment, certainly. But may I just get something straight? Am I to understand that in the past fortnight you have been from London to Rotterdam and from Rotterdam to Berlin, and then from Berlin to Vienna and from Vienna to Geneva, and then from Geneva to Paris and thence back to Berlin, and from Berlin to Ostend, and from Ostend to Flushing, and finally from Flushing to Harwich?'

'That is correct. I was delayed finding passage from Flushing to Harwich, but apart from that I was able to maintain a fairly accurate schedule.'

'And the Germans did not object to this?'

'Oh, they objected, John. They seemed to think I was not taking the fact of Europe being at war seriously enough. But I did not let their objections concern me. I am an American citizen. And an international entrepreneur.'

'Hm,' Drummond said. 'Hm. And what do you intend to do next?'

'Is there any news from America?'

'I'm afraid not. Except indirectly. Mr Petersen has withdrawn his backing deposit from Coutts Bank. This isn't important at the moment, of course, as no one is using Superb traveller's cheques at the moment, and I do assure you that it will not in any way hinder your raising the financing for the Paris venture, but . . . I don't much like the look of things there.'

'Nonsense,' Mina said. 'He has to send for me, and I have to refuse to go, before there is any breach of contract. And until he does send for me, I have no intention of going. So, I shall go down to Epsom tomorrow, and spend some days with Harry and Aunt Bettina – he's going to school next month, you know; apparently there's a good school right there in Epsom.'

'And after that?'

'Ah, once he's settled in at Epsom College, I'm returning to Ostend.'

'You mean you're going back?'

'Of course I am. I've an hotel to repair, John. I'm afraid my departure, both from Ostend and from Antwerp, and from Flushing as a matter of fact, was always rather on the spur of the moment. I certainly intend to see what can be done about the Ostend Superb.'

'I see,' Drummond said, apparently to himself. 'Mrs Petersen . . . look, may I call you Mina?'

'I should be delighted if you would.'

'Well, Mina, may I be so bold as to inquire on which side your sympathies lie, in this war?'

Mina gazed at him. 'I would have thought that should be fairly obvious.'

'Yes,' Drummond said. 'Well, then . . . there is a gentleman who is anxious to meet you. He works for Military Intelligence.'

'Oh, yes,' Mina said.

'Would you have any objection to lunching with him, and with me, of course, at the Café Royal tomorrow?'

Colonel Morrison turned out to be a dapper little man with a breast full of multi-coloured ribbons, and wearing highly polished boots. Save for the fact that his uniform was khaki instead of grey-green, he reminded her of every German officer she had ever met, and for that reason she did not immediately take to him. But she was interested in what he had to say. 'Information such as you could provide, my dear lady, would perhaps save, well . . . I cannot say. But thousands, perhaps tens of thousands of lives. I mean to say, you visit Berlin, and can see for yourself the actual food and morale situation there, and in Vienna, and then you travel west, to the very front line, surrounded by German troop movements, and then you spend some time in Ostend, watching U-boats coming and going all the time . . . you are operating in the very heart of the German war effort.'

'And you, sir, are asking me to become a spy,' Mina pointed out.

'I suppose that would be one way of looking at it. But I don't think such a description technically applies. You are a neutral citizen who from the requirements of her legitimate business spends her time in travelling around Europe. I presume you travel with your eyes open. Thus I do not think anyone could criticise a lady who, dining with her friends here in London, relates some of the adventures she has had, the sights she has seen, the conversations she has had, on her travels.'

'Don't you suppose the Germans might look at it the way I do?'

'Supposing they ever find out. But if they do find out, Mrs Petersen, what are they going to do about it? They have aroused sufficient anger in your country by sinking the *Lusitania*. Your President has had some difficulty in keeping you out of the war. I don't think the Germans would wish another incident. No, no, should they ever suspect you of relaying information to us, they would merely tap you on the shoulder and request you to leave their occupied territories, and not come back. That would be regrettable, but not personally disastrous. I can assure you that we will monitor your whereabouts at all times, and make the devil of a fuss should you ever be arrested.'

'And what about my hotels? Wouldn't the Germans immediately confiscate those?'

'My dear lady, the Germans can confiscate what they wish. As they are going to lose the war, all the property they have already confiscated, with interest, is going to be returned to its rightful owners.'

Mina gazed at him, and finished her wine. Surprisingly, in view of the obvious failure of the Allied summer offensive – which still dragged on – she didn't really doubt the truth of anything he was saying. And the prospect was exciting, as well as satisfying – far more so than helping a nameless British officer to escape. Only the concomitants were daunting. Daunting? She might well have to sleep with Claus Freilinghausen again. Might? She would have no choice, if she went back. And sleep was a euphemism if ever there was one. They certainly had not slept, that afternoon. As he had done nothing for her, sexually – save fill her with distaste, but that had nothing to do with him personally – she had had to act, but she had learned how to act in bed, and she had done a great deal for him. And in fact she *had* enjoyed it. Not the sex, but the fact that she had been getting her own back on a German, by hoodwinking him into believing she could love a member of the nation which had murdered her son, and even because, by committing adultery of her own accord, she was getting some of her own back on Felix – and safely, because he could never know. But to be a spy . . . and yet, she did want to do anything she could to end this war, as rapidly as possible, with an Allied victory.

'Ahem,' Morrison said, glancing at the anxious Drummond. 'I may say that I know of your involvement, already, Mrs Petersen.'

Mina frowned at him.

'Lieutenant Brassard was required to make a full report on his miraculous escape from Ostend,' Morrison explained. 'Of course he is still interned in Holland, but our ambassador was able to interview him. In the strictest confidence, of course. He mentioned a Mrs Petersen, an American lady, who not only arranged his removal from Ostend to Antwerp, but accompanied him, and there further arranged for him to change clothes with a Dutch worker and get across the river. Again accompanied by her.'

'Are you trying to blackmail me, Colonel?'

'Good Lord, no, Mrs Petersen. I am merely explaining how we came to approach you at all, and why we have always felt sure that you would be willing to co-operate with us. Having already chosen sides, so to speak.'

Mina glanced at Drummond in turn, who shrugged. 'I think you wish to weigh the pros and cons very carefully,' he said.

Mina sighed, considered, and then smiled. What did she have to lose? She certainly did mean to go back to Ostend, Claus or no Claus. 'I shall be making a longer stay than usual, this time,' she said. 'As I am hoping to have some work done on my hotel in Ostend. But I shall be back for Christmas, certainly. Will you join me for dinner, at the London Superb? Say on Christmas Eve?'

* * *

'Happy Christmas!' John Drummond raised his glass. 'Here's to 1917.'

'And to us.' Mina brushed his crystal with her own. They were dining tête-à-tête in her suite at the Superb, this year, where the previous Christmas Morrison had of course been with them, taking notes as she had talked. This year that was already done, and she need not spoil her meal by discussing German food problems or U-boat movements in and out of Ostend.

Besides, she enjoyed dining alone with Drummond. He knew all of her secrets, the only man in the world in possession of so much . . . and yet he had never tried to take advantage of them. She wondered why? He must know that the life she had lived for the past year and more had to have involved her in sex with at least one German; why not one Englishman as well? There was no way that Felix could find out about them, either. But of course, knowing so much about her, he would also know how repugnant she found physical relationships. Besides, he was her lawyer, and in many ways her father figure as well. If he certainly occasionally dreamed of her – that she could tell from the way she sometimes caught him looking at her – he preferred to leave it that way. So he alone of all the men in the world she could absolutely trust. Now she smiled at him. 'Do you remember this time last year?'

'Morrison? He was over the moon. Do you regret meeting him? I feel very guilty about that.'

'Well, don't,' Mina told him. 'I certainly don't regret anything. It's been exciting.'

'And dangerous? When I think of poor Edith Cavell . . .'

'You tried to call the whole thing off for me. I know, and I'm grateful, John. But if anything, knowing they had shot so gracious and heroic a lady merely made me the more determined than ever to carry on. Because she was a real heroine, you know.'

'Only in degree, Mina. You helped an allied officer to escape.'

'I helped one, as you say. She helped hundreds. And I'm untouchable, because I'm an American. Anyway, I don't actually take any risks. I don't make notes or take photographs. I just travel. I think the Germans regard me as a very large nuisance, but then, so do the French, with my insistence upon obtaining everything I can for the hotels, and the way I arrive and depart so abruptly, but nothing more than a nuisance.'

'And how are the hotels?'

She winked. 'The Ostend Superb will take years to put right, at the present rate of work. But isn't that what you want? And need? Right now? Years?'

He sighed. 'I don't know, Mina. Really I don't. Everyone thought this year would be it . . .' Another sigh.

'So you threw away sixty thousand young lives in one afternoon,' she said. 'Is that any way to win a war?'

'We are winning,' he insisted. 'Taken all together, there are more British and French and Italians than there are Germans and Austrians. But we know we are winning in more ways than by just killing Germans. We know the blockade is slowly but surely taking effect. You tell us that. You know that you couldn't be enjoying a meal like this, in Berlin.'

'Oh, yes, I could,' she said. 'If I was dining in my own hotel with a German general.'

'But not if you were dining with a German soldier in his own home.'

'Now that is something I never knew before,' she said. 'That British soldiers dine on champagne and pâté de foie gras when at home.'

'You know what I mean. Their families aren't starving.'

'And they are in Berlin,' she agreed. 'Oh, I know what you mean, John. It just seems to me that starving women and children to death is a horrible way to go about winning a war.'

'It has to be better than blowing them up, or drowning them, Mina.'

Their eyes met, and it was her turn to sigh. 'Yes.'

'Believe me, I didn't mean to drag it up. But . . .'

'You have something on your mind.'

'I'm afraid I do. A letter from Felix.' He felt in his pocket, laid the envelope on the table. 'I must admit I opened it, in your absence.'

Mina did not pick it up. 'He wants me back?'

'It is rather a formal application. I would say he's been talking with his attorneys.'

'That figures. Do you know the swine never even wrote a note of condolence after James' death? Much less inquired after *my* health.'

'I'm afraid being solicitous, or even loving, is not written into your contract, for either of you. He points out that you have now been away eighteen months. That was a month ago.'

'Well, I guess he's right about that. He was always pretty good at arithmetic.'

'So what are you going to do?'

Mina finished her champagne. 'Tomorrow I am going down to Epsom, to spend Christmas with Harry and Aunt Betty and Grandad, and on 6 January I'm booked for Rotterdam.'

'And Felix?'

'Felix can wait.'

'You're handing him live ammunition.'

'There's a lot of it about, isn't there? Write to him for me, John, and tell him I'm presently stuck on the Continent, but that you know I'll be on my way the moment I return.'

'And will you?'

'I don't know. And that's the truth.' Because it was. Having spent eighteen months away from Felix she didn't know if she'd be able to force herself to go back, without James, without Jessie . . . to that. 'But if I decide not to, I'll call Morrison, and you, John, as witnesses. No court is going to condemn me for fighting for a righteous cause.' She gazed at him. 'It *is* a righteous cause, isn't it, John?'

She had no doubt that it was. Her instincts told her that, even had there not recently been arising a tremendous clamour on the part of her own people for an ending to this most bloodthirsty of all conflicts, a cessation of hostilities which more and more Americans seemed to feel would have to be imposed on Germany by force of arms, especially if unrestricted submarine warfare, hastily abandoned as a means of bringing Great Britain to her knees following the furore over the sinking of the *Lusitania*, were to be resumed, as the German naval experts were recommending.

'What do you do, Mother, when you go away on those long trips?' Harry asked.

They walked together over the Surrey Downs, their boots leaving indistinct splodges on the light dusting of snow which had fallen during the night, while Grandfather Doberley's golden retrievers, three in number, bounded to and fro in front of them, certain there were rabbits to be raised beneath the white covering.

Mina sometimes thought her days here at the Doberley house were the happiest she had ever known. It was where she had belonged, from birth. It was fascinating to consider that, had Father not been a rebel and dutifully married Bishop Aubrey's daughter, this house was where she would have spent a large part of her childhood. She would probably have been married from here, a huge reception to honour her husband, who would have been some future captain of British industry.

Save that had Father married Bishop Aubrey's daughter, she wouldn't be Mina. She'd be somebody else altogether. She preferred to be her.

Even if she walked a tightrope between success and disaster? She was used to that by now. More difficult was it to keep reminding herself that there was a day of reckoning which had to come, and not merely from possible German action or possible legal problems with Felix. The only problem she was prepared to worry about was walking beside her.

Harry was fourteen, now. He was tall and well-built, and seemed to enjoy school. Presumably he had made friends there; according to Bettina, he sometimes brought a companion home for holidays, although not of course for Christmas. But he was almost a stranger to her. She wished it could be otherwise. She loved him more than she would ever dare show him; he was in fact about the only remaining living creature that she did love. But, loving Harry, and bearing such a burden of guilt as she did on her shoulders for James' death, she could only exist by fighting her way back to the top, so that he could inherit a fortune.

Because he would do that. No matter what happened. And when the war was over they would settle down together, because in only a few years he would be old enough to start learning about the business. And old enough to start controlling his memories, too. Because she did not doubt that he had as many nightmares as she, even if he had never mentioned the *Lusitania*. But then, he had never asked her any questions, until now, either.

She smiled, and hugged him. 'I have hotels to look after. Hotels which are one day going to belong to you.'

He made no reply, so after a few moments she said, 'Don't you want to own a lot of hotels, Harry?'

'I think that would be so grand,' he said. 'Will I really.'

'Really and truly,' she promised, her heart singing.

'Will that mean I'll have to be a hotel manager?'

'An owner. Not quite the same thing.'

'But I'll have to learn all about the trade.'

'Well, yes, of course. You'd need to do that. Don't you want to learn the hotel trade?'

'I'd thought of becoming a lawyer. It's a decision we have to make, pretty soon.'

'Oh,' she said. 'Well . . . I guess being a lawyer isn't a bad thing, even for a hotelier. You know Mr Drummond? He comes down here to see us sometimes. He's a lawyer, and he handles nearly all my business for me. So you go ahead and be a lawyer, if you wish.'

He glanced at her. 'Can one do anything one wishes, Mother?'

'Sure. If one's determined enough.'

'I wish we could go home.'

Mina stopped walking. 'We will go home,' she said. 'Just as soon as this war is over, Harry.'

'But not until then?'

'No,' she said. 'Not until then. I have to stay, Harry. And I couldn't bear to be separated from you.'

He gazed at her. 'But you are separated from me, Mother. Most of the time.'

Mina sighed, and held his hand as they turned for the walk back. 'That's only until the end of the war, Harry. Once the war ends, you and I are never going to be separated again. That's an absolute promise.' She squeezed his gloved fingers. 'And you know what? I don't think that's going to be too long delayed, now.'

She was not the only one who had that possibility in mind. 'What will you do, Mina, if your President declares war on us?' asked Claus Freilinghausen.

Mina sat on the edge of the bed and brushed her hair. They had already made love, because Claus seemed to need to make love to her within minutes of being in her company. In many ways he reminded her of Jimmy Morton. Many ways. Except that he was even more unimaginative, more anxious only to hold her in his arms, for which she was truly thankful.

But she didn't want him brooding on the possibility of American intervention. 'I doubt if it will truly come to that,' she said. 'You've been reading too many East Coast, pro-British newspapers. President Wilson has to weigh good and bad for the nation, and then he has to persuade Congress to do the same. You know, he has the power to tell our sailors to shoot back if you people start shooting at them, but he can't go to war all on his own. Your admirals would have to do something very agressive to make all of Congress want to start shooting.'

'Suppose they did?' His hand slid up and down her arm.

She frowned at him. 'You'd better say what you have on your mind.'

'Do you remember a conversation we had, oh, nearly two years ago now, just after you first came back to Berlin, following the death of your son?' He sighed. 'I have a terrible feeling that the win-at-any-cost believers are again seeking control. I suppose because they can see that unless we win at any cost, we will not win at all.'

'You mean your government *is* going to resume unrestricted submarine warfare.'

'It has already begun.'

Her heart seemed to give a lurch. 'Can you really even attempt to justify anything so barbaric?'

'One can justify anything, if it is a case of victory or death. Because do not mistake the situation. To lose this war means the death of Germany as we know it.'

'And you reckon you can win that way, even if it means bringing us in against you? There are an awful lot of Americans, Claus.'

'But would even your millions be of any avail if we could force Britain and France to make peace before you could mobilise?'

'You really think that's going to happen, don't you, Claus?'

His eyes gloomed at her, and for just a moment his fingers tightened on her arm. 'I know it is going to happen, Mina.'

She stared at him. But he could know nothing of the truth

266

about her. That simply was not possible. 'Then I would have to go home, Claus.'

'To your husband?'

'That is correct.'

'Whom you have told me that you do not love? Whom you hate, in fact.'

Mina shrugged. 'I would be going home to America, Claus. Felix is merely an unfortunate aspect of American life. But he is the only one.'

'But you have an alternative, Mina. You could stay here.'

'With you?'

'I think I could propose that, now that I know you better. Now that I know that I can make you happy. Germany is a splendid place to be happy in, Mina. Oh, I know that we are sometimes prepared to do terrible things to secure our future, but that is because we are confident our future is the best, for us, and for Europe, and perhaps even for the world. And you have a stake here, Mina. While, when the war is over, and we have won, why . . .'

The amazing thing was that he meant every word of what he was saying. He honestly thought he did make her happy, and that she wanted nothing more in life than to lie in his arms. Just as he honestly thought that she had nothing against the Germans, even if they had murdered her son. She had made him believe that, she knew; she remembered thinking once before, how many centuries ago, that she would have made a marvellous actress.

'That is an awfully big decision, Claus,' she said. 'I can only pray it is one I shall never have to make.'

But if it was one he thought was imminent, or if his government *was* meaning to resume sinking merchant vessels without warning, then she had to make the decision, and follow it up by getting out of Germany, and out of any German controlled territory as well, just as quickly as she could. Claus might suppose it would simply be a matter of internment, or expulsion, which he could overcome, were she to declare herself his mistress. But she simply could not do that. Even if she had the slightest desire to move in with him on a permanent basis, in effect to abandon Harry until the end of the war, she would never be able to act her way out of the hatred and loathing she would feel for him and all his people, a loathing which, although she did not like admitting it, had been dwindling over the past year as she had observed the courage with which they were facing a rapidly growing certainty that here was a war they could not win – and losing which, as Claus had remarked, would involve disastrous consequences.

Equally, she could not take the risk of anyone learning about her activities, or the risk that Morrison might blow the whistle on her if she were to opt to remain in Germany – because how could he then be sure she had ever been straight with him at all? She still did not really think that America was going to become involved – she just could not imagine it of the America she had left nearly two years before – but if there was even a chance of that happening, however slim . . .

Panic was going to achieve nothing, however. It was simply a matter of taking her usual route, visiting Ostend, thence going on to Holland, and thence taking a passage to England. Exactly as she had done six times before in the past year and a half. Once she was in Holland she was safe. But she would be happier in England. And meanwhile, she would smile and be her usual elegantly confident self, and if she held her new mink coat a little tighter against herself on the railway platform, that was surely because it was an intensely cold February morning; messages had been coming in of rioting in Petrograd, as the Russians had renamed St Petersburg – where apparently it was freezing and the bread shortages were even greater than in Berlin – and Russia was supposedly an Allied power, whom the British blockade was designed to help. She could not escape the feeling that the whole of Europe was descending into a pit of catastrophe.

Claus accompanied her to the station, as usual, although his duties on the staff no longer allowed him the time to travel with her. 'I should not be telling you this,' he confided, 'but you will find the situation in Belgium somewhat different to last year. We are making some tactical withdrawals in certain places. It is all a plan, you see, to trap the British. Our spies tell us they are about to launch another great offensive, as soon as the weather improves, and Ludendorff has decided to let them expend their artillery on barren ground, and occupy worthless territory. There is nothing for you to worry about . . .' He gave her arm one of his familiar squeezes. 'We are not giving up Ostend. It is too valuable to our navy. But there will be a salient into our lines, and so I am routing you to Aachen. There you will change trains, and travel direct across north Belgium to Antwerp, and thence down the coast to Ostend. It will mean, I am afraid, entering Dutch territory, briefly, and then leaving it again, but it is by far the safest way to travel. I hope you do not mind?'

Mind, she asked herself, as her brain danced. It was what she would have proposed herself, had she dared. Once in Holland, she could change trains again at Maastricht, and travel direct to Rotterdam, without entering Belgium, or any German controlled territory again. Of course once she did that she had burned her bridges; she would not be able to return either to Berlin or to Ostend until the end of the conflict – the hotels would certainly be confiscated. But if the Allies did win, as Morrison had assured her, the property would be returned, with interest.

And she would be safe. With what tremendous information to give the British. Morrison would be happy to let her go into honourable retirement after she had brought him up to date on Ludendorff's plan 'to trap the British', as Claus had put it.

Of course, having retired, she thought sombrely, she would have no choice but to go home to Felix. But even that might be a relief, once the Atlantic crossing was behind her. She had not realised until last night how tense had been the past few months. 'Of course I do not mind, Claus,' she said, and kissed him goodbye. 'I have no desire to be blown up, believe me.'

He was gone, waving goodbye as the train slowly pulled out of the station, and she could relax. It was about eight hours to Aachen, and they would not arrive before dusk. But she was at least on her way.

The first-class compartment was crowded with officers, as the entire train was crowded with enlisted men, on their way back to their units after a brief Berlin leave, or a spell in hospital. They were all very jolly at first, although they treated her with the greatest respect; they had all seen her kissing General Freilinghausen goodbye. And soon even their slightly hysterical high spirits dwindled into somnolence as the train chugged on, occasionally stopping at a station in a main town such as Hanover to take on yet more soldiers. Mina read her novel for a while, and then lunched from her picnic basket; the train was simply too crowded to attempt the dining car. Then she dozed, allowing her hat to drop forward over her face, and awoke with a start as they pulled into yet another station. She peered out of the window. It was already dark, and she couldn't see a sign, but the porters and the stationmaster were undoubtedly German.

Her head turned as the door to the corridor opened; the compartment was already full. Two men stood there, one in the uniform of a police officer and the other in civilian clothes, looking in.

'There is no room, comrades,' said one of the seated officers.

'Then we will make room,' the civilian said, and pointed, at Mina. 'Get up, Frau Petersen. You are under arrest.'

Mina was so surprised that she could not speak for the moment, and at a gesture from the civilian, the policeman stepped into the compartment to grasp her arm and pull her to her feet. She was not used to physical violence, even from Felix, and found herself breathless.

'I must protest,' said the young officer who had been sitting next to her throughout the journey, and who now also got up. 'That is no way to treat a lady.'

'Sit down, Herr Lieutenant,' the civilian said. 'This woman is a well-known *agent provocateur*. Take her outside.'

Mina was dragged into the crowded corridor. People stared at her, and she stared back, not actually seeing any of them. She knew she had to think, quickly and accurately. But she could only think about details. 'My things,' she said, looking at her travelling case on the rack.

'They will be taken care of. Haste, now.'

There were two other uniformed policemen in the corridor, and these bundled her along, pushing people right and left, causing her to lose her breath all over again, until she found herself on the platform with the cold air whipping into her face and scattering her hair; only then did she realise that her hat had fallen off in the train. Which was now pulling out.

'My things,' she said. 'My hat. My . . .'

'Be quiet, Frau Petersen,' the plain-clothesman, as she now

270

understood him to be, commanded. It was the second time he had used her name. She could no longer even hope that it could be a mistake.

But it had to be a mistake, even if he did know who she was. In fact, that made it more of a mistake than ever. She drew a long breath, and with a determined effort got her thoughts under control. 'I am an American citizen. You cannot do this.'

'I have a warrant,' the detective said.

'My government will crucify you,' Mina snapped, now getting angry.

Another train was pulling into the station, heading the other way, the way she had just come from, back to Berlin. One of the policemen opened the door of a compartment, gestured the people inside out, and went in himself. The detective and the other two policemen pushed Mina in behind him; she tripped on the step and was jerked to her feet, head spinning. The evicted passengers were protesting loudly and one of them tried to get back on, but the detective shook his head. 'This compartment has been requisitoned,' he said. 'Find seats further down the train.'

The door was slammed, and one of the policemen locked the corridor door and drew down the blind. For the first time Mina's bewilderment and anger at what was happening were replaced by apprehension; she was quite alone in this locked compartment, with these four thugs. But she could not let them see that she was afraid. 'Where are you taking me?' she demanded.

The detective, sitting opposite, gazed at her. 'To Berlin.'

'And you say you have a warrant for my arrest? Am I allowed to know the charge?'

'If you wish. You are charged that on the fifth of August, 1915, Frau Petersen, you did aid and abet the escape of an English officer, Lieutenant Brassard, from Ostend to Holland.'

'Brassard?' she cried. She had almost forgotten the incident.

'You cannot deny it, Frau Petersen. Monsier Chaffaux has been arrested, as well as the driver of the laundry truck, and the chef from the Splendide Hotel. Under . . . interrogation, they have confessed everything, and implicated you.'

She gazed at him, as viciously as she could. 'Under interrogation? You mean you tortured them, you savage.'

'We persuaded them, Frau Petersen. Now, I am sure you

271

would not wish us to have to *persuade* you, to tell us the truth.'

'I will tell you nothing.'

The man shrugged. 'As you wish. Then we may well have to hurt you a little.'

'You . . .' Her stomach seemed to be dancing a jig.

'And to what avail?' he asked. 'Those three, Chaffaux and the others, have already been shot.'

'Shot?' she shrieked.

'Of course. They were guilty of crimes against the Reich. As you are.'

'You . . . you monster,' she shouted. 'My God, I will see that you pay for this. And you think you can browbeat me? Well, think again. I am an American citizen. I wish to see the United States Ambassador. I am also a well-known international figure, mein Herr. You had better consult with your superiors, just as quickly as you can. Because there has been a mistake for which someone is going to pay. I give you my word on that.'

The detective smiled. 'My warrant was signed by my superiors, Frau Petersen. And they do not make mistakes. I had never even heard of you, down to the day before yesterday. But my superiors have, apparently. M. Chaffaux was arrested several weeks ago, in connection with aiding another British prisoner to escape. It was just after your last departure from Ostend. He confessed very quickly, it seems. Not a very strong character. And so he has been shot. But his confession remains. My superiors merely waited for you to return to Germany, you see, and for certain other, shall we say, favourable developments to take place.'

'Favourable developments?'

'Yesterday your President broke off diplomatic relations with Germany.'

'My God,' Mina said. 'But that does not yet make us enemies.'

'Indeed not. But war will certainly be declared. President Wilson has seen fit virtually to issue us an ultimatum, that we either abandon our projected plans for unrestricted submarine warfare, in order to complete the defeat of the British, or he will declare war. Well, I can assure you that Germany has no intention of being dictated to by an ex-schoolmaster. So, very soon, America and Germany will be at war. In arresting

272

you, and various other American agents, we are merely anticipating the actual moment. That will give us the necessary time to . . . interrogate you. And then, when war is declared, we are going to put you against a wall and shoot you, Frau Petersen. Just to show the Americans how we deal with those who would fight against the Reich.'

Chapter 13

Once again Mina had to fight against the panic which was clawing at her mind. She felt that she had to be in the middle of a nightmare, and would awaken at any moment in Claus' arms.

But as she knew it wasn't a nightmare, it was necessary to exercise great self-control, to remind herself that she was Mina Petersen, and even more, Mina Doberley, that she had survived the cholera epidemic on board the *William McKinley*, and the icy waters off the Irish coast when the *Lusitania* had been torpedoed, not to mention being driven full tilt into a lamp-post; no German detective should be able to frighten her.

But it was necessary to think very clearly and very seriously. Who could possibly have suspected that little Chaffaux would have helped other British soldiers? And without telling her? And had he actually implicated her in the other escapes? Or only with Brassard. Had he actually implicated her at all? She had been shown no documents incriminating her. And Chaffaux was dead. While this man who had arrested her, as he had just admitted, was an underling who merely carried out orders. Orders which had been given by some superior. But not necessarily a very superior superior. Probably some colonel in military intelligence, a German Morrison, who had been given too much power by the exigencies of warfare.

She further reminded herself that it was all really rather amusing, for they apparently had no idea what she had really been doing the last eighteen months, were intent upon nailing her for a single rather irrelevant crime. But in that they did not have a leg to stand on, legally. When she had committed that crime, it had not been a crime, because she had been a neutral, entitled to take whichever side she chose. She frowned. Technically, she was still a neutral, and yet was under arrest. But she had already observed how the Germans were prepared to bend the rules, and the truth, to gain an advantage. Well, she must simply be prepared to bend the rules, and the truth, back in her favour, as indeed she had been doing for more than a year. Only now she would have to do it more forcefully, and more convincingly, too.

She gazed at the detective. 'I presume you are not aware that I am a friend of General Freilinghausen?' she asked.

He stared at her.

'A very close friend,' Mina said, meaningfully.

Still he stared at her.

'And I can tell you,' Mina went on, 'that the general will be very angry, very angry indeed, when he learns what has happened to me. He himself put me on this train, and if you look through my handbag you will see that he himself signed the pass allowing me to cross the border into Holland.'

'The general is no doubt unaware of your perfidy,' the detective said.

'I assure you that the general knows all about me,' Mina said. 'You have made a serious mistake, my friend. Or your superior has. So take me back to Berlin. That will suit me very well. General Freilinghausen is in Berlin. But the moment we get there I wish to see him.'

The detective stared at her for several more minutes. Then he said, 'This woman has not been searched. Why has she not been searched? Who knows what weapons may be concealed about her person?'

Mina opened her mouth to protest, and closed it again with a snap, as two policemen seized her arms and stretched them along the cushions, pinning them there, while the other came round in front of her. She considered kicking him, but decided against it, as it could only make her more vulnerable to assault. Instead she panted with anger and outrage as he felt in her armpits, slid his hands down her ribs; patted her thighs; actually, the man seemed even more embarrassed than she was, and hurried through his task in a most perfunctory fashion.

'She is not armed, mein Herr,' he said.

'Do you call that a search?' the detective demanded. 'I have dealt with these female *agents provocateurs* before. They carry small pistols concealed in their drawers, next to their skin. Search her, man. Find me that weapon.'

The man hesitated, licking his lips.

'If you lay a finger on me,' Mina whispered, trying to snarl.

'You are afraid of a woman,' the detective said, and in a quick movement gathered her boots from the floor, holding her ankles and tucking them under his arm; now she did try to kick, but he was stronger than he looked and she could not free her legs, while the effort, added to his tug, pulled her down the seat and left her hopelessly vulnerable, her skirts already riding up. 'There you are,' the detective said.

The policeman hesitated again, bit his lip, and then threw up her skirts and plucked at her drawers. She actually felt his fingers on her flesh for a moment and gave a convulsive heave which chased him to the far side of the compartment. 'There is no weapon, mein Herr,' he gasped.

The detective nodded, and the other two policemen hastily released Mina's arms and moved as far away as they could. She pushed herself up, desperately anxious to drag her clothes back to their proper places but determined not to do so before these scoundrels. 'I am going to have you sent to prison,' she said. 'All of you.'

'You have an over-inflated sense of your importance, Frau Petersen,' the detective said. 'As of this moment, you are a nothing. A nothing, you understand. I forbid you to speak again until we reach Berlin. If you do I will have my men search you again, and this time they will strip you and do a proper job.' He smiled. 'You are a friend of General Freilinghausen, you claim. Well, meine Dame, I will ask the general to come to see you, as soon as we reach Berlin. Until then, I advise you to be quiet. Save your breath, meine Dame because when the time comes, we are going to require you to say a great deal.'

However much it went against the grain, Mina decided her best course was to obey him. He seemed to feel that he possessed unlimited power over her, and while they were in this train he did. No doubt he would like nothing better than to have an excuse to manhandle her some more – well he was not going to get it. But that did not mean she was going to allow herself to be afraid of him. It was simply a matter of keeping her nerves under control. Until Berlin.

But, as the train chugged into the night, courage became

increasingly difficult to sustain. She kept having to remind herself that she had committed no crime. At least, so far as these people knew. She must simply maintain that, and deny everything else, and then set to work to escape Claus, and Germany, before Wilson actually went to war – and meanwhile hope that he would not go to war at all. If he hadn't over the *Lusitania*, which had involved the deaths of more than a hundred American citizens, it seemed rather pointless now, when so far as she knew no American had yet been killed.

At last she even managed to doze, from sheer weariness, for it was after midnight before the train pulled into the Tiergarten. Immediately she was hustled into a taxi cab and driven off to an official-looking building with a flag outside – some sort of police station, she presumed. Inside she was taken along corridors and up flights of stairs, past offices crowded with men, and with women, she saw to her surprise, all still working despite the late hour, until she was shown into a small room containing only a table and two chairs, and no windows. 'You will wait here,' the detective who had arrested her said. 'Grete will stay with you.'

A large, blonde young woman stood beside the door. At least that was better than a man. Mina sat down, waves of exhaustion creeping over her. And the exhaustion was again making her depressed and afraid. But if they were really sending for Claus . . . she made herself sit up, and attempted to straighten her clothes, and even to smooth her hair, which was a tangled mess. To her utter surprise, the detective returned a little while later with a cup of coffee, which made her feel much better – although it did not in the least alter her determination to have him punished just as thoroughly as she could.

But were they meaning to keep her sitting here all night? She smiled at Grete. 'Does no one in Berlin sleep?' she asked.

Grete merely gazed at her, face expressionless.

Surely they could not be getting Claus out of bed? Mina decided to rest while she could, however uncomfortable her situation; she rested her head on her arms on the table, and actually dozed off again, to awake with a start and severe backache as the door opened once more. Because there he was.

'Claus!' she cried, springing to her feet with such violence she overturned the chair. 'Oh, Claus!'

277

Claus jerked his head, and Grete left the room, closing the door behind her. 'Do you know what I have just been told?' Claus asked.

'Yes,' Mina said. 'Claus ... I can explain.' She went towards him, but the grimness of his expression made her check.

'They have told me that no matter how angry I may be, how betrayed I may feel, or how humiliated, I must remember that you are still technically a neutral, and that in any event I must not mark your face or break any bones, because you will have to appear in a court of law to be tried.'

She stared at him, her jaw slowly sagging. 'Not break ...' She licked her lips. 'They are very amusing.'

'You think so?' He looked down at the sheet of paper he was holding. 'The fifth of August, 1915. I remember it well. The fourth of August was a night I shall never forget, Mina. It was the most splendid of my life. And while you were ... entertaining me, Chaffaux and his people were removing the Briton from the Superb, is that it?'

'I ...' She bit her lip. 'It was an impulse, Claus. That poor man was half-starved, and so sad. And I wasn't sending him back to England. He was interned, in Holland. No doubt he is still there. He can't ever fight you again.'

'Was it also an impulse that made you seduce me that night? An impulse suggested I remove the sentry from your hotel?'

She gazed at him. She knew she desperately needed to think very quickly and very accurately – but her brain was so tired.

'And every night that you slept with me since?' he demanded, his voice harsh. 'When you crawled naked into my bed and wriggled your arse with joy, were those also nights on which Britons were being smuggled across our borders?'

'No,' she shouted. 'I swear it. No.'

'Those endearments you whispered in my ear, did you ever mean a single one of them?'

Mina stared at him, a calamitous hesitation.

'You are a *slut*,' he shouted, and hit her across the face. The force of the blow was beyond anything she could have expected. She had the impression of flying through the air while her head was travelling much faster than the rest of her, found herself on her hands and knees, coughing and gasping, while her mouth filled with blood.

'Now your face is marked,' Claus said. 'I should not have done that.'

'No,' she whispered, turning on her knees, her mind consumed with a quite vicious anger. 'I am going to have you *shot*.'

'I should have kicked you instead,' he said, as if she hadn't spoken, and did so. His boot thudded into her thigh and she rolled across the floor, the pain too excruciating for words. She landed on her face, and he kicked her again, while she was unable to move, and then seized her by her hair and her mink and dragged her back into the centre of the room, sprawling her on her back, while he knelt above her and drove his fists into her stomach and breasts. She tried to ward off the blows, opened her eyes, and even through the pain saw to her amazement that he was weeping, even as he hit her.

'I loved you,' he moaned. 'I *loved* you.'

She realised that he was quite out of control of himself, and at the same time so angry he was quite capable of beating her to death. She rolled away from him, drawing up her knees and tucking her arms in against her ribs in an attempt at least to protect her breasts and stomach, while attempting to make a noise, to shout, to scream, to call someone to her aid.

And apparently succeeding. The door burst open, and she heard men, and women, speaking loudly. The hammering blows on her ribs and kidneys stopped, but that did not mean immediate relief. She was seized by the ankles and the wrists, dumped on some kind of stretcher, and taken out. Dimly she was aware that a man in a white coat was prodding her chest and using a stethoscope, but it was all merging into the general nightmare with which she was surrounded.

Mina awoke to a world of women, more completely so even than in her first days at the Superb. There had been men at the Superb, however they had been excluded from the private world of the girls. Here there were no men. Only women. Presumably there were Ednas and Bettys and Lucys and Claudettes, but those she saw only from a distance. Her world was composed of Mrs Youngs, old Mrs Youngs and young Mrs Youngs. They dominated her days, and equally they dominated her dreams. They decided when she would awake

279

and when she would sleep, when she would eat and when she would wash; they had never apparently come into contact with actual bathing. Her only conversation was with them, when they chose to speak with her, which was seldom. Her exercise periods, as an enemy alien, were different to those of the other female prisoners, and while she saw the others on the far side of the yard, they could not communicate with her – not that they showed any great desire to do so. They were only criminals; she was an enemy.

She supposed in many ways she was fortunate; she suffered no sexual assaults and no deliberate brutality. In the beginning, while she still ached from the beating Claus had given her, when she could still see the huge purple marks on her thighs where he had kicked her – it was a miracle no bones had been broken – this was a tremendous relief. Had she been beaten then she knew she would probably have gone mad. But after a month or so she would have welcomed brutality. It was possible, as she remembered from Mrs Young, to set up a certain relationship with a woman who was beating you. It was impossible to set up any sort of relationship with women who did their best to ignore you, who dominated your life as they dominated the dust on the floor, and treated you with as much respect. They did actually hit her from time to time. Each wardress carried a leather strap, and when one of their charges was the least bit slow in standing to attention at their entry, or in obeying a command, the strap whipped across knuckles with a paralysingly sharp snap of pain. This was intensely humiliating. But it was quite impossible to feel there was any human emotion, such as anger, involved in the punishment; no doubt it was written down in a rule book, somewhere.

Only once did they show any interest in her. It was the day they heard a tremendous shouting from outside the prison walls, and even the guards had been interested, and in her reaction, to that. 'Your President has declared war,' they said. 'The schoolmaster would fight against the Reich. Do you hear that noise, American? They are burning an hotel, the property of an American. Do you know the hotel, American?'

So confused had she been, that was the first time she had actually realised that she was still in Berlin.

They were burning the Superb. Poor Adolf. The Superb had

been his great pride, the summit of his ambitions, as he had often told her. She could only hope he had not been inside when the mob had set fire to it.

And had it not also been the summit of her career? She supposed it had. But it all seemed terribly irrelevant now, when she was about to be put on trial and shot, at any moment. 'When America declares war,' the detective had said. She wondered how she would stand up to being put against a wall, tied to a stake, blindfold attached to her eyes. Edith Cavell had faced her murderers without flinching. Did she have that much courage? And when they tortured her, as apparently they first intended to do, would she be able to withstand them without breaking, and confessing to all the other crimes she had committed against the German war machine?

Considering these possibilities was as great a torture as any the Germans could have inflicted. Because it never happened. But it was always about to happen. She spent every day trying to make her peace with . . . God? No, she still refused to do that. Besides, she had no doubt at all that He would wish nothing to do with her, after everything she had done, or accepted, during the years. The peace had to be made with herself. She had driven herself onwards, surmounting obstacle after obstacle, accepting humiliation and mistreatment after mistreatment, in search of what? There was the damning, unanswerable question. She had thought only of expanding. Berlin had been going to be a stepping stone to Cairo, and Moscow, and Tokyo, and San Francisco, and heaven alone knew how many places in between. But what then? She had never considered that. Because she had expected to die before her ultimate dream was reached? She had not been aware of that. But to have expended so much energy, sacrificed so much – her own son – accepted so much – Felix's sexual sadism – risked so much . . . to wind up in a German cell, waiting to be shot. Why? Simply because she had never refused a challenge? There seemed no other reason, when she could so easily have refused Morrison's proposal, and gone back to Felix, and his dwindling capabilities, and her financial empire, and said to herself, what the hell has Europe to do with me?

Instead, she would die, twelve bullets smashing through those breasts Claus had longed to hold, and Jimmy had loved to

281

fondle, and Felix had loved to mistreat – and Philip Clancy had once said were the greatest tits in all the world. Twelve bullets, and then oblivion.

That it was not going to happen dawned on her only slowly. She didn't know why there had been a delay, and she was reluctant to try to find the answers, at first. But she suddenly realised that she had been in prison an awfully long time, without trial or even formal accusation – and that she was being held to all intents and purposes in solitary confinement. The understanding of her situation, as much as the sense of injustice, drove her into a fury. She was Mina Doberley, and she had her defence all ready to prove her innocence of any crime on fifth August 1915. For her just to be locked up . . . her shouts and her bangs on the door at last awakened a reaction from the wardresses, who descended upon her in great numbers, stripped her naked, and then bound her up in a strait-jacket and left her. After she had spent twenty-four hours in this ghastly contraption, overheated from the hips up, trembling from the hips down, she had been released, forced to stand beneath a freezing water hose, and allowed to dress again. To her pleas to be allowed to see the governor, or a lawyer, or an accuser, or even an executioner, no one had paid any attention at all.

In despair, and continuing anger, she very nearly surrendered to the temptation to shock them by declaring herself to be a spy, by forcing them to do something about her by the very extent of her revelations. Fortunately common sense came to her rescue. It even occurred to her that this might in itself be a form of torture, to which she had very nearly succumbed. But she would not. She would sit it out for as long as they did.

But slowly time itself became her enemy. She had been arrested on a freezing February evening. Before she had properly come to terms with her situation she was sweltering in the heat of summer. By then the daily humiliations of being a prisoner no longer seemed relevant. Emptying a full latrine pail, standing to attention whenever the cell was inspected, falling hungrily and even gratefully upon the black bread and cabbage soup which was her normal food, seemed a perfectly acceptable way of life, even for the erstwhile toast of two continents. With the coming of hot weather they shaved her hair. Felix had shaved her groin, often enough; these women did that as well as her head. To prevent lice, they explained; they could not risk typhus in the prison. She supposed they were right, and that she should be grateful to them for worrying about her health. She remembered that her head had been shaved before, after her accident, and that her hair had grown back more luxuriantly than ever. As had her pubic hair. And they were at least impersonally efficient.

But then it became autumn again, and she realised that for some reason which was beyond her understanding she was neither going to be tortured nor shot, but was merely being left in solitary confinement to rot. Then she began to consider other things. She begged for a message to be sent to England, to John Drummond for relaying to Aunt Bettina and to Harry, telling them she was still alive – it hadn't seemed important when she had been about to be shot. The wardress wrote down the message, but she had no means of knowing if it had ever been sent – there was never a reply. She wondered what Felix thought about it all, and found some faint amusement in that. Which rapidly turned to anger as she thought of him taking over her hotels. And then to tears, as she thought of the Berlin Superb, burned to the ground. What had happened to all the other Superbs?

What had happened to her dream?

She spent a lot of time brooding on the past. Because it was impossible to convince herself that she was not being punished for that past. By God, of course. He had sought to punish her for years. And always she had defied Him, and escaped Him, and dived deeper into sin. She had married Jimmy Morton without love. She had borne James and Harry, without love. They had been on the one hand stepping stones, on the other hindrances, on the way to the realisation of her dream. That she had suddenly come to love both the boys was neither here nor there, because by the time she had done that it had been too late: one was dead, and the other was far away.

She had sold herself to Felix, deliberately and cold-bloodedly, to get the financial backing she required. Well, she had paid for that. She had deliberately refused to allow herself to make friends with any man or any woman, save for Jessie and John Drummond – and Jessie was now also dead. While Drummond probably soon would be. And finally, she had

283

deliberately deluded Claus Freilinghausen into believing she loved him. And she had suffered for that, too.

What had she gained, out of all of that, which could be considered of the least value to her in this desolate cell? She could at least feel secure in the knowledge that Harry was being looked after by Bettina and Grandad, and she could feel a certain warmth that she had after all been reconciled with her father's family. It was not something she had ever intended to allow to happen. She could feel secure in the knowledge that the New York Superb and the London Superb were both no doubt prospering, as much as that was possible in wartime, and no doubt the shell of what was going to be the Paris Superb was still standing . . . but they were all far away, and she was here, for day after deadening day, after deadening day, with nothing to do but think. Planning was not possible, where there seemed no future – and without her plans she had always been only half a woman. Only memory was left to her, and too much of that was bitter.

God had finally caught her up.

And slowly, as the autumn became winter again, and winter once more became spring, and spring became summer and the wardresses came in to shave her again, and then summer itself faded into yet another autumn, even memory became impossible. The woman of whom she had been thinking seemed like a fantasy from the past. She had long since abandoned any attempt to count the days, but the mere change of seasons convinced her that she had now been in this cell for well over a year. Without trial. Without a visit from anyone, save the wardresses. Even they changed from time to time, and the other prisoners certainly changed, so far as she could see – but old and new apparently laboured under the same instructions: speak to the American only as was absolutely necessary. While she remained in solitary confinement, staring at the walls, dreaming and remembering, with dreams and memories becoming increasingly confused, but determined that she would not go mad, existing as best she could on a steadily dwindling supply of poor food, waiting, listening, and hearing nothing, except one day rifle shots close at hand. She asked about these, and for once the wardress answered, shrugging as she did so. 'Police, firing on the mob,' she said casually.

So Berlin did have a mob after all. The mob which had

burned her hotel, no doubt. She wondered whose hotel they were burning today?

Amazingly, only a few days afterwards, the door of her cell opened, and for the first time in nearly two years Mina found herself gazing at man.

His appearance, short and dapper and very well dressed, made her instinctively aware of how dishevelled and unfeminine she must appear – she had not been allowed the use of a mirror in all the time she had been in this cell, just as she had not been allowed the use of a hairbrush – although her hair was growing out again – or even a toothbrush, much less soap or perfume. She left her cot to stand against the far wall, staring at him, and past him, at the wardress standing there, face as impassive as ever.

'Wilhelmina Petersen?' the man asked, very formally.

My God, Mina thought. The executioner. After all this time, the executioner had finally come for her. He could be no one else. Her tongue seemed stuck to the roof of her mouth.

'She cannot speak?' the man asked.

'She has had no one to speak to, for a long time, mein Herr,' said the woman.

'But it is she?'

The woman shrugged. 'That is what it says on the door, mein Herr.'

The man glanced at her. 'You may have much to answer for, Fräulein,' he said, and stepped into the cell. 'Mrs Petersen?' He spoke English, and raised his hat. 'I am Josef Tiene. I am a representative of the Swiss Government. Will you come with me, please?'

Mina opened her mouth, closed it again, and opened it again with an effort. 'Where?'

Tiene smiled in relief. 'I really thought you had lost your tongue, my dear lady. To my home. My car is outside, and my wife is waiting to assist you.'

Mina frowned, and looked at the wardress. Of course it had to be some kind of a trick. But the woman continued to look disinterested.

'It is cold outside,' Tiene continued. 'But there is a warm coat in the car. Will you not come, Mrs Petersen? Do you not

285

understand? You are free to leave this place.'

'Free?' Mina muttered. 'No, Herr Tiene. I do not understand. Why am I free to leave?'

Tiene took her hand, and half pulled her towards the door. 'Because the war is over, Mrs Petersen. Germany has surrendered. And I am under instructions to take care of you. Do you know what we are going to do?' He continued to hold her arm as he guided her along corridors and through barred doorways, past other impassive wardresses – presumably the fact of the war being ended would make no difference to *their* professions. But to her? She still did not properly grasp what he had told her; she was afraid to, in case she should discover that it wasn't true.

'We are going to take you home,' Tiene continued, 'And we are going to give you a hot bath, and then a square meal, and then we are going to put you to bed for just as long as you wish to stay there, and then, why, Mrs Petersen, when you feel up to it, a passage is arranged for you, back to England. Won't that be marvellous?'

They were in the outer courtyard, and had to wait while a wardress unlocked the door to the street. Tiene was now frowning. 'Please try to understand, Mrs Petersen,' he said. 'You *are* free.'

'Mrs Petersen!' Pierre Raizman seized Mina's hands and kissed them, several times. 'We have all been so worried, madame, so very worried. We have missed you so. But to have you back, and looking so well . . .'

Mina smiled at him; she was close to tears. Presumably she did look well; John Drummond had sent some of her clothes across to meet her, and if they hung on her because she had lost over a stone in weight, that fact was concealed by the new mink he had also sent; her hair was largely concealed beneath her fur hat, and could have been piled on the top of her head– no one could tell it was still short, just as no one could see the little silver threads running through the deep gold. She had spent long hours in a hot, scented bath, and was again wearing her favourite perfume; no one could suspect she had recently smelt like a sewer. Just as, if her movements were slow and uncertain, everyone understood that she had not, apparently, been very well over the past two years – no one suspected that with every step she anticipated a barked command telling her she had gone far enough.

Even her teeth were white again; only she knew her gums still bled every time she brushed them. 'I thank you, Pierre,' she said. 'And you, you have done wonders.'

Because there was no argument about that. There were one or two places where she would have liked to see fresh paint, and the carpet was a little worn, here and there, but the hotel looked as prosperous as ever, the flowers bloomed as brilliantly as ever, both in the vases and in the garden, and the staff looked as busy and as enthusiastic as ever.

'Ah, madame,' Pierre said. 'You should have been here on Armistice Night. We had a party until two in the morning. It was a great occasion. But not so great an occasion as this. Having you back will be like opening night all over again. You will be staying with us for a while?'

Mina glanced at Drummond, attentive at her elbow. 'I don't know, Pierre. There is so much . . . I don't know.'

Drummond's hand was on her elbow, as he guided her to the elevators, and a few moments later she was in the privacy of her own suite. Exactly as she had left it, her own clothes hanging in the wardrobe. She wanted to throw herself into her own soft bed and stay there forever. But she couldn't, because Drummond was waiting. Because, as she had told Pierre, there was so much to be done.

So much yet to be discovered. He had hardly spoken of anything save niceties during the drive from Victoria Station. He had clearly been calculating his moment, and had opted for now, when she would be back in her most confidence-inspiring surroundings.

'Well,' she said, and sat down. 'Do you suppose I could have a drink?'

He went to the bar, and poured them each a glass of champagne. 'Do you know, we honestly thought you were dead, at one stage?'

'I have no idea why I'm not.'

'I suppose because of Freilinghausen.'

Mina frowned at him. 'Claus?'

'Well, after what happened . . .'

'What did happen? Believe me, John, I have been told nothing about anything for the past two years.'

'You didn't know he shot himself?'

Slowly Mina put down her glass. 'Claus Freilinghausen shot himself?'

'On the night of the fourth of February, 1917.'

'But . . . that was the night I was arrested. The night . . .' She bit her lip. How she had been beaten was no business even of Drummond's.

'Yes,' he said. 'I imagine you know more about that business than I do. But the fact is, as far as we have been able to gather, the German General Staff took his suicide as an admission of guilt, of his implication in your activities. He left a note, you see. Just three words: 'I loved her'. Well, the 'her' had to be you. And when they started to think about it, they remembered that he had been with you in Ostend the night Brassard was smuggled out. And had spent a lot of time with you ever since. It seems they were terrified that, were they to put you on trial, or even have you interrogated, you might tell how he had been a traitor, and thus bring the whole German Staff into disrepute. You know how seriously they take, or rather, took, their military top brass over there. And Claus was a very important member of the staff. He had access to almost every military secret. The effect on morale, at so critical a period of the war, could have been disastrous.'

'So they just shut me up and tried to forget I had ever existed,' Mina said, half to herself. 'I loved you,' Claus had wept, as he had hit her. 'I loved her,' he had written, seconds before blowing out his own brains. Poor, bedevilled Claus. Oh, poor, poor Claus. She felt a tear trickle down her cheek.

Drummond hastily refilled her glass. 'Well, anyway, you survived, Mina. As a matter of fact, when a few days had passed and although we knew you had been arrested no word came in of your trial or execution, when we were quite sure the Germans would make a song and dance about it, I began to feel sure you would survive. Because, as I told you once before, remember, you are one of nature's survivors.'

One of nature's survivors, she thought. Luck? Or, as she had once prided herself, toughness. And what was toughness, really, but self-centred determination? In prison she had wanted to change all that. Now she wanted to do that more than ever.

'So now, I suppose, you're ready to start picking up the pieces,' Drummond said, watching her carefully.

He has absolutely no concept, she thought, of what it's like to spend twenty months in prison, and in solitary confinement within that prison. One goes in, he thinks, and the world necessarily stops. One comes out, and the world starts revolving again. Nothing more than that.

'Now,' she told him, 'I am ready to go down to Epsom to spend Christmas with Harry and Aunt Bettina and Grandad. You did tell them I was coming home? You know, I was half hoping you'd have Harry up here to meet me. But I guess this way is best.'

John Drummond put down his glass. 'Mina . . . Harry isn't at Epsom any more.'

Mina just stared at him; her brain seemed to have gone dead.

'Well, you know your grandfather is dead?'

'No,' she said. 'No,' she shouted. 'How could I know? Where is Harry?'

'Easy, Mina, easy. Harry is fine. The fact is, when news was received that you had been arrested on a charge of aiding British prisoners to escape, well, after what had happened to Edith Cavell everyone thought you were certain to be shot. And when you just disappeared . . . well, your mother-in-law came across herself to see to Harry.'

'My mother-in-law?'

'A Mrs Elizabeth Morton.'

'Good God!' Mina said. 'But . . . Aunt Betty . . .?'

'Well, as I was trying to tell you, Mina, your grandfather had just died. I imagine the shock of your disappearance was the last straw as far as he was concerned. And Bettina, well . . . she naturally had quite a lot on her plate. Her brothers have all died as well, you know. You and she and her sister are the very last Doberleys. So I don't suppose she protested too hard. And I must say, Mrs Morton was awfully nice, as well as awfully courageous to cross the Atlantic in the summer of 1917. The U-boat menace was at its height then, you know. I met her myself, and she explained how Harry was her last remaining flesh and blood, and how she would never be able to forgive herself if he was neglected as well, and, well, she is a wealthy woman . . . and she did in fact have a legal claim, if you were dead. I suppose the final factor was that Harry himself seemed glad to see her, so . . .'

'Oh, don't worry about it, John,' Mina said. 'I'm sure you did the right thing, in all the circumstances.' Because at least it meant Harry was in good hands; Elizabeth had always worshipped both the boys. She sighed. 'The only drawback about the situation is that I suppose I have absolutely no excuse for staying over here. Going back means facing Felix. I suppose he has been ranting and raving, as usual?'

'Ah . . . I suppose you could put it that way. Mina . . .'

But in fact she was suddenly feeling the adrenalin pumping through her veins, and recently she had been wondering if it ever would happen again. She was a woman who thrived on plans, and on putting plans into action. For too long she had been just stagnating. So maybe Drummond was right. Her world *had* stopped, and was now starting again. Mina Petersen was back in circulation. There was an exhilarating thought.

She gave him a bright smile which checked what he had been going to say. 'And I was dreaming of resting up for a while. Hell's bells, as the song goes, I've been doing nothing else for the past two years. Now, John, you must give me a complete breakdown of the situation. All the bad news, so I can sit down and have a serious chat with Felix when I get home. Berlin I know about – the Superb is a heap of rubble. But we still have the site. And shouldn't we get some compensation from the Germans, especially as they've lost the war? Ostend I know about; things aren't much better there. But again, can't we screw some compensation out of someone? Paris I know about; we have to start from scratch. But London seems fine. And I imagine New York is fine. I would like up-to-date balance sheets and income and expenditure accounts, with special reference to staff wages just as soon as they can be prepared. I would also like estimates for redecoration and recarpeting. But I am assuming that we shall be able to tick over very comfortably until I get things started again. As I am going back to Felix anyway, I shall persuade him to redeposit that two million with Coutts, to cover the traveller's cheques. I suppose I am also going to have to approach the old devil for some financing, at least until we can sort out the compensation angle. Ah, well, it's been so long I suppose I can even stand a bit of him.' She winked. 'And he *is* several years older. So am I. Maybe grey hair will turn him off.'

'Mina . . .' Drummond hesitated. 'About Felix.'

'What about Felix? Don't tell me he's dead too?' She wasn't sure whether that would make her jump for joy or weep for lost financing.

'Ah, no. He's very much alive. I suppose like everyone else he supposed *you* were dead. He stopped corresponding. But I felt obliged, the moment Herr Tiene reported that he had found you, to send the good news across the Atlantic. Mr Petersen did not reply himself, but the day before yesterday this arrived.' He laid the document on her desk.

'What is it?' she asked, as if she didn't know.

'Formal notice of divorce proceedings. The grounds are desertion, and, of course, breach of contract.'

Mina picked up the heavy envelope, and then laid it down again. Nothing has changed, she thought. Not a single thing. Save me. But have I changed? 'Has he grounds for that now?' she asked. 'I have been a prisoner, in Germany, for two years. I could not return to him, however much I wanted to.'

'That is correct. But the very fact of your imprisonment infers that you never did intend to return to him.'

Mina frowned. 'I have no idea what you mean, or how such a thing can possibly be inferred. Morrison . . .'

Drummond sighed, and looked terribly upset. 'The fact is . . . there are a great many things which are not quite as they seem, and must never be as they seem. And there are a great number of things about this war which must never be allowed to see the light of day.'

'Would you mind speaking English?' If her tone was brusque it was because she could just feel the walls closing in on her again.

'Brigadier Morrison has asked me to make it perfectly plain to you that he can make no admission that you ever worked for him, or for the British Government. He cannot even admit that he has ever met you.'

'Am I allowed to ask why?' She was fighting back the waves of panic which were making her feel almost physically sick.

'It is actually at least partly due to a request from your own people. They learned of your, ah . . . activities, and were deeply distressed. You may know that not all of your countrymen approved of President Wilson's decision to involve America in the war, a decision which, even in the less than a year during which American troops were fully engaged, cost a large number of American lives. In addition, there is an even larger proportion of your population who are not really keen on continued American involvement in the European scene, something which both your administration, and our government, I may say, regard as absolutely essential to the future of world peace. Now, President Wilson's attitude is that he was forced to go to war because of Germany's unrestrained aggression and her breaking of so many rules and treaties and conventions; he has stressed time and again that never, in any way, were the Germans offered any provocation by the Americans, save where self defence was necessary. There are dozens of factors involved, but to put it in a nutshell, it is felt that it would be injurious to the plans of our respective governments for it ever to be made public that a well-known American businesswoman, who is also an internationally known personality, spied for the British for a considerable time before your government declared war. The official line is therefore that you were arrested by the Germans for aiding British prisoners to escape, without any encouragement or directives from His Majesty's Government, and that, as I told you, you escaped execution because of the suicide of your German lover.'

Mina felt as if a large horse had trodden on her stomach. It was some seconds before she could speak. 'Felix knows this?'

'I am sure he must do. But you will note that he is not naming Freilinghausen as a co-respondent.'

'Meaning that the State Department has got at him too?'

'Meaning, I would say, that he is doing everything on his lawyers' advice. He might find it difficult to prove your liaison with Freilinghausen, and in return you could raise the point that you were doing something pretty heroic. But there is no question of your desertion. You left New York on 3 May 1915, and it is now 20 November 1918, and you have not only never been back, you have never answered any of his letters.'

'And saying that I was in prison for two of those years is no defence? I just don't understand that.'

'You went to prison, Mina, mainly as the result of an adulterous love affair. Felix is playing it very cannily; you must give him credit for that. You are only accused of desertion and breach of your peculiar contract. But he *knows* about Freilinghausen, and is keeping it as an ace up his sleeve. You know, I did warn you about breaking your conventional marriage vows.'

'For God's sake, John . . . can't you understand it was in the line of duty? I'm sorry, believe me I'm sorry, that Claus committed suicide. But *I* never loved him.'

'But you can't prove any of that, Mina. Because if you attempt to involve Military Intelligence they are going to deny everything and prove you a liar, which won't do your case any good, while if *you* introduce the matter of Freilinghausen, you are merely making Felix's case for him. He'll say, all I am doing is accusing her of desertion in view of her gallant war effort, trying to keep scandal out of it, and here she is brazenly throwing an adulterous affair in my face. And in the face of the court.'

'You're beginning to make me feel like the woman who never was.' But what she really felt was a growing sense of anger, and of outrage, dormant for so long, beginning to grip her system. 'And what does Felix want, exactly?'

'He wants his twenty million dollars back.'

'Oh, yes? And where am I supposed to find that?'

'Well . . . with everything inflated, if you were to put both the London and New York Superbs on the market, I think you could realise such a sum.'

'And what then? I'd be the proud possessor of one burned-out vacant lot, one totally decrepit seaside shack, and one run-down and unusable Paris pension.'

'Yes, well . . .'

'*You* are recommending that to me?'

'Mina . . . you wouldn't ever starve. I'd see to that. Mina . . . well . . . I . . .' He licked his lips.

She stared at him in total consternation, realising that for the first time in his life, no doubt, this sixty-six-year-old bachelor, this perfect English gentleman, was about to propose marriage. 'Oh, John,' she said. 'A self-confessed adulteress?'

'Do you think that would matter to me, Mina?'

'Of course not, John. It was a silly thing to say. Maybe I'm

293

feeling just a trifle hysterical. But seriously . . . I am enormously flattered, believe me. And honoured, more than I can possibly tell you. But . . . I guess I'm just too restless a spirit to settle down to being a housewife. I'd drive you to an early grave. And I don't like being beaten. If Felix wants a fight, by God, he'll have one.'

'On what grounds? I've told you . . .'

'That I can expect no support from anyone. But I can fight him over the terms of the contract, can't I? You said I had a case there, six years ago.'

'I said you *might* have a case. But . . .'

'But I had acquiesced. Maybe. But then I ran away because it was too beastly to stand any longer.'

'Would that be the truth?'

'Is anything the truth, John? Am I alive, if your government or my government doesn't want it to be so?'

'Mina . . . to go into court, and relate the details of your married life with that man would destroy you.'

'People have tried to destroy me before, John,' she said. 'And they haven't succeeded. But by God I'll destroy his filthy contract. And him with it.'

'Mina . . .' He hesitated, and then finished his drink. 'No one is asking you to make a decision right now, or even tomorrow. In any event, transatlantic shipping is in such a mess there is no chance of your securing a passage for New York before next week. Think about it.' He flushed. 'Think about everything we've discussed, Mina. Please.'

Mina smiled, and held him close for a moment while she kissed him on the cheek, and felt very close to tears. 'I will. I promise. And John, thank you, so very much, for everything.'

She closed and locked the door behind him, went to the bar, poured herself another glass of champagne. She thought she might very well get drunk, alone up here in her private suite. Because, remarkably, having been almost entirely alone for two years had not made her wish for human company any the more. She was too used to being alone, even in the midst of a crowd. Now she was more alone than ever. But she was in her own suite, in her own hotel, in the heart of her own empire. That was a lot better than being in a cell.

And here she could prepare to fight. Because there could be no doubt, now, that she was going to have to do that. They were trying to take two, no, three years out of her life and tear them up. They. The nameless names who thought they were the lords of creation. But she had encountered them before, head on, and not yet given her best. As for Felix, that creeping lump of shit . . . she was angry where for too long she had been resigned. She had come out of prison wanting only to spread goodness and light all around her, and she had walked into a den of wild animals, seeking to snap her up. Only Elizabeth had turned up trumps. Good old Elizabeth. Although it was strange she had not written her a letter . . . but Felix, by Christ . . . her fingers tightened so hard the champagne glass snapped in her hand. She gazed at it, at the blood welling from the small cut, in surprise, and her head jerked as there was a knock on the door. 'Oh . . . what is it?' She stamped across the room, tore the door open, and gazed at Philip Clancy.

Chapter 14

For just a moment Mina could not believe her eyes. The man wore the uniform of a captain in the United States Army, and was most definitely a man where she remembered only a boy. Yet the face belonged to Philip Clancy. But it was a face which had looked on tragedy too often for comfort; she could see that in the eyes. Yet it *was* the face of Clancy.

'Clancy?' she whispered. 'Phil?'

'Mina?'

'Phil,' she screamed, and was in his arms. He lifted her from the floor and she kicked her heels in sheer ecstacy. Just when life had been composed of nothing but enemies . . . Phil. An officer. 'Oh, Phil.'

He carried her into the room, set her on the floor again, closed the door. 'Mina! The grand Mina! I've read so much about you, Mina. I've been so proud.'

'Read about me? Proud . . .?' She hurried to the bar, poured the last of the champagne, picked up the telephone. 'Room service? This is Mrs Petersen. Send up another bottle of champagne. No, make that two. And lunch for two. Oh, I don't care. Caviare and oysters. Haven't you? Then send out and get some. There must be oysters available somewhere in London, even in November.' She replaced the phone. 'Philip, oh Philip. If you knew how glad I am to see you.'

'Are you, Mina? Are you?' He drank his champagne very quickly.

She refilled his glass from her own. 'Oh, yes,' she said. 'Oh, yes. But . . . however did you find me?'

'You're not hard to find, Mina.'

'But . . . I've been away.' She had to think, before deciding how much of her recent past she wanted him to know about – if any.

'I know that,' he said. 'Do you know, I had a furlough last year, and I came here and asked for you, and they said you were away, but were soon expected back. And I came again twice more, and they told me the same thing. The last time was only a week ago. I really thought they were putting me off, but last week they said you were expected back, some time soon. So I tried again . . . and here you are. Oh, Mina.'

She was in his arms, and he was kissing her, holding her tightly. The way she remembered being held, and the way she remembered being kissed. For the first time in seventeen years she was being held as she wanted to be held; for the first time in seventeen years she *wanted* to be held.

There was a knock on the door, and they stood apart, like young lovers, while the floor waiter wheeled in the lunch trolley; he looked rather taken aback at the sight of the Army captain, who had obviously just been kissing his employer.

'I am sorry to have been so long, Mrs Petersen,' he said. 'But the oysters . . . it was necessary to send out to a restaurant. I went myself. They are absolutely as fresh as any in London.'

'I am sure you did very well,' Mina remarked, indicating with her gaze that she wanted him to go, but he just stood there, gazing back at her. Was he expecting a tip? From her? 'You may open the champagne,' she suggested.

'Of course, madame.' He opened one of the bottles, poured, and then placed the lunch on the table, before waiting again, staring at her.

'That will be all,' Mina said, coldly.

A last hesitation, and then he left the room. But the magic had been dispelled, at least for the moment.

'The standard of service seems to have slipped,' Mina remarked, and handed Phil a glass. 'I shall have to have a word with Pierre.'

'Well, no doubt he knows I'm not your husband. Maybe I should . . '

'Stay right where you are,' Mina said. 'I make the rules in the Superb, Phil. Nobody else. And the most important of those rules is that nobody questions a guest, by look, word, or deed. If someone wants something quite impossible, or really outrageous, then the waiter goes to Pierre Raizman, but he never allows the guest to suspect any criticism. I'll deal with that oaf later. Right now, let's forget him. Right now, there's you and there's me. Nobody else exists. I want to hear all about you. A captain?' She served caviare, offered toast, sitting opposite him. 'All in two years?'

'I was lucky,' he said. 'Or maybe not.'

She looked into his eyes again. 'I guess you saw a lot of action.'

'Yes,' he said.

'But you don't want to talk about it?'

'I'd rather talk about you, Mina. They tell me you've been travelling, all over Europe, while the war was on.'

'Well . . .'

'And you've cut your hair.'

How much *did* she want him to know about her? How much could she risk his knowing about her? Probably nothing at all. He could never know of her and Felix. That would be to disgust him. And he could never know about her and Claus. That would be to horrify him.

She smiled. 'It was simpler, while travelling. I didn't always have a room with a bath. But it's growing now. Maybe you've noticed it's not quite the same.'

'It's beautiful,' he said. 'You're beautiful, Mina. More beautiful than I even remember.'

'Do you remember, Phil?'

They gazed at each other, and he flushed. 'And the hotels?'

He was in awe of her, until this minute. 'Oh . . . there's one in Berlin, I guess. Burned down. And there's one in Ostend, probably fallen down. And there's one in Paris. And there's this one. And . . .'

'There's the old Superb, in New York. Gosh, Mina, do you remember the old Superb?'

'It's the new Superb now, Phil. Do you mean you've never been back?'

'I've an idea it's just a little out of my class.'

'You'll go there with me,' she said, and bit her lip. Because if she fought Felix in the courts, Phil would have to know, at least about that. The whole world would have to know. And she *was* going to fight Felix.

'But you reckon it's still a little out of my class,' he remarked, his smile twisted as he observed her hesitation.

Mina gazed at him. John Drummond had said there was no hope of obtaining a passage for a week. Therefore, for that week, no matter what might be happening around her, time had to stand still, for Mina Petersen; she could do nothing for herself until she reached New York and saw Felix. One week. She thought she deserved a week of happiness, after two years of hell. Because here was happiness. Here was the only man she had ever wanted to go to, without reservation, without ambition, without anger.

'No, Phil,' she said. 'It's not out of your class. Neither is the London Superb. Will you stay here awhile? Guest of the management?'

'Here?'

'Right here, Phil. This suite is the best we have to offer.'

He swallowed. 'Mina . . .'

'I left Felix several years ago, Phil. We're only now getting around to a divorce, what with the war and everything. But the papers are filed. I'm a free woman, Phil.'

Still he hesitated, but she could see the longing in his eyes. 'I've only a three day pass,' he said.

Mina smiled, sadly. That was to be the limit of her happiness. Three days, in exchange for two years. 'Then,' she said, 'we don't want to waste any of it, do we?'

'I want no calls,' Mina told Pierre Raizman on the telephone. 'Not even if it's the President of the United States. No one is to communicate with this suite until further notice, except for room service as and when required. And talking of room service, Pierre, would you have the floor waiter replaced, please.'

'Alphonse,' Raizman said. 'I know he can sometimes be difficult. But he was in the trenches, you see, and . . .'

'He gives me the creeps, Pierre. And if he gives me the creeps, try to imagine the effect he has on all the other guests. I'm sorry if he suffered in the war, but he just isn't the right material for the Superb. Give him two months' wages in lieu of notice and to tide him over, and then fire him. And remember, no interruptions before Monday morning.'

'And it will all be done without question,' Clancy said. 'Because you're the Boss.'

'Does that bother you?'

'I don't think so,' he said. 'Not any more.'

299

'Then we're wasting time.'

It had been so long. Too long? She refused to accept that. Because if it had been too long, it had been too long for her, not for him. And it was never going to be too long, for her.

'Mina,' he said. 'You're so thin.'

'It's fashionable,' she said. 'Actually, I've been ill,' she added, as she saw where he was gazing as she removed the last of her clothes. 'They had to shave me. But that's several months ago, now. Last May. It's nearly good enough to scratch. But it also has one or two silver threads. Does *that* upset you?'

Because she remembered how he had kissed her, the first time.

'Oh, Mina,' he said. 'My dearest, darling Mina.' And he kissed her again.

Where before she had wanted to hurry, now she wanted time to slow, even to stop. Was it too long? Could she ever go to a man again, totally joyous and happy, knowing that orgasms was awaiting her, but, far more important, that even if it wasn't, the happiness would still be there? Because she had never known that in her entire life before. She had supposed so, the first time, with this same man – but then there had been no orgasm and he had been terrified at the realisation that he had taken her virginity, so even the happiness had been so fleeting as to be non-existent. Since then there had been orgasms, quite often; Felix was a master at handling a woman, quite literally. But no happiness. Now . . .

'Mina?' he asked, watching her frown.

She smiled. 'I never married for love, Phil,' she said. 'I guess you know that. Where one never gives love, one never receives it. Be gentle with me, Phil. Be gentle.'

'Do you want to love now, Mina?'

She lay with her head on his shoulder, her leg thrown across his body. She was happy. There had been no orgasm, but it had hovered close, and in fact she had not wanted it. She wanted a special relationship with this man, before that came into it. 'Yes,' she said. 'I want to love, now. And I want to be loved in return. By you.'

As if that could be possible. When she was already lying to

him, in everything. And when she must either renounce everything she had spent her life fighting for, or have him know that she had lied, and how much she had lied, very soon. Once again she was dreaming. But wasn't she the woman who made dreams come true?

'I should like that,' he said. 'Mina . . . I'm still an accountant.'

She smiled, into his flesh. 'With Rigby and Smith?'

'That's right. You mean you remembered? But I'm number three, now. They gave me leave of absence to join up, of course, but when I get back there's a good chance of a partnership. Rigby, Smith and Clancy. And we're talking about maybe twenty thousand dollars a year.'

'Suppose I offered you a job, as chief accountant for the entire Superb Travel Group. Twenty-five thousand a year.'

'Can you do that?'

'I own it, Phil.' Just for the moment, she thought. No, for ever and ever, no matter how hard she had to fight, no matter what she had to do, to keep it.

'Gee,' he remarked. 'You really are a bit too much for me, Mina. You mean . . . I mean, I knew you were president, or whatever, but you mean you actually own all this? What about the shareholders.'

'I'm not incorporated, Phil. I own every stone of this building. And every stone of the New York Superb as well. Does that bother you?'

'Well . . .'

She pushed herself up, knelt beside him. 'To get it, to get everything, I had to do some pretty crummy things, Phil.'

'Such as marrying Felix Petersen?'

'That's right. Can you forgive me for those things, Phil?'

'I can forgive you for anything, Mina. Now. I guess once upon a time I was just a stupid kid. Now . . .' Once again the shadow passed across his eyes. 'I know one has to live, Mina. Just as far and as fast as possible.' He sighed. 'But . . . work for you . . .'

'That's a formality, Phil. People want formalities. And we have to live with people. I'd be working for *you*. For your happiness. Our happiness. And we would be happy, Phil. You and me. We would be happy.'

She could see the uncertainty in his eyes. And she had gone

301

far enough for one night. She had two left. She lay down again, her head on his arm. 'Give it a thought, Phil. Like you said, one has to live. Just as far and as fast as one can.'

She slept, more deeply and soundly than she had for several years, but awoke when he left the bed, about two in the morning. She rolled on her back and watched him leave the room, not, surprisingly, to go to the bathroom. Instead the light went on in the sitting room, and she heard the bar door opening. A moment later he stood in the doorway, gazing at her while he drank from a tumbler, silhouetted against the light. Thinking about her, as she had asked him to. Thinking about this life, which could be his.

It was only after he returned to bed, still supposing her asleep, and she smelt his breath that she realised he had been drinking neat whisky.

Yet the knowledge made her feel more secure. Just as it made her even more anxious to take him for her own, to help and protect him, to ignore and defy her professional instincts which kept telling her that to employ an alcoholic accountant for a company as widespread and involved as Superb Travel would have to be a disaster. Because she knew he drank to eliminate memory, so far as he could. He had seen, and smelt, and felt, and heard, far worse things in the trenches than she could ever conceive – and she thought she had experienced it all. And now she was facing him with an enormous decision. He was enough of a masculine Irishman not to wish ever to be inferior to any woman, however much he wanted her. And she was enough of a Doberley never to give up one cent of her empire, as he well knew. They wanted each other, and they were entirely suited to each other, and they even needed each other, but they lacked the courage to come together as they should. Because she equally lacked the courage. Or she would have told him everything. And everything she planned to do.

But how could she, now? When she had only these precious few hours to bind him entirely to her? Supposing it could even be done. Besides, she tried to convince herself, he would not wish her to confide all her past secrets to him, certainly not now, perhaps not ever. She was asking nothing from him, as to the women he had loved, and how, during the past seventeen years. He must take her as she was, as she was become, surely.

As she must take him. He was not the boy she remembered from long ago. But she had not fallen in love with that boy. She had wanted to, but she had refused to let herself, because she had known, instinctively, that such a love could not last. Now, if he had shed the callowness she had feared, he had accumulated worse, to go with his manhood. These things she must accept. These things she wanted to accept. Because now she wanted to love – him.

Yet she hoped he would tell her about it, talk to her about it, allow her to help him, found herself surreptitiously watching him, knew instinctively that when he left her soaking in the bath, he was going to the whisky bottle. But he would talk to her about it. In due course. When he was hers. Because this was their future, not a spectre from the past. Nothing could be allowed to interfere with that.

'What are your plans?' she asked, on the third morning at breakfast.

His smile was as shy as ever. 'Have you withdrawn your offer?'

'No.'

'Well . . . I have to rejoin my unit. We aren't scheduled to return to the States until the New Year. Could be a few months.'

'I'll wait, Phil.'

'Well . . . I'll come to see you the moment I land.'

'I want you to. Phil . . .' She held his hand. 'I don't want ever to lose you again. But I want you to know . . . as I said, I'm in the middle of divorcing Felix. Or maybe he's divorcing me. But it could be a sticky one. He thinks I owe him a lot of money, and I don't think I do. I'm going to try to talk some sense into him the moment I get over there, but if it comes to a fight, well, I guess I have to fight. That'll mean a lot of publicity. You know what the newspapers make of things like that.'

'And you think it may bother me?'

'It won't be pretty.'

He squeezed her fingers in return. 'I have got to rush. Mina . . . I love you. I have always loved you. Now I've got you, there's no way I 'm ever going to let you go again. I'll see you in New York.'

She kissed him, and watched the door close. How she wished she had been able to bring herself to tell him the truth. But there would be time enough for that, in New York.

'Mrs Petersen. Oh, my dear, dear Mrs Petersen.' Howwinger looked ready to embrace her, so Mina embraced him instead, to his obvious delight. 'My dear Mrs Petersen,' he said, quite overcome.

'I'm back, George,' she said. 'Oh, I'm back. And it is so good. So very good.' She gazed at the lobby, the reception desk, the potted palms . . . she might never have been away. 2 May 1915 was the last time she had stood here. Very nearly four years ago. And four such years. But now she was home, and the only thing different she could see was the closed travel desk. But she would be opening that again just as soon as she could. If only *she* need never leave this first stage of her dream, ever again. 'Mr Stark?'

'Mrs Petersen.' He kissed her hand.

'Mrs Young?'

'Oh, Mrs Petersen. Oh, *Mina!*' Mrs Young burst into tears.

Old friends. She had known them all for seventeen years. In fact, she realised with something of a shock, they were all approaching retirement age. But the idea of the Superb without these three stalwarts . . . or without Anatole, waiting for her in the kitchen.

'Madame!' he said. 'To see you . . . mmmMM!' He blew her a kiss. 'I have invented a new dish, for the occasion: Oysters Superb à la Petersen.'

Mina shook her head.

'You do not like it?' Anatole was horrified.

'I do like it, Anatole, save for one thing. I would like you to call them Oysters Superb à la Doberley.'

Anatole smiled. 'Of course, madame, of course. And madame . . . in that matter, we are all on your side, eh?'

Because they all knew of the impending divorce. Did they also know of the impending scandal which was about to break over their heads? But as she followed Mrs Young through the rooms, gazed at the bed behind which poor Laura Freindship had hidden her cosmetic case, remembered the vigorous, forceful woman who had returned here to fetch it, she once again felt the adrenalin flowing, and knew that she only had to fight, to win.

But there was an awful lot of fighting to be done.

'We have pleaded the war, of course,' Howwinger said, sitting her at her desk and placing huge folders in front of her. 'But there are certain necessary redecorations, and more important, the matter of an increase in staff wages, which require urgently to be considered. I have refused any concessions up to now, in your absence and in view of the national emergency, but now that you are back the union has already asked to have a meeting.'

'Put them off for a day or two, George,' Mina said. 'I do understand all of these things have to be attended to, and I shall start getting down to them tomorrow.' She closed the folders and stood up. She had only landed that morning. 'But right now, I have some very important calls to make.'

She couldn't tell him she didn't even know if she still owned the hotel.

'Wilhelmina?' Elizabeth Morton swept across the drawing room floor to greet her unexpected guest. 'But you *have* aged. In a most becoming fashion, of course.'

'I've had some pretty horrendous experiences in the past few years,' Mina acknowledged. 'Where's Harry?'

'At school.' Elizabeth's eyes were like pieces of green flint, Mina realised.

'So tell me where, and I'll go pick him up.'

'I have thought it best to send him to an academy, for the time being,' Elizabeth said. 'He is fifteen years old, you know, and frankly, I don't think he learned much more at that English public school than how to play a perfectly horrid game called rugby football. We all wish him to get to college, don't we?'

'Of course I do,' Mina said. 'And he will. Where is this academy? It's just about time for them to break up for the Christmas vacation. I really am surprised you don't have him here to meet me, Elizabeth. You knew I was coming . . .'

'Yes,' Elizabeth said.

Mina frowned at her. 'Just what do you mean by that?'

Elizabeth sat down and arranged her lorgnette. 'It was the knowledge that you were returning to America that made me decide that it would be best were Harry not to return to New York for this vacation. I have arranged for him to spend Christmas with some dear friends of mine in . . . well, a very nice part of the country.'

'*You* have decided where Harry shall spend Christmas?' Mina could not believe her ears. 'He is *my* son, in case you have forgotten. My son, whom I have not seen for two years and more.'

'I do know that, Wilhelmina,' Elizabeth said. 'And that is the crux of the matter. You have not troubled to see your son for two years or more. Before then . . .'

'I was in a German prison for two years!' Mina shouted.

'My dear girl, everyone knows that,' Elizabeth pointed out. 'But you chose to go there, did you not?'

'I . . .' Mina was absolutely speechless.

'Leaving your son behind,' Elizabeth went on. 'Just as you decided to take both your sons across the Atlantic in time of war, regardless of the danger. I am afraid I have begun to wonder if you are truly fit to be a mother.'

'You, have begun to wonder if I am fit to be a mother? You . . ?'

'And others. And now I am informed that you are to be divorced.'

'Is that any business of yours?'

'It may well be. Your husband is suing you for divorce on the grounds of desertion. It is a pity children are not allowed to sue their parents for desertion. I should think Harry has a very good case. As for poor, dear James . . .'

'You are trying to keep Harry away from me,' Mina said, pointing. 'If you do not have him brought to New York and to me at my suite in the Superb Hotel within twenty-four hours, I am going to see *you* in court.'

'Yes, my dear,' Elizabeth said. 'I think that would be a very good thing. But don't you think it might be a good idea to have your own life tied up first? Otherwise you won't have a leg to stand on. Not that you have in any event. You are condemned, Wilhelmina. Comdemned by your own every action, even before my Jimmy killed himself on your behalf, as a thoroughly selfish, irresponsible woman, totally unfit to be responsible for anyone, much less two teenage boys. That is *proved*, by the way you let poor James drown. After having let him contract infantile paralysis in the first place, while you were gadding about. You are irresponsible, Wilhelmina. Just plain irresponsible.'

Mina was so angry she could not speak. Anyway, she knew that if she opened her mouth it would simply be to spit in this woman's eye, and then she would certainly throttle her to death.

But her wartime experiences had taught her a great deal of self-control. 'You shall see me in court, Elizabeth,' she said, quietly. 'And I am going to have you sent to prison.' She left the house; her car was waiting. 'The Superb,' she told the driver. She had come back to New York, as she had gone back to England, wishing only to make things different, to make everyone happy, to spread a glow of pleasure around her, the pleasure she found in having survived, in being alive. And this was how she was being greeted. Well, she thought, by *God* . . . I am going to make all of them *grovel*. She did not remember ever having been so angry in her life, and yet was surprised, as she entered the Superb lobby and caught a glimpse of her face in a mirror, how relaxed and even calm she looked, save for the rest of her jaw. 'Well?' she demanded of Joe Stark. 'Is he here?'

'Waiting for you, Mrs Petersen,' Stark said.

Mina swept through to her office, gazed at Mr Surple. 'Mrs Petersen,' he said. 'Welcome home. Oh, welcome home.'

'I have yet to discern the slightest sign of a welcome, Mr Surple,' Mina pointed out. 'Except from my staff. And now from you.' She threw her coat in a chair, threw her gloves and umbrella on top of it, and then, to his obvious amazement, took off her hat and threw that on top of the lot, then shook out her hair; he began to look distinctly nervous.

Mina sat behind her desk. 'First thing, Mr Surple, do you know of a good private detective?'

'Ah . . . I think so, Mrs Petersen.'

'Then I have a job for him.' Mina told him what she wanted done, and Surple looked grave. 'Well?' she demanded. 'I can't possibly be breaking any laws in looking for my own son?'

'Of course not, Mrs Petersen. And I am bound to say that Mrs Morton has behaved in a rather high-handed way. On the other hand, while you were missing, presumed dead . . . it

307

became quite a common phrase during the war, you know . . . I suppose . . .'

'I am not accusing Mrs Morton of kidnapping in taking Harry from England, Mr Surple. Although I think even that was rather high-handed, as you put it. But she is breaking the law in not returning my son to me now that I am here. That woman is guilty of kidnapping. I want Harry found, and I want you to be standing by with writs of habeas corpus, or subpoenas, or whatever it is you need to bring him here, and I want charges brought against Elizabeth Morton.'

'Ah . . . yes,' said Mr Surple, unhappily. 'Would you like to discuss the forthcoming divorce proceedings, before we continue?'

'Why?' Mina inquired, coldly. 'What has my divorce to do with possession of my son? My son, Mr Surple, not Mr Petersen's. He has nothing whatsoever to do with the matter.'

'I understand that, Mrs Petersen, in cold terms. But it is possible that the outcome of the divorce case, or even what is said there, could affect the outcome of a possible court case between you and Mrs Morton.'

'You will have to explain that.'

'Well, Mrs Petersen, Mr Drummond has seen fit to acquaint me with your proposed defence to the breach of contract suit.'

'Oh, yes?' Mina asked.

'I do not wish to discuss it in detail, Mrs Petersen,' Surple went on, 'except to say that I am horrified by the very existence of such an unholy pact, if I may be permitted an opinion. But, in all the circumstances, and more particularly in the light of the circumstances you have just outlined to me, I must echo my learned English colleague and beg you to reconsider.'

'Reconsider what?'

'Well . . . your decision to make public the intimate relationship between your husband and yourself, and the, ah, rather involved financial arrangements.'

'It is not my intention to reveal a single detail of my married life more than I have to, Mr Surple,' Mina said. 'But I must defend the suit. I have been accused of breaking a contract with my husband. I believe I can prove that I did not break that contract. I believe I can do that without revealing anything which might disturb anyone. But I know my husband, Mr

Surple. And if he or his lawyer attempt to prove me a liar, then I shall fight them with every means at my disposal, even if I have to tell the judge exactly what was required of me under the terms of that contract. This is a suit I *have* to win, Mr Surple. If I do not, I am bankrupted, and everything I have endured for the last eleven years has been a total waste of time. Cannot you understand that simple fact? And if I admit desertion and do not dispute the legality of the arrangement I entered into with Mr Petersen, I lose. I am also accepting all the guilt in the breakdown of the marriage.'

'But if you defend by revealing all, Mrs Petersen, which as you say may well come down to specific details of your married life, well, while you may involve Mr Petersen in your own social ruin, which may be very satisfactory to you, I cannot see that it will necessarily alter the legal situation. You are both, as I understand it, guilty of . . . ah, illegal sexual acts. It is even possible that criminal charges could be preferred. But the salient point is that at the time these acts were committed, you agreed to them.'

'I was only twenty-three at the time,' Mina pointed out. 'And when I discovered that I had in fact agreed to certain acts I did not even then know were possible, I accepted the situation. But my husband later exceeded the terms of our contract.'

'Yet you did not raise the matter then, or sue him for divorce?'

'I raised the matter with *him*, Mr Surple, and was paid extra for accepting the situation.'

'Mrs Petersen, do you seriously mean to go into court and declare that?'

'If I have to.'

'Jesus Christ!' he commented. And flushed. 'I beg your pardon.'

'Don't. However, there seems to be one vital factor which you and John Drummond and even Felix are all overlooking. I am *not* contesting the divorce. Felix can be shot of me tomorrow. I am contesting the return of the twenty million dollars Felix paid to me, on certain conditions. I have fulfilled all of those conditions. All you have to do is point that out to my husband, and there need be no recriminations and no scandal. When are we to meet?'

'Ah . . . your husband refuses to meet with you, Mrs

Petersen. He sent to say that he has no desire ever to look on your face again.'

'Is that so? Then you'll have to explain my position to his attorneys.'

'I have of course discussed the whole affair with Mr Marley,' Surple said. 'Like myself, he finds it difficult to believe that you could consider going into court and, ah, baring the facts of the marriage bed.'

'And on that little fact they are basing all their strategy,' Mina remarked. 'Well, you can tell him from me that he had better believe it. On the other hand, you can also tell him that if Felix withdraws his demand for the return of the money, I will not contest the suit. I won't even go to court, and he won't *have* to look on my face again.'

Because she had realised that retention of what she had was the most she could now hope for. So there could be no further expansion at least for some time. If she couldn't obtain compensation for the Berlin Superb she might never be able to rebuild. As for Paris . . . but she'd still have the New York and London hotels. And she was only just thirty-three years old. There was still time to make every dream come true.

'How soon is the hearing, incidentally?' she asked.

'Well . . . next week.'

'Next *week?*'

'Well, it was to have been last month,' Surple explained. 'At that time it was assumed you were not even acknowledging the plea. As soon as Mr Drummond informed us that you were back in circulation, so to speak, I applied for an extension, but I could only gain a month. Mr Petersen's attorneys naturally opposed any extension at all.'

'Next week,' Mina muttered. 'But that . . .'

'Quite,' Surple agreed. 'That will hardly give us time to find your son.'

'And you are worried that he may be upset by the divorce? It certainly gives us time to bring charges against Elizabeth Morton, Mr Surple. As for Harry, he is *my* son. He is not going to be upset by any courtroom revelations, believe me. But it would obviously be to everyone's advantage if you would persuade Mr Petersen's attorneys that I do mean to fight, to the very last ditch, unless they drop the financial suit.'

'I did put these points to Mr Marley,' Surple said. 'And I

have to tell you that he would not consider it. His attitude is that you do not have a leg to stand on, and while he concedes that you have the power to cause a scandal, his opinion is that such a scandal would hurt you even more than Mr Petersen. He asked me to request that you think very deeply about all the possible consequences before proceeding.'

'Well, then,' Mina said, her mouth forming a hard line. 'We shall just have to tell it to the judge instead.'

'Jesus Christ,' Mr Surple said again.

'Petition of Divorce,' Mr Marley, who was large and shaggy, sounded unutterably bored. 'I represent Mr Felix Petersen, and Counsellor Surple represents the defendant, Mrs Petersen. Mr Petersen seeks to terminate his marriage with his wife Wilhelmina, née Doberley, on the grounds of desertion and breach of contract.'

The courtroom was almost empty; one sleepy reporter sat in the press section, there were a couple of the usual hangers-on with apparently nothing else to do but watch court proceedings. Even Judge Brown had been looking tolerably somnolent. He was a sleepy-looking man who vaguely resembled a bloodhound, but Surple had been pleased to see him – he apparently not only had a reputation for very liberal thinking, but also for a dry wit, both of which the attorney had no doubt were going to be essential before this day was out. But now he was showing some signs of waking up. 'Is that accurate, Mr Marley? I had meant to speak with you about the wording on this plea before. A marriage is a contractual matter, and therefore any wish to terminate it must involve a breach of the marriage contract, somewhere. Would you explain?'

'Well, Your Honour . . .' Marley looked down at Felix, seated beside him. And then across to the other table, where Mina sat beside Surple. Felix had refused to look at her as they had entered the room. Now he sat with his back half-turned to her. She thought he was being unutterably child-ish. But she was pleased to note how old he was looking. On the other hand, perhaps he was thinking the same thing about her. Yet the important thing now was to get it over with. For a week everything had stood still; it had been almost the most miserable period of her life, save for the two years in prison. Everyone had been very sympathetic – she had even managed to have the meeting with the union postponed. But all the efforts of Surple's detective had failed to turn up Harry, and on her attorney's advice she had agreed not to press charges against Elizabeth until after the divorce had been settled; he was sure the resultant publicity would be bad. There had not even been a letter from Phil, although she knew she had no right to expect one, with the mail still in a tangle. Yet the fact was that life *had* stopped, and could not begin again until this battle had been fought and won. Because she knew she was fighting for more than money, or even survival. She was looking for revenge for all the humiliation and misery this man had heaped on her, and she was looking to regain her self-respect, now and for ever. And perhaps she was even looking for her soul.

'This marriage was undertaken, Your Honour,' Marley was saying, 'between two parties of greatly disparate ages and backgrounds, and was therefore entered into more as a business partnership than what we would call a love match. In addition to the breakdown of the marriage, therefore, there are contractual matters of a financial nature which need to be resolved.'

'A modern marriage,' Judge Brown remarked, without explicit disapproval. 'And I am expected also to give judgement on the financial question?'

'Yes, Your Honour, because it is, ah, intimately bound up with the marriage itself.'

'No doubt you'll spare the time to tell me what is involved as the case goes on,' Judge Brown said.

'Indeed I am about to do so, Your Honour. And I may say that there is a great deal of money involved. A matter of twenty million dollars.'

Judge Brown raised his eyebrows. 'Twenty *million* dollars?'

The lone reporter sat up.

'My client is a very wealthy man, Your Honour,' Marley explained.

'And would you care to tell me *how* this astronomical sum of money came to be involved?'

'As I have said, Your Honour, this marriage was strictly a business relationship. Mrs Petersen agreed to marry Mr

Petersen if he would invest the sum of twenty million dollars in her hotel business.

'Hm,' Judge Brown remarked. 'Peanuts, I presume. And now he wants his money back.' His tone was disparaging. Surple squeezed Mina's hand. Could it be that they *did* have a friend on the bench? But now the judge was looking at them, although still addressing Marley. 'And Mrs Petersen doesn't want to *give* it back. I'm beginning to get a glimmer of light. You have a copy of this extramarital contract, Mr Marley?'

'Right here, Your Honour.'

Judge Brown read, all the while scratching his head. 'I don't much care for the morality here,' he commented at last. 'But it seems a straightforward document, signed by both parties. Have you any comment on it, Mr Surple, before we commence?'

'My client acknowledges that she entered into such a contract, Your Honour,' Surple said. 'She is even prepared to concede that Mr Petersen is entitled to a divorce if he wishes one. However, she disputes that she has ever broken that contract.'

Judge Brown frowned at him. 'It seems to me that there is some double thinking, and even some double talking, going on here. That I don't like. Would both you gentlemen, and your clients, approach.'

Surple gazed at Mina, who shrugged. They got up and went forward. Felix also advanced, with Marple, to stand immediately before the judge. The reporter hurried through the door to find a telephone.

'Now you folks listen to me,' Judge Brown said. 'This is a court of law, not a society for semantical debate. A marriage is a contract. This contract you have been talking about is an offshoot of the marriage contract, nothing more. A divorce suit implies that one or other of the parties considers the marriage contract has been broken. Mr Surple, either your client agrees to that fact, in which case let's just hear the proof of desertion and go home, or she disputes that fact. She can't have it both ways.'

Surple sighed, and gazed at Mina; he had warned her this would almost certainly be the court's attitude.

But Mina had already formed an alternative plan to her

313

original. She looked at the judge. 'I dispute that I have ever deserted my husband, Your Honour.'

'Then it looks like we may have a case to hear after all,' Judge Brown said. 'So let's get on with it and try to have it sorted out by lunch. Mr Marley?'

They returned to their seats. 'You realise that you could wind up still married to him?' Surple whispered.

'That,' Mina said, 'is going to be his problem.' The adrenalin was starting to flow. She did love a scrap.

Marley cleared his throat. 'The facts of this case are very simple, Your Honour.' He glanced at the press section, where there were now three reporters. The public section was also very rapidly filling up as the magic words, twenty million dollars, had seeped through the building. 'As stated, Mr and Mrs Petersen signed a contract when they got married, which required that Mr Petersen would invest twenty million dollars in Mrs Petersen's business, such money to be in the form of a permanent, interest-free loan, to be repayable only should Mrs Petersen ever fail in her, ah, conjugal duties.'

'Which was to go to her husband's bed every other night,' Judge Brown observed, and shook his head. 'I guess your client likes to lead an orderly life, Counsellor.'

'Yes, Your Honour,' Marley said, a trifle wearily. 'However, to continue, the defendant left her husband's house, and therefore his bed, on the evening of 3 May 1915, and has not returned, despite repeated requests from Mr Petersen that she do so. She has not even replied to any of his letters.'

'Getting on for four years,' Judge Brown commented. 'That's got to be something like seven hundred nights she's in debt.'

'Quite, Your Honour. Therefore my client is seeking a divorce, as stated, on the grounds of desertion, and he is also seeking restitution of his investment, under the terms of the marriage contract.'

'I assume you're going to offer evidence?'

'I am, Your honour.'

Judge Brown looked at Surple, who was on his feet. 'You have a problem, Counsellor?' His tone indicated that Surple did indeed have a problem.

'No, Your Honour. I simply wish to say that in the interests of time, my client will not dispute the fact that she left her husband's house, and indeed New York, on the night of 3 May, 1915, and that she returned here for the first time since then one week ago.'

Judge Brown scratched his head. 'Your client is well on the way to a citation for contempt,' he pointed out. 'Is she defending this petition, or not? If she is, how can she admit to the desertion on which the petition is based?'

'My client maintains, Your Honour, that being absent from this country, and away from her husband's bed, for nearly four years, as you have said, does not constitute desertion, under the terms of the marriage contract.'

'Now, you are going to have to convince this court of that, Mr Surple,' the Judge said, in tones which indicated that he did not consider such a thing possible, and which boded no good for either Surple or Mina when the attempt failed. 'By direct evidence. Let's start from the top. You are prepared to concede that your client left New York on 3 May 1915 and returned last week. Do you propose to offer any further evidence of desertion, Mr Marley? If so, let's have it.'

'My evidence is concerned with the desertion, Your Honour. If the plaintiff is willing to concede that, I am content, and would ask for a judgement in favour of my client.'

'I suspect the plaintiff only concedes that on condition she is allowed to prove her own peculiar point. I am inclined to let her do that, if she can. But you have the right to call your witness first.' He looked meaningly at the clock.

'Does the defence concede the desertion?' Marley asked.

'The defence concedes my client's absence from New York between 3 May 1915 and 28 November 1918,' Surple said.

'Then I am content, Your Honour,' Marple said.

'Okay,' Judge Brown commented, obviously relieved. 'Now let's get this thing moving. You have the floor, Mr Surple, but you'd sure better make it good. And brief, if you will.'

'I will ask Mrs Petersen to take the stand,' Surple said.

Mina sat beside the judge, took the oath. She stared at Felix, but he continued to look away. Marley met her gaze, outwardly confident, but with one finger tapping tensely.

'Wilhelmina Petersen,' Surple said. 'Will you tell the court when you married Felix Petersen?'

'28 November, 1907.'

'Then last week was your eleventh wedding anniversary,' Judge Brown remarked. 'And the day you came home? I hope you celebrated, Mrs Petersen?'

'I did not, Your Honour. The day after tomorrow is my birthday. I'm not sure I'm going to celebrate that, either.'

'Oh, I am sure you shall. Or should. You may continue, Mr Surple.'

Surple, who had been waiting patiently, gave a little sigh. 'Will you tell the court why you married Mr Petersen? Did you love him?'

'I did not love him,' Mina replied. 'I wanted his money, and he wanted my body.'

Two more reporters had reached the press section.

'It was, in effect, a business deal, as described,' Surple said.

'That is correct.'

'Now, Mrs Petersen, His Honour has the original contract before him, but I am going to have to ask you for the interpretation of it, by your husband and yourself, over the eleven years of your marriage.' She could see the prayer in his eyes. But she was quite prepared to avoid trouble as far as she could.

'Basically, as we each recognised the other's business and social interests, we agreed that we would spend four nights out of every seven together, as man and wife. But this was the overall picture. It was recognised, from the beginning, that if I needed, as I often did, to be away from home for any long periods of time, in connection with my business, I would make up the time on my return. Thus, for instance, if I was away for four weeks, I owed Mr Petersen sixteen consecutive nights on my return.'

'And when you left New York on the *Lusitania* on 3 May 1915, it was on a business trip?'

'Certainly. I was going to Paris to buy an hotel.'

'You had every intention of returning?'

'Of course. I left most of my clothes and jewellery in the house.'

'But you were prevented from coming home when you intended, by circumstances beyond your control?'

'That is correct.'

'And you are perfectly prepared to return to Mr Petersen's bed and board now?'

'Certainly,' Mina lied, looking straight at Felix. Who appeared to have swallowed a fly.

'The defence rests, Your Honour,' Surple said.

'Well, it seems to me that this whole thing could be a case of monumental misunderstanding,' Judge Brown remarked. 'If I adjourn, Mr Marley, can't your client and Mrs Petersen get together? I reckon they have a whole lot of time to make up. Seven hundred odd nights! Great balls of fire.'

'With respect, Your Honour,' Marley said, 'I do not think that a reconciliation would be possible. Simply because neither my client nor myself believe a word of the evidence we have just heard, or the protestations made by Mrs Petersen.'

'Your Honour,' Surple protested, 'my client gave evidence under oath.'

'And is therefore guilty of perjury,' Marley said. 'Am I allowed to cross-examine, Your Honour?'

'Well, it looks if you'll have to,' Judge Brown said, 'having said all that. I'm sorry, Mrs Petersen, but I'll have to remind you that you are still under oath.'

Mina nodded. She was quite prepared to do battle. Because this *was* the real battle.

'Wilhelmina Petersen,' Marley said. 'It may well be that when you stormed out of your husband's house on 3 May 1915 . . .'

'Objection,' Surple said.

'Anyone would suppose this was a murder trial,' Judge Brown remarked. 'May I remind you that you don't have any jury to impress today, Mr Surple. However, I'd be obliged if you'd pick your words a little more carefully, Mr Marley.'

'Yes, Your Honour,' Marley agreed. 'When you left Mr Petersen's house on 3 May 1915, Mrs Petersen, it may just be that you then had no certain plan to desert him. However, I put it to you that you very soon did form such a plan.'

'I did not,' Mina said.

'Then would you tell this court why you did not return for nearly four years?'

'I was prevented.'

'By what?'

317

'By the war, Mr Marley.'

'But you were a neutral citizen, at least until April 1917, travelling on business around the continent, were you not? There was nothing to prevent you returning to the United States. Yet you did not even answer your husband's letters.'

'They were couched in most disagreeable terms,' Mina said evenly. 'I never answer letters which are rude to me. As for returning, may I remind you that I spent two years in a German prison?'

'Ah, of course,' Marley said, while Surple sighed. The wall had at last been breached. But had Mina trapped them, or had they trapped Mina?

'Is that so?' inquired Judge Brown. 'May we know why?'

'I was accused of aiding a British officer to escape from occupied Belgium, Your Honour.'

'Good heavens,' the judge commented. 'Then we have a heroine in our midst?'

'Not really, Your Honour.'

'You are too modest, Mrs Petersen. You may continue, Mr Marley.'

Marley looked ready to spit. 'I am sure the court, and indeed all America, honours and respects your courage, Mrs Petersen. However, you have not yet explained why you did not return during the very nearly two years between your departure and your arrest by the Germans. Were you helping British soldiers to escape all of that time?'

'Tut, tut, Mr Marley,' Judge Brown said. 'Unworthy. Oh, unworthy, sir.'

'I was engaged in some very intricate and important business,' Mina said.

'Business connected with a certain General Claus Freiling-hausen?'

'Certainly not.'

'But is it not true, Mrs Petersen, that you were arrested because of your paramour's suicide following his treason to Germany, on your behalf?'

'That is ridiculous,' Mina said. 'I was arrested before Claus . . .' She bit her lip. She had nearly fallen into a trap.

'Yes? Mrs Petersen?' Marley invited.

'Now hold on just one minute,' Judge Brown said. 'What's

this paramour business? Adultery is no part of this petition, unless I have misread it.'

'You are correct, Your Honour,' Marley said. 'Simply because my client wished to spare his wife as much pain as possible. However, in view of her attitude . . .'

Surple was on his feet. 'I really must object, Your Honour, to the introduction of adultery in any way into this hearing. As it is not in the petition.'

'I am introducing it, Counsellor,' Marley pointed out, 'as a means of proving Mrs Petersen's perjury and her desertion of her husband.'

'You can't prove a thing,' Mina told him. 'You have absolutely no proof that General Freilinghausen and I were ever more than good friends.'

'Now everyone, and that means you too, Mrs Petersen, just be quiet,' Judge Brown said. 'This is *my* court, and that means I'm the one who says who can do what, and who speaks next. The next person who utters a word out of turn *is* going to be cited for contempt. Mr Surple, you have my assurance that whether or not your client committed adultery with this General fellow is going to have no bearing on my judgement in this case, as such. However, I intend to hear the rest of this evidence, because as Mr Marley says, whether or not your client had a love affair with a European gentleman may well have a bearing on her decision whether or not to return to this country, and to her husband's bed and board. Now, Mr Marley, the defendant says you cannot prove she had an affair with anyone. Will you kindly do so, now, or withdraw the question.'

'Did you or did you not have a love affair with General Freilinghausen?' Marley asked. 'An affair which lasted from the night of 4 August 1915 to the night of 3 February 1917? I would remind you that you are under oath.'

Mina looked at the judge. 'Am I allowed to take the Fifth Amendment, Your Honour? Without prejudice?'

'You are certainly allowed to take the Fifth Amendment, Mrs Petersen. Mr Marley?'

Marley glared at her. 'Did you or did you not spend the night of 4 August 1915 at the Splendide Hotel in Ostend, Belgium, in the company of General Claus Freilinghausen?'

'I spent the night of 4 August 1915 at the Hotel Splendide in Ostend, certainly,' Mina said. 'There were approximately twenty-five German officers also staying there that night, so it is possible to say I was in their company. And one of them, I believe, was General Freilinghausen. Does that answer your question?'

'Counsellor?' Judge Brown was looking delighted at the exchange.

But, strangely, Marley was not looking as displeased or angry as he should be. Mina had the feeling that even the glares he was giving her were false. Suddenly she began to worry.

'Well, then, Mrs Petersen, will you deny that when General Freilinghausen committed suicide, he left a note which read, "I loved her".'

'I have heard that he did. I have not seen the note.'

Judge Brown looked at Surple to see what his reaction might be to the introduction of hearsay evidence. But Surple was obviously perfectly willing to let Mina look after herself at this stage.

'And was not the "her" in the note you?' Marley asked.

'I have no idea,' Mina said.

'Do you categorically deny that you have ever had an affair with General Freilinghausen, or with anyone else, during the period when you refused to return to Mr Petersen's house?'

'I have already taken the Fifth Amendment on that subject, Mr Marley,' Mina said. 'And I have already said that I spent a large part of those three years *trying* to return to Mr Petersen's bed and board.'

'Counsellor?' Judge Brown was beaming.

'Well, then, Mrs Petersen,' Marley said, with a resigned air. 'Perhaps you will also wish to take the Fifth Amendment when I put it to you that you spent the nights of 20, 21, 22 November last, just two weeks ago, when, as you put it, you were trying so desperately to return to your husband and were at last in a position to do so, locked away in your private suite at the Superb Hotel in London, an hotel which you own, Mrs Petersen, with a certain Captain Philip Clancy of the United States Army.'

Mina's head came up in consternation. How on earth had the wretch discovered that? And Phil . . . what would he *think* when he read the newspapers?

320

Surple was on his feet, understanding that at last she needed rescuing. 'Your Honour, this is becoming a travesty. Counsel for the plaintiff seems intent upon linking my client's name with everyone in Europe while she was there. Without a shred of proof to back up his insinuations.'

'I'm afraid Mr Surple is right, Counsellor,' Judge Brown said. 'We could be here until Christmas. Throwing out these accusations isn't going to get us anywhere unless there's some proof around.'

'Your Honour,' Marley said, with the air of a magician confident in the knowledge that he possessed a very large white rabbit secreted about his person. 'If I could be allowed to interrupt Mrs Petersen's evidence, I *can* produce proof of her relationship with Captain Clancy.'

'Proof, Mr Marley?'

'An eye-witness, Your Honour.'

'To adultery?' Judge Brown gazed at him for a few seconds, then looked at Mina, who was desperately trying to think, and then at Surple, who already had his mouth open.

'Your Honour, the introduction of fresh evidence for the plaintiff at this juncture would be a highly irregular proceeding. Mr Marley has waived the right to present evidence at all.'

'He waived the right to present evidence of desertion, Mr Surple, on your decision not to contest that point. My task here today is to decide whether or not, as she claims, Mrs Petersen was acting within her rights in remaining away from her husband for four years, and *that* seems to me to depend largely upon her proven intentions to return. Clothes in a closet is one thing. Falling in love with another person is something else again.' He looked at Mina, as if daring her to point out that it was not necessary to fall in love with someone to have an affair with him. 'However,' the judge continued, 'I am bound to ask, Mr Marley, why, if you possess proof of Mrs Petersen's adultery, isn't she cited for that? In which case we could all have gone home over an hour ago. And in view of what has been said in this court today, don't give me any nonsense about sparing her feelings.'

Marley appeared only marginally embarrassed. 'Proof of Mrs Petersen's liaison with Captain Clancy only emerged within the last week, Your Honour,' he explained. 'To have withdrawn the petition and begun anew would have caused a great deal of delay, nor did it appear possible to my client and myself for Mrs Petersen to defend the suit as it then stood. Indeed, we did not even know she was returning to this country to appear. So why raise the question of adultery? Now it has become necessary, in view of her absurd attempt to claim that she was *entitled* to remain away for as long as she liked, even if that were to be for several years.'

'Yes, yes, Mr Marley,' Judge Brown said, a trifle impatiently. 'However, there is no doubt that those are valid points. Even if the question of Mrs Petersen's marital fidelity is not at stake here today, and I promise you that it is not, Mr Surple, I must repeat that the question of her *intentions* must certainly be at issue, as it is the only means of arriving at a decision. And if she did commit adultery, then those intentions are certainly to be called into question. It may also help us to save some time. I'm sure you will agree that for Mr Marley to name names and Mrs Petersen to take the Fifth Amendment from now until Kingdom Come is an absurdity if it is possible to *prove* one of these desertions?'

It occurred to Mina that his earlier sympathy for her had obviously dwindled at the suggestion that she might have perjured herself, or be prevaricating. But proof . . . an eye-witness. She just could not think.

'So therefore, Mr Surple,' Judge Brown continued, 'I am going to allow this interjection.' He held up his finger. 'Don't tell me, this is irregular. But this is an irregular case. It seems to me that there is some kind of dispute going on here which is not being aired in this court, but which is very well understood by Mr and Mrs Petersen. And I intend to find out what is the real point at issue here before I give judgement. You are excused, Mrs Petersen. Mr Marley, call your witness.'

Mina hesitated, then rose, and seated herself next to a visibly trembling Surple. 'If only you'd told me about this Clancy,' he whispered.

'It didn't seem important at the time,' Mina replied. She was watching Marley, who had given the judge a brief bow of acknowledgement, and was turning to look at the press gallery, which was now absolutely packed, as indeed was the rest of the court.

'I call Alphonse Melas,' Marley said.

Chapter 15

'Who the Sam Hall is Alphonse Melas?' Surple wanted to know.

'I have no idea,' Mina whispered back. 'But . . . oh, my God!'

She gazed at the dapper little man who was taking his seat next to the judge; the last time she had seen him he had been wearing a floor waiter's uniform, in her suite at the London Superb. She had quite forgotten his existence.

'Bad?' Surple asked.

'It's going to be dirty,' she agreed. 'They don't *know* how dirty.' Oh, Phil, she thought; you are just going to have to forgive me. But he would. He had said he would.

How much, she wondered?

Alphonse had taken the oath. 'Now, Mr Melas,' Marley said. 'Would you tell the court your present position?'

'I am butler to Mr Felix Petersen,' Alphonse replied.

'And what position did you hold before that?'

'I was floor waiter at the Superb Hotel in London.'

'Will you tell the court why you left the Superb?'

'I was dismissed on the orders of the proprietress, sir, Mrs Petersen.'

'Why?'

'For discovering her *in flagrante delicto* with a man.'

Surple looked at Mina, who shrugged. 'I told you, it didn't seem to matter at the time.' This gutter rat, she thought, this crawling thing must have crossed the Atlantic on the same ship as herself, hurrying to Felix, and his revenge.

'What exactly do you mean, *in flagrante delicto?*' Marley asked.

'They were in each other's arms.'

'Were they dressed?'

323

'Yes, sir.'

'Then what leads you to suppose they were anything more than old friends?'

'Because this man remained in Mrs Petersen's suite for three days, and I heard the hotel manager, Mr Raizman, say that Mrs Petersen was not to be disturbed during that time.'

'Ahem,' commented Judge Brown, and looked at Surple.

'I *must* object,' Surple whispered. 'That's hearsay.'

'Forget it,' Mina said. She was slowly tensing herself up, aware of a burning anger which seemed to be gripping her mind.

Judge Brown, having waited for several seconds, sighed, and nodded to Mr Marley, who was looking suitably contrite – but even more pleased.

'You say this man you saw in Mrs Petersen's arms remained in her suite for three days. How do you know this?'

'I saw it.'

'How? You say you were dismissed. When did this happen?'

'On the second day. I knew this was because of what I had seen. And up to then, certainly, this man had not left the apartment. But after I was dismissed, I stayed, watching the car park. This man had come on a motor bicycle. That motor bicycle never moved until the Monday morning.'

'I see. And did you ever discover the name of this gentleman in whose company Mrs Petersen did not wish to be disturbed, for three days?'

'His name was well known to the hotel staff, sir,' Alphonse said, 'because he had been to the Superb several times already, asking for Mrs Petersen. It was Captain Philip Clancy, of the United States Army.'

'I have no further questions, Your Honour.' Marley sat down.

'You may cross-examine, Mr Surple.'

Surple stood up. He had a job to do, to the best of his ability, even if his client seemed totally disinterested in what was going on. 'Mr Melas, you have testified that until quite recently you worked for Mrs Petersen?'

'That is correct, sir.'

'But now you work for Mr Petersen?'

'Yes, sir.'

'Is that not a rather strange coincidence?'

Alphonse looked dumbfounded. 'I came to New York looking for work. I have emigrated, because conditions in Europe are very bad. And this Mr Petersen, he offers me work.'

'Are you not aware that this petition for divorce was filed nearly a year ago?'

'No, sir.'

Surple glared at him. 'I put it to you, Mr Melas, that you were employed by Mr Petersen, while still working for Mrs Petersen, to spy upon her and, if necessary, fabricate evidence of misconduct against her?'

'Oh, no, sir.'

'But you did feel it necessary, having come to this country and so *fortuitously* found employment with Mr Petersen, to tell him what you had seen?'

'I give my employers total loyalty, sir,' Melas said.

Surple hesitated, looked over his shoulder at Mina, who was inspecting her nails, and sighed. 'I have no further questions.'

'You may step down, Mr Melas,' Judge Brown said, and looked at the clock. 'We have just one hour left to lunch. Now, gentlemen, I know you are both as anxious as I am to get on and quite frankly I have heard enough. However, out of fairness to the lady, I would like to put one or two points to her myself, before I offer judgement. I assume you have no objection?' He looked from one to the other. 'Thank you. Mrs Petersen, would you return to the stand? And just in case you feel called upon to say something, I would remind you that you are still under oath, however little this fact seems to have weighed with you during your past evidence.'

Mina obeyed. She was aware that she was sweating, but no one else could see that. She kept her hands still, folded in her lap. But if the judge also wanted a fight, he was welcome to it. It was as if her entire body was in a white heat of anger. They had dragged Phil into the mess. And perhaps ruined her life. She didn't know that, but she knew that was what they had intended. To pre-empt her. But now they had shot their bolt; they simply could not harm her any more. Phil was either going to come to her, after having been named, or he was not; nothing she could now say or do would alter that in the slightest.

But she could now start harming them. And was she going to do that.

Even Judge Brown seemed a little taken aback by her

325

expression. 'Mrs Petersen,' he said, not unkindly, 'I want you to think very carefully about what I am going to say, and take your time in answering. When asked a direct question, just now, as to whether or not you had ever committed adultery, you took the Fifth Amendment, as you were quite entitled to do. However, it would now appear that Mr Petersen has had it proved to his satisfaction, and I have to tell you that it has certainly been proved to my satisfaction that you did indeed commit adultery, while in Europe, with Captain Clancy. As to whether or not you committed adultery with General Freilinghausen, that is hardly relevant. As I have reminded you several times, the point at issue is not your morals, but your statement, made under oath, that you have always fully intended to return to your husband's bed the moment you were allowed to do so, because that is the crux of this case. Now, madam, can you still swear that, having committed adultery with Captain Clancy, and at least given your husband grounds for supposing you had also done so with General Freilinghausen, you always intended to return to him?'

'I can and I do,' Mina said.

'But can you possibly claim that your husband would still want you back, after a four year separation, and in possession of the facts we have heard here today? Merely to insist that you intended to return, while knowing full well that you would not be accepted back, is hardly a defence to the charge of desertion.'

'Your Honour . . .' Surple was on his feet, but hesitating; he had never queried a judge's questions before. 'You have assured me that the question of my client's adultery was irrelevant to this case.'

'It is, as adultery. But, Mr Surple, I am trying to ascertain, firstly, whether your client has perjured herself, and secondly whether or not this marriage should be dissolved. Your client keeps claiming that she has always been willing to return to her husband's bed, no matter how long she may have been away, or what she may have done during that time. She seems certain that her husband will want her back, regardless. But Mr Marley has told us that Mr Petersen doesn't want her back. Now it seems to me to be relevant indeed for us to discover *why* Mrs Petersen feels that she would be welcome. You don't have to answer my question if you don't wish to, Mrs Petersen, in view of your attorney's very proper interjection, but if you do not I shall be forced to draw my own conclusions as to whether or not you have merely been wasting this court's time here today, and I will have to base my judgement of this case, and the financial matters arising from it, on those conclusions.'

'I never doubted my welcome, Your Honour,' Mina said, 'because adultery is not and never has been an issue between my husband and I.'

'I agree it has not been named in this petition, which might lead one to suppose that Mr Petersen has been a somewhat indulgent husband in the past, and one who perhaps preferred not to drag his wife's good name through the dust . . .'

'With respect, Your Honour,' Mina said. 'But that is poppycock.'

'Come again, Mrs Petersen?'

Mina took a long breath. 'Adultery has never been an issue between Mr Petersen and myself Your Honour, because he not only always condoned it, he has made me perform it, in front of him, so that he could watch.'

There was a moment's utter silence, then three reporters tried to get through the door at the same time, while the packed courtroom began to hum. Judge Brown used his gavel, and silence was restored. 'I would remind you that you are under oath, Mrs Petersen,' he said.

'I am well aware of that, Your Honour,' she answered.

'And you maintain that your husband forced you to commit adultery in front of him?'

'Several times.'

Judge Brown stared at her, and then looked at Marley, who might just have swallowed hemlock. Felix's face was hidden behind a handkerchief. Judge Brown seemed to think this was a good idea; he also produced a handkerchief and patted his brow, while using his gavel again. 'You've never objected to this?'

'I couldn't, ' Mina said. 'When I married Mr Petersen, it was a straight business deal. Forget about all this talk of his investing in my hotels. The deal was that he would give me twenty million dollars to invest as *I* chose, in return for absolute control of my body four nights out of every seven. The word *was* absolute.'

Judge Brown broke his gavel. Extra police moved into the courtroom, and two people were evicted.

'Let me get this straight,' Judge Brown said. 'Twenty million dollars . . . you'll have to excuse me, Mrs Petersen, but you must have a lot of body'.

'I do,' Mina said. 'And my husband wished to do a lot with it.'

Judge Brown gazed at her for several seconds, obviously attempting to deduce the accuracy of her remark beneath the mink coat and the winter suit. Then he said, 'Including farming you out for his entertainment, eh?'

'Yes, Your Honour,' Mina said. 'But I refused to accept it.'

'But you have just told the court . . .'

'I have said that he forced me to do so, Your Honour. I regarded this as breaking our contract, and told him so. The terms were that *he* could use my body for . . .' she gazed at Felix, 'whatever bestial purposes *he* chose; nobody else. However, in return for this breach of contract, Mr Petersen provided me with a further ten million dollars of backing, and this I was prepared to accept.'

Judge Brown gave up, and left the restoration of order to the police, of whom it seemed half of New York's strength had been despatched to this courtroom. Reporters rushed in and out. So did other people.

Judge Brown leaned back in his chair. 'I guess you would like to ask some further questions, Mr Marley.'

Marley stood up. Now the hemlock was obviously taking effect. But he was a fighter himself. 'Is it not true, Mrs Petersen, that it was *you* approached Mr Petersen, and proposed this marriage?'

'That is quite true, Mr Marley,' Mina said. 'I was twenty-three years of age, in desperate need of money, and I knew that Mr Petersen was in love with me. I assumed it was with *me*, and, in any event, at that time I thought there was only one thing a man could possibly do with a woman. I discovered differently later, when he wished to sodomise me.'

'*What* did you say?' Judge Brown asked, but Mina could hardly hear him above the nosie.

She waited for it to die down. 'I said, when he wished to . . .'

'That's enough, Mrs Petersen,' Judge Brown said. 'Make the request, Mr Marley, and I'll clear the court and hear the rest of this evidence in camera.'

Marley looked at the reporters. The damage was done. 'That

will not be necessary, Your Honour,' he said in a crushed voice. 'I have no further questions.'

'Just one moment, Mr Marley,' Judge Brown said. 'I want to get something straight. Mrs Petersen has made some very remarkable assertions here today. Do you mean to tell me that your client does not mean to refute any of these?'

Marley looked down at Felix. Felix got up, and hurried from the courtroom, handkerchief still held to his face; as the door to the lobby opened, there was an explosion of flash-bulbs.

'No, Your honour,' Marley said. 'My client does not wish to pursue this matter further.'

'I see,' Judge Brown declared. 'You'd better step down, Mrs Petersen. I think you have said quite enough for one hearing.' He waited for her to seat herself next to Surple, while gazing over the restless courtroom. 'I have to say,' he said, loudly, 'that this is quite the most remarkable marriage I have ever heard of, and one which reduces the accepted relations of a husband and wife to a travesty of what I believe they were intended to be. I accept that there seem to have been faults on both sides, in that Mrs Petersen appears to have been prepared to do anything to obtain financing for her hotels. But I also have no doubt that she was ruthlessly taken advantage of by a very rich man, to whom a few million dollars was nothing, provided he obtained what *he* wanted. Something of what he wanted we have heard here today. I therefore say without reservation that this marriage will be ended, as indeed it should never have been undertaken in the first place. I believe this to be in the interests of both parties, and indeed the desire of both parties.

'I now come to the matter of the financial arrangements between Mr and Mrs Petersen, arrangements which are set out in this contract.' He picked it up, as if it might have been a piece of dirty toilet paper, and let it drop again. 'This document calls for certain conditions to be fulfilled by Mrs Petersen. Now, I believe that Mrs Petersen, reluctantly, fulfilled these conditions, difficult, distasteful, obscene and certainly outside the law as they were, for as long as it was physically possible for her to do so, and I also believe that she had every intention of continuing to fulfil these conditions, so long as she could also hold on to her hotels. This may not be admirable, but it is what is required by the contract. I therefore find, that, although the marriage should be terminated, by reason

329

of the unwitting desertion of the defendant from the plaintiff, as set out in the suit, the defendant has no reason to accuse the plaintiff of any breach of contract, in that she seems to have fulfilled her conjugal duties up to and beyond the limits required in that contract, and equally in that Mr Petersen does not choose to contest the allegations because it was he who first broke the contract, by what we might term his extramarital arrangements. I therefore find that there need be no adjustment of the financial settlement originally agreed between Mr and Mrs Petersen. You are dismissed, Mrs Petersen. I cannot say whether or not the criminal authorities may wish to have a word with you.'

Marley's face was cold. 'We shall appeal, Your Honour. On the grounds of the numerous irregularities you have permitted.'

'As such irregularities were mainly intended to assist your client, Mr Marley, and having regard to the uncertain legal position in which he now finds himself, you will do that at your discretion and in your professional judgement. And the best of luck to you.'

'My word,' Surple said. 'My congratulations, Mrs Petersen.'

Marley was also there, as form demanded. 'You have won a singular victory, Mrs Petersen,' he said, and kissed her hand. 'I wish you joy of it.'

Joy of it, Mina thought. She gazed at the reporters who surged around her.

'I am authorised to offer you one hundred thousand dollars for the serialisation of the story of your marriage, Mrs Petersen,' said one of them.

'One hundred thousand?' Mina asked, unable to believe her ears.

'That is nonsense, Mrs Petersen,' said another young man. 'I am authorised to offer you two hundred thousand dollars . . .'

'Two hundred and fifty thousand dollars, Mrs Petersen . . .'

'Five hundred thousand dollars, Mrs Petersen . . .'

'Did you say, five hundred thousand dollars?' Mina asked.

'Mrs Petersen,' Surple was whispering urgently.

'Forget these fellows, Mrs Petersen,' said another young man. 'The *World Globe* is prepared to offer you one million dollars to relate the exact details of your life with Felix Petersen.'

'One million dollars?' Mina asked. One million dollars would re-do the Ostend hotel and set the Paris hotel on the right road.

'Cash on the barrel,' the young man said.

'Mrs Petersen,' Surple begged, more urgently than ever.

'You come to lunch,' Mina said. 'And bring your contract with you.'

'I do wish you would reconsider, Mrs Petersen,' Surple begged.

Mina drank champagne, provided by a beaming Howwinger. 'What do I have to reconsider?'

'Well . . . signing that contract, telling that story, will make you . . . well . . .'

'The original scarlet woman? Am I not going to be that anyway?' Because her bridges were now burned. She opened the newspapers the next morning with an almost breathless expectancy. And found exactly what she had expected. "Divorce court sensation!" "Amazing revelations!" "He made me have sex with other men in his presence, declares famous hotelier!" "I was forced to accept illegal sexual acts, declares hotelier Mina Petersen!" "Marriage for sale!" "Twenty million dollars worth of sex!"

And, from the *World Globe*, "Exclusive! Mrs Petersen's story, in every sad and sordid detail, will appear in these pages beginning next Saturday!'

'Oh my God, my God, my God!' Surple came in while she was still in bed, drinking coffee. 'Oh, Mrs Petersen.'

Mina had been writing to Phil, to explain why she had had to tell the court the truth, and how she certainly had no knowledge, or intention, that his name would be introduced. Now she gazed at her attorney. She actually felt remarkably calm, so long as she concentrated on detail. 'It happened, Mr Surple. I need that million.'

'My dear lady,' Surple said. 'My dear, dear lady, money isn't everything.'

'It is to me,' Mina pointed out. 'I need a lot more than a million to get things started again, but a million is sure going to help. And I'm not going to reveal very much more than is already in these papers. Just a few details. And I'll make that bastard squirm.'

'My dear lady,' Surple said again. 'The effect on your reputation, on your business . . .'

'That we will just have to wait and see,' Mina remarked.

'And on your son . . .'

'If and when you find him,' Mina pointed out.

'Mrs Morton is bringing him in to see you today,' Surple said.

Mina leapt out of bed, careless of nudity, scattering sheets and newspapers. Surple hastily averted his eyes, but she caught his shoulders. 'What did you say?' she shouted.

'That Mrs Morton and your son are coming to see you today, Mrs Petersen. We didn't make the arrangement. I'm afraid my man didn't even succeed in finding the boy. But the District Attorney's Office rang my office early this morning, and said it was time you and Mrs Morton got together and sorted out the young man's future.'

'The District Attorney's Office?'

'Mr Plover.'

'Ah,' Mina said. Eric Plover was an old friend. Or was he a friend? He had been a friend of Jimmy Morton's in the old days; they had raced yachts together, and thus she had not known him very well. But he certainly knew Elizabeth. How well?

But it was not going to do her any good to bring the Governor with her. 'Well,' she said, 'that's some progress, at any rate. Now, Mr Surple, you just get hold of a warrant for Mrs Morton's arrest, and a police officer to serve it, the moment she appears.'

'Don't you think you should wait and see her, and Mr Plover, first, Mrs Petersen? I'm afraid, well . . .'

'Afraid?' Mina demanded. 'You are always afraid, Mr Surple. What *are* you afraid of now?'

'That is not a good press you have there, Mrs Petersen.' Surple at last looked directly at her, flushing as he did so, and Mina wrapped herself in her dressing gown. 'I actually had a word with Mrs Morton's attorney, and he claims that his client was acting in the best interests of your son in protecting him from just such unfortunate publicity. There is a crowd in the lobby, you know. Waiting for you to come down. They want to take photographs for their scrap albums as well as for the newspapers. They want to interview you. And some just want to look at you. At this moment you are the most famous woman in the entire United States of America.'

'That woman is trying to take my son away from me,' Mina said in a low voice. 'I am going to see her punished.'

'I am sure we can all come to some amicable agreement on the matter, Mrs Petersen. Especially as your son will be here himself. But, Mrs Petersen, I am bound to give it as my professional opinion that for you to seek another favourable court judgement at this precise moment, especially in the matter of a child, where you, if I may put it that way, would be in the position of your husband yesterday, would be a grave mistake. Please at least attend the meeting first. You can lose nothing by doing so. I promise you that. Nothing.'

'Harry,' Mina said. 'Oh, Harry!'

She held him close. But his body remained stiff, as his face was cold; because of all the people, no doubt. But still . . . 'Harry?' she asked.

'It is good to see you, Mother,' he said.

Mina looked from face to face. She had reached her office by a circuitous route through the hotel, to avoid the crowds in the lobby, and found this large room just as crowded. Surple was on her side, presumably; Howwinger was on her side, she knew. Elizabeth and her attorney were obviously in opposition. And the District Attorney, Eric Plover, she had to believe was neutral, whatever his background. But Harry?

'It *is* good to see you again, Mina,' Plover said. 'And looking so well. Do you think we could sit down?'

Mina gazed at him, hesitated, looked at her huge mahogany desk. She did not wish to sit behind that, and pontificate about her son. 'Maybe you'd like to take the chair, Eric.'

'Thank you, Mina.' Plover sat down. Mina chose the settee against the far wall, still holding Harry's hand, so that he was obliged to sit beside her. Elizabeth promptly sat on the other side.

'I have taken the exceptional step of coming here today,

333

because of the rather exceptional circumstances,' Plover explained. 'And because of my deep regard for both Elizabeth and yourself, Mina. I only discovered yesterday, you see, that Mr Surple here has filed charges of kidnapping against Mrs Morton. Apparently he was ignorant, and I assume you were also, Mina, that Elizabeth had previously applied to the courts for the rights of guardianship over her grandson . . .'

'*She* applied to the courts?' Mina cried. 'I want her arrested, for kidnapping.'

'Please hear me out, Mina. Elizabeth's application was made over a year ago, when she first returned from England with Harry, and when you were presumed dead. Her application was therefore granted. It therefore follows that, until that guardianship is rescinded in your favour, she has broken no law in continuing to regard herself as being responsible for Harry.'

Mina glared at him, but kept her temper. 'Okay,' she said. 'So I didn't know about that. But I suppose you can see that I'm not, after all, dead. So now I would like that order rescinded. Immediately.'

'Unfortunately,' Plover said, 'Elizabeth has found it necessary to apply to the courts once again, for a continuance of her guardianship. She did this the moment she discovered you were indeed alive.' He looked at a sheet of paper he had taken from his briefcase. 'Elizabeth's grounds are that you are an unfit person to supervise the upbringing of the young man, because he is a young man, now, isn't he? She cites your abandonment of him over considerable periods of time, your wilfully taking him into danger, a course of action which in fact caused the death of his brother, and above all, the mode of life you have pursued for the past eleven years.'

'You,' Mina said, turning to Elizabeth. 'You unutterable, hypocritical bitch.'

'Mrs Petersen, please,' Surple begged.

Mina glanced at him, then at the red-faced Harry, sandwiched between herself and his grandmother. 'I am sorry, Harry,' she said. 'But really, to have her creeping around the fringes of my life, like some coyote round a campfire, just waiting to snap up something . . . and you,' she said to Plover, 'you mean you believe all of that?'

'I have to say I took it with a pinch of salt, until I read this morning's newspapers.'

Mina looked at Surple, who waggled his eyebrows; she had no idea if he was trying to be sympathetic, or conveying an 'I told you so.'

She could feel the anger beginning to bubble in her belly and in her mind. Another fight. Well, so be it. 'So,' she said, 'you think I'm unfit to be a mother, do you, Eric? Well, I think we shall let a court decide that, if you don't mind. And until that happens, Harry stays here with me.'

'Now that is just not going to be possible, Mina,' Plover said. 'Elizabeth acted entirely properly, as I have said, in assuming control of Harry when you were presumed dead. Now she has made very grave charges against you, for neglect of your children, charges which to a certain extent appear to have been substantiated by the testimony offered in your divorce case. In view of that, and on request from her attorney, such request having been made, the courts have had no option but to make an order of wardship, at least until the matter of proper guardianship can be sorted out. Now you, at your discretion, may object to Elizabeth continuing as guardian under the court order. She in return has already objected to you resuming responsibility for Harry. In such circumstances . . .'

'He goes to an orphanage, eh?' Mina said. 'Or some place. What *is* this, anyway?'

'This, Wilhelmina,' Elizabeth said, 'is merely the logical and deserved outcome of your wilful neglect of your children. You stood up in court yesterday and described a home life which is unthinkable for any growing boy. You have been found guilty of sleeping with half the men in Europe, and of having been prepared to do anything, however unspeakable, in return for money. You . . .'

Mina reached round Harry and slapped her mother-in-law on the face, as hard as she could. Elizabeth's head jerked backwards, and blood trickled from her lip. 'You keep your lousy opinions to yourself,' Mina snapped.

'She hit me!' Elizabeth screamed.

'Mother!' Harry shouted, attempting to catch Mina's hand in case she was going to repeat the blow.

'Mrs Petersen!' Surple begged, grasping her other arm.

'Madame!' Even Howwinger was shocked.

'We shall be bringing charges of assault against Mrs Petersen,' Elizabeth's attorney remarked, producing a hand-

335

kerchief and holding it to his client's mouth.

'Jesus, Jesus, Jesus,' Plover commented. 'Ladies, please!'

'If you think that I am going to sit here, in my own office, in my own hotel, and listen to that harpy . . .' Mina said.

'Mina, *please!*' Plover insisted. 'I am trying to save you as much grief and unfortunate publicity as I can. Right this minute you are about the most notorious woman in America. To go to court now and drag the whole thing out again in public, and over the care of a teenage boy, well . . . it isn't going to do you any good. Elizabeth *does* have a case. The court *does* have discretion to appoint a legal guardian. And that legal guardian may very well be the boy's grandmother, in the absence of any other suitable person. I think Elizabeth may well be able to convince a court that over the last two years Harry has been living a more normal and cared for life than ever before.'

'And you expect me just to sit back and accept all of that?' Mina demanded.

'I want you to think very deeply about your situation. But more important, I want you to think about Harry's situation, and his future. Because that is what this is all about, isn't it? Not possession. But Harry's well-being.'

Mina stared at him.

'You are an international entrepreneur, Mina,' Plover went on, clearly sensing victory. 'You have an empire of hotels. One or two of which have been pretty badly knocked about during the war. Aren't you going to rebuild those, to get your empire back on its feet?'

'Why . . . of course I am. I must.'

'On the evidence of the past few years, that isn't going to leave you too much time for Harry.'

Mina looked at Elizabeth, who had stopped crying, Howwinger having thoughtfully provided her with a glass of brandy; beside her, Harry looked petrified. But the sight of that frightened little face, when she could remember him laughing as he had romped with the Doberley dogs at the Epsom house, only made her more angry than ever. Besides, she had always won in the past, through righteous anger and determination.

'I take it you have been retained by Mrs Morton, Eric?' she asked.

'Mina, please try to understand my position. For God's sake,

336

I don't have to be here, you know. I can just wash my hands of the whole lousy business and let Elizabeth and yourself stand up in court and slang each other from here to Kingdom Come. But I happen to be a friend of yours, and I was a friend of Jimmy's. And as a friend I have to tell you that in my professional opinion you don't have a hope in hell of winning a custody suit right this minute. But you have every prospect of earning yourself a lot more notoriety, notoriety which will rub off on Harry. Maybe ruin his life. Don't you think you should talk to him about it, hear what he thinks about it, before rushing off to court?'

Mina gazed at him, then looked down at Harry, whose lips were trembling.

'He *is* fifteen years old,' Plover said, gently. 'Not a babe in arms.'

'Why, yes,' Mina said. 'I would very much like to talk with my son, after . . .' She hesitated. Every time she opened her mouth she seemed to be incriminating herself. 'After so long. Would you mind leaving us alone?'

'Never,' Elizabeth Morton declared.

Mina glared at her, feeling the anger returning.

'God knows what she'll say to him, how she'll bully him,' Elizabeth said.

'And haven't you been bullying him, while you have had him alone, for the past two years?' Mina inquired, her voice brittle.

'Ladies,' Plover begged. 'Perhaps, if one independent witness was to remain . . .'

'Oh, shut up,' Mina shouted, quite losing her temper. 'So I'm some kind of an ogre, am I? Unfit to bring up my own children, am I? Well, you can all damned well stay, and listen. Listen very carefully. Harry . . .' She sat down again, next to him, picked up his hands, and then let them go again as there was no answering squeeze. 'Harry, I guess a lot of things have happened these past few years you don't really understand. Okay, so maybe a lot of things I did have seemed to be wrong. I was trying to do right, for you and James. That was all I ever wanted to do. A lot of people drowned on the *Lusitania*. Over a thousand. You remember Mr Vanderbilt, and Mrs and Mrs Frohman, and Mr Hubbard? They all drowned. Nobody supposes they were irresponsible for being on that ship. They thought she was safe. Just as I thought she was safe. And then, afterwards, I couldn't bear the thought of bringing you back, across that same ocean, through the submarines. I didn't know I was going to be imprisoned, Harry. It just happened. I wanted to spend every moment I could with you. But it didn't work out that way. I'm sorry it didn't, just as I'm sorry James died. God knows I'm sorry. What more can I say? I did what I thought was right, and it was wrong. But I'm home now, Harry. Okay, maybe I'll have to go away occasionally in the future. But it'll never be for very long again. And we're going to live here, in this hotel. You and me. Won't that be grand, Harry? It'll be so grand. You and me, here, so that when I'm away you'll have all the company you need. And we'll do things together. I promise. We'll have fun together, just as we used to with James and Jessie. Oh, Harry, I do love you so. More than I can ever tell you. Harry . . .'

She watched the trembling lips dissolve, and the eyes fill with tears. He *was* only fifteen, and he had had a tragic life. A lot of which was her fault, she knew, even if she would never admit it to these vultures. But now . . . 'Harry?'

The tears cascaded down Harry's cheeks, and he turned, and threw himself into the arms of his grandmother.

Chapter 16

'Mrs Petersen?' Howwinger's voice was anxious. The curtains in the bedroom were drawn, the room was stuffy. And he had only the reports of the chambermaids to go by.

Thus he had brought support. 'Do you think we should call a doctor?' asked Mrs Young, equally anxiously.

Memory! Seeping back. Of things she didn't want to recall. Of staring at shocked faces in her office, unable to believe what had happened. Of running away from them, not even using the elevator for fear of encountering someone. Of stumbling in here, panting, and throwing herself across the bed. Of crying until she had thought her heart would break.

And then of sending a cablegram. Somewhere there was someone who loved her. He would reassure her, and come to her, and hold her in his arms and stroke her hair, and tell her it didn't matter, nothing mattered, because they had each other.

But that was all in the past.

She rolled over. 'I'm not dead, Hilda,' she said. 'Just tired. Oh, draw the curtains. Is it raining?'

'Snowing,' Mrs Young said, and allowed brilliant daylight to flood the room. Howwinger coughed, gently, and Mina pulled the sheet over herself. But she could not so easily disguise the half-empty glass, or the empty gin bottle which waited beside it.

'Are you sure you're all right, Mrs Petersen?' Howwinger asked, cautiously.

Mina stretched. She really didn't know. She felt lightheaded, combined with a slight ache, but physically, from the neck down, she actually felt on top of the world. Presumably those were all the after-affects of half a dozen aspirins taken with a tumbler of gin, after several other tumblers of gin. She had gone out like a light and remained out for just about twenty-four hours, and she had never slept so well in her life. She might even have died, and then come back to life again.

Had she wanted to die? She rather thought that might have been the case. So did she want to die now? Because the physical well-being was surely going to wear off the moment the misery which was her brain and her soul came back to her. But that need never happen, if Clancy's reply to her telegram arrived first. As it would. 'I'm fine, George,' she said. 'Is there a wire for me yet? It'll be coming from England.'

'I'm afraid not, Mrs Petersen.'

Because things were still in a mess. But there would be a message. Soon.

'You haven't eaten in two days, Mina,' Mrs Young said, attempting severity. 'You must be starving.'

Mina considered, and realised that she was more anxious to lock herself in a bathroom for several hours. But she was also starving. 'Yes,' she agreed. 'Let's start with breakfast.'

'I'll see to it right away,' Mrs Young said, and hurried from the room.

'Don Axelman is waiting to see you,' Howwinger said.

Mina blinked at him, and wriggled up the bed, propping pillows behind her head. 'I'm not with you.'

'The accountant, Mrs Petersen. Don't you remember?'

'Not really.'

'He feels that we simply must have a meeting.'

'Has he any good news?'

'Ah . . . I can't say. I know he's been in touch with Mr Drummond. And then there's Tommy Krakowski, from the union.'

'Ugh!'

'I know, Mrs Petersen, but I'm afraid I can't put them off any longer. They were all here yesterday, you see, and I sent them away then. I can't put any of them off, any longer. There's this Miriam Jurgen, as well.'

'Who?'

'A lady from the *World Globe*.'

'I spoke with a man.'

'I know, Mrs Petersen. But they apparently feel your story would be best told to a woman. She's here to discuss the overall layout, and the first instalment.'

'My God,' Mina remarked.

'And then, well . . .' He hesitated.

'Yes?' Mina asked.

'Well, there's a police sergeant.'

Mina gazed at him.

'I don't think he's after *you*, Mrs Petersen, save as a witness,' Howwinger said.

'What time is it?' Mina asked.

'Ah . . . a quarter past ten.'

'Well, I have to have a bath, and something to eat. I'll see Mr Axelman first, at eleven, and Krakowski at twelve. The rest will have to come back after lunch.'

'They won't like it, Mrs Petersen. They were here yesterday, too.'

'Well, I can't see everybody at the same time, George. They'll just have to wait. But I'll see them all today, some time. You can promise just that. Just give me half an hour.' She got out of bed, and Howwinger rapidly left.

Half an hour, she thought, as she soaked in her tub. And then she had to start picking up the pieces. But the pieces of what, there was the question? The pieces of whom? There were, in fact, no pieces left worth picking up. Until Clancy's telegram arrived.

There was a vase of red roses, sitting on her desk, waiting for her. From Surple. Because he had promised her she would not lose by meeting with Elizabeth and Plover. He must be worrying about his retainer, she supposed.

That was her mood. She had bathed and eaten, and felt fighting fit. And once again like fighting. She sat behind her desk and gazed at the anxious faces. But for the moment only Don Axelman mattered. He was tall, thin, and disturbingly young, and wore horn-rimmed spectacles which increased his earnestly confident air. Mina did not suppose he was any younger than herself, actually, but she suddenly felt very old. She did not know him very well; he had been the junior accountant back in 1915, but the senior, Roger Burton, had retired. She was out of touch.

She wondered how she would get around to telling him that she proposed to bring in a new senior? But did she? Did she have anyone senior to introduce?

341

Did she have anything at all, except a horde of people waiting to stare at her, and take photographs of the notorious Mrs Petersen. She had, as both Drummond and Surple had warned her, won her case, saved her money – and lost everything else.

And now, she supposed, she was about to be told, by this obviously efficient young man, that in real terms she no longer even had any money. But did that really matter? What did she have to live for, and fight for, with all the relentless determination which had driven her for so many years? Because all the time she had thought she was winning, had been looking forward, at least subconsciously, to a future day when she would sit back in triumph, her every dream accomplished, her son and his children at her side, her faithful hotel managers and other senior staff gathered round, she had been being undermined, by her own temperament, her willingness *to* fight, her very single-mindedness, as much as by any outside factor. Until, two days ago, that aggressive self-confidence had wilfully dug a deep hole, into which she had then tumbled, head first. Because, after having defied them all to do their worst and, in effect, declared her intention of abiding by Harry's decision, she had been left with no choice but to do just that.

'I have obtained all the relevant figures from Mr Drummond,' Axelman said, placing an enormous sheaf of papers in front of her. 'And I've put together a rough scenario of the situation. An overall look, shall we say. First of all, income. We have been holding our room prices at five dollars a double since 1914. Well, in part we've been obliged to by the war. But obviously we've only been operating at about half capacity, or less, the last couple of years; the travelling public just hasn't been travelling. For comparative purposes, the last time every room of the New York Superb was full just about every night of the year, we grossed just over half a million dollars, and in addition made a good profit on the restaurant and even more on the bar. Outgoings were down to a hundred and seventy-five thousand a year, and so we were making a profit of approximately three hundred and fifty thousand a year. Allowing even for taxes and depreciation, that was working out at over two hundred thousand. This year, we shall just about break even, but that is before we begin to consider redecoration or staff wage increases.

'Then again, in 1913, we were clearing close to a hundred thousand a year from Superb Travel. For the last four years this has been nil. This is not as serious as it sounds, except as a further diminishment of the total profit; obviously as there have been no outgoings in this regard we haven't actually been carrying a loss here. Now, the London Superb has also not been doing as well as pre-war. In fact, it has done worse than over here, and both in 1917 and this last year it has shown a loss. This loss is now up to a hundred and seventeen thousand pounds for the two years. In other words, we are talking about a total group profit of some four hundred thousand dollars a year now turned into a loss of half a million.'

'You are a most cheerful fellow, Mr Axelman,' Mina observed.

Axelman grinned at her. 'A lot others have done a lot worse, Mrs Petersen. There ain't anybody not affected by this war. But now let's look on the bright side. The war is over, and we can surely look to business to return to normal. Much depends on how soon that happens. But I would estimate that, providing we raise our prices commensurately, at least to equal inflation, we should be back in the black to the tune of at least a quarter of a million a year by the end of next year. I think that, with wartime inflation, we can reasonably increase our prices by as much as fifty per cent. Outgoings have of course also increased considerably, but I still estimate that profit figure is attainable. Unfortunately, that, taken over two years, is just about going to restore things to normal, as of course you committed all your surplus funds to Ostend and Berlin, during 1913 and 1914.'

'The money I receive from the newspaper serial will of course go into the business as well,' Mina told him. 'So that will be a million more available.' As ever, when there were facts and figures to be considered, challenges to be faced, plans to be laid and decisions to be made, the adrenalin was starting to flow.

She began to feel almost optimistic. Things were not actually as bad as she had feared. If she no longer had a son, and could not even be sure if she still had a lover, she still had her hotels, and her dream.

'Ah, yes,' Axelman said. 'I have not yet had the time properly to evaluate the possible effects that your court appearance and your proposed . . . revelations may have on trade. Some people are putting the downturn as high as twenty-five per cent. Others are thinking that you might actually attract more trade. I'm afraid we shall just have to wait and see.'

'But you think it will drive people away?' Mina asked.

'I haven't formed an opinion yet, Mrs Petersen.'

'George?'

Howwinger cleared his throat. 'Three guests have checked out over the past two days. They were permanents you understand, Mrs Petersen. And all were, well . . . somewhat elderly. I am sure that when travel picks up again, as Mr Axelman has said . . .'

'I see,' Mina remarked.

'Now I have,' Axelman resumed, smiling encouragingly, 'with the aid of Mr Drummond's figures, produced an estimate of the required sums to, shall we say, set your empire back on its feet. To begin with, we can estimate the New York Superb as being worth approximately five million dollars at present, and I would estimate the London Superb as about half that. Say seven point five million, against which we should be able to borrow at least five million. However, as you know, one million of that is already committed as security for the projected Paris Superb. That leaves a total availability of roughly four million dollars until we get on our feet, say, over the next two years, which is going to be the vital period, when the largest expenditure would have to be undertaken, to restore the status quo, as it were.

'Very roughly, the required figures look like this. Redecorating and refurbishing the New York Superb, three quarters of a million. Redecorating and refurbishing the London Superb, ditto. Rebuilding the Ostend Superb, probably a million. Rebuilding the Berlin Superb, a million and a half. Virtually rebuilding the Paris Superb, a million. And of course, supposing we realise the borrowing possibilities to the limit, approximately a million over the two years in interest and mortgage repayments. There will also have to be a deposit of at least two million dollars with Coutts Bank to re-establish the traveller's cheque guarantee that Mr Petersen has now abandoned, and they may indeed require a lot more; you may recall that Mr Petersen's deposit with them was two million *pounds*, that is, even with the recent fall in the value of the pound, very nearly ten million dollars. You would also, I calculate, need a float of approximately a million to re-establish your premier rating with the transatlantic shipping companies. To this I am afraid we will have to add some realistic staff increases, both here and in London. We shall know more about what is involved after we have spoken with Mr Krakowski, but really these should not amount to greatly more than two hundred thousand dollars over the next two years. However, we must also expect a loss on the entire European organisation until we get it started again. Something like a million in the first year, between the three hotels. But I would expect that we should at least break even during the second year. So we are talking about a required outlay of approximately ten million dollars to get everything back on its feet. That is, supposing Coutts will settle for a guarantee of two.'

'Ten million dollars.' Mina wrote down the figure, and regarded the four million she had first written. 'That puts us five million short, if we include my serial money. At the very least.'

'Quite so,' Axelman agreed. 'So it will have to come down to a question of priorities. Now, Mr Drummond is fairly sure that there will be *some* compensation from Germany for the Ostend and Berlin Superbs. But when that will be is impossible to calculate. In view of all the hummings and hawings presently going on in Paris, and remembering that we do not even have a peace treaty with Germany as yet, I cannot include any such speculative figures in our two year projection. However, if you were to let the Berlin site remain vacant, for the time being, that would save one point five million right there; you would, of course, still own the site. Now, secondly, I wonder if you have considered the possibility of not creating a Paris Superb at all? I believe you paid one million for the existing building and site, three years ago. I think you got a real bargain. Prices are going to increase in Paris fairly rapidly. In fact, we have evidence that they are already doing so. Were you to place the Paris hotel on the market, as it is, you would not only save that million you have tied up as security for the purchase price, but I believe you would make a substantial profit, say as much as half a million, together of course with the million I have allocated for the renovation of the building. That's four million. But in fact, if you were to abandon your European venture altogether for the time being, that is, forget Ostend as well, you would have no financial worries at all, and you would still have two, if I may say so, superbly viable hotels, here and in London.'

Sell the Paris Superb? Not rebuild the Berlin Superb? Forget Ostend? To this young man it *was* all just a matter of figures. He did not understand how every hotel, even when it was only being planned, was a part of her entire being.

'On the other hand,' Axelman went on, watching her expression, 'if it really is your intention to maintain a European presence, as it were, I would strongly recommend that you give some thought to going public. I don't think there would be any difficulty about that, given the value of the properties and your trading record over the past six years or so, and we could make sure that you retained effective control. That way you could well raise several million dollars, very quickly.'

Effective control, Mina thought. There was some distance between that and ownership.

'Thank you, Don,' she said. 'Thank you an awful lot. You have worked so hard, and done a magnificent job. I shall have to consider the various alternatives, for a day or two.' She looked at Howwinger. 'What's next on the agenda, George?'

'I'm afraid it's the union, Mrs Petersen. They really have been very patient.'

'Our people have been very patient, Mrs Petersen,' said Mr Krakowski, a heavy-set man who, although he had obviously shaved that morning, had not done so very effectively. 'They have not asked for an increase in the four years you have been away, not only because of your absence, but because of the international situation, while in that time the cost of living has gone up a good fifteen points.'

Soft talk, Mina thought, before he puts the boot in. Her mood of defiant anger, against all society, had been building all morning. But she kept her voice even, and quiet. 'I understand that, Mr Krakowski, and I appreciate it,' she said. 'Unfortunately, it will be a little while before business picks up again.'

'How little is a little while, Mrs Petersen? Like maybe next month?'

'I'm afraid you're being a trifle optimistic, Mr Krakowski.' Mina looked along the faces at the table; on the right,

Howwinger and Joe Stark, and Mrs Young, as well as Don Axelman; these were her team. On the left, with Krakowski, there was another union official, and Walter, the assistant head chef, who apparently was the Superb shop steward.

'We don't think so, Mrs Petersen,' Krakowski said. 'We think we're just being taken for a ride. There's all this talk in court about millions here and millions there, and the *World Globe* is putting out how it's paying you millions for your story . . .'

'Those are all exaggerations, Mr Krakowski,' Mina said, still keeping her temper, no matter how she wanted to throw him out. Representing her staff! He knew nothing about the Superb, about the people who worked here, who were a part of her carefully selected team. 'I do assure you. You don't seem to understand that there are other things which have had to stand still because of the war. All my hotels need redecoration. Two of them need complete rebuilding, and one has to be completely renovated. This is going to take every last cent I possess. Once this rebuilding and redecorating is completed, and the Superb Hotels once again move into profit, why, then the whole situation can be considered from a more optimistic angle. My employees have never found me an unfair boss before. They will not do so now, I do promise you.'

'Mrs Petersen, my job is to represent your employees here in New York. Nowhere else. Sure I understand you may have problems with some of them foreign hotels. That's not something we can afford to take into account. Maybe you expanded too far and too fast.'

Mina's eyes were cold. 'Are you trying to tell me how to run my business, Mr Krakowski?'

'No, ma'am. I am trying to tell you that us Americans aren't about to starve so that a lot of Germans can stay employed. We beat them, didn't we? And we've bent over backwards to be patient. Now we have to have results.'

'I see,' Mina said. 'What sort of results do you have in mind?'

'We are demanding an across the board pay increase of twenty-five per cent for all our people, as from 1 January 1919. Not retroactive, mind. We want to be fair. Just from the beginning of next year.'

'Which happens to be the week after next,' Howwinger pointed out.

'So?' Krakowski asked.

'That is quite impossible, Mr Krakowski,' Mina said, getting all the ice she could into her voice. 'It would be impossible even had you *asked*, instead of demanding. However, as I would agree that your members have served me loyally during my absence from this country, I would be prepared to consider an across the board increase of five per cent.'

'Five per cent?' Krakowski cried. 'You must take us for a bunch of apes.'

With an effort Mina did not make the reply she wanted to. 'Mr Krakowski,' she said. 'There just isn't any more. Not one red cent.'

'There has to be, Mrs Petersen. Tell us how you would have paid, if you'd lost that divorce suit?'

Mina gazed at him. 'I would not have paid up, Mr Krakowski. I'd have declared bankruptcy, and all your members would have been out of a job.'

'But you didn't lose,' Krakowski pointed out. 'Okay Mrs Petersen, it goes against the grain, because I'm letting our people down, but I'll play ball with you. I'll settle for twenty. But that's it. Twenty per cent, or I'm going to call our people out. Right away.'

'You dare to sit in *my* office and threaten *me* with a strike?' Mina shouted, finally exploding into too long suppressed anger. 'There has never, never been a strike in a Superb Hotel. *My* people would laugh in your face, Mr Krakowski. My offer is on the table. I do not propose to alter it. Five per cent, with a revision in two years' time. Take it or leave it.'

Krakowski got up and left the room, his aide at his side. After a moment's hesitation and an apologetic smile, Walter followed them.

'I reckon he'll be back when he's had some lunch and a think, Mrs Petersen,' Axelman said. 'Jobs are tight right now, and they'll get tighter as the army comes home. He'll come down to fifteen per cent, then if you go up to ten, you'll probably be able to settle it for twelve and a half, which'll be pretty much in your favour. But I agree with you that it's important to get the figures right, because Mr Drummond says the British unions will almost certain base their claim on what we settle for here.'

'I am not paying that man any twelve and a half per cent, Mr Axelman,' Mina said. 'I am not going above the five I have already offered.'

'But Mrs Petersen, we can afford twelve and a half. Like I told you . . .'

'You told me we're six million short, to begin with,' Mina declared. 'And maybe a lot more, depending on the Coutts guarantee. So we need to save every cent. Equally, you say that at this moment we are making no profit at all. So what am I supposed to pay staff increases with? Accumulated capital? You tell me I don't have any accumulated capital. Five per cent is as far as I am prepared to go, and that's final. When we're back on our feet, say in two year's time, then they can have their twenty-five per cent. Not until then.'

Axelman opened his mouth, closed it again, and looked at Howwinger. Who shrugged.

'Well,' Joe Stark said, 'you're the boss, Mrs Petersen.'

'Thank you, Mr Stark,' Mina said. 'George, I don't really feel like facing crowds at this moment; would you have them send in a plate of cold turkey sandwiches and a bottle of Bollinger? Then I may just be ready to face the police sergeant.'

'I've been sent along, Mrs Petersen,' said Sergeant Cowan, 'to find out if you'd care to make a statement regarding the various illegal sexual acts your ex-husband made you perform.'

Mina gazed at him, and he flushed. But she was slowly beginning to feel human again. The champagne was helping there – just as it was helping to keep the lurking misery at bay, and allow her to think. But this . . . these people wanted to lock Felix up. They wanted to put him in a cell and leave him there, just as she had been put in a cell and left there – only he would deserve to go.

Perhaps she could make a deal with him, money in exchange for *not* sending him to prison.

Oddly, she discovered that she did not wish to do either of those things. She would take no part in locking *any* human being up, no matter what they had done. Anyway, Felix was out of her past, and she had to forget about that past if she was going to stay sane. Why, she wondered? Was she pretending that she had a future? Was it shame? Or guilt? She would not have put up with Felix's requirements for so long if she had not had some pleasure from them. Or was it a sudden desire to prove to the world she was not as bad as they thought her. Yet she hated that world. She thought she hated it more than ever, now. But did she hate even Felix enough to drag his story through the pages of a newspaper, even in return for a fortune? Then she had been angry. Now she was only aware of being tired.

Yet she had signed a contract. But had not yet been paid a penny. On the other hand, she was already six million short of what she required. Two million, three . . . such astronomical figures had never seemed important, to her or to others, while she had had Felix's backing.

It occurred to her that she was no longer planning, but merely responding; like a wounded, hunted animal, withdrawing here, snapping there, seeking only shelter and peace, and some comfort . . . where there was none to be had. But surely Clancy had replied to her telegram, by now. It would arrive at any moment.

'Mrs Petersen?' asked the sergeant.

Mina raised her head. 'No, I would not care to make a statement regarding my husband's sexual activities,' she said. 'If you want to read about it, Sergeant, buy a newspaper.'

'We can subpoena you, Mrs Petersen,' the sergeant pointed out, 'should it be decided to bring charges. Hell, we can even charge *you* with being a party to an unlawful sexual act.'

'Why don't you just goddamned well leave us alone?' Mina asked, her voice still quiet. 'What we did, in our own bedroom, is our own affair. Not yours. So we fell out and I had to drag out all the dirty linen to win my case. That's still our affair, not yours, and not the New York Police Force's, and not anybody's in the whole wide world, save us. You tell your superiors I said so, Sergeant. Just leave us alone.'

'Krakowski's back,' Axelman said. 'Now, Mrs Petersen, just a little give and take can solve this whole business, to everyone's satisfaction.'

Mina had been sitting at her desk, staring in front of her at the empty office. Now she raised her head.

'Like I was saying,' Axelman went on. 'I think he wants to talk turkey, Mrs Petersen. If you would . . .'

'Show him in, Don,' Mina said. 'And ask Mr Howwinger to step in as well, would you? And Mr Stark, of course.' She gazed at Krakowski, who as usual was accompanied by his two aides. 'It's being one of those days, Mr Krakowski. I shall be glad to see the back of it.'

'Me too, Mrs Petersen. Me too. You understand I have a job of work to do. No hard feelings?'

'No hard feelings, Mr Krakowski. Come in, George and sit down. Mr Krakowski would like to review the situation.'

'I guess you could put it that way, Mrs Petersen. We've been out and talked things over, and, well, we're prepared to be reasonable, because we're reasonable men. We always have been. You drove some hard bargains when you started this here enterprise, and we went along with those. We thought the Superb Hotel was going to be one of the best. Well, we weren't wrong. It is one of the best. And we're proud that our people helped make it so. But we know it wouldn't have worked so well if you hadn't expanded, and kept on expanding. So we aim to meet you half-way, Mrs Petersen. We'll settle for fifteen per cent. That'll just bring us up to the cost of living increase these last four years. Not a cent more. Nobody can ask more than that.'

'I appreciate your generosity, Mr Krakowski,' Mina said. 'But I'm afraid there just isn't the money. My first task, and the first task of all my employees, must be to put the Superb Hotel Group back on its feet. As you have just acknowledged, we stand or fall together. That means some of the profits, a large part of the profits we make here in New York over the next few years, have to go into the re-establishment of the other hotels. Now, my accountant here tells me that we should be back on our feet in two years. I am willing to give you my word that in two years' time I will grant staff increases in line with whatever cost of living increases have taken place between Christmas 1915 and Christmas 1921, as it will then be. Until then I can only offer you five per cent a year.'

'Lady, you're pushing your luck,' Krakowski said. 'I came here to negotiate, but you, you don't seem to want to do that.'

'That is correct, Mr Krakowski,' Mina stated. 'I am not negotiating, because I am not in a position to do so. I have told you what Superb Hotels can afford. There just isn't any more.'

'Then you won't afford anything,' Krakowski snapped. 'I'll see you bankrupt, just like you should've been, last week.' He left the room, his two aides hurrying out behind him.

'Well,' Don Axelman said. 'Looks as if we may have a strike on our hands.' He was as determinedly cheerful as ever.

'Oh, nonsense,' Mina retorted. 'I know our people better than that blowhard. He made me so *angry*.'

'Well . . . maybe it'd be a good idea to speak with your staff, Mrs Petersen. Howwinger?'

'Yes, I think that *would* be a good idea.' Howwinger looked at his watch. 'Lunch is still being served; they'll all be at full stretch for a while yet. But this afternoon . . . I'll call a meeting of the entire staff, save essentials, for five o'clock. How about that Mrs Petersen?'

'There's the telegraph boy,' Mina said, looking out of the window. 'Mr Stark, I wonder if you'd be so kind . . .'

'Of course, Mrs Petersen.' Joe Stark hurried from the room.

Howwinger cleared his throat. 'Five o'clock, Mrs Petersen?'

'Eh? Oh, yes, of course, George. Five o'clock. Thank you, George.'

He hesitated, then left the room, followed more slowly by Axelman, who was clearly worried. But he didn't know the staff either, she thought. They'd support her, because they always had in the past, and they knew their future was with her, not with Krakowski. And by five o'clock she'd have had her cable, and she'd actually *feel* like facing them . . . she looked up eagerly as Stark came in. 'Yes?'

'Nothing for you at this time, Mrs Petersen. But . . .'

'Yes?'

'That lady from the *World Globe* is still waiting to see you.'

'Oh, Lord,' Mina muttered. 'I'd forgotten all about her. Show her in, Joe.' She leaned back. Of *course* the wires were all still in a tangle. She was worrying needlessly. Of course . . .

'Hi,' said the young woman, carefully dressed and made up, and obviously as hard as nails. 'You lead a busy life, Mrs

Petersen. Or should I call you Mina, seeing as how we're going to be working together for a while?'

'Mrs Petersen will do,' Mina said. 'Because it is actually going to be a brief acquaintance.'

'Oh, I think we can stretch it to at least a dozen episodes,' the young woman said, not apparently disturbed by Mina's coldness. 'In fact, I'm just thinking that we could run on into a series about Mina Petersen, business executive. I think that would do rather well. Woman at the centre of things. There are a lot of latent suffragettes still knocking about, you know. My name is Miriam Jurgen, by the way. Now . . .' She opened her briefcase and spread various sheets of paper on Mina's desk. 'I have some suggested chapter headings here, gleaned from the newspaper reports of what was said at the hearing. I imagine you'll want to change one or two, and maybe add one or two more. Then I thought we'd sit down and decide exactly how far we'll take episode one, and just how we'll treat it, and then I'll leave it with you overnight to think about, and tomorrow I'll be in with a tape recorder. It shouldn't take more than a couple of hours. Then I can have the tape transcribed, and bring the typescript here for you to look over. We've already lost a day, and we have to be ready for press on Friday, which doesn't give us all that much time. But we'll make it. Right?' She smiled, as brightly as ever.

Mina also smiled, as coldly as before. 'I don't think all of that will be necessary . . . Miriam,' she said. 'I've changed my mind.'

'About what?'

'About telling that particular story.'

Miriam's smile faded. 'We have a contract with your signature, Mrs Petersen.'

'So sue me, for the return of your money,' Mina said. 'I assure you that I haven't spent any of it, mainly because I haven't received any yet.'

Miriam Jurgen stood straight. 'We can sue you, Mrs Petersen, for breach of contract, whether any money has actually been paid or not. We've already accepted additional advertising revenue in view of the probability of increased sales for Saturday's edition.'

'Then I suggest that you go and set the wheels in motion, or whatever,' Mina said.

Miriam Jurgen stared at her. 'You can't change your mind about things like contracts, Mrs Petersen, the way you might change your hat.'

'I can change my mind about anything,' Mina told her. 'I am a woman. And I am Mina Petersen.' It was all she had to hold on to now. Her rock. But at least there was now time for a rest before she had to address the staff. And who was to know, by five o'clock there might be a telegram from Clancy.

'Mrs Petersen? Mina?'

Mina opened her eyes, gazed at Mrs Young. She had lain down on her bed in her underclothes and had been sleeping deeply. Perhaps a residue of the pills and gin. Perhaps just the exhaustion which seemed ever-present these past few weeks; prison, the long months of poor diet and lack of exercise, had taken more out of her than she had supposed.

She looked at her watch. It was just after four. Too early . . . she sat up. 'Has a telegram arrived? From England?'

'No. Nothing has arrived from England.'

Mina gazed at her. She had never seen Hilda Young looking quite so distraught. 'What's happened?'

Mrs Young drew a long breath. 'The staff, Mrs Petersen . . . they've left.'

'Left?'

'Even my upstairs girls. I thought I could count on *them*. But they've all gone, Mrs Petersen.'

'*All* gone?' All gone. Her Hotel . . . Empty?

'Well . . . save for Mr Howwinger and me. And Mr Stark, of course. And Anatole. And the two under-managers. Oh, Mina . . . what are we to do?' Her eyes were filled with tears.

Mina got out of bed, ran to the door, opened it. And listened. There was utter silence, where usually there was always at least a distant clank of crockery.

'Mina, you can't go out like that,' Mrs Young protested.

Mina came back inside, pulled on a dressing-gown, thrust her toes into slippers, and ran to the elevator, Mrs Young at her heels.

'Mina . . .'

Mina stared at her as they went down. 'How many guests have we?'

'One hundred and seven.'

'Well, go find Mr Howwinger, and tell him and the under-managers to start telephoning to find them accommodation at other comparable hotels. At our expense, Hilda. Then you and they will have to see each guest individually, and explain the situation, and arrange their transfer. Again, at our expense. Quickly, now.'

'But what are we going to do, Mina?'

Mina smiled at her. 'Just look after the guests first, Hilda. There's a dear.'

She left the elevator and ran into the kitchen. Anatole stood there, gazing at the food he had been laying out for the evening – and also at Walter, who wore his street clothes but had forgotten to take off his chef's hat. Apart from the two of them, and now herself, the huge room, always so filled with people and bustle, was empty and still.

'Mrs Petersen!' Anatole cried. He also looked close to tears. 'These wretches . . . my dinners! My creations! My speciality tonight was braised duck with sauce à la Superb. And now . . .'

Mina looked at Walter, who clearly wished the floor would open up and swallow him. 'I'm sorry, Mrs Petersen,' he said. 'But Mr Krakowski . . .'

'You'd rather go on the street with him, than stay and work with me?' Mina asked.

'Well . . . maybe it won't come to that,' Walter said. 'When you and Mr Krakowski have your next meeting . . .'

'It has come to that,' Mina told him, 'because I am not having any more meetings with Mr Krakowski. I am not surrendering to blackmail. I just don't understand your attitude. I thought here at the Superb we were a team. I thought you people were loyal.'

'You've been away too long, Mrs Petersen,' Walter said. 'Sure we're loyal. But to our union. Things have changed, since 1914. You've been away too long, Mrs Petersen.'

'You realise that rehousing all of these people is going to make one big hole in your bank balannce, Mrs Petersen?' Axelman asked. 'And you don't have to do it, you know. It's become pretty well established in law that management cannot be held liable for inconvenience or even damage caused by industrial action on the part of the staff.'

'I have never let any Superb guests down in my life, Don,' Mina said. 'And I don't mean to start now.'

'But surely it isn't necessary,' Axelman argued. 'Look, Mrs Petersen, I can get Krakowski back in here in half an hour. We can even have dinner on the table on schedule. Believe me, Mrs Petersen.'

'All depending on whether I give him his fifteen per cent.'

'Well . . . I don't reckon he'll come below that. Not now.'

'I am not going to do that, Don,' Mina said. 'I'd have to be licking his boots for the rest of my life.'

'But the alternative . . . Mrs Petersen, I've cabled Mr Drummond, and he has replied that he recommends negotiations and acceptance. He is very worried about the possible effects on the staff of the London Superb when this news hits the newspapers. Mrs Petersen, you just have to face facts. When you had better than a hundred million dollars in the background – when you were married to Mr Petersen – the unions were afraid to get tough, because they knew you could close down the whole operation and not give a damn. Now they know you're not in a position to do that. And they are in a position to close *you* down, and leave you with nothing. Please, Mrs Petersen, there comes a time for all of us when we just have to acknowledge that the other guy is on top. And hope for a change.'

Mina's brain seemed filled with lead. He had cabled Drummond, and received a reply. All in twenty-four hours. She had cabled Clancy several days ago . . . and got no reply at all. Her hopes that everything was still in a tangle had been so much nonsense. He had read the newspapers, and he just wasn't going to reply.

She realised everyone was staring at her, and looked at Howwinger.

Who sighed, and shrugged. 'There doesn't seem much alternative, Mrs Petersen. I know it goes against the grain. But without the staff, we don't have a hotel.'

I don't want a hotel, Mina thought. I don't want anything, save to be alone. Alone, alone, alone . . . without even wardresses to disturb her and bully her.

Then she would *be* alone. 'Well,' she said, amazed at the calmness of her voice. 'Maybe we all need a good rest. You are all on three months' leave, as of this moment. On full pay, George. I'll see you next year.'

They took some persuading. But did, eventually, leave. Because they could see she wanted them to, even if they worried at the thought of her, all alone, facing . . . what?

Merely the fact of being alone. But this was what she wanted. Besides, there were private pleasures, things she had long wanted to do, and never had the time. There was the Superb itself. Because she realised that, however well she knew this building, however much time she had spent in it over the past eight years, she still did not *know* it all, not even as well as she had known the old Superb. Now it was empty, and all hers. She could climb to the very top, and stand in the girls' dormitory. It was, of course, an entirely different place to the room where she had been hazed that first night, which had led to Jimmy's interest, and where, so soon afterwards, he had been sitting on her bed, waiting for her; she had deliberately made it so, but just standing there brought back memories of that first night, made her think of the girls she now employed, or had employed down to yesterday, who slept here and gossiped and flirted with the boys, and hazed each other . . . and perhaps even dreamed.

She went to Mrs Young's apartment, where she had been so shocked by the reality of the life she was suddenly involved in; this at least looked the same – Mrs Young had seen to that. But the bedrooms, where Jimmy had first tried to seduce her – she could not even remember the number, although she did remember it was on this floor – were totally different. Again, her own design. Style. Comfort and efficiency. Her watchword and the source of her fame. All brought to nothing by human greed. Or by her own intransigence? But had she not been intransigent, all of this could never have happened in the first place. If only people could understand that.

She could wander through the suites, and remember Lord Fanning and Laura Freindship; she could stand in the restaurant and remember the night they had opened, and remember too the frantic dash back from the *Mauretania*, and

357

that even more frantic dash out of the harbour in the police launch. Those had been great days.

Which had now gone forever? She realised that they could well have. It was not necessary. She could surrender. She could do exactly what Don Axelman with his clear, cold, accountant's brain – did Clancy have, had Clancy ever had, a clear, cold, accountant's brain? – had recommended. It all made very good sense. It was even what she had been prepared to do when she had first come out of prison. Abandon Europe, for the time being. As Axelman had said, she wasn't the only one who had been caught short by the war. But Europe would still be there, after she had put New York and London back together, recreated Superb Travel . . . if she concentrated upon just those objectives, she had no real financial worries at all. If she went public, she had even less. She could even surrender to Krakowski, and pay him his fifteen per cent; that was only fifty thousand dollars extra a year. It required just a simple act of will, like picking up a telephone, and all her troubles would be over.

But she would be over, too. Mina Petersen, Mina Doberley, had only ever triumphed by her sheer refusal to admit defeat. Her intransigence.

So, instead of surrendering, she could simply end everything herself. Don had been wrong in suggesting that the union could actually harm her. They were as powerless to do that now as when she had had Felix's immense backing. She could place both hotels on the market, sell the Paris building and the Ostend and Berlin sites, and retire, a multi-millionairess.

With nothing to do for the rest of her life but grow old in her loneliness, and die.

So, maybe they could harm her after all. The choice was as simple as that. So, *was* there a choice?

There was not, for the old Mina. There was not, for this Mina, if she cared, any more. But did she care any more? Did she have anything to care for, any more? Did she care if the world were to come to an end, here and now? It could not happen at a better moment. She was in the building she had created, the heart of the empire, of the world, that she had created. She was alone, wandering the corridors, with all the ghosts of those who had walked here, and laughed and loved, and probably stolen, despite her precautions, and probably even sold sex, despite her precautions. She could stand on the great staircase and see the tuxedo-clad waiters, the gorgeous girls in their deep blue evening gowns, revealing just the right amount of cleavage, hurrying back and forth. She could die, now, seeing all of that, remembering all of that, for all eternity.

As perhaps she should have died, when the *Lusitania* went down. That was it. She should have got back out of that lifeboat and stood on the deck, and held Alfred Vanderbilt's hand, and with him gone looking for James, and with him, cigar in mouth, drowned. It would have made no difference to anything. Harry would still have survived, and would still have wound up in his grandmother's care. And the Superb Hotels would still have disappeared from the face of the earth.

How terrible, to know one had survived, where one should have died.

She prepared herself meals in the kitchen, ate at the table in there. She drank vintage wine. And she slept. How she needed to sleep. She thought that if she could sleep for a month she might be able to regain some of her old energy, her old decision, even her old determination. She might even know what she had to do.

She was troubled only by doorbells. They rang often, at the tradesmen's entrance. Even the lobby doors sometimes trembled. Just as a steadily mounting pile of mail came through the letter box. But they could only be bills. Just as the telephone jangled, continuously. But she ignored this too. Upstairs in her suite it was not audible. But today, she did not know which day it was, this persistent banging and ringing would not cease. Mina went down the stairs to the staff pantries and the store rooms, and down the corridor to the staff entrance, slowly unbolted and unlocked and unlatched the door, gazed at the snow-clad street, and the two men who stood there.

'Merry Christmas, Mrs Petersen,' said Don Axelman. 'Now you see, Captain Clancy, I told you she was in there.'

'Clancy,' Mina said. 'Oh, Clancy,' she shouted. Because that was his name. Phil had always been a mistake.

He had stepped forward, and she was in his arms. Don

thoughtfully closed the street door, with himself still on the outside. She smelt alcohol on Clancy's breath, and loved it. It meant there could be no mistake.

'Oh, Clancy,' she said. 'When you didn't reply to my wire . . .'

'What wire?' he asked.

'You mean you never got it? My God . . . but Clancy . . .'

'I've been away from my unit for the past ten days,' he explained. 'First of all waiting for a ship, and then on my way home. I got compassionate leave, you see, because my father had died.'

'The sergeant? Oh, Clancy. I am so terribly sorry.'

'Well,' Clancy said. 'I guess he was older than he looked. He was retired, you see, two years ago. He wasn't the sort of man who could really retire. So he just died, I guess. But Mina . . .'

She stood away from him, to stare at his face. 'Then you don't know?'

'About the divorce? Sure, I've read about it.' He gave one of his shy smiles. 'It hasn't been easy to avoid, these last few days.'

'And you're still here?'

'You said something about a job.' The smile widened, but was even more shy than before. 'Besides, well, I guess . . .'

'You've realised I'm not so highfalutin after all?'

'You're highfalutin, Mina. You're the most highfalutin dame I ever did see. But I love you for it. No, I was thinking, maybe right now you need me. At last.'

She held him close again. 'Oh, I need you, Clancy,' she said. 'How I need you.' She held his hand and led him along the corridor, and up the stairs to the lobby.

'But this place . . . Don Axelman has been telling me how you've quarrelled with the union, and they've all gone on strike and closed you down. Mina . . . what are you going to do?'

'Do?' She put her arm round his waist, and waltzed him around the lobby, remembering the strains of the orchestra which used to play here. 'There's nothing I can't do.' Because the orchestra would play here again. 'There's nothing *we* can't do, Clancy. Now and always.'

Chapter 17

They made love, and then Mina got some bottles of champagne from the cellars, and they sat up in bed, naked, drinking champagne, and making love as they felt like it. Mina Petersen's final descent into hell, she thought. But hell was such a reassuring place.

And anyway, it was only a temporary sojourn. Because his appearance, his acceptance of the situation, *had* reinvigorated her. She felt she could think again, and plan again . . . and even feel again.

'Hate,' Clancy said thoughtfully. 'It's a non-productive emotion.'

'You'd be surprised,' Mina said, 'what you can do on hate.'

'And you hate everybody, right?'

'Not you, Clancy, not you. And not George Howwinger or Hilda Young or Don Axelman. Not even Joe Stark. I've never actually liked the man. But he's always been faithful to me.'

'That's your criterion,' Clancy observed. 'You'll be telling me next that you hate Harry.'

Mina gazed at him. 'Sometimes I do,' she said.

'I won't believe that.'

'Maybe hate isn't the right word. Hate I use for people like Tommy Krakowski, who came along to kick me when I was down, where he always bowed and scraped when he felt he couldn't harm me. No, I don't hate Harry, Clancy. If he was to walk through that door right this minute, and say, Mother, I've come home, I'd say welcome.' She sighed into her champagne glass. 'But he's not likely to do that.'

'Mina . . . if you really want me to move in . . . well, you and I . . .' He bit his lip.

Mina shook her head. 'I'd love to have a child by you, Clancy. There's nothing I would like better. But you can't replace one child with another, you know. That doesn't happen. Anyway . . .' She smiled at him. 'I'm too old.'

'Old? At thirty-three? You ain't never going to be too old, Mina.'

'Sometimes I feel very old. And I know I wasn't cut out to be a mother. A lot of the things Elizabeth said about me were quite true. Are quite true, I guess. Which doesn't mean that if she came through that door this minute I wouldn't break this bottle and twist the glass in her face.'

Clancy kissed her. 'I think you try to act tougher than you really are, Mina. Anyone who can see the other person's point of view can't be all bad.'

'I have to be tough, Clancy. Don't you see? It's me against the world.'

'Us.'

'Us,' she agreed, knowing it was a lie. It was still her, however much Clancy might be always at her side from here on. Simply because he wasn't tough at all. He had no burning ambition, no mind-consuming determination. There was not a ruthless bone in Clancy's body. While she . . . now more than ever was a time for ruthlessness; for using the surgeon's knife, and not only on Berlin and Ostend and Paris, as Don had suggested. It had to be used on her as well. On her pride. Not only to give up those symbols of success, but also to surrender to Krakowski. That was going to be the most difficult thing of all. She did not know if she would be able to do it. But if it brought her hatred back up to the right temperature, it might be worth it.

'Let's get something to eat,' she said, and pulled on a dressing-gown before leading him down to the pantry, to hear the bell at the tradesmen's entrance once again pealing.

Suddenly, doorbells could only be good news. Where Clancy gazed down the stairs in dismay, Mina ran down them. 'It's probably Don Axelman,' she laughed over her shoulder. 'Come back to find out if I've eaten you alive.'

At the bottom she paused, for the first time in several days aware of the letters pushed through the box; letters, amidst which were several telegrams. From John Drummond, no doubt. Dear John Drummond. To tell her that the London

Superb was also on strike? But she felt she could even deal with that, right this minute. Once she had dealt with whoever was at the door.

She released the bolts, pulled it open, was surprised at once by the darkness outside and by the cold which seemed to rush in. But equally by the man who stood there. He was tall, dark complexioned although certainly white, and wore evening dress with a white scarf and a black coat and Homburg hat – even in the gloom she could tell that his clothes were flawlessly cut.

She had the strangest sensation that he might be the devil. Once she had thought that of Felix. But that had been a sick joke.

He raised his hat. 'Mrs Petersen?'

'Why . . . yes.' She was suddenly breathless.

'Merry Christmas. The name's O'Leary. Sean O'Leary.' He paused, as if expecting her to know it, but she didn't. Instinctively she looked past him, because such a man could not just materialise; there was a black sedan on the far side of the street, and she knew there were other men in it. But they were not getting out.

'Oh, yes?' she asked.

'We actually have met,' O'Leary said. 'But it was a long time ago. Nearly twenty years.'

'Sean?' Clancy said from behind her. 'Sean O'Leary?'

'Philip!' O'Leary seemed genuinely pleased to see Clancy. 'Won't you introduce us again, and perhaps, ask me in? I'm sure Mrs Petersen is freezing.' He looked at Mina's dressing-gown and slippers; it wasn't difficult for him to deduce that she was wearing nothing underneath. And in fact, she *was* freezing, now she thought about it.

'Sean and I were kids together,' Clancy explained, with some embarrassment, Mina thought. But that figured; Sean O'Leary was no accountant. 'Maybe you don't remember him,' Clancy went on. 'But that day you ran away from Morton's motor car, and then . . .' He checked, his embarrassment increasing.

'The other boy on the bicycle,' Mina cried. 'Of course, I remember now. Come in, Mr O'Leary. Please. I'm sorry. I guess I'm a little confused this evening.' Confused, she thought: she hadn't even known it was evening.

O'Leary stepped inside, closed the door behind him. 'Eerie,' he said. 'To be in a hotel like this, just the three of us. I love the Superb, Mrs Petersen. I've dined here often.'

'Oh.' She didn't know what to say. She certainly had never seen him before. 'Have you ever used Superb Travel? I've been concentrating on that the last six years or so.'

'That's why we have never met since . . . well, since I could afford to come here. No, dear lady, I have never used Superb Travel. Because I never travel. New York is where I was born, New York is where I am living, and New York is where I shall die.' He held up his finger as he pulled off his gloves. 'Which is not to say I do not know of, and place value in, the rest of the world. As I hope to convince you. Philip, old friend . . .' He shook hands, with a yet more embarrassed Clancy, 'A war hero, I'm told, and grieving for your dear old dad. Well, you know, so am I. They don't make them like Sergeant Clancy any more. And I want you to know that I do not bear any grudges. Mrs Petersen . . . is this hallway where you have currently made your home?'

It occurred to Mina that he was the most confident man she had ever met. Even more confident than Felix. She had always thought of herself as a confident woman, but suddenly she felt like a schoolgirl. 'Oh, I am sorry,' she said. 'Clancy . . . Philip and I, were just going to fix ourselves some supper. Will you join us?'

'Thank you,' O'Leary said. 'But no. I have already eaten. But I would not say no to a glass of ginger beer.'

Mina, already turning for the steps, checked in surprise. 'Ginger beer?'

'That is all I ever drink.'

'Oh . . . well, Clancy . . . Phil, would you see if we have any ginger beer? You don't mind if *we* eat, Mr O'Leary? I'm ravenous.'

'Please go ahead.' He followed her up the stairs. 'And I would be flattered if you'd call me Sean. After all, we have known each other for twenty years.'

'Why, I suppose we have.' She led the way into the pantry, opened the refrigerator, took out some cold ham and tomatoes, set them on a plate, still aware of his gaze, seeming to shroud her. And yet, not in the sexual manner that she had known from so many men. This man did seem to *shroud* her. She turned to look at him, take in his features, for the first time; they were long and cadaverous, yet certainly not old – he was of course approximately the same age as Clancy himself. 'Mr O'Leary,' she said. 'Sean. May I ask the reason for this visit?'

Sean O'Leary sat down and crossed his knees. 'It occurs to me, Mrs Petersen . . . Mina, if I may . . . that you and I should become partners.'

Mina, about to slice tomatoes, nearly removed her thumb. Clancy set down the bottle of ginger beer and a glass with a thump.

O'Leary smiled at them. 'I will be perfectly frank with you, Mrs Petersen, as I expect you to be perfectly frank with me in return. I am a businessman, who needs, shall I say, certain investment outlets. Both for money and for goods. Now, I'm told you are currently in need of a considerable financial injection. I am prepared to make that injection in return for a share of your profits. Not a large share. Thirty-three per cent, that's all I'm asking. And in your profits, not your gross income.'

Mina stared at him. Some friend of Clancy's who had made good in a rather flashy fashion. And wanted to ride gallantly to her aid. She smiled. 'I don't think you have any idea what sort of money I would be talking about, Sean,' she said. 'Even if I was interested in taking a partner, which I'm not. My business is going through a temporary difficulty, that's all. Caused entirely by the war. The war is now over, and I anticipate that my difficulties will soon be over as well.'

O'Leary smiled at her in turn, and drank some ginger beer. 'You need at least six million dollars to get back on your feet, Mina. You also need a staff who aren't going to rush out on strike whenever Tommy Krakowski snaps his fingers. I'll offer you a cash investment of eight million dollars, and I'll offer you your own staff back at work. All I want is a third share of your profits, worldwide. I'll expect a third interest in your hotels, of course, as security for my investment. That's business. But I'll be a silent partner. So silent you won't even know I'm around, save once a quarter. But there's more. I can save your costs, as well. One of my outlets is liquor. I can supply you with liquor at better prices than any wholesaler, providing you undertake to sell it at a good enough profit margin. That way we both get rich, eh?' He sipped his ginger beer.

Mina absent-mindedly ate some ham and tomato, while looking at Clancy. Clancy did not look happy. But that was probably sheer jealousy. If only she dared believe what she had just been hearing. Eight million dollars . . . there had to be a catch. 'I think you should know I'm not prepared to knuckle under to Krakowski,' she said.

'I wouldn't be interested in doing business with you, if I thought for one moment that you were,' O'Leary replied.

They gazed at each other.

'Then how do I get my staff back?' Mina asked. 'They belong to his union.'

'You leave that end of it to me. They'll be back within forty-eight hours of us signing a contract.'

Once again she gazed at him. Undoubtedly he was a sinister man. But he talked very big. She would never like him. But then, she had never liked Felix. And this man . . . 'There'll be no monkey business,' she said. 'You ever attempt to lay one finger on me, and I'll brain you. And the deal will be off.'

'My dear Mina . . .' He looked genuinely shocked. 'I never mix business with pleasure.'

She looked at Clancy.

'I think maybe you want to think about this pretty carefully, Mina,' Clancy said.

O'Leary smiled. 'Philip is trying to warn you, Mina. I've been inside. Isn't that what you were going to say, Philip my boy? Sent up, I was, for stealing an automobile. Arrested by Sergeant Clancy himself. When I was nineteen, would you believe it?'

'And what are you stealing now, Mr O'Leary?' she asked.

'I learned my lesson,' O'Leary told her. 'Once was enough. I run a liquor business now. And it has been successful. But it ain't going to last. I know that. Once the Volstead Act passes Congress, and I believe it is going to pass . . .'

'The Volstead Act?'

'I forgot, you've been out of circulation. You've been sent up too. That kind of makes us kindred spirits, wouldn't you say? The Volstead Act is what temperance societies have been dreaming of since Moody and Sankey started preaching. No more booze, Mina, anywhere in public.'

Mina frowned at him. 'Can they do that?'

'I guess Congress can do anything it wants to. And it seems it may want to pass this one. Sure, it depends on the election, but signs are the Republicans may take it; the people seem mighty fed up with Wilson. And the Republicans are the do-gooders. Now, as to whether they can enforce it, that's a different matter. People will drink, just as people . . .' he winked at her, 'like to sleep together in their own way. No law is going to stop them doing that, as you have found out, Mina. But it's all going to be illegal, and like I told you, I've learned my lesson. From here on, everything Sean O'Leary does is going to be on the up and up. So I'm looking for an investment, see? I reckon they sure ain't going to stop drinking in London and in Paris, in Ostend and in Berlin. And I don't reckon they'll stop staying in hotels, either. So there it is. When I heard you were having a little financial difficulty, I figured right away we could do business together.'

'You have other interests apart from liquor,' Clancy said, quietly.

'Sure I do. I run a scrap metal agency, and I own a couple of used car garages. They make a profit. I won't ever starve. But booze is where the real money is. I would sure hate to have to lower my standard of living. Mina, Philip here has every reason to be suspicious of me. But you're welcome to come down to my warehouses and see for yourself. You're even welcome to look over my books. Help yourself. Bring your accountant. Bring Phil here. Come and see. But do it soon.' He finished his ginger beer and got up. 'Sleep on it, Mina. I'll give you a call tomorrow morning. Maybe you'll have made up your mind by then.'

'He's as crooked as they come,' Clancy said. 'Okay, maybe he's only been to prison once, but he's been suspected of a whole lot of crimes which couldn't be proved. And not just car stealing. There's been strong arm stuff as well. And there's more than a suspicion of vice. And he's not in the charitable business, either. If he's prepared to invest a lot of money in your hotels, it's with Sean O'Leary in mind, not Mina Petersen. At the very least it's hot money, owed to the IRS or something like that. More likely he's looking for outlets for his booze and vice markets.'

Mina stood at her bedroom window and gazed out at the snow. Eight million dollars. Of course, it involved taking a partner. But that was preferable either to going public or surrendering to Krakowski. And with eight million dollars . . .

Clancy caught her wrist, sat her on the bed beside him. 'Have you been listening to a word I've been saying, Mina?'

'Sure I have. But . . .'

'Eight million dollars,' he said.

She sighed. 'It's not just the money, Clancy. Really and truly. It's the right to do what I want, my way. To expand where I want. Okay, O'Leary is crooked. I don't doubt that. But he's not muscling into my business. He's to be a silent partner, and I mean to see that he is a silent partner. As long as he gets his third of the profits every quarter, there's nothing he can do about making *me* a crook. So maybe I'll be using crooked money. For God's sake, all money has been through crooked hands, some time.'

'And you really think you can stop him from muscling in?'

'I promise you, he'll only try it once,' Mina said.

Clancy's turn to sigh. He released her and lay down. 'Sometimes your confidence frightens me.'

'It isn't meant to do that. It's meant to give us both strength.'

'But you won't follow my advice and give Sean the thumbs down.'

'No,' she said. 'I can't. He's the best hope I have. I can't knuckle under to a thug like Krakowski. To go public is well on the way to losing control of my own hotels. And I can't just sell up and retire, Phil. Like your Dad, I'd be dead in a year. It's me against the world, you know. They've taken away my son, and my self-respect, and everything I thought was good about me. They wrapped it all up and chucked it into the gutter. Well, I don't mean to follow it. The hotels are all I've got. I'm going to make them so big that every time anyone says the word hotel he'll mean a Superb. I have to do that, Phil. Can't you see?' She knelt beside him. 'You're not going to walk out on me again? Promise me that?'

He smiled. 'I might, if I thought it would change your mind.

I.think you're about to make the biggest mistake of your life. But it's your life, and you know how you want to live it. I just aim to be around from here on, to pick up the pieces.' He lifted her hand and kissed her fingers. 'Do I get the job?'

'They're coming in.' Hilda Young was breathless.

Mina got up from her desk and hurried into the lobby, to watch her staff return. Walter was there too. They stared at each other. 'Your day, Mrs Petersen,' he said.

'But . . . I didn't really expect . . . I had a communication from Mr Krakowski, of course, saying that he had reconsidered the situation, and had decided, in the interests of his people, to accept the five per cent pay increase over the next two years. But I didn't really believe it.' She was gabbling, and saying far too much. But it didn't matter; she realised that she was looking at a very frightened man.

But the staff seemed happy enough. She ran to greet them. 'Happy New Year. Oh, Happy New Year.'

She shook their hands and kissed the girls. It was like beginning all over again. She went into the kitchen, where Anatole was beaming. There was so much to be done, so much cleaning and preparing, so much ordering . . . but she could order what she liked. 'Now,' she said. 'We are going to remain closed for six months, while the hotel is completely redecorated and renovated, and we are also going to expand. I am adding a wing which will have an extra hundred and fifty bedrooms. That will mean, Walter, that I am preparing to take on an extra fifty staff. Isn't that splendid?'

'Yes, Mrs Petersen,' he agreed. 'That is splendid.' He didn't return her smile.

She returned to her office, where Howwinger and Stark, Axelman and Clancy, were waiting for her. 'I think Walter is a little dazed,' she said. 'But you have to admit that Mr O'Leary delivers the goods.'

'He does that, Mrs Petersen,' Axelman agreed.

Mina frowned at him, then looked at Howwinger. 'Just what is going on here, George? Some kind of conspiracy of silence?'

'You mean you haven't heard, Mrs Petersen?'

'I haven't heard a thing,' Mina said. 'I've given up reading newspapers.'

369

'Well . . .' Howwinger looked at Axelman.

'Tommy Krakowski is in hospital with both his legs broken,' Axelman said. 'They say he fell down a flight of stairs.'

'And Walter's kids have been threatened,' Joe Stark told her.

Mina looked from face to face in temporary bewilderment. She had always supposed she had seen most of the seamy side of life, but this was outside even her experience. Yet she was offended rather than frightened. She picked up her telephone, dialled; O'Leary had given her his private line. 'Did you strongarm Tommy Krakowski?' she asked. Her stomach was rolling, but the feeling of offence was slowly crystallising into anger.

'Me? What an idea. My dear Mina, I've told you, I've turned my back on all that sort of thing.'

'I'm talking about your goons, acting on orders from you,' Mina said.

'What the devil are you complaining about? You wanted your staff back at work, and I guaranteed to talk them into coming back. That was the deal. You should be happy.'

'I don't like the way you talk to people, O'Leary,' she said. 'Not one little bit. Now, it so happens that I need your money. So we have a deal. But you're the silent partner. Just remember that. If you mess about in any more of my affairs, *any* from now on, or with any of my staff, the deal's off, and you can try suing me. If you dare.' She hung up, looked at the anxious faces. 'I reckon you all think I'm a bit of an ogre.'

They gazed at her.

'Okay,' she said. 'So, I've gone into partnership with a crook. Maybe that was necessary to get things moving. Because we are going to get things moving. My way. Don, I want you to draw a cheque for fifty thousand dollars and pay it into Tommy Krakowski's bank account.'

'Fifty thousand . . . he'll never accept it. Not from you, Mrs Petersen.'

'So he won't ever know it's from me,' Mina said. 'It'll be from an anonymous well-wisher, and if he ever shows his nose in my hotel again I am going to have him thrown out. But see that he gets that money. Then get together with Walter, and tell him that Superb Hotels have agreed to grant an across the board increase of twenty-five per cent to all staff.'

'Twenty-five . . .' He stared at her with his mouth open, then looked at Howwinger.

'That is very generous of you, Mrs Petersen,' Howwinger said. 'But really . . . we had supposed you would not consider that kind of figure.'

'I said I would not be blackmailed. But I also said I would grant such an increase the moment funds became available. Funds are now available.'

'But twenty-five per cent,' Don protested. 'There's no need to go that far, Mrs Petersen. I mean to say, they'd be over the moon with twenty, or even fifteen. Twenty-five per cent was just a figure to start negotiating from.'

'Twenty-five per cent is the figure I want paid,' Mina said. 'Starting now. Thank you, gentlemen. But would you stay behind for five minutes, Don. You too, Philip, if you would.'

The others filed out. Axelman, starting to rise, subsided into his seat.

The door closed behind Joe Stark. Mina placed her elbows on her desk. 'This is very difficult for me,' she said. 'I just want you to listen and understand. You especially, Don.'

'Mina,' Clancy said, uneasily. 'Now is not the time.'

Mina shook her head. 'Bear with me. Now is always the time, for everything. Don, the work I've seen you do, the figures you have put together, the alternatives you have come up with, since my return here last month, have been stupendous. I want you on my side, now and always. I don't want to lose you, no matter what happens. I would like to offer you twenty-two thousand five hundred dollars a year, to stay with the Superb Hotel Group.'

'That's very nice of you, Mrs Petersen,' he said. 'I'm only getting fifteen now, you know. Even adding twenty-five percent on to that don't make twenty-two thousand.'

'I didn't know what you were getting,' she told him. 'And you're outside the norm, as far as I'm concerned. I think you're worth twenty-two five. You happy with that?'

'I'd have to be a fool not to be happy with that.' But he glanced at Clancy, obviously puzzled.

'As an assistant accountant,' Mina continued.

Don frowned.

'Phil Clancy will be taking over as accountant,' Mina said.

'Now, Mina,' Clancy protested. 'Are you sure?'

'I'm sure,' Mina said. 'That's my business, being sure. I want you both. So, Phil will be the boss. He takes the responsibility. I don't care which of you makes the decisions, as long as they're the right ones.'

Don Axelman gazed at her for several seconds. Then he shrugged. 'You're the boss, Mrs Petersen.'

'No way,' Clancy said. 'Don is a much better accountant than I can ever be.'

Mina appeared to hesitate; but wasn't that the decision she had been praying he would make? 'Okay,' she said. 'You're on twenty-five thousand a year at this moment, Don. So are you, Phil. You're joint chief accountants. Every suggestion or recommendation has to be signed by you both. And you'll bear joint responsibility. I want the very best, every time. And I think I've got the best, every time. Now let's get on with it. There is one hell of a lot to be done.'

Suddenly life was flowing again. More than ever before, because there was no Felix to go home to. Having warned O'Leary off, she was utterly and completely her own boss, her own woman. She saw O'Leary often enough; he did not seem to resent her tongue-lashing, and made a habit of eating at the Superb, always immaculately dressed in his black tuxedo, and requiring his guests to meet his standards. Indeed, she soon set a special table aside for him, and would stop and have an after-dinner brandy with him, from time to time. That the fact they were business partners was widely known could be gathered from the gossip columns, but oddly enough – or perhaps she thought, reasonably enough – neither that fact nor the sensational divorce case affected her custom in the least; more than ever before people wished to be known as having stayed at the Superb, if only to show that they too were the ultimate in sophistication, and they were even more anxious to contrive to be noticed speaking with the famous Mina.

All the same, she could not blame O'Leary for keeping an eye on his investment; it was eighteen months before even the New York Superb began again to show a profit.

But they were a happy, crowded eighteen months, during which she was busier than ever before in her life, and again feeling the surge of winning, of things falling into the places she had chosen for them – neither the District Attorney's Office nor the *World Globe* brought any actions against her, simply because they knew that they would have appeared in the wrong by seeking to drag out her sexual misdemeanours for a sensation hungry press.

Indeed she would have welcomed a trial, on whatever count. Once again she felt fighting fit, and anxious *to* fight. Their refusal to do battle left her energies free to be devoted to her first love, Superb Travel, which was almost immediately the most viable of her businesses. Because O'Leary had been quite right in his prediction that the Volstead Act would be passed by Congress, over President Wilson's veto, and on 16 January 1920 America officially became dry. Mina herself supervised the destruction of all the fine wines and spirits which had accumulated in the Superb cellars during the previous ten years, watching them being poured down the drains; that same evening she caught the *Mauretania* for Southampton, and got pleasantly tight over dinner, as soon as they were beyond the three mile limit. A large number of wealthy Americans apparently felt the same way. Suddenly the London Superb was more popular than ever, so much so that she was forced to re-open sooner than she had intended – she had closed the Park Lane hotel as well for total redecoration. But this was a happy decision. Her only problem with London was Drummond's desire to retire. He was getting on for seventy, and she knew he had to go. But he had served her so faithfully and well, had avoided the strike risk in the grim days of 1919 by his adroit handling of the union claims . . . she did not know how she would replace him, and finally decided to send Don over to England for a spell as overlord of her European investments – every day taught her how sharp and incisive and worthwhile were his opinions and his decisions.

Not even Don could get things moving on the Continent with any speed, however. Europe was shattered, emotionally as well as physically. Building in Berlin was not a possibility while the mark plunged to ungraspable depths of inflation, and Ostend, like all of Belgium, would clearly never be the same. Belgium was a place of ghosts. When the post-war continentals could again afford holidays, they began to turn to the increasingly cosmopolitan Mediterranean. Reluctantly she decided to abandon the North Sea site, where she felt she had done the only uncalculated and entirely good thing in her life, however much she had eventually suffered for it, and concentrated all her efforts on Paris, which was recovering far more quickly. The Paris Superb opened its doors on 6 June 1923 to an explosion of publicity. By then the profits were rolling in as fast as ever in the past. Sean O'Leary was a happy man. And Mina could start thinking again. Of Cairo. But she had no more intention of sharing her future with Sean O'Leary than she had had with Felix Petersen – her immediate goal was to be able to buy out his share in the business, even if she realised that he might not wish to leave. But she did not doubt she could cope with some Irish layabout who had big ideas.

She hurried through life, hardly pausing for breath. This was necessary. She wasn't only hurrying from her thirties into her forties, with all the concomitants of lost and irretrievable youth that that involved, even if her very energy appeared to slow down the inevitable physical consequences of approaching middle age. Pauses also involved thinking about herself. That involved remembering that somewhere she had a son, who did not even send her Christmas cards, although she kept as close a watch as she could on his progress, and sent *him* a card when he graduated from Harvard Law School. Thought also involved recognising that she was in partnership with a crook, a gangster, to use the term recently coined to describe those who broke the law and surrounded themselves with strongarm men, both for their protection and to impose their will upon others. O'Leary's activities, as Prohibition began to bite, and even the less wealthy American citizenry started to feel like a drink, became ever more illegal. Soon he was making his own gin and whisky, she knew, and smuggling some good stuff in from Bahamian rum runners. He had opened a couple of speakeasies, where behind locked doors, and after sufficient police pay-offs, a selected clientele could drink and gamble to their heart's content. He even suggested that the Superb could be used for that purpose, with enormous profits to them both. She refused. She was taking no chances. Even so, the hotel was raided one night, to the embarrassment of the Police, the amusement of the guests, and the fury of Mina, who demanded, and got, a public apology. But the incident only made her the more determined to get rid of her silent partner the moment it could conveniently be done.

Thought also involved recognising that the old rapprochement with the staff was gone. With the retirement of George Howwinger and Joe Stark in 1924, it definitely ended. Hilda Young had gone two years before. Only Anatole was left, and he was relatively new, having only been there for fifteen years. She promoted Walter to maître d', but took over the management duties herself while grooming the two under-managers to handle things during her frequent absences; one of them, Robert Benton, was obviously George Howwinger's eventual successor, alike in energy and flair and his determination to succeed.

These changes would in any event have led to some diminution of the old intimacy. But the feeling was aggravated by the staff's knowledge of what had happened to Tommy Krakowski, who had retired from union activities when released from hospital, and that she had been a part of that, however tacitly. They worked for her, faithfully and well, because they were the best paid staff in all New York, and because they had the best working conditions. But even more, they worked for her, faithfully and well, because they were afraid of her. Or at least, of the tall, dark figure who stood in the shadows behind her.

So, she would think, whenever she made the mistake of allowing herself to relax, Mina Doberley had at last scaled the very heights of power, with everything at her fingertips, with no one in all the world daring to oppose her. But without a friend in all the world, either. Save perhaps Don Axelman. And, of course, Clancy.

But pauses also involved thinking about Clancy.

He was more than a friend, of course. He was the dominating factor in her life. In every way. To her surprise and relief, and total gratification, he proved to be as brilliant an accountant as Don, in a totally different way. But this was part of the problem. Where Don discovered what she wanted, and then set out to get it for her, Clancy was inclined to have an opinion of his own. He did not, of course, approve of her connection with Sean

O'Leary, which he was convinced would ultimately prove a disaster, and while he recognised that this might have been necessary in the circumstances of the time, he held it to be her number one priority to accumulate the necessary capital to pay O'Leary off before she even considered anything else. He regarded Paris as a risky overextension. And he was not afraid to say so.

In many ways even this gratified her. If she knew that his alcoholism was a disease, it was a relief to know that he did not allow his work, or his basic personality, to be affected by it. At least, not yet. And it was a disease which she was sure could be cured, and would be cured, by her. Because she had no doubt that she was partly responsible for his affliction. He had apparently started drinking before the war, out of sheer lonely frustration at having lost her. The war, with all its horror, had merely accentuated his feeling of futility, of total irrelevance. Only she could make him aware of his true value, his true place in the world.

The easy way, of course, was to marry him. But this she could not bring herself to do. She told herself the reason was that she had had enough marriage to last her a lifetime. But she knew that was not the truth. The real reason was that she was afraid to take on something she might not be able to handle, which might distract her from her goal, from the self-centred drive which was essential to her success.

Yet she loved him. It was as simple as that. She had wanted to love this man almost since her first night in the Superb, and had refused to allow herself to do so, even then, because it had been necessary to love other men first, in order to climb that ladder to which she had clung so firmly throughout her life. Now she could afford to love him unreservedly – and was afraid to do so. His drinking made very little difference to their private lives, because he was innately such a gentle person; it was difficult to imagine him leading his company 'over the top' and through German barbed wire, and yet he had apparently done so, with enormous élan and success – he had the medals to prove it. When he was moody and even desperate in his uncertainty as to who and what he was, and why he was, she was content to mother him. He was at once the cross she knew she had to bear, and the son she wished she had. As well as the lover she did have. And the husband she wanted and needed –

and was afraid to take, legally. She had long ago come to terms with her situation; Mina Petersen lived the most perfect of lives, in the eyes of the world, in which everything always fell into place exactly as she decreed should happen – until she closed her private door upon herself. Then nothing happened quite right. But that was God's will, and she knew now that He had only ever been playing with her, allowing her to run here and there, but always holding the end of her leash, with which He could jerk her back to reality whenever He felt she was bounding a little too freely, and with which, she knew, He would one day snap her neck.

She no longer resented this, no longer, she thought, even hated. But hatred aside, she still could not resist challenging the Omnipotent. It appealed to her Sagittarian sense of derring-do, her instinctive desire to gamble. Thus she gambled, not only with her time and her money, but with her very deliberate arrogance. Money was in fact very little gamble at all, in her opinion, as the economy suddenly seemed released from all the fears and doubts which had from time to time beset it before the war, and boomed as it had never done before – or appeared to do so. Mina put all of her profits into the stock exchange, willingly selecting the highest of risks, revelling in watching scrip bought for a hundred dollars today doubling itself in a month. Clancy of course shook his head and made doleful predictions about the situation actually being less stable than ever before, and about Wall Street teetering on the edge of a precipice. She did not believe him, but even if she had, she would not have been able to resist throwing out this fresh challenge to the forces of society and capitalism. Besides, she could remind herself, it was necessary, if she was going to expand further. But, in fact, she didn't, although by the summer of 1928, as even the German economy began to boom again, she had completed the rebuilding of the Berlin Superb; she celebrated the re-opening on her forty-third birthday, 6 December 1928, with Don at her side in preference to any German general, because although the military were in at least temporary eclipse in the new German Republic, one never knew –and she did attempt to learn some lessons from her various experiences.

She now had a personal worth, apart from her properties, of approximately sixteen million dollars, at least on paper, and could easily have afforded both to buy out O'Leary and build, or buy, a Cairo hotel, and thus implement Plan Four, simply by selling her portfolio. But this she did not choose to do, at this moment. If the bull market *was* temporary, as Clancy seemed to be convinced, then it seemed to make sense to milk it for everything she could, and the moment it began to slide, *then* sell out and go into Egypt. Playing with figures was a new and exciting game, the like of which she had never known before. It soon became her principal relaxation.

Playing with people's opinions and emotions was a different matter, but equally enjoyable. She liked making entrances, just to remind everyone of who she was, and as every time she entered the lobby of the New York Superb, her mink thrown carelessly over her shoulder, sometimes smoking a Balkan Sobranie through a silver holder – she did not like smoking but she liked the effect it created – the world seemed to stop, she often went out for half an hour's drive in her Rolls, simply down to the Battery and back, in order to make a new entrance. She knew she was about the best hated woman in the city, simply for that arrogance. And she loved it. This was the role God had decreed for her, and she would live it to the very hilt. What happened when she could no longer sustain it she dared not consider. But that, too, was a magnificent gamble.

And she still hated, from time to time. Mostly nameless forms, all the people she imagined had done her down, or all those who hated her, for her wealth and her power and her success. She was quite willing to feel that way in return. Only for one or two was she prepared to feel an actual personal loathing. Thus her entire body seemed to tingle the night she swept into the Superb restaurant and saw, seated at one of the special tables reserved only for her personal friends, Felix Petersen.

He was accompanied by an extremely brassy blonde, about half her age, Mina estimated, and terribly modern, with her bobbed hair and showing as much knee as she was bosom. And looking unutterably bored, although Felix was making animated conversation.

'What is that man doing here?' Mina asked Walter. 'And at that table?'

'Well, madame, Mr Petersen . . .' Walter hesitated.

'As he's here,' Mina said, 'he will have to stay. But I do not wish him charged for this meal.'

'Not charge him? Madame?'

'We will accept not one cent from that man, Walter, now or ever,' Mina said, and made her entrance. Clancy was already seated at her table, and rose to hold her chair for her. Everyone in the room, as always, observed her entry, Felix amongst them, but she ignored him.

'I really didn't know what to do,' Clancy confessed. 'I mean, he is still one of the wealthiest men in the world.'

'Forget it,' Mina said, watching the gossip columnists, there were always one or two scattered around the restaurant, scribbling notes. At least there could be no photographs; she allowed no cameras in her dining room. And probably, she thought to herself, after nine years, no one even remembered she had once been married. But still . . .

'Here he comes,' Clancy muttered.

She raised her head.

'Mina!' Felix bowed. 'May I say that you look more beautiful than ever?'

'I cannot say the same for you, Felix,' she remarked, with perfect truthfulness. The once splendid figure was bowed and obviously attacked by arthritis, from the way he moved; the once handsome face had collapsed into jowls induced by crash dieting and lines of disappointed dissipation. 'I don't think you've ever met Mr Clancy, my accountant.'

'Clancy.' But the name clearly didn't register; Felix gave him no more than a glance, and then sat down.

'I did not invite you to join us, Felix,' Mina said, coldly.

'But I wish to speak with you,' Felix said. 'First, to thank you for not going through with that revelation. I should have thanked you long ago.'

'I doubt it would have mattered,' Mina said, watching Walter summoning his various minions from all about the lobby, just in case the going got rough. 'It would only have been a nine days' wonder.'

'Perhaps. Still, I had expected the worst, and I was spared that. Just as I have been spared a prosecution, I have learned, by your refusal to testify against me.'

Mina shrugged, and drank orange juice. Actually, it was

Buck's Fizz, as O'Leary kept her supplied with champagne, but only the staff knew that.

'Mina . .' Felix leaned forward, and then glanced at Clancy for a second time. 'Do you think you could find yourself something to do, Mr Clancy? Like adding up a book or something? Just for ten minutes?'

Clancy looked at Mina.

'Mr Clancy stays, Felix,' she said. 'And I really have no interest in anything you may have to say.'

'Mina . . .' He tried to pick up her hand, but she withdrew it. 'Mina, I surrender. Horse, foot and guns. Mina, I'm an old man. I . . .' He hesitated. 'There never was anyone like you, Mina. These young girls . . . Mina, they laugh at me. Mina, I'll give you anything you want. I'll finance any and every project you have in mind. Just name it, ten million, twenty . . . it'll be a gift. If you'll come home. Marry me again, Mina. Come back to me. Mina, just to have you there . . . Mina . . .'

Mina looked up. Walter was standing there, with four other waiters. 'Mr Petersen is just leaving,' she said. 'Perhaps you would show him where the door is. Please make sure his, ah . . . companion goes with him. And Walter, remember, his dinner was on the house.'

'He was utterly humiliated,' Clancy remarked. 'I don't believe you have an ounce of pity or forgiveness in your body.'

Mina blew him a kiss across the bed. 'Once you told me that I wasn't half as tough as I pretend. Don't tell me you're changing your mind.'

'Oh, I changed my mind a long time ago. It's not that you mean to be so tough, or so cruel. I think. It's just that you allow yourself no checks, no balances. You just obey your instincts. When I think how absurdly generous you were to Krakowski, and the staff, back in 1919, and compare that with how brutal you were to Petersen, tonight . . .'

'So I won't ever need a psychiatrist,' she said.

'So it's my personal opinion. I'm just glad I'm not at the end of one of your hates.'

'So am I, Clancy,' she said. 'So am I.' But in fact, seeing Felix had been good for her. It had reminded her that she had things to do, and that she had been allowing life to pass her by. Well, she could not allow that to happen. 'Now,' she said, 'I have a surprise for you. We're going to take a long holiday, you and I. The entire summer.'

He raised his eyebrows. 'What about the hotels?'

'I think Robert Benton is quite capable of holding on here for a few months. And Don is quite happy to run the European show. But we'll be seeing Don, anyway. Because, when I say holiday . . .'

'You're going to look at hotels.'

'That's right. I would say we're completely back on our feet now, financially. It's time to move ahead. But Clancy . . . not a word to a soul, especially O'Leary.'

They left in June 1929, travelling by the latest queen of the Atlantic, the *Bremen*, which flew the German flag, going to Berlin, and thence visiting Don in Paris on their way to Marseilles. There they joined a ship for Alexandria, and cruised through the magic sea for several days. Finding what she wanted was remarkably easy, although the place would certainly require a small fortune to be spent on it. But it *was* what she wanted, and she paid her deposit without hesitation, before starting for home again, after the happiest three months of her life, she thought. She thought Clancy was happier than she had ever seen him before, too. Much more relaxed. Even if his brain still ranged over the problems which lay ahead. 'You do realise,' he told her, 'that this little venture is going to cost something like twelve million dollars, if you include paying off O'Leary?'

She nodded. 'You'll have to decide which stock we sell.'

'It'll mean liquidating almost the entire portfolio. On the other hand, that may not be a bad thing, right this minute. The market is getting increasingly fluttery, by all reports.'

For a moment the thought of what she was doing frightened even her. But only for a moment. Although he knew she would need all of her troops in the front line. So they stopped again in Paris on the way home, to pick up Don. 'I need you in New York,' she told him, 'for a couple of weeks. There are some pretty big decisions to be made.'

But she was actually wildly excited. Plan Four, at last. Because this had been so long delayed, it had become the most important of all her plans. Egypt had answered her wildest expectations, even in the all-pervasive presence of the British as compared with the ageless monuments of Egyptian greatness, the pyramids towering above the river and the city. She could envisage a Superb Travel Group taking the Nile up to Abu Simnel, all as the climax of a journey which would have begun in New York.

Here was all the enthusiasm of her youth coming back, to which was added the ever-present enthusiasm of returning to New York itself, of walking through the lobby of her hotel, and of sitting down to dinner once again in her restaurant, with Don and Clancy seated beside her, with Walter hovering attentively at her elbow, to know that everyone in the room was whispering, that no doubt all of New York was whispering, 'She's back!'

Oddly, this night Sean O'Leary was not at his table. But she was rather pleased about that; she had not yet worked out exactly how she was going to go about having a showdown with him. But she felt in the mood for a showdown, the moment she was in a position to write him a cheque for eight million dollars. Then she would put everything else into Cairo. That would leave her once again out on a financial limb, but only for a little while, and everything was going so well she did not consider that really a risk.

'Onwards and upwards,' she smiled at Don and Clancy, toasting them in carrot juice, and staring past them in total consternation, as the restaurant doorway suddenly became filled with blue-clad policemen, at the same time as the entire hotel was filled with the shrilling of police whistles. Women screamed, men shouted, and Walter threw the light switch, increasing the pandemonium.

Mina was on her feet in an instant. 'Walter,' she bawled across the noise. 'Put those goddamned lights back on.'

He obeyed, and people stared at each other. And at the police. And at Mina, as she went towards the captain in charge. 'I'm going to have you *busted*,' she declared. 'This is the second time you have come charging in here, with no reason at all. You goddamned well know we don't serve liquor on these premises.'

He looked her up and down. It was Cowan, from so many years ago. He had been promoted. 'I'm not looking for liquor, Mrs Petersen,' he said. 'I'm here to put you under arrest.'

'Me? Under arrest? You have got to be crazy. On what charge?'

'I have a warrant here,' he told her, and pulled it from his pocket. 'For possession of narcotics with intent to distribute.' He grinned at her. 'I guess you're going to *have* to testify this time, Mrs Petersen.'

Chapter 18

'See her?' asked one of the prostitutes. 'That's Mina Petersen, that is. I've seen her before.'

'Mina who?' asked the second prostitute.

'The hotel woman,' said the pickpocket.

'And sex,' said the loitering-with-intent, enigmatically.

'I remember about that,' agreed the first prostitute.

Mina sat in the corner of the cell and gazed at them. She was in evening dress and they were in rags. It was a total insult to have placed her in here at all. But Cowan had been seeking revenge. Well, he was not going to get more than this cheap effort. She was totally unafraid of these deadbeats, and she was totally consumed with anger. Someone was going to suffer for this. And she had no doubt at all who it was going to be.

'Tell us about the sex, Mina,' said the second prostitute.

'Why don't you drop dead,' Mina suggested.

'Hark at her,' scorned the first prostitute. 'You want to be respectful, darling. This ain't your hotel, you know.'

'You be rude to us, and we might just scratch that pretty face of yours,' said her companion.

Both got up.

'You come one step closer to me,' Mina told them, 'and I am going to break every bone in your bodies.'

The prostitutes considered her, added to her height and her obvious fitness the expression in her eyes and the set of her jaw, and returned to the far side of the cell. 'So be stuck up,' the first one said. 'You think we give a damn?'

Mina turned her back on them and watched the corridor and, soon enough, Surple. Yet he seemed to have taken an eternity.

'They asked a million dollars bail,' he whispered as the woman sergeant unlocked the door. 'Thank God both Clancy and Axelman were around.' He hurried behind her down the corridor. 'That's an enormous amount of money, even if they do seem to have a very strong case. I mean to say, Mrs Petersen, carrying the stuff loose in your suitcase . . .'

'Do you honestly think I did that?' Mina inquired. 'Oh, really, Charles, it was a plant. That's obvious. And somebody tipped Cowan off to arrest me before I even got around to unpacking properly. Although I think the stuff was put in the suitcase after I got to the hotel.' Her anger seemed to be growing to furnace heat.

'Yes,' he said, not entirely convinced. 'But there seems to be other evidence as well. Apparently the Superb has been being used as a distribution centre for the past three months. Still, a million dollars . . . you'd think you were on a murder charge.'

'That's right,' Mina agreed, signing for her mink and her rings. 'So you bustle off, Charles, and arrange for another million. Because that is very likely to be the next charge I'll be on.'

The man was large, and looked larger because of the padded shoulders of his jacket, the tightly pulled in waist; he entirely filled the aperture left by the half-opened street door. He wore dark glasses, although it was just after midnight. 'What makes you think Mr O'Leary is here, doll?' he asked. 'You got a watch?'

'I know the time,' Mina said. 'I also know that Mr O'Leary spends most of every night here. You tell him Mina Petersen wants a word.'

Her anger remained at white heat, and she had refused to pay any heed to Surple's pleas for consideration before acting, or at least that she should return to her hotel and fetch Clancy and Don and perhaps some others as well. But those were her employees, not her friends, or her aides. Except for Clancy. But she did not wish to involve Clancy in what might lie ahead; she could not be sure of his reactions. So she had no friends, when it came to the crunch. And she did not need any. She was Mina Doberley, and she was quite capable of dealing with this gutter rat by herself.

'Mina Petersen? Jees!' The door was slammed shut, and Mina stamped her foot impatiently. It had been a cool autumnal night, and it was distinctly cold at one o'clock in the morning; she wore only a mink wrap over a pale blue chiffon gown, which, in keeping with the current fashion, ended immediately above her breasts, save for two straps, and also immediately below her knees – her hair was kept in place by a diamanté band.

'He says you can come up.' The door was open again, and the man was standing aside.

'You're so kind,' Mina commented, and stepped past him. She walked along a corridor, conscious of the man at her shoulder, and then down a flight of stairs to another corridor; now she was aware of sound behind the wall to her right. This would be the speakeasy. Another corridor, another sound, and now there were several men around her and moving with her. She felt no fear of them. She was too angry, for one thing and, besides, she was Mina Petersen. If this cheap Irish hoodlum thought he was going to use her hotel for narcotics trading . . . but there was even more involved than that.

A door opened before her, and she found herself in a sort of enclosed gallery, where there were several more men, mostly looking down through glass windows at the crowded room beneath them; here she was past the speakeasy and in the gambling room. Several of the men looked up as she came in, but she felt that was more because women were rare in here, and good-looking and richly dressed women were probably even rarer, than because they actually knew who she was. But at the rear of the gallery a door was opening, and Sean O'Leary was there, wearing his inevitable tuxedo, and smiling at her, framed in the light from within. 'Mina,' he said. 'How wonderful to see you. Do you know, I only just learned you were back from your holiday?'

'I want to see you alone, O'Leary,' Mina said.

He raised his eyebrows, but stepped aside, and she entered a very richly furnished office-cum-sitting-room. But tonight she was not in the mood to appreciate other people's tastes in décor. She turned to face him as he closed the door. 'I have just spent four hours in a cell,' she said. 'Accused of narcotics smuggling, and of using the Superb for distribution.'

'Good Lord,' O Leary said. 'That's a dangerous business, Mina. You should've known better.'

His effrontery was quite staggering. 'You're damned right it's a dangerous business,' she said, 'for those who do it. It seems that the superb Hotel, *my* hotel, O'Leary, has been under surveillance for some time, some months, because of suspected narcotics transactions taking place there. Some time, O'Leary. Some months. But not more than three. And I've been away for four. But the police have evidence. Oh, bags and bags of evidence.' She pointed. 'All mine. I warned you to keep your dirty nose and your dirty hands out of my affairs. I reminded you that you were a *silent* partner. So that's it. As of now, our partnership is dissolved. My accountants will deliver my cheque for eight million dollars tomorrow morning, and you are out. But not quite, O'Leary. Not quite. They tell me I'm well on the way to a Federal charge. Well, I can prove my innocence of drug peddling, because I wasn't there when it happened. I can prove that some underling of yours must have planted the stuff in my suitcases before I had the time even to unpack. And I can almost certainly prove that someone telephoned Captain Cowan and told him that now was the time to nail me. But I am not having my senior staff or my hotel splashed across the newspaper headlines as being involved in drug peddling. This is one rap you are going to have to take, O'Leary. I don't care how you do it. I don't care who you bribe or who you fix, but you are going to get those coppers off my back.'

'You amaze me, Mina,' he said. 'The way you think you can charge through life, giving orders, issuing ultimatums, telling people where they get off . . . oh, don't remind me, you're Mina Petersen.' He walked past her and sat at his desk, pressed a button. 'Well, I think I've had just about enough of Mina Petersen. I actually thought that a long time ago, but I had to wait for the right moment. You may not yet realise it, dear lady, but you are on the way out. I was letting you go easy, on a narcotics rap. So you'll go to gaol, for two, maybe three years, with good behaviour. But you've been to gaol before. You know the score. You'll survive. But it seems that you also need a lesson in how to behave towards your betters. Well, you're going to get one.'

Mina saw his eyes move, and turned to look at the door, which had opened to allow four men to enter. She was aware of being breathless, although she still could not believe that anything was about to happen to her. She was Mina Petersen. Even more, she was Mina Doberley.

'You lay one finger on me, O'Leary,' she said, 'and I will kill you. There's a promise.'

O'Leary smiled. 'I am not going to lay a finger on you, Mina. They are. Work her over, boys. Do it here; I want to watch. But try not to break anything. Just make her feel.'

Mina looked left and right, but the men had surrounded her. She summoned all her dwindling breath, and screamed, suddenly truly afraid for the first time in her life. But as the men did not seem disturbed, and she realised that she could hear nothing of the hum from the gambling tables outside, the office had to be soundproofed. She turned, in an attempt to reach the door, and had her hair seized, jerking her head backwards, while a gasp of pain escaped her lips. Another man stood in front of her, and when she struck at him, the other two held her arms. I've been beaten up before, she reminded herself, desperately. I've been beaten up, and survived.

But that had been by one man, not four. And that one man had been in love with her. She did not suppose these goons knew the meaning of the word, as they certainly did not know the meaning of the word pity, or decency, or even respect for beauty. They tore her gown down the front, tugged at her bra and knickers while her body jerked to and fro, and at last the elastic burst; they laughed at her. They hit her in the stomach, and then let her go, so that she fell to her hands and knees, and vomited. They stood on her hands so that she could not move, and could only whimper with pain, while they used their belts on her back and buttocks and thighs. They let her go again, and when she rolled in agony they kicked her in the ribs. They pulled her about the room by her hair and her breasts and threw her to and fro between them; they put their hands between her legs to toss her into the air, and then stepped aside to let her crash to the carpet. Once she almost lost consciousness, and they poured a bottle of whisky on to her upturned face. She choked and retched, and they stood on her stomach until she lost control of her muscles, and then dragged her up and down the floor by her ankles.

Then they let her go again, and she lay, waiting for the next punch or kick, seeming to be locked up in a pain-crazed world, a world of unutterable humiliation and disgust, and of other emotions, too, but these were only lurking at the edges of her fading consciousness. And gazed at Sean O'Leary, bending over her. 'Are you awake, Mina?' he asked. 'So listen to me, very carefully. I'll be coming in to lunch at the Superb, this morning. When I do, Mina, you will smile, and buy me a drink. And for God's sake wash your face.' He straightened. 'Take her out and dump her. Somewhere along the waterfront will do. Let's see how she gets home from there.'

Mina realised she was cold, because the breeze was cold, playing over her naked body. And she ached. There was no corner of her body which was not in pain, and some of it was sharp. But she also hated. There was no room for any other emotion to exist, either in her mind or in her heart.

Save for the determination to survive – for at least the next twelve hours.

Survive. She rolled, and pushed herself to her hands and knees, and tasted the vomit in her mouth. She remembered being in the car, while the men had continued to torment her with their fingers, before throwing her out on to this dock. She didn't even know which dock. How far it was from the Superb.

She tried to stand, and fell again, striking the concrete heavily, and rolling, gasping for breath. The Superb. Her dream. Finished. Come cascading down in the ruins of a woman's life. But if she was going down, she was going to take that bastard with her. She had no doubt about that. It was all she wanted to do, to go out in the biggest explosion in history. Just her, and Sean O'Leary.

To do that she had to get home, and find some clothes, and have a bath, and try to stop hurting . . . and get herself a gun. There was nothing else. But all of those things had to be done.

She moved again, got to her knees, and heard laughter.

'See what I told you?' a man said. 'That's a naked woman, that is. Spotted her a mile off.'

'Jesus *Christ*,' said another. 'You don't touch that dame, Bryn. She's taken one hell of a beating. That means she's mixed up with some of these goons that hang around here.'

'Maybe we should call a cop.'

'Maybe we should just sidle off and pretend we didn't see

her, you mean. Those boys play rough. And they could still be around.'

'You afraid of that mob?' asked a third voice. For some reason she could not fathom, Mina thought she had heard this one before. But her head was spinning too much to be sure.

'Please,' she whispered. 'Could you lend me a coat, or something? And call me a cab? Please.'

'Jesus Christ,' said the second man again. 'She's alive.'

'Shut your trap,' said the third voice, the familiar voice. 'By God . . .' Rough, but strangely gentle hands grasped her shoulders and pulled her to her feet, while great shudders of pain tore through her body. 'By God,' he said again. 'Mina? Mina Doberley?'

Mina blinked at him. He wore a pea-jacket and a seaman's cap, and he hadn't shaved in two days, at least. His breath smelt of rum. But it was the breath that brought memory flooding back. 'Charlie?' she whispered. 'Charlie Stark?'

'Mina? Jesus Christ, girl, what's happened to you?'

'Lend me your coat, Charlie. And fetch me a cab.'

'Sure,' he said. 'Sure thing. Mina . . . get your asses off,' he roared at his companions. 'Find the lady a cab. Hurry now.' He took off his pea-jacket, and wrapped her in it; it came to her thighs, and she suddenly felt warm. 'Mina?'

'I'm all right, Charlie,' she said. 'I'll be all right. When I get home.'

'But who did this to you, Mina? By Christ, if I ever get my hands on them . . .'

'Forget it,' Mina said. 'I'm going to get my hands on them.'

'There's a cab,' cried one of the sailors, running back to them. 'Say, you really know this dame, skipper?'

'Sure I do,' Charlie Stark said. 'I'm her oldest living friend. Ain't that right, Mina?'

'That's right, Charlie. That's right.' She leaned against his shoulder, feeling and strength flowing out of his arms into her body.

'And I'm going to take her home,' Charlie announced. 'So you guys shove off.'

'Yes,' Mina said. 'Please take me home, Charlie.' But even through the pain and anger, her brain was working again. 'But first . . . Charlie, do you have a gun?'

390

'Sure I have a gun,' he said. 'Everybody needs a gun, nowadays. It's on board. But Mina . . .'

'We'll take the cab,' she said. 'But we'll go fetch your gun first, Charlie. I want you to lend it to me. Just until lunchtime.'

Mina lay on her face, across her bed, and coughed. And tried to stop coughing, because it was so painful, and whenever she coughed, she tasted blood. But she was increasingly aware of people, clustered around her.

She raised her head. 'Clancy?' She looked from left to right. 'Don? Robert?'

'Oh, Mina,' Clancy said. 'If only you'd come home first.'

'We know where you went,' Don said. 'Mina, we are going to *get* that guy.'

'No,' she said, pushing herself to her knees; someone had thoughtfully draped a dressing-gown over her shoulders. 'It's between him and me.'

'Mrs Petersen,' Benton protested. 'You can't take on the mob.'

'Watch me,' Mina said, and frowned. 'What happened to Charlie Stark?'

'Was that old geezer the famous Charlie Stark?' Don asked. 'Well, holy cow.'

'What happened to him?'

'He left,' Clancy said. 'Said he had to see a man.'

'Oh, my God,' Mina said. And then frowned again. Stark had no idea who had beaten her up.

'Well, we thought he was just getting out of here in a hurry,' Don explained. 'Before we started asking questions. Seeing as how it was he brought you home. But Mrs Petersen . . .'

'It's my problem, Don.' She looked from face to face. 'My problem. Nobody else's. And I'll handle it. But there is something I'd like you to do for me: telephone Captain Cowan at the New York Police Department, and ask him to stop by and have lunch with me. One fifteen, sharp. Tell him I have a statement to make. Please, Don.'

Axelman glanced at Benton and Clancy, and then gave a slight shrug. 'Anything you say, Mrs Petersen.'

He left the room, and after a moment's hesitation, Benton followed him.

'Clancy,' Mina said. 'Did Captain Stark leave a parcel?'

'Yes, he did,' Clancy replied. 'But Mina . . . it's a gun.'

'So I'm taking up target shooting,' Mina said. 'Every girl has to have a hobby.'

'Mina,' he protested. 'You're badly hurt. Really badly. I think a couple of your ribs are cracked. I didn't call a doctor, because I wanted to talk with you first. But Mina, you really need to have an X-ray. Look, let me get hold of a doctor, and let me bring Cowan up here. You can prefer charges against O'Leary . . .'

'What charges?' Mina asked.

'Well . . .'

'There was nobody else there. Except for his goons. So forget the doctor. I'll be all right. And I can look after my own dirty linen.'

'With a gun? That's crazy. As Benton said, you can't take on the mob. Nobody can do that, Mina, save the police. That's what they're paid for.'

'I'll do it *my* way,' Mina snapped. 'And I don't want you cluttering up the place with your long face, either while I talk with your friend O'Leary, or while I'm talking with Cowan. So maybe you should lunch out today. Right?'

Clancy hesitated, and then shrugged. 'Sure, I'll lunch out, if that's what you want.'

She wanted to weep. She was sending him away, because she didn't want any harm to befall him, and because she didn't want him to see what was going to befall her. But how she wished he had defied her, and stayed. Because wasn't this what she had always feared, that when the chips were really down he would duck out? She had no right to grumble now. But she could feel very sad.

'And take Don Axelman with you,' she said.

Mina soaked in a hot tub, and felt a whole lot better. She took a quick look at herself in the mirror, and then turned away. Her entire body seemed discoloured, and the pain in her side was quite severe now, while the flesh over her ribs was pink and blue, and the taste of blood was always in her mouth.

Undoubtedly Clancy was right, only she suspected the ribs were broken rather than cracked. But she was content. The pain kept her aware, and angry. She knew there was only one thing left in her life for her to do.

One thing, and then the end of all those fabulous ambitions. And yet, she thought, not of Mina Petersen. She was going to go out in such a blaze of glorious mayhem she had no doubt that she would become more of a legend after her death than before it. And she knew she was a legend already. But nothing else mattered, now. All of the antagonisms she had known, which had driven her through life with such single-minded determination, had now centred in a single human being. On him she would be avenged, not merely for what he had done to her, but for everything all society had done to her, for twenty-eight years. And then she would be content, to walk with a steady step to either the electric chair or the hangman's noose. She could see no further than that. She wanted to see no further than that.

Thus there could be no evidence of pain, or even discomfort. She powdered herself all over, dressed with great care in a black lace dinner gown with crêpe de Chine lining – it had a flesh-coloured georgette top but she omitted this – although adding flesh-coloured georgette stockings and silver shoes, draped a string of pearls around her neck, added silver bracelets to her arms, and tucked Charlie Stark's pistol safely into her handbag. She had never handled a gun before, had never even touched one before this morning. But it seemed straightforward enough; she only needed to pull the trigger once. Her hair she wore up in a chignon, and she made up her face so carefully that no tear or bruise marks could be seen. Then she telephoned the desk, and asked to be informed the moment Sean O'Leary arrived, and had been shown to his table.

She spent the next hour writing letters. One to Surple, expressing her exact requirements; he already had a will, dividing her estate between Clancy and Harry. Then she wrote Clancy, telling him what had happened to her and what she intended to do. And then to Harry, telling him the same, but also attempting, once again, to explain the driving force which had carried her through life for so long. She no longer wept, or even felt like weeping. This was the hand God had given her to

393

play, as she had always known He would one day deal her a loser. But not even God could tell her how to play it. That was her secret.

The telephone buzzed. She picked it up, feeling her heart beginning to slow, even as her brain began to buzz. 'Mrs Petersen? Front desk. Mr O'Leary is at his table.'

She looked at her watch. It was fourteen minutes past one. 'And Captain Cowan?'

'The Captain has just entered the hotel.'

'Well, show him to my table, please, and tell him I'll be right down.'

She stood up, looked at herself in the mirror, gave herself a little smile, and went to the elevator. She rode down, the handbag held in both hands, and emerged at the bottom, the boy giving her a little bow. She nodded both to him and the others, and to Benton, who came to walk at her elbow. 'Thank you, Robert,' she said, as she reached the restaurant doorway; she had no desire to involve him in what was about to happen, either, again simply because she was quite sure that he had no wish to be involved. The same went for Walter. 'Good morning, Walter,' she said. 'Don't bother to come across. I am going to have a word with Mr O'Leary, first.'

She paused, for just a moment, looking over the restaurant, more crowded even than normal, because of course the morning newspapers had all carried the story of last night's drug raid, saw Cowan already at her table in the far corner, looking at her. As was everyone else. Mina Petersen, making one of her entrances.

She nodded, and smiled to her guests as she crossed the dining room, stood above O'Leary's table; he had two of his men with him. She couldn't remember whether they were the ones who had beaten her up or not, but it didn't matter. The men last night had been automatons, acting on their master's orders; without him, they would simply fall apart.

'Mina!' O'Leary stood up. 'How good to see you.' His gaze drifted up and down her body, and he smiled. 'Did you get home safely this morning? I was so worried for you.'

'I got home safely, thank you,' Mina said.

'That's great. I see Cowan is here. Going to make a clean breast of things, are you? That's always the best thing to do. But first . . . you were going to buy me a drink, I think.'

'No,' Mina said, and drew the pistol from her handbag. 'First, I am going to kill you, Sean. Remember?'

O'Leary stared at the gun in absolute terror, his colour fading to leave his features dead white; his two aides seemed paralysed, hands apparently turning to stone on their way to their shoulder holsters. Then a woman screamed, and chairs scraped as people tried to reach the floor and the walls. Out of the corner of her eye Mina saw Cowan, also on his feet, his face a picture of consternation.

'Our partnership is dissolved, as of now,' she said, and squeezed the trigger.

There was a click, and then another, as she squeezed again. O'Leary continued to stare at her, but his colour was beginning to return. 'Your little joke, Mina?' he asked, in a low voice. 'By God, but you are going to suffer for that.'

Mina looked down at the gun, and laughed. The final hideous joke had been played on her. Charlie Stark had assured her the gun had been loaded, and she had not bothered to check. There was nothing she could do, but laugh.

'So you just get down on that floor,' O'Leary said, still speaking in a low voice. 'Right here and now. Kneel, Mina, and kiss my boots. Now, Mina. Now.'

Mina's smile faded as she stared at him, watched him nod. The two men stepped up to her, while her entire brain as well as her body seemed to have gone numb – she only knew that, were they to touch her, she would go mad. But they did not touch, while she remained staring at O'Leary, and watched him frown. Then she turned, to look at Clancy and Don Axelman, flanked by Walter and Robert Benton, standing immediately behind her.

'What the hell do you want, drunkie boy?' O'Leary asked.

'You,' Clancy said. 'And them. We want you outside, Sean. We're going to beat you, the way you beat Mina. Only we're going to *hurt* you.'

'You and who else?' O'Leary snarled. But he was looking left and right, and discovering that there was a cordon of waiters and bell-boys, and even waitresses, drawn right around this corner of the room. 'Let's get the hell out of here,' he snapped, and jerked his head towards the kitchen doors, behind them.

The three men left the table, and backed towards the doors, facing the room, hands hovering close to their pockets, but afraid to make the irrevocable move of actually drawing their weapons. Mina stared at them, while the pistol slipped from her fingers to clatter to the floor. She could not understand what was happening. These people weren't her friends, because she had no friends. They were simply her employees, who worked for her because she paid them, and despite hating and fearing her. They had no business to be risking their lives for her.

She looked past O'Leary and his men, and saw the kitchen doorway also suddenly fill with people. With . . . she could not believe her eyes. Charlie Stark stood there, and Joe Stark was at his shoulder. Anatole stood beside them, a meat cleaver in his hand.

One of the gunmen also noticed that the entrance was blocked. 'Jees,' he muttered. 'Boss . . .'

O'Leary turned his head, looked at the men behind him. The Stark brothers were grey-haired now, but they were still big, tough men, and there was no doubting their determination. Then he looked at the men and women in front of him. Then he looked at Mina. Then he thrust his hand into his jacket and drew his gun. 'Just freeze,' he said. 'Nobody move. We're walking out of here. Nobody even breathe, until we're outside.' His men had also drawn their weapons. Now they moved forward, O'Leary in front, a man at each shoulder.

'O'Leary,' said Captain Cowan, up to now a passive spectator. But he had drawn his revolver. O'Leary's head turned, just an inch, and Clancy launched himself through the air. The gun exploded, but O'Leary went bowling over, Clancy on top of him. The Starks had moved quickly forward to seize the first gunman, Don and Walter had seized the other. O'Leary got back to his knees, and Clancy hit him a round-house right on the jaw; he fell backwards and struck the floor.

Someone started to clap, and then the whole room broke into cheers. Cowan hurried across, holstering his gun and pulling out a pair of handcuffs instead, and then checked, to stare at Mina.

Mina stared back at him. To her surprise, she was sitting in a chair. She certainly hadn't meant to sit down. But she suddenly felt entirely breathless, and someone had given her a terrific thump in the chest, with his elbow, she thought; at least the blow had had the effect of quite numbing the pain from her cracked ribs. But if only she could breathe.

'Holy Mother of God!' Cowan said, and caught her as she slipped from the chair to lie in the blood soaking her dress.

Everything seemed so familiar. The pain, the vague glimpses of white-clad figures, the drifts into the wildest of dreams. She was sure she could remember recovering from hitting the lamp-post, but obviously *that* had been a dream, because now she could see nothing but the lamp-post, rushing at her. Only it had a face on it, and the face was that of Sean O'Leary.

She kept asking for Jimmy, but he never came. Yet eventually there was a white-clad man, surrounded by white-clad women. This too was familiar, even if she recognised none of their faces. 'Jessie,' she said. 'I must speak with Jessie.'

They smiled, and went away, and eventually came back again, when she felt much stronger, and almost able to decide what was real and what was not.

'You have had a very lucky escape, Mrs Petersen,' said Dr Loveridge. 'Did you know that you had two broken ribs, ah . . . *before* you took on the mob? O'Leary's bullet smashed two more. But only just nicked your lung. Had it been an inch to the right . . .'He patted her shoulder. 'You spent several days in a coma, and for a while, well . . . but you are one of nature's great survivors.'

O'Leary's bullet? She remembered no bullet. She remembered Clancy, throwing himself at his old friend . . . 'Clancy,' she said. 'Philip Clancy. My accountant. I wish to see him.'

'Soon,' said Dr Loveridge. 'Soon.'

She had heard that routine before. She began to fret, and they gave her sedatives. When she awoke she found herself looking at Captain Cowan.

'I've brought you some newspapers,' he said. 'Thought you might be interested.'

Mina licked her lips. 'Am I under arrest?'

He raised his eyebrows. 'What for?'

397

'Well . . . everything.'

'I guess you're thinking of the narcotics charge. That's been dropped, in view of the fresh evidence.'

'Fresh evidence?' She had no idea what he could be talking about. 'Where's O'Leary?'

'In gaol. He comes up for trial in a couple of weeks. There's quite a list. Narcotics smuggling and distribution, operating an illegal gambling house, serving alcoholic drinks on his premises, attempted bribery of a police officer, carrying an unlicensed gun, attempted murder, conspiracy . . . oh, and income tax evasion. You name it.'

'I was also carrying a gun, Captain,' Mina pointed out.

'Were you? Hell, so you were. Some unloaded and out-of-date weapon belonging to a Captain Charles Stark. It was unlicensed too. But Stark has paid the fine.'

'I don't understand,' Mina said.

'Why should you? But the fact is, Mrs Petersen, all your troubles stemmed from going into a partnership with a crook. I guess you never knew how much of a crook he was. How could you? But now that he has confessed everything . . .'

'Sean O'Leary?'

'Well, you see, with you so badly shot up, I had to kind of look after you first, fetch an ambulance, try to stop the bleeding, and that kind of thing. That meant I had to leave O'Leary in the custody of those accountants of yours, Phil Clancy and Don Axelman, and just to make sure he didn't escape, I asked the Stark brothers to keep an eye on him too. Well, what do you know? When I'd seen you to hospital and come back, O'Leary offered to sign a complete confession of how he had attempted to implicate you in his narcotic dealings to take over the Superb. He confessed to all those other things too, but he certainly completely exonerated you.'

'Captain,' Mina said. 'I do not believe a word you are saying. Sean O'Leary? He'd never confess to anything.'

'Well, it surprised me too,' Cowan agreed. 'I guess he just wasn't as tough as he thought he was. Mind you, those lads of yours had problems with him. He did try to break out. And they couldn't stop him, apparently. But they had a stroke of luck. Seems after busting out, he missed his footing at the top of the stairs, and fell right down to the bottom. Broke both his legs. Well, I guess that kind of discouraged him.'

Mina wanted to laugh, but it was too painful. So she smiled, instead. Amongst the flowers which festooned her room, there were roses from Tommy Krakowski.

She was too tired to look at the newspapers. She wanted to see Clancy. There was so much she had to say to him, to them all.

'Mr Clancy is very busy right now, Mrs Petersen,' Sister told her. 'Well, he would be. It's like a madhouse down there. You can't ever have seen anything like it.'

'A madhouse?' Mina asked. 'Down where? Not the hotel?'

'Oh, not the hotel, Mrs Petersen. Wall Street. We've been trying to get hold of Mr Clancy, or Mr Axelman, to tell them you're awake and lucid at last, but neither of them can be found. They're busy, I guess, like I said. But they'll be along. One or other has called here every day. Now, we do have a very important visitor waiting to see you.'

Mina blinked at her, hardly hearing what she was saying. Madhouse? Wall Street? Nothing made any sense. Neither did the face of the young man who came through the door and stood by the bed.

'Harry?' she whispered.

'Mother? Oh, Mother!' He kissed her forehead, and held her hand.

She smiled, through the tears. 'Elizabeth won't be pleased.'

'I guess I don't please her very much, any time,' Harry said. 'Mother, I am so very proud of what you did. Everyone is. If a few more citizens had the guts to behave like that we could clean this town up.'

'I did nothing but make a fool of myself,' Mina declared. 'And get in the way of a bullet. It was my staff. And my friends.' How marvellous to be able to say that.

'Yeah,' he said. 'I guess you have that knack, of making people love you. But it's your guts they love, Mother. Mother . . . can you forgive me?'

'Uh-uh,' she said. 'Can you forgive me, Harry?'

He kissed her again. 'I just wish . . . well, that things weren't in such a mess right now. But Mother, I want you to know, whatever has happened . . . look, I have some capital put by. Not much, but it might help to tide you over for a while, just in case . . .'

'What in the name of God are you talking about?'

He frowned at her. 'You mean you don't know?'

'I don't know anything,' Mina cried. 'I haven't exactly been in circulation these past . . . God, I don't even know how long I've been in this bed.'

'Five weeks,' Harry said.

'Five *weeks*? Good Lord. Five weeks. But Harry, what's been happening? You simply have to tell me.'

He hesitated, and glanced at the door as it opened, with some relief. 'Here's Mr Clancy,' he said. 'I think he should do the telling.'

'Clancy?' Mina tried to sit up, found she could not; in any event Sister hurried forward to restrain her.

'You simply must lie still, Mrs Petersen,' she said. 'You have been very badly hurt, and you are still very weak. Any sudden movement and you could start to haemorrhage again. You must lie still.'

'Clancy,' Mina said again, subsiding into the pillows.

'Mina.' He stood by the bed. 'Gosh, it's good to see you looking better. There were times . . .'

'Mr Clancy has been here every day,' Sister explained, proudly.

Mina stared at him. Because this was certainly Clancy. But then, not Clancy. She felt exactly as she had on that November day in 1918, at the London Superb. Only in reverse. There was something . . . 'Aren't you going to kiss me, Clancy?' she asked.

He hesitated, then lowered his face and kissed her on the forehead. And she knew what had happened. The spring in his step, the air of alertness signified that his suspicious distrust of the very air he breathed had gone . . . along with the smell of alcohol on his breath.

'Clancy,' she said. 'Oh, Clancy.'

He looked embarrassed. 'There hasn't been any time for . . . well, relaxing, since . . .'

'Since you took the bullets out of Charlie Stark's gun?'

He raised his eyebrows, and then grinned. 'It seemed a good idea at the time. The mood you were in you could have killed somebody. Charlie sends you his love, by the way. He'll be along to see you, now you're over the hump. They all will. Your staff really does worship the ground you walk on, you know. But Mina . . .' He held her hand. 'I didn't reckon on you stopping a bullet. My dearest, darling Mina.'

Was this confident, ebullient, romantic man really Clancy? Because at last she *had* really needed him, in every way? Perhaps that was the only thing that had been missing from his life, all of these years. But for all his ebullience, he still had something on his mind. 'I didn't either,' she said. 'And I know, just how marvellous the staff have been, Clancy. Knowing that, seeing you, I'm happier than I have ever been in my life. Now tell me the bad news. I can stand it, really and truly.'

Clancy looked at Sister. 'How strong is she?'

'Strong enough, I guess,' Sister said. 'Dr Flaxton knows she has to be told. I'll leave you. But don't let her move about. And if she gets agitated, ring immediately.'

She gave Mina an encouraging smile, and left the room.

'What *is* this?' Mina demanded. 'What the devil is going on? Anyone would think the world has come to an end, or something. Oh, Clancy, I don't think you've ever met my son, Harry?'

'We've met,' Clancy said. 'He's been coming here every day too.'

'Have you, Harry? Have you?' She squeezed his hand. But she was still looking at Clancy. 'Now, Clancy, please. Even the doctor says I have to know what's happened.'

Clancy sighed. 'Well, I guess you could say the world *has* come to an end. The financial world, anyway. There's been a slump on the stock exchange. Some people are calling it a crash. Others are calling it a holocaust. I guess the market was simply operating on too much credit, and it only required a couple of big operators to default, and another couple to decide to pull out, and zing! Wall Street is in a mess. The whole country is in a mess. Banks are going bust all over the place. So are people. It's been the grimmest fortnight any of us can remember, and right this minute the only way ahead looks down.'

She stared at him. 'So?' Her heart began to pound; the blood pumping through her battered arteries was intensely painful.

'Well . . . I had to take some pretty hard decisions. I guess I held on a shade too long, as it was. But you were in here, dying, for all anyone knew. I was the only one with power of attorney. So . . . I finally unloaded everything.'

'Everything?'

'Everything anyone would buy. We salvaged a million.'

Her brows slowly drew together into a frown. 'My portfolio was worth sixteen million dollars, when last I looked, Clancy.'

'On paper, Mina.'

'Right this minute it's not worth the paper it was printed on, Mother,' Harry said. 'It was all high risk stuff. You couldn't even give it away, today. Clancy took the only decision he could.'

'*You* took the decision, Clancy?' Mina asked. 'You?'

'Well . . .' He shrugged. 'There was nobody else, Mina. So I guess you can fire me.'

'Oh, Clancy,' she said, and squeezed his hand. What a torture he must have gone through, she thought. But he had done it. And he had done more than that. He had come here to tell her he had lost her fifteen million dollars, without needing a drink. 'A million,' she said. 'So I can still buy lunch. Oh, Clancy, how can I ever thank you?'

'Don't, yet,' he advised. 'Sure, there's a million. But Mina . . . O'Leary wants his capital back. Now.'

'Can he do that?' Instinctively Mina looked at her lawyer son.

'I guess he can, Mother. He may be all kinds of a crook. He may be on his way to prison for a long time. None of that affects his legal rights. And the deal entered into with you was legal.'

'And he's sure going to need the money, to pick up the legal fees he's going to have to face,' Clancy said.

'Eight million dollars,' Mina groaned. 'Oh, God, eight million dollars. Oh, Clancy, why didn't I take your advice and sell out in the spring?'

'Why should you have?' He grinned. 'Even I didn't know there was going to be a crash quite like this one.'

'You had a feeling. Well . . . I don't know how long they aim to keep me in here. They're muttering about some more weeks. So you'd better arrange for the bank people to come in here and see me, and I'll organise a loan. I know it means forgetting about Cairo for a while, and I guess I'll lose my deposit. But we'll just have to pull in our horns for a bit.'

'Ah . . .' Clancy looked at Harry.

'What now?' Mina inquired.

'It can't be done, Mina,' Clancy said. 'There is no bank in this country capable of picking up a loan of eight million dollars, right this minute. I don't think they could pick up eight thousand.'

Mina frowned at him. 'Are you trying to tell me I'm bankrupt, Clancy?'

'Well . . . I wouldn't put it quite like that. Including current bank overdrafts and various debts, you need to find pretty near ten million in a hurry. But I reckon if you were to put the European hotels on the market . . . that will have to include the London Superb, I'm afraid . . .'

'Now, wait just one moment,' she said. 'Are you saying that to raise ten million dollars I have to sell Berlin, and Paris . . . and London? That's crazy. Those hotels are worth seven million each.'

'Last month, Mina, maybe. Right now, well . . . nobody's buying anything. You might not even get the ten. But you'd still have New York. And hell . . . things must improve.'

'When?'

'God knows. But they must. I mean to say, a country like the United States can't *stay* bankrupt.'

Mina sighed. 'I guess not,' she said. 'Maybe you'd better just let me sleep on it. I'm so very tired. But Clancy . . . ' She squeezed his hand. 'I'm so proud of you, for everything. So proud, Clancy. So proud.'

How people would laugh at her, Mina supposed. And Sean O'Leary, even as he stepped through the door of Sing Sing Prison, would laugh loudest of all. She had been overreaching herself all of her life, and had always come up smiling. But now she had finally gone and done it. She would have deserved it all. No one would have any doubt about that, simply because she had taken up with a crook.

God's will. He had finally given the jerk on the leash to bring her back down to earth with an almighty thump, as was His prerogative.

But hadn't she, in real terms, gained more than she had just lost? She would still have the Superb, and more than that. She would have friends. People who had been prepared to risk their necks for her. People like Charlie and Joe Stark. But even more, people like her own waiters and waitresses. And she had Harry back again. And she had Clancy, for the first time, she thought.

But more than any of those, she had her self-respect, and the respect of all New York. That was all she had ever wanted, from that first day, twenty-eight years ago, when she had gone ashore in her borrowed clothes, and been laughed at. So who could say she had lost, anything?

'Can you get hold of Mr Clancy and ask him to stop by?' She asked Sister next morning as soon as she awoke. Because the sooner it was done, the better.

'Right away, Mrs Petersen. But there are two gentlemen here to see you, already.'

Mina looked at the card. 'Oh, show them in,' she said. 'May as well get all the bad news over at once.' Because there could be no more truly bad news, not when she considered all those assets of hers. 'Charles,' she said. 'How nice of you to call.'

'Mrs Petersen.' Surple looked as anxious as ever. 'May I introduce Mr Rogers, of Rogers, Winston and Graham?'

'Mr Rogers.' Mina shook hands.

'It's splendid to see you looking so well, Mrs Petersen,' Rogers said. 'And may I say how much I admire your courage and resolution in sending that thug O'Leary where he belongs.'

'Thank you, Mr Rogers. But I guess he's also sending me where I belong, into virtual liquidation. You've spoken with Phil Clancy, recently, Charles?'

'Mr Clancy and I have been in close touch throughout your illness, yes, Mrs Petersen.'

'So you'll know that there is a little cash that needs to be found?'

'Ah, yes. However, we have come about another matter.'

'Oh, Christ,' Mina said. 'Who do I owe now, Mr Rogers?'

'It is actually to do with the estate of your late husband,' Rogers remarked.

'My . . . did you say, *late* husband?'

'Mr Petersen died of heart failure three weeks ago. You were of course still in a coma. He had been ill for some time, and he was of course approaching seventy.'

Felix, dead? While she had been in a coma. She had attained the age of forty-four, all but, and she had still never been to a funeral. Not even, remarkably, her own. 'Well,' she said. 'I guess somehow I had supposed he would live forever. Oh, don't bother to tell me, Mr Rogers. His estate wants to raise the matter of that twenty million dollars all over again.'

'Twenty million?' Rogers asked. 'Oh, no, no, Mrs Petersen. The amount is much greater than that.'

Mina stared at him. She hadn't ever considered the possibility of something like compound interest. 'I'll see you damned,' she said. 'I won that money, in court, And you're going to have to take me to court all over again if you want to touch a cent of it.'

Mr Rogers looked at Surple, eyebrows raised.

Surple cleared his throat. 'I don't think you quite understand, Mrs Petersen. Mr Rogers is talking about the total value of Mr Petersen's estate, which has been probated at one hundred and three million dollars.'

'Yeah,' Mina said. 'Mine was valued at sixteen million down to last week.'

'My dear Mrs Petersen . . .' Rogers was clearly shocked. 'There are no stocks or shares involved in that figure. Mr Petersen never played the market, except for fun, and with, ah, irrelevant sums. The estate comprises three copper mines in South America, two shipping lines, coastal, you understand, and a gold mine in Australia. And, ah . . . I'm afraid an airline, would you believe it? Mr Petersen kept active in business to the very end and, frankly, his business judgement was beginning to slip a little. I mean to say, an *airline*.' He allowed himself a sad smile. 'However, that is neither here nor there. What I do wish to discuss with you is the cash balance, because I have to say that I am acutely worried about the situation.'

'Cash balance?'

'Mr Petersen always kept a considerable amount of his money in cash, so that he could always take immediate advantage of any profitable deal which arose. To be precise, there was eighteen million dollars on deposit when he died. That was just as this unfortunate slump was gathering speed, so to speak, and I received a tip-off that things were rapidly going to get worse, and that there would almost certainly be a run on the banks. So I acted on my own initiative, withdrew the money, and have kept it in cash ever since, in a safe deposit box. However, it does worry me, sitting there . . .'

'Mr Rogers,' Mina interrupted. 'Why are you telling me all of this?'

'Because it's yours, Mrs Petersen.'

'Mine?' Mina looked at Surple.

'You are the sole beneficiary, Mrs Petersen,' Surple confirmed.

'Felix left his money to me?'

'Every red cent,' Surple said.

'One hundred and three million dollars, with eighteen million in cash?' Mina spoke very slowly.

'In grateful thanks for the only happy years of my life,' Rogers quoted from memory. 'So, Mrs Petersen, I would be greated relieved if you would tell me what you would like done with all that cash . . .?'

The reporters, male and female, crowded round, as Mina came down the hospital steps. She walked slowly, because she was still convalescing, but she was supported by her son Harry on one side, and by Clancy on the other; Don Axelman walked immediately behind. She had lost a great deal of weight, and her clothes hung on her, while there was a lot more silver than gold in her hair now – but no one could doubt her radiant health.

'How does it feel to be up and about, Mrs Petersen?'

'It feels great,' Mina said.

'What do you think of O'Leary's sentence, Mrs Petersen?'

'Well,' Mina said. 'Once I thought I would never wish to send any human being to gaol. But in his case, I think ten years is just a little generous.'

'Where are you going now, Mrs Petersen? Back to the Superb?'

'Of course,' Mina said. 'The Superb is my home. That's where my friends are.'

'But aren't you taking a holiday, Mrs Petersen? Aren't you and Mr Clancy booked on the *Bremen* tonight?'

'We are sailing on the *Bremen*.' Mina smiled. 'But it's not strictly a holiday. We are going to Cairo, to oversee the building of the Cairo Superb, and then we shall be taking the inaugural Nile voyage of Superb Travel. On the other hand . . .' She looked from face to face. 'It will also be a honeymoon.'

'You and Mr Clancy?' Flashbulbs exploded, while Clancy flushed.

'Then you're on your way to City Hall now, Mrs Petersen? Before the Superb?'

'No,' Mina said. 'We are on our way to church, before the Superb.'

'To church, Mrs Petersen?'

'Why not?' Mina asked. 'I am no longer a divorcée, you know. I am a widow. I can be married in a church, and I never have been, before.'

The young woman did not look embarrassed. 'I wasn't thinking of that, Mrs Petersen. I was thinking, well . . . you've always given the world the impression of being something of an atheist.'

'Why, do you know, ' Mina said, 'I was, down to a fortnight ago. In fact, this afternoon will the first time I have entered a church since leaving Devon, twenty-eight years ago. I used to think God played games with people. Now I know He does. But I've kind of grown to like the games He plays. Besides, I want to thank him, personally, for the game He's been playing with me, the last twenty-eight years. So, ladies and gentlemen, if you'll excuse us, we have a wedding to catch.'

A selection of bestsellers from SPHERE

FICTION

HOOLIGANS	William Diehl	£2.75	☐
UNTO THIS HOUR	Tom Wicker	£2.95	☐
ORIENTAL HOTEL	Janet Tanner	£2.50	☐
CATACLYSM	William Clark	£2.50	☐
THE GOLDEN EXPRESS	Derek Lambert	£2.25	☐

FILM AND TV TIE-INS

SANTA CLAUS THE NOVEL	£1.75	☐
SANTA CLAUS STORYBOOK	£2.50	☐
SANTA CLAUS JUMBO COLOURING BOOK	£1.25	☐
SANTA CLAUS: THE BOY WHO DIDN'T BELIEVE IN CHRISTMAS	£1.50	☐
SANTA CLAUS: SIMPLE PICTURES TO COLOUR	95p	☐

NON-FICTION

HORROCKS	Philip Warner	£2.95	☐
1939 THE WORLD WE LEFT BEHIND	Robert Kee	£4.95	☐
BUMF	Alan Coren	£1.75	☐
I HATE SEX		£0.99	☐
BYE BYE CRUEL WORLD	Tony Husband	£1.25	☐

All Sphere books are available at your local bookshop or newsagent, or can be ordered direct from the publisher. Just tick the titles you want and fill in the form below.

Name _____

Address _____

_____

Write to Sphere Books, Cash Sales Department, P.O. Box 11, Falmouth, Cornwall TR10 9EN

Please enclose a cheque or postal order to the value of the cover price plus:

UK: 45p for the first book, 20p for the second book and 14p for each additional book ordered to a maximum charge of £1.63.

OVERSEAS: 75p for the first book plus 21p per copy for each additional book.

BFPO & EIRE: 45p for the first book, 20p for the second book plus 14p per copy for the next 7 books, thereafter 8p per book.

Sphere Books reserve the right to show new retail prices on covers which may differ from those previously advertised in the text or elsewhere, and to increase postal rates in accordance with the PO.